Slowly and confidently, the circle of hopping ravens tightened around Brenn, singing a song of death, decay, and dire prophecy.

❖❖❖❖❖❖❖

They would feast on his eyes and entrails, and with his feathers they would thick their nests.

Brenn had heard enough. With a swift, shuddering wingbeat he was aloft, his pursuers close behind him with their harsh, icy laughter.

Then the first of them struck his side with a resounding blow, sending him hurtling into another of them. He slowed, tumbled from his precipitous climb, and all of a sudden the ravens were upon him.

Around his face and eyes the sharp bills darted like the tails of scorpions, the claws of crabs. They dropped on him like dark hail, razored and deadly, and twice he felt the tips of his wings brush the ground.

With a shriek, Brenn burst upward through a dense squadron of ravens, headed towards the clouds and higher still. The black wings parted in front of him readily, and one bird alone—a blue-black thug, its talons outstretched—stood between Brenn and the open sky . . .

❖❖❖❖❖❖❖

A FOREST LORD

MICHAEL WILLIAMS

WARNER BOOKS

A Time Warner Company

WARNER BOOKS EDITION

Copyright © 1991 by Michael Williams
All rights reserved.

Questar® is a registered trademark of Warner Books, Inc.

Cover illustration: Edwin Herder
Cover design: Don Puckey
Map: Teri Williams

Warner Books, Inc.
666 Fifth Avenue
New York, NY 10103

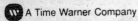 A Time Warner Company

Printed in the United States of America

First Printing: October, 1991

10 9 8 7 6 5 4 3 2 1

Acknowledgments

The second volume of a trilogy offers its own pleasures and challenges, and accordingly, requires its own list of acknowledgments:

First of all, thanks to all my cousins: though the cousins of this book are not necessarily based on you, your multitude and oddness and goodness were their inspiration.

Thanks again to Peggy Leake, whose help blossomed in these pages, to John Fitch for his crystalline comments, to Cheryl Plain for her healing touch, and to Russell Peck, who went hiving off for answers to obscure long-distance questions.

A special thanks to Galen, Cracker, and Kelpie—the boofers who dance for bread and cheeses in our own caravan.

And finally, there is my wife Teri, who helped explore and develop the ideas in this book, read manuscript, and offered suggestions and revisions. In all senses of the phrase, it is her book as much as mine.

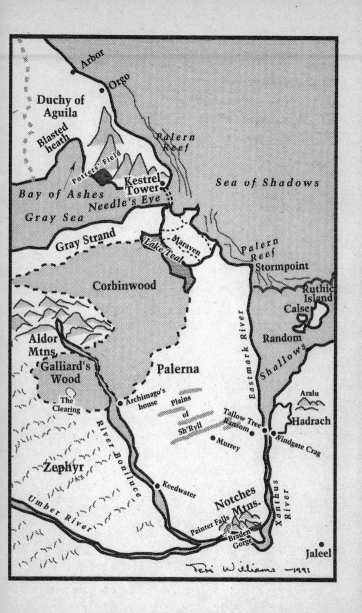

>>> **Prologue** <<<

Ravenna clutched the stones of the parapet.

She stood on the great East Balcony, overlooking the Sea of Shadows. The light in the doorway behind her seemed to fade as the sunrise overwhelmed the guttering light of the candles in the shadowy chamber. Her black eyes still glittered with the effects of the drugs, of green acumen and bolstering borage, and the Great Witch blinked painfully in the new light.

The wizard was out there somewhere, beyond the East Wall, no doubt halfway to Hadrach with that venomous boy in tow.

A great weariness accompanied the sunlight washing over her tangling black hair. With a hand as deft and pale as a court assassin's, she drew a black veil across her face and stared through its gauzy shadows onto the gibbet-lined causeway and the clustered buildings beyond it, over the bronze dome of the Burgher's Hall and past a point where she lost clear sight in the hazy streets of Maraven.

"Out there somewhere," she whispered. "Where the four winds carry the stink of death and the tide washes up the hands of the drowned."

She paused, breathed in the mist off the Gray Sea, rich with the dark smell of the Corrante—that dangerous, encircling current. Salty, it was, riding the odor of kelp and sulfur ash and decay.

"But it is not crucial," she reminded herself, lifting her hands from the stones. "What will come to pass will come to pass regardless of this night and this morning."

She turned with a dark billowing of robes, entered the chamber, and walked to the center of the room, where the floor was inlaid with a stone map of the subcontinent. Stepping onto the glowing surface, onto the engraved straits of the Needle's Eye, she extended a long mirror-black nail toward the nearest of the candles. At once the sputtering flame steadied, then bent toward her as though it yearned for her hand.

"But now . . ." Ravenna breathed, arching her graceful, thin eyebrows, her hand encircling the taper, ". . . now to survey those . . . who will bring it to pass."

A smile uncoiled on her pale face, and her eyes faded to a pale gray; then, finding what they sought in the center of the candle flame, they flashed black again, swallowing its light. For a breath, two breaths, she stared into the fire and stepped to the east.

Haloed by the candle, seasoned armies and horsemen moved silently and efficiently through the easternmost streets of Wall Town.

The army was King Dragmond's, the deadly Maravenian Watch who marched through the nightmares of the poor. Two hundred of them were assembled at the East Gate, nor were they the typical thugs that went about the king's business in Ships and Grospoint and Wall Town.

Ravenna's eyes narrowed in admiration. These were crack troops. Only last week they had patrolled the Gray Strand with General Helmar's legions, in search of Zephyrians and rebels. Some of them, and not necessarily the oldest, remembered the invasions of Baron Macaire, when, all along the Gray Sea, the Maravenian Guard waded up to the ankles in Zephyrian blood. Reassigned now to a tamer duty, they prepared for a march into inland Palerna.

Ravenna smiled to see them arrayed in their red leather armor, their spears and curved swords at the ready. Though she had neither furnished nor equipped them, these men were hers. Her plans had mustered them, her design had given them purpose, and now that purpose was to flush from hiding the wizard Terrance and his snot-nosed brat.

To underscore that purpose came a rider out of the edge of the candlelight, as though he was emerging from the wings of a stage. On a pale horse he moved gracefully through the ranks of the guard, his armor draped with a white cloak against the unseasonable morning chill.

"Captain Lightborn," Ravenna whispered huskily, her eyes fixed into the flame through which she watched the man. "Captain Lightborn. My favorite murtherer."

Gracefully the man in white lifted a handkerchief to his face. With a scarcely visible movement of his gloved hands, he tied the silk cloth over his nose and mouth, masking himself against the mist. Then he swiftly raised his arm and the East Gate opened wide in front of him in a flurry of rope and pulley and creaking. The fog already burning off the road in front of him, Lightborn rode in the middle of the column as the army lifted itself and marched, free of the sheltering walls as it made its way, deadly and seasoned and ever so attentive, toward Stormpoint.

"So for the east," Ravenna proclaimed, and, candle in hand, stepped toward the west of the map, over its slate Gray Strand toward the outline of Zephyr, her black eye never leaving the heart of the flame. "Now to the west, over ashes and the cwalu."

When she thought of the cwalu, the walking dead, even the Great Witch shuddered. They were sleeping now, struck down by the sunlight and by something else—something Ravenna could not yet determine. Strewn across Potters' Field they lay, along the glittering black sands of the Aquilan coast and floating in the Bay of Ashes itself, forming a grotesque sargasso of bone and hair and tattered cloth in the far waters.

Ravenna looked into the flame, as she might stare across a battlefield or across the bodies on the streets of Wall Town, brought from the houses by hooded guards when the plague struck fiercely in the summer nights. Whatever had stopped them, the cwalu would return at her bidding.

But now was not the time. Instead, it was the time to call on the other creatures.

Over beaches she looked, over Potters' Field and the great necropolis of Maraven, where arranged rows of graves and tombs sprouted like broken teeth from the dark ascending slopes of the coastline. Ravenna lifted the candle and stared through its flame, fixing her gaze on a point in the black sky west of Aquila, somewhere over the vastness of the Parthian Desert where legends say that everything dreamed a thousand years ago still rushes and wavers over the dunes that forget nothing.

Her chant rose to fill the vaulted room at the top of the tower as she began:

> *By this the dreadfull Beast drew nigh to hand*
> *Halfe flying, and halfe footing in his hast,*
> *That with his largeness measured much land*
> *And made wide shadow vnder his huge wast;*
> *As mountaine doth the valley ouercast.*

Through the lifted flame of the candle she saw the sky brighten and bristle at the edge of her sight. The air took on form and substance, sprouting scale and claw and wing as the dragon emerged from the twisting sand and wind.

The Great Witch continued, the candles wavering with the hushed urgency of her words.

> *Approching nigh, he reared high afore*
> *His body monstrous, horrible, and vast*
> *Which to increase his wondrous greatnesse*
> *   more,*
> *Was swolne with wrath, and poyson,*
> *   and with bloudy gore.*

Ravenna paused. The monster was fully formed now, wheeling westward like a deep and pitiless shadow.

"Good!" she hissed, wrenching her eyes from the heart of the flame. To the north were mountains, an impenetrable wall of rock through which not even a wizard could pass.

And yet . . .

There were three ravens sat on a tree
  Down a down, hay down, hay down . . .

The song began as she stepped to the northernmost point of the map, where black obsidian ended in gray wax-spattered stone. Ravenna's thin, high voice was strained, unaccustomed to music. A tune in a minor Umbrian mode it was, filling the tower with a deep melancholy, a deep sense of doom and boding. In the anteroom to the chamber, the Great Witch's handmaiden paused above her clumsy embroidery, gray eyes shifting toward the door behind which her mistress brooded and plotted and sang.

Out in the tangled, neglected gardens of Kestrel Tower, well out of earshot of the singing, two sentries paused and stared desolately at one another beneath a shaggy, half-dead elder tree. Even though they could not hear the song, the breeze around them died with an ominous stillness.

As she sang, a dark cloud rose like vapors from the earth around the sentries and rose to the top of the tower, where it settled on the battlements, swirling angrily, boiling with a life of its own.

There were three ravens sat on a tree
  With a down
There were three ravens sat on a tree,
They were as black as they might be.
  With a down, derry, derry, derry, down, down.

Above the heads of the melancholy guardsmen, in the bare, topmost limbs of the dying elder, worms began to whip about the branches. They were small, hideous things, at home in the shadows and the rotting wood. Ravenna curled her lip in disgust, like a too-proper child who lifts a rock and recoils at the frantic wriggling life she has disturbed. The witch drank yet again from the flask of acumen, and suddenly the worms seemed larger, more defined in the stark white moonlight. The creatures swelled, sprouted feathers and wings, and with a rattle of stagnant air arose from the branches. Circling the tower once, they sped toward the mountains, croaking and cawing.

Then to the oldest verse of the song the Great Witch turned, singing in full voice now, her black eyes lidded and weary and unnaturally bright . . .

> *Mony a one for him makes mane,*
>   *Down a down, hay down, hay down . . .*
> *But nane sall ken where he is gane;*
>   *With a down*
> *O'er his white banes, when they are bare,*
> *The wind sall blaw for evermair.*
>   *With a down, derry, derry, derry, down, down.*

More ravens rose from the branches and flew to the south, as Ravenna turned her gaze toward the Gray Strand and Corbinwood beyond it.

"To the rebel's forest with you," she breathed to the birds. "And all that you see, you will bring to my eyes and my ears."

Then kneeling over the green spot of the map, the sculptured jade by which some ancient artisan had chosen to represent Palerna's greatest forest, she looked once more into the heart of the candle.

A flurry of arrows flew straight at her face. Shrieking, the Great Witch dropped the candle and covered her eyes. Slowly, cautiously, she parted her fingers.

She was unharmed. It had been an illusion. The candle burned on the floor in front of her.

"Damn him!" she exclaimed through clenched teeth, snatching up the taper. Drinking the final swallow from the flask of acumen, she stared once more into the flame to make sure.

The man in green stared back at her, pointed at her, and winked. Behind him, almost invisible in the shadows, a woman watched him, smiling enigmatically.

"Galliard!" Ravenna hissed. "Damn your foolery!"

Behind her the door to the chamber opened. The slight, gray-eyed maid peered respectfully into the room and, seeing her mistress intent at the window, stepped silently inside and, broom and cloth in hand, swept the floor and polished the candelabra while the Great Witch seethed and saw nothing.

They all bore watching, Ravenna thought, oblivious to the

girl behind her. The dragon somewhere over Partha, the birds high above Corbinwood and Aquila, Captain Lightborn at the head of his seasoned company, and even Dragmond.

Especially Dragmond, who slumbered a floor below her, entangled in the nightmares of kings and the bedsheets of the Great Witch herself.

She did not know the king was awake, his pale hands linked behind his head, his vigilant eyes on the stars outside the western window.

Green Pytho had moved through the belt of the Forest Lord. Now the planet—the favorite of prophets and philosophers—whose place in the sky foretold the fall of cities and the death of kings, had moved to the sign of Draco, the great dragon whose wingspan touched both horizons and whose tail linked a dozen stars.

Perhaps the omens have passed me this time, Dragmond thought. He closed his eyes for a moment, looked into himself for peace, for slumber. *Perhaps they have something to do with Alanya, where the philosophers spend half their time stargazing, or perhaps it is something about the wars far away in Europa, or a signal that the plague is passing . . .*

Uneasily, he shifted on the bed, dazed by possibilities.

It was already dawn, and even the brightest stars were fading in the whitening sky. Soon he would be up and about the business of the kingdom—dispatching messengers and soldiers and reading the city for signs of unrest. For one thing was sure: the troubles would return to him. Whether from the mountains, the deserts, or from the fastness of woodlands, the troubles would return.

The sunlight, harsh and restless, swallowed the last of the stars.

Slowly the king arose, wrapping the bedsheet about him. He coughed and set his bare feet gingerly on the marble floor. In the shadows of the chamber he seemed to float from the bed to the open window like a restless ghost. The ashen shores of the Gray Strand lay desolate to the south, where his cavalry searched through the rubble and sand.

But the wizard and the lad are long gone by now, the king thought, wrapping the sheet more tightly about him. *They are no fools, and they are long gone.*

Nevertheless, he mused, *there are things that can bring them back.*

As he thought of the girl a slow, deadly smile spread across his face.

For in the tumult of crowns and nations, we cannot forget that the lad is a lad, drawn to the firmness and fragrance of a girl. Of this girl in particular.

The King of Palerna shivered as he breathed in the fresh salt air at the window. Upon it, so faintly that he thought he dreamed or remembered it, he tasted the sharpness of decay, as though the air had turned around him. He lifted the sheet to his face, smelled nothing but the strong, bewitching perfumes of his mistress.

Despite the scent and the spells of the witch, he considered the girl Faye and his thoughts burned.

A floor above him, Faye thought of little, of next to nothing, as she swept the dust and ash and pried the cold wax from the floor of Ravenna's chamber. The witch stood motionless on the inlaid map, and Faye knew not to bother her in the depths of augury.

Listlessly the girl knelt, gathering the refuse into the dustpan. *There is something I am supposed to remember*, she said to herself, looking up through her matted hair to where Ravenna raised her black-nailed hands in a ceremonial gesture as old as magic itself.

Faye sighed as the Witch began to chant at the parapets.

Whatever it is, she mused, *I expect I shall think of it sooner or later. As for now, the mistress cannot conjure in a sty, and the world's a mess enough without laziness from the likes of me.*

With a sort of dim cheerfulness, Faye closed the chamber door behind her, descending the stairwell as Ravenna's chant rose behind her, filling the air with menace and poison.

With a down, derry, derry, derry, down, down, she sang. *With a down, derry, derry, derry, down, down.*

>>> I <<<

Terrance lurched out of a dreamless sleep and found himself in the seat of a moving wagon, the reins slack and slipping from his hands. The little team of horses he had hitched the night before waded aimlessly through the high grass, pausing to nuzzle and graze and sniff the rising wind.

For a moment, panic rushed over the wizard, as his gray eyes rifled the landscape for prominent trees, for familiar hills and declivities, for road or distant cottage or fading stars in the morning sky.

He did not have to look far. Ahead of him was Corbinwood, dark green and expansive, at the limit of his sight. It had to be Corbinwood. Within a thousand miles there was no other forest so large and dense.

Terrance sat back on the seat of the wagon. A long sigh issued from under his broad-brimmed hat, and his shoulders sagged in relief.

Good. It was as though the horses had known the way.

Brenn stirred and coughed in the wagon bed behind him, and the wizard turned. The lad was still asleep, his head resting on the flank of the old dog Bracken, but he was flushed and fitful,

9

tangled in a frayed blanket and small, almost frail, amid the bags of belongings he and Terrance had shoved into the wagon in their rushed departure the night before.

The wizard frowned. It was not good, this coughing. If what he feared was true, the swelling would follow, the sweating brow and the black sores. For when the coughing began the sick were past retrieval by potion and herb, past even the most powerful fever-drawing spells that Terrance knew. Then the plague took its course and the patients died or recovered, depending on something within them—something undefinable that emerged in dire circumstance: when the plague struck, or despair threatened, or the battle turned dire and nasty.

If the boy survived, he was the stuff of kings.

But his survival was very much in question as the wagon moved slowly south across the Palernan grasslands and the wizard, awake now and vigilant, guided the horses toward higher ground and twisted the reins anxiously in his hands.

Above him, in the high thin branches of a poplar, a solitary raven settled with a quiet folding of wings.

The forest was always at the edge of their thoughts, a sign that no matter how much they hewed and built and governed and civilized, there would always be something large and unmanageable beyond them, enormous and threatening beyond the momentary borders they had made. So the people of Palerna made stories about Corbinwood, filling it with legend and with the greatest fears they could imagine.

In the farthest reaches of the countryside, along the banks of the Eastmark River where the forest was only a traveler's tale, folks believed that its borders were white with the webs of spiders the size of small dogs. The creatures, it was said, would wrap their victims in white cocoons of webbing and suspend them from the branches of oak and poplar until the edge of the woods itself was heavy with dangling wayfarers.

Of course the more worldly laughed at the stories about those spiders. *Old wives's tales*, they maintained. *The largest spider is the sarcofago, the hand-sized Parthian creature that burrows in the great desert. Its bite makes the victim dance himself to death. There are no such exotic beasts at the edge of Corbin-wood. But deeper in the forest . . .*

Deeper in the forest, they maintained, was the panther who killed with its breath, or the hippogriff, or the porpentine. It depended upon who told the story. Terrance had run through most of the legends he remembered as the wagon drew to the wood's edge. Now he could see into the green shade beyond the first imposing row of trees.

Softly, he began to chant.

> *Fair quiet, have I found thee here,*
> *And Innocence thy Sister dear!*
> *Mistaken long, I sought you then*
> *In busie Companies of Men.*
> *Your sacred Plants, if here below,*
> *Only among the Plants will grow.*
> *Society is all but rude,*
> *To this delicious Solitude.*

Solemnly he chanted, carefully as old Archimago had taught him a half-century before, taking care to pronounce the *unciales*, that slight twist and rising in the voice that the old spell-casters wrote down as the capital letter. Finishing, he stared intently toward the margins of the forest.

A weak light flickered beyond the line of trees, and then a green glow, faint but steady, arose from the heart of the wood.

"Not much," Terrance grumbled. "Trees of this age are hard of bark and harder of wood. You can't persuade them and you can't win them over with flattery." He snorted, then stopped himself with a harrowed smile. Even though the apprentice was fast asleep, the master continued to puff and lecture.

He turned and cast a protective look over his charge. Curled up beside the young man, Bracken looked up at the wizard brightly, wagging his ragged tail.

"Where . . ." Brenn rasped suddenly, and the mage's gaze riveted itself to the restless lad in the bed of the wagon. "And Faye and Dirk . . . where is . . ."

"Hush, boy," Terrance soothed, his eyes returning slowly to

the border of the forest in front of him. "Dirk is fine. I know no Faye."

Not a lie. Not really. What did he know of the girl? And now was not the time, amid perils and fevers, for young romance to make the blood hectic and the actions reckless. It was a king in the wagon bed, no thrall of valentines and sonnets and youthful biology.

The less he thought on the girl, the better.

"Hush," Terrance soothed. "All will be well, I wager. Including you, my young friend."

Setting the reins on the driver's bench beside him, Terrance fumbled in the folds of his cloak. "It's in here somewhere," he muttered. "In the place I put it. Wherever *that* was."

Gently he produced a pen and inkwell and, shaking his head as he held them to the light, set them atop the reins and rummaged deep into the dark cloak again. A sparrow came next, its head flickering out from beneath its wing as the wizard brought it forth into the noonday light. It took wing, and Bracken grumbled once before falling back to sleep.

Now Terrance drew forth a book, and then another, then an astrolabe and an abacus. The seat beside him stacked with texts and instruments, the wizard's right hand snaked up his left sleeve, slipping over his shoulder, where he found the item he had been groping for.

"Ah!" he exclaimed, and drew forth the claridad apple—the green, luminous fruit from a long-dead tree. He had picked it in a place not far from here, but a half century ago, in a time that seemed so remote, so fragmented, that sometimes the wizard wondered if he had dreamed its finding and its story filled with sorrow and romance.

"Whatever the story, it's all the light I have," he assured himself. "And when we're past the spellglow, may the gods of wind and sun and stars grant that it is all the light I need."

For into the depths of the myth-shadowed forest the wizard planned to go, of course. Past the imagined hippogriffs and the enormous, iron-eating estrich bird, past the pards and mantichoras of children's stories to the very real robbers who prowled the banks of the Boniluce. For of all the rumors that Terrance had heard surrounding Corbinwood, there was only one story that mattered in this hard and dangerous time.

The rumors went that Galliard, the rightful Duke of Aquila, had found sanctuary in the green interiors. The Forest Lord, the Palernan peasants called him, after the green star whose passage signaled upheaval and change. With his numerous cousins and a small but loyal band of followers, he had made a stronghold on the Zephyrian side of the river, where even an occasional maneuver or a harmless "show of strength" by Dragmond's army might strike the fierce Zephyrian athelings as an act of aggression on their homeland.

There, safe in the midst of Palerna's traditional enemies, the King's cousin found safety and a peace of sorts, emerging only on rare occasion to unburden a rich Alanyan or redirect a shipment of Umbrian wine. Always the money found its way to the peasantry, to the yeomen farmers or the poor rivermen who reeled a meager living from the Boniluce or the Eastmark. And yet Duke Galliard was gone so quickly that the people had no chance to thank him. He was even more wary of common folk, it seemed, than he was of the crack Maravenian troops that searched for him along the Gray Strand and the Palernan plains.

"An odd sort," Terrance said aloud, setting the claridad on his lap and pulling the reins from the pile of belongings on the seat beside him. "Odd, but what we have in these times and these circumstances. I expect he will do, and do nicely."

He cast a worried glance behind him. The lad's brow was sweaty; his eyes spiraled and raced beneath the veil of the lids.

"And may his knowledge of herb and flower extend beyond my own," Terrance added quietly and passionately, as he flicked the reins and the tired horses began to move again, the shade of the trees surging over them.

In the leafy wet shadows, the air was loud with mosquitoes and midges. Brenn tossed fitfully in the bed of the wagon, jostling against Bracken, who rumbled amiably and curled up behind the lad's knee.

Leaning back over the seat, Terrance lifted the claridad. The leathery fruit warmed in his hand, and as he breathed regularly, rhythmically, the glow at its heart began to spread and swell. By its faint blue-green light the wizard peered at his sleeping apprentice.

Terrance gasped. The lad's condition had passed from feverish to alarming in almost no time.

"Now the swelling," the old man murmured. "Next 'twill be the chills and the black sores. Then the plague takes complete hold of him, and he looks into the face of the Dark Lady."

Wearily, he looked beyond the colonnade of trees for a sign of rescue. He dimly imagined the Forest Lord, young Galliard himself, striding to the rescue out of the encircling woods, bearing herb and ointment and perhaps the healing touch. For a moment, at the edges of green light, he saw the man, dressed in summer and gold.

Terrance blinked, shook his head, " 'Tis Duke Galliard's *father* I remember," he chided himself. "Perhaps even the grandfather. And whoever the man, it has been thirty years. By the assembled hamadryads of all these trees, I couldn't recognize Galliard if he stood before me!"

He lifted the claridad and stared into the looming shadows of the central woods. The strange green light of the fruit failed ahead of him, as though it was swallowed by the encircling darkness. Terrance felt alone and desolate, swallowed by his own dark thoughts.

On the wizard fared, slowly and cautiously. Once he heard noises in a deep thicket to his right—a mewling sound like a baby crying. Fooled for a moment, Terrance stood in the wagon, the claridad lifted in his hand. Then something crashed through the thorns and shrubbery—something large and menacing and no doubt predatory, and the high, frail sound faded, changing quickly to a growl just before it passed out of earshot.

Terrance shuddered and sat down again, his pale hand passing over the cold, polished, wooden club beneath the seat.

Next it was the smell of the sea, rising subtly and surprisingly from an oak-lined footpath at the edge of the wizard's side. Salt and kelp and the faint earthy smell of decay rode the breeze out of the heart of the wood, and if he closed his eyes and breathed deeply, Terrance could almost imagine he was back home, standing atop his ramshackle tower in Maraven, the sea wind sweeping past him from the north.

But the woods were breezeless, close and humid, the odor of decay rising until it overpowered the others, and in the light of the glowing fruit, the oak-shrouded path seemed to whiten with webs, to glitter with trapped and dying life.

"That's one path we're not taking tonight, Brenn," Terrance announced quietly, his back to the sleeping boy, and turned the horses to the left, toward what he thought was the sound of water.

It was a little while before a light, amber and brilliant, began to gambol amidst the trunks of the trees at the edge of the wizard's sight. At first he dismissed it as a product of his own fatigue, as the watchful eye's hunger for light after a long time of peering into darkness. But still the light continued to flit from branch to branch in the distance like a large and luminous bird, and a strange whistling filled the air around Terrance, the wagon, the dog and the sleeping Brenn.

"Hmmm," the wizard murmured, and reached just under the seat of the wagon, producing a twisted, club-shaped cypress knee the size of his arm. Without ceremony he set it on the seat beside him, assurance against whatever menace lay in the distant light. Under his watchful eye the light encircled the wagon, moving from tree to tree. With its circuit completed, it blinked out altogether, vanishing as rapidly as it had risen out of the forest dark.

Terrance sighed and stepped into the bed of the wagon, two dried sprigs of bittersweet in his hand. It was not yet time for the lethe—not while Brenn still fought against the fever and gave them all good heart.

And even if he lost that struggle, if the fever rose and the boy sank further . . . well, there were other, more desperate things that a wizard could try.

"I cannot give up and settle on making your dying easy, boy," Terrance whispered. "Not like I did for the others in Wall Town. Because the fates of nations are bound with your living. You must not die, no matter your pain and your fevers. Sometimes the simple drawing of a breath is most cruel and most kind, all at once and altogether."

✻ ✻ ✻

He had lived not far from here as a boy.

Yes, and somewhere to the south, where the Boniluce broke from the thick and impenetrable trees, Terrance's old master still dwelt in a wooden house, stilted precariously over the driving waters. Though it looked ready to drop into the currents at any moment or movement, the house only creaked and sighed. Its gray board sides sprouting green, feathery sprigs and anchoring roots, it was made from the "ever-living" wood. No doubt by this hour the fires were low in old Archimago's dwelling, the long alchemies of the day translated to slumber and the ancient man's loud and relentless snoring.

Terrance chuckled to himself and wrapped the blanket more tightly around his shoulders. It was the deepest part of the woods, where bears or assassins or even harmless trespassers were fashioned from vaporous shadows by overactive eyes and ears, not to mention an undue relish of gin.

Indeed, Terrance had just imagined that the trees were moving. Twice, three times, he had lifted the claridad and marked the location of twin cedars in the midst of a white stand of birches. At first the shadows had seemed different around them, and when he looked again, sure enough, it seemed that the two scrawny evergreens were farther apart. Perhaps he had dreamt them otherwise, or perhaps the sunlight had filtered somehow through the network of branches and leaves, shifting and fragmenting and creating the illusion that the trees themselves had moved.

Or perhaps the faeries had moved them.

Terrance chuckled again, lifting his broad-brimmed hat and producing a slim flask from underneath where it had lain, safe and easily found atop his head. He opened the bottle and took in the fresh smell of juniper. A brief swallow of the strong Zephyrian gin dazzled his nostrils and the back of his throat, and the wizard leaned against the side of the wagon. Soon he would need more warmth than the flask could provide.

He reserved judgment on the faeries. He had seen them only once, and fancied them long gone from this part of the world. But who knew what legends came to life among these gnarled and ancient branches?

What was the old warding Archimago had taught him? Something about circles and . . . and . . .

He had laughed at it then. Called it Archimago's gin. How the times had changed.

Terrance drank from the flask once more, a bit amused at how these simple tricks of light, easily explainable as foxfire or as vagaries of sunlight through leaves, could conjure up fairy tales to bother and unsettle a learned, if somewhat exhausted and cold, wizard. He sipped once more, then again for good measure, and, reaching into the wagon bed, set the flask precariously beside the boy and the dog. He leaned back again and cast another worried look at the boy, whose raging illness was no child's story or woodland legend.

It was then that Bracken growled, his long snout tipping over the flask as the dog rose from the entanglement of apprentice and blanket and fur in the wagon bed. Terrance called to the horses and flicked the reins, and the tired beasts surged left down a narrow trail.

It ended at once in an enormous net of rope, in which four straw men turned and dangled like moths in a spider's web. Laughter echoed around the wizard, as though the trees were mocking him.

Terrance turned the horses through brush and undergrowth, reaching for the cypress club. Then he heard rustling in the shadows to his left. Swiftly the wizard turned, lifted the weapon in his most formidable and fierce growl . . .

. . . and saw himself grimacing back, holding a cypress club.

Staring at the polished mirror, Terrance reined in the horses. He squinted into the distance beyond the light of the claridad, and saw men rising from the sea of leaves and greenery. All around him the forest burst into calls and whistles, as his ragged assailants—anywhere from a dozen to a thousand, it was confusing to tell, and their numbers were multiplied by mirrors—sprang from low-hanging limbs and rose out of bushes and undergrowth, knives in hand and bows nocked at the ready.

"Brenn!" the wizard hissed, the cypress club now tightly in his hand and Bracken circling the boy in the wagon bed, growling, his hackles raised. "Brenn!"

There was no answer. The lad murmured, stirring fitfully with a rustle of straw.

"Damn it!" Terrance muttered, his thoughts cascading over spells and charms and wardings he remembered only dimly, searching desperately for a word or a song or a token to spirit away his apprentice.

"Not yet!" he breathed. "Whoever they are, whatever their knives and numbers, they won't have him. Not yet!"

It was as though the woods responded. From somewhere in the foliage, surprised no doubt by commotion and torchlight, a hawk swooped over the wagon and eastward out of the woods. Terrance ducked as the bird passed above him, then smiled as the dark level wings flashed out of sight, his memory in tow behind them.

"How did it go?" he murmured, as someone shouted on the webbed trail ahead of him and the oak leaves rustled. He chanted, slowly at first, but more quickly as the ancient words came back to him and the men around him drew near.

> *Thence gathering plumes of perfect speculation,*
> *To impe the wings of thy high flying mind,*
> *Mount up aloft through heauenly contemplation*
> *From this darke world, whose damps the soule do blynde,*
> *And like the natiue brood of Eagles kynd,*
> *On that bright Sunne of glorie fix thine eyes,*
> *Clear'd from grosse mists of fraile infirmities.*

His back to the bed of the wagon, Terrance watched the approaching enemy. Suddenly, he heard a rustle of wings, a scraping and scrambling, and Bracken's surprised grumble. The wizard turned in time to see the eagle rise from the straw and the blankets straight into the humid forest air, surging through the branches above them like an arrow, like rocketry.

"It worked," he said wearily, sinking to his knees as a tight ring of torches formed about the wagon. "And it might be worth the risk."

Rough hands grasped the side of the wagon, then settled firmly on Terrance's shoulders. After a brief growl of protest, Bracken, never a formidable watchdog, gave up and burrowed behind the canvas bag in which Brennart had packed his belongings—a cloak, a knife and a new pair of boots and a large, mudstained scroll of vellum—things that no longer availed the lad as he rode the night wind and the moonstruck clouds of the Palernan sky.

"May it all be for the good," the wizard whispered, as his captors dragged him from the wagon.

After all, did not the scholars say that the eagle renews its youth? And what the scholars said was not always a lie.

So he thought as they bound his hands behind him roughly, as a black hood slipped over his face and blotted out torchlight and stars. The rest of the night he recalled by ear and smell and touch: the brush of a branch against his face, Bracken grumbling somewhere behind him, the snort of the horses and the creak of the wagon wheels, the cough of a man at his shoulder, and the smell of woodsmoke.

They led him through entanglements of woods toward the distant rush of the Boniluce. None of them, not even the most alert of the lookouts, posted at the point and the tail of the column, noticed the thousand amber eyes that watched intently as the men passed from tree to tree.

>>> **II** <<<

"Godspeed, lad," Terrance whispered through the dark hood, as branches and spiderwebs brushed over his arms. The forest was loud about him, rustling with the sound of moving men, with rough breathing and the creak of metal on leather.

Brenn was somewhere above the forest, he figured. Airborne and circling, acquainting himself with his new form and his new freedom. For a moment Terrance's thoughts soared after the lad, but they failed against wind and air. He could not reckon what had befallen his apprentice, there in the high thin winds. The spell had been a desperate one, after all—too volatile and mysterious to try unless you were hard-pressed, plague-ridden, surrounded by enemies.

Unless, indeed, it had been your last choice.

The wizard winced as someone behind him tightened the ropes at his wrist. Quickly he ransacked his memory for spells of light and escape, for conjury to loosen bonds, lift veils, and banish soldiers. Nothing came to him except a chant Archimago had taught him when he was only seven and fresh to apprenticeship, a simple chant of courage and resolve, learned before even the most elementary of magics.

> *The man of life upright,*
> *Whose guiltlesse hart is free*
> *From all dishonest deedes*
> *Or thought of vanitie,*
>
> *The man whose silent dayes*
> *In harmeles joyes are spent,*
> *Whome hopes cannot delude,*
> *Nor sorrow discontent,*
>
> *That man needes neither towers*
> *Nor armour for defence,*
> *Nor secret vautes to flie*
> *From thunders violence.*

Terrance smiled. The chant was an old one—so old that he could not be sure whether it had served as song or proverb or spellcraft. Having spoken it, he clenched his teeth and willed away the pain in his tightly bound hands. As if drawn by the power of conjury, or by simple fortune alone, the smell of the river rose to meet him.

The Boniluce, Terrance thought in surprise. *We are not returning to Maraven at all.*

For the first time since he had seen the torches in the darkness, hope returned to the old man. For this veiled procession was on its way into Zephyr, and the Forest Lord's camp was in those Zephyrian woods.

"I do believe I am rescued," Terrance whispered. He would have spoken aloud then, but the point of a spear prickled the back of his neck and a low voice behind him urged him gruffly to hold his tongue, if he knew what was good for him.

Silence was good enough for now, the wizard thought, his confidence rising. Breathing deeply the clean, moist air, he walked compliantly amid his captors, a spring and vitality returning to his strides.

It was an hour before the party jostled to a halt. One of his captors lowered him to the ground, bound his feet, and removed his hood. Blinded by the sudden intrusion of light, Terrance blinked uncomfortably. He turned to catch a glimpse of the man, but lost him in the bottle–green evening sun, dimly aslant through the layered thickness of trees.

Terrance's eyes adjusted, and he gasped at the camp in which he found himself.

It must have been the oldest part of Corbinwood—the vast interiors that had remained untouched and looked much as they had thousands of years before. A wide-girthed cedar grew in the midst of the clearing, spreading its shady branches, smothering nearly all undergrowth so that the ground was spongy, well-trod, covered only with a few hardy, shorter trees. Acacia grew there, and pine, and cypress, the wizard's favorite.

Terrance shifted his feet uncomfortably. The dried needles rustled on the ground beneath him. He breathed in the clean, watery smell of cedar, catching a whiff of woodsmoke so strong that it startled him. He turned to find a large central fire, low and magically smokeless, at the edge of the clearing, around which a dozen men stood and crouched and sat.

They were a ragged lot, his captors—their robes were a motley of grays and browns and forest greens. But they were healthy enough, and some seemed of a scholarly bent: One crouched over a sketch pad, charcoal in hand, while yet another thumbed through the worn pages of a book. Several others listened intently to a ruddy, handsome woman in her early middle age. Seated on a rickety oaken stool, her straight, slim back to the fire, she faced her audience and spoke to them merrily. On her knees she balanced a wooden bowl, while her rough hands deftly sliced a long yellow root that, despite his considerable schooling in herb lore, Terrance could not identify.

One of the men by the fire—a short, bearded fellow with pale gray eyes—rose, knife in hand, and moved quickly, casually, toward the wizard. For a moment Terrance caught his breath, foreseeing circumstances plummet from terrible to even worse. But the man slipped behind him and suddenly cut the ropes that had bound Terrance's hands. Just as suddenly, even before the wizard could thank him, the stocky man turned and vanished behind the bole of the monstrous cedar that dominated the center of the clearing.

The real show, however, lay a hundred feet above dried needles and fires, high in the branches of this enormous central tree. The wizard's eye followed a single thin strand of smoke as it snaked up the rough cedar trunk into the vault of branches over his head. There, half lost amid thick clusters of needle and cone, a dozen or so houses perched on the glassy air, as though floating atop a thick green rack of cloud. Terrance squinted, looked for supports, for braces—for anything that held the buildings aloft.

"Nothing," he breathed finally, admiring the ingenious architecture. "The trees themselves have grown around them."

He had seen it before in fence rows that bordered thick and encroaching woodlands—frail little battlements of paling and post, set by optimistic farmers and naive old wizards to ward out the woods and its disruption. For a while it had seemed to work: the forest would stop at the fence line, giving up, it seemed. Then, just when you had forgotten about it, the woods had covered the fence, swallowing it in greenery, and the rails of the fence vanished in the encircling trunks of the trees—live wood growing over and around the lumber as though living things were reaching back to claim their own from among the dead.

Nor did the wonders stop at the houses themselves. The wizard thought of his guest room, of the huge black maple that twined through the windows—for dozens of smaller trees were grafted to the cedar, sprouting at odd angles as though the cedar had taken it upon itself to shelter the lot of them. Acacia grew there, and pine, and cypress . . .

Again those particular trees. Terrance scratched his beard in puzzlement. And whatever hand had grafted them long ago had been a wise one, its skills surpassing his own so much that the wizard felt new and ignorant. It was as though a town, complete with its own groves and gardens, had grown and taken sustenance from the spreading branches of the cedar.

All of this ancient architecture, in all its height and vastness, seemed to house no more than two score men—fifty at the most. It seemed that the stories in Maraven had magnified greatly the strength of the "wolves's head" forces—the outlaws on whose head Dragmond had placed a sizeable bounty.

Or so the wizard was thinking when a half dozen rope ladders tumbled from the village perched above him, and yet another score of men—as ragged as the others—descended, armed with bow and arrow and long deer-skinning knives.

"We'll know soon enough," Terrance muttered, "if I am guest or hostage." He shifted himself with a crackle of dried leaves, and a small squirrel darted from his robes. Delighted at the prospect of so many trees, the animal took to an old acacia at the corner of the wizard's sight. The motley men, their feet now anchored firmly on the forest floor, encircled the wizard, and, after an irritatingly long silence in which Terrance stirred dried needles in front of him and murmured again the little song of courage, one of them—a slight, dark-eyed young man of twenty or so—spoke at last.

"I expect I should know you," he said, his hand resting lightly on the pommel of a polished short sword at his belt. "Your countenace is that of old Maraven, and in it is something of my own coasts and, alas, of the dark halls of Kestrel Tower."

Court Palernan, the wizard observed. *Self-important formal jabber, with its shoulds and countenances and words ass-backwards. The lad's a schooled nobleman, for all his ragged tunic and leather leggings. He's no doubt used to receiving visitors with bowing and scraping and dodging sentences.* Terrance responded with cautious silence only, his eyes darting from one bandit to another in the encircling ranks.

Sometimes they don't play fair, he thought. *Sometimes the one who greets you is not the one you should be talking to.* And he remembered everything he could of phrenology, of physiognomy, of all the other sciences of appearance he had always fancied a lot of balderdash, as he searched the faces for signs of leadership, for some special mark of insight surpassing that of the high-voiced, hesitant lad in front of him.

He settled on a larger young man—about the same age as the courtier, but with more assurance about him, a sort of quiet serenity. He was the only one not looking at Terrance. The big fellow towered at the side of the little spokesman, brandishing a club he did not intend to use. There was something about this blonde colossus that said he had found wisdom in the woods— just the thing Terrance expected from one who went by the name of Forest Lord.

"Know me ye might, young man," he answered the spokesman cautiously, his eyes all the while on the larger woodsman, "though by my reckoning you'd have been scarcely out of diaper and dress the last you saw me in Kestrel Tower. Terrance, I am: counselor to the late King Aurum and currently between employments."

Glances flickered through the ranks of Terrance's captors as they took in the surprising announcement. The wizard reached up, extending his hand for the clasp of friendship customary in Aquila, but the green-clad man who faced him folded his arms and regarded him skeptically.

The hands of the others rushed to the hilts of their swords.

"And how," he asked, lifting a hand to brush his black hair from his eyes, "do you regard the man who sits Aurum's throne in his stead?"

Off beyond the clearing, back toward where he imagined the Boniluce lay, Terrance heard a shrill, inhuman shriek—whether aloft or aground he could not tell, though something in him feared for Brenn at once.

"For King Dragmond," the wizard began, his thoughts racing and disrupted. "I can claim no . . . close affections."

The big man snorted and, hefting his club atop his broad shoulder, turned and placed his foot upon the nearest rope ladder.

"His news may not interest you, Ponder," the little dark man said, politely but intently, his eyes never leaving Terrance. "Nonetheless, I believe 'tis courtesy to hear him out."

Terrance sighed wearily. The menacing sounds of the deep

woods seemed farther away now. With creaking, popping knees he rose, feeling as though he had passed through all imaginable dangers to a time and a place where he could rest, restore his strength, and take heart for the rest of whatever lay ahead. The big man turned, extending a huge hand to help the wizard to his feet.

Terrance swayed precariously on his bound ankles and scowled at the lot of them.

"Of course," the dark young man continued, pulling his hood over his face and extending his right hand, into which a boy of twelve or so placed an enamelled, ebony shortbow, "sometimes to hear a man out takes days, or weeks, or even months. For what goes before him on the wind heralds more than his passing words, and what follows him echoes the counsel of his true heart."

The young man turned to this giant, this Ponder, and winked solemnly.

Terrance squinted in perplexity. He was used to his own doubletalk, and quite enjoyed veiling his teachings to exasperate young Brennart. But these forest proverbs were baffling, and he vowed to be more direct and less general when Brenn returned.

Providing he did return.

"There's a way of speaking in Corbinwood, it seems," the wizard observed, trying to appear calm as he brushed the dried needles from his leggings, "a way of speaking that tends toward parable, which may be fine for some ears. But for an old man whose brains are addled by time and travel, it's a mystery. Pray tell, Galliard—if that is who you are—just how you plan to *hear me out*."

"Galliard I am," the man in green conceded with a strange, crooked smile. "And by the gods, I know not whether you are in truth that Terrance of whom the forest itself has told me. That one, I have heard, travels this way, but he comes with a boy in his fatherly care—a boy to whom all honors are due. Or so the wind says."

Carefully, Galliard turned his attention to the bow in his hand. Quietly, with a swift, deft intensity bred of years in the hunt, he strung the weapon.

"I see no boy with you," he observed. "Indeed, all I have

seen are a hundred and twelve soldiers who follow your trail, each in the red armor of Dragmond's Watch.''

Terrance's eyes widened. It was the first he had known of this. They had made their way from Maraven, he and Brenn, under cover of night and of screening magic, but Ravenna's thousand eyes were sharp, and the noses of her commanders keen.

And Galliard knew to the number. The man in green was no green youth.

''I do not know why the soldiers come after you,'' Galliard continued, and Terrance, lost in thought and in worry, scarcely heard him. ''I do not know whether they hunt you or await your command. But as for now you will stay here, and we shall inspect those armed followers at our leisure.''

Galliard smiled again and, nodding to Ponder, walked off across the clearing. Three, then four other woodsmen joined him, each of them armed with bow and sword.

The Forest Lord wheeled about suddenly and stared at the wizard with a gaze disarming and direct.

''Rest for now,'' he said. ''I shall be with you anon, and together we shall determine what kind of Terrance you are. Meanwhile, I regret that I must bind your hands and enjoin your silence. Gesture and word are the stuff of magic, I understand, and though these woods are known to spoil and bend the best of conjury, I shall take no chances with the conjurer himself.''

Then, his followers beside him, Galliard vanished into the dappled shadows of the undergrowth. In an instant, the brush and branches settled into their former stillness, and Terrance coughed nervously, looking about him at the seasoned guerrillas who, after a brief, expectant moment, returned to whatever had occupied them. The handsome woman by the fire regarded him cautiously, her amber eyes flickering on a distant point behind him, as though she kept a private vigil from across some wide, unfathomable gulf.

He could produce the boy. The gods knew it would be tricky, involving a spell he was not sure he remembered, a forest in which dense growth baffled sight and sound, and the bird in question aloft and elusive, and probably very confused. Nonetheless, it could be done.

"But do I *want* to do it?" Terrance asked himself. The guard beside him turned, looking askance at the muttering old man in his custody. Terrance cleared his throat, closed his eyes.

For the eagle renews itself, is reborn on the wing. But who is to say that Brennart will return in health—that when again, or if, he puts on flesh and limb and hair, he will not dress himself in the plague as well?

So he thought through the lengthening day, as the faint smell of sulfur reached the clearing, and with it, the distant, muffled cries of man and horse.

>>> **III** <<<

The branches and leaves rushed darkly downward, and then there was nothing above him but sky and sunlight.

Brenn turned on a high breeze and circled about a tall stand of poplar. Dazzled by sudden wakefulness, he struggled to remember where he had been, what had brought him here . . .

He recalled only a wagon and leaves, a heaviness of wing and a damp disease. The old man had been perched on the wagon seat, and the whine of midge and mosquito filled his ears unmercifully. Even as these things came to mind, they were difficult to assemble, as though he remembered them from ten, a hundred, a thousand years before . . .

And so he forgot them for the moment, instead delighting in the lift of the air, in the sun over the lip of the woods and on the thousand sounds of the afternoon around him and below him. Twice he banked over the poplars, his bright eyes piercing through layers of forest to a line of torchlight dim amid the leaves.

The men were traveling toward the river.

There was something about them he was supposed to remember.

Brenn circled lower, intent on the men and the torches. They did not move in a line. Not like the others.

A wave of unease passed through him. So there were others. He could not remember.

But these men were quiet, were woodswise, spreading out and traveling in a long, foraging file toward the sound of the water. Quickly they passed through the spangling amber lights —light amid light unnoticed—and rejoined at two spots on the banks of the river.

At one of those spots the cover broke. Brenn, circling over that clearing, watched them ford by the fractured torchlight on the water.

The old man was among them—the one perched on the seat of the wagon. Brenn swooped lower in an effort to see and remember more.

Something about warmth and nurture came to him. Something gentle amid the thoughts of the high places and the hunt. Brenn remembered feeling much worse than he did now, and that the man had something to do with his feeling better.

But there was also the call of the sky above him. There was the need to hunt, and something more than that need—an impulse toward height and loneliness and the thin, washed air among the glowing clouds. So he banked his long wings and turned, his eyes on the sun. Swiftly he dove and passed one last time above the moving wagon, then climbed aloft into the lowest clouds. In the wagon his feathers had grown. He remembered as he surged back into light, as a lark twittered and banked from him in panic.

Before . . . he was in the wagon . . . was . . . mottled and ill at ease, and the man had . . .

The memory vanished, like a rabbit into the safe dark of its underground warren. Brenn circled back again, trying to recover the thought, but halfway back to the wagon he found himself borne aloft again.

The feathers had bristled on his back as they grew. It was like a part of him had opened, extended itself to the night air, offered itself to shadow and light and the cold breeze.

South his circling took him, over the glittering river. Beyond it were prospects of grasslands and fat mice. Brenn wheeled on a gust of warm wind and circled back over the woods and onto the pasturelands of Palerna, the sun behind him now and his shadow wavering red over fence and thatched roof, over copse and pond and warren.

For a moment he breathed in the high air exultantly. The breeze was brisk on his face, and the clean, watery odor of lightning rode in its wake. At once Brenn recognized the smell of the storm and swooped into a low glide over a hayfield. Bright and fragrant, the ricks seemed to rise to meet him, and he rode the sweet smell of drying grass over a thatched village, where a solitary farmer, hoe on his shoulder, shielded his eyes and looked up at the source of the flitting shadow above him.

He looks . . . Brenn thought, and the words failed him. As his wings swept through light and shadow, so his thoughts raced from human to bird back to human—from brief, barely reflective moments in which he was aware of his wings and his feathers, knowing he had not always been aloft and clothed in wind, and then to a wordless, instinctual alertness, when he saw the fur of small things bristle in the high grass, as they stiffened or scrambled to cover at his passing.

He looks . . . *like* . . .

A rabbit broke from the shadows of a capsized wagon, its back legs hammering as it raced under railing, then back into sunlight and across the cropped grass of a pasture.

Brenn tilted his wings as the hunger grew in him. His eye on the skittering prey, he began his dive, descending from the clear sky like lightning. Inches from the ground, he spread wide his wings and tail feathers, arched his talons and swooped from behind at the dodging rabbit—

At that moment, another part of him stopped short of his catch in a sudden, unexplainable terror. Something large and dangerous, afloat on the far horizon, moved over the wide, sunstruck fields. At once, the rabbit, doomed only a second before, leapt across a small brook and lost itself in bramble and high weeds.

Brenn flapped awkwardly and regained his balance. Steadily he surged to a vantage point in the sky, where sunlight and cloud would conspire to obscure him from the dark, approaching shape to the east.

It was not long until he could make out the black, leathery

wings, as the air caught fire and blazed around them with a fierce white light.

Dragon! the human voice within him exclaimed, and fighting down the powerful instinct to scream, gather the sun behind him and swoop down into battle, Brenn rose even higher, climbing into a sun-reddened cloud, where he hovered and circled and waited for the monster to pass.

It was some time before the dragon passed below him. By the time Brenn smelled it and felt the heat of its wings, he had almost forgotten it was approaching. The human part of him wrestled with his memory, saying *remember! remember!* It was only that persistence that kept him from breaking free of the thermal and exposing himself to tooth and talon and fiery, venomous breath.

His sharp eye piercing the mist below him, Brenn watched as the dragon surged under him, moving uncertainly westward.

It had a wingspan ten times his own and a sleek, reptilian body like that of the python, the green prophetic snake for whom the wandering star was named. And yet there was no prophecy in this monster—only a hungry, sinister searching as it passed, its wings burning away the mist around it.

Brenn banked and followed it closely, his sharpened senses racing over the leathery wings, the carrion smell, the hiss of the boiling air as the beast passed through it. Straight toward Corbinwood the dragon flew. It was as though high August followed the creature—the burning air, the drought, the charred grass, the days without prospect of comfort and relief.

Safely behind the monster, his gaze fixed on its laborious movement, Brenn felt a wave of desolation pass over him, a sadness too deep to be anything but human. He cocked his head, his glittering eye on the steaming crest of the dragon, and to his ear there came the high-pitched sound of wailing, as though a choir of gnats swarmed over the head of the beast. Curious, Brenn sailed even closer to the creature, until the heated air wavered and crackled on his feathers, forcing him to a greater height, to a cooler breeze.

There had been words in the wailing—of that Brenn was certain, though his human thoughts struggled so fiercely with those of the eagle that he had found no time to make out the words. Nor did he know whether the voice had come from the dragon itself or the incandescent air around it.

But there was something about its tone and pitch that Brenn remembered. Somewhere across a wide expanse of water, he believed, or somewhere in a dream—he was not certain. But he had heard it before.

Now directly above the creature again, he felt the air ripple about him, saw cinder and ash and smelled burnt hair. In the hot air the voice rose also, and Brenn concentrated, dipping uncomfortably as he strained for the words in the wailing.

Somewhere between chant and requiem it was—a lament for lost joys.

> *With what delight could I have walked thee round*
> *If I could joy in aught, sweet interchange*
> *Of hill and valley, rivers, woods, and plains,*
> *Now land, now sea, and shores with forest crowned,*
> *Rocks, dens, and caves; but I in none of these*
> *Find place or refuge; and the more I see*
> *Pleasures about me, so much more I feel*
> *Torment within me, as from the hateful siege*
> *Of contraries . . .*

A terrible lament it was, a harsh infernal muttering. It was a woman's voice, Brenn knew, and he combed his memory—fighting away false recollections of eyries and high rocks and the warm metallic taste of blood—for a thought of the woman herself, an image, a history.

Firelight. He remembered firelight, a dark gondola in the distance upon a lake and the faint glow of moonlight on skin pale as teeth or tombstones. Laughter . . . harsh laughter on the water, and the sound of singing and incantation.

The voice was dangerous. He was sure of it now. Though he could not remember the woman's name nor why he feared her, for a moment he saw her adrift against incredible darkness, her black hair flickering in a midnight breeze and the silhouettes of ravens in dark enamel on the side of her boat.

Startled, Brenn mounted the charged air in a powerful climb

through a bank of clouds, to a height where it seemed there was nothing between him and the sun but the thinnest expanse of air. It was like a huge and lidless eye; Brenn felt vulnerable, exposed.

The dragon turned and, with a single ponderous beat of its wings, skirted the edge of the woods in a northward glide. The branches and underbrush were seared behind it—withered and black and ruined—but the big beast seemed reluctant, even unable, to pass above the green, untouched sea of trees to its west. Silently it continued, the voice in and around its crested head dying away into the distance.

For a moment Brenn turned and flew north after the creature, catching a faint hint of sea air above its scalding stench. Far beyond the dragon, at a great remove on a shimmering horizon he recognized as the water's edge, he could see the dark mass and hovering smoke of a city.

It was a place that repelled him now.

He had come from there, he remembered vaguely. From a place where fear ruled. And where the sickness had settled like mist on the streets.

Suddenly Brenn wished he could lose the part of him that remembered and worried and feared deep within the instincts of the bird. He would be safe then, far from sickness and fear. His thoughts could rest, and he could delight in the wind passing over him, the buoyancy of the thermals and the smells and long sights of perpetual hunting.

For a moment the prospect seemed like heaven. He savored it, circling in a high arch and gliding south into the moist air over the river.

He would be an eagle forever. It was as simple as that.

But there in the warm skies over Palerna, Brenn had no idea how to begin with such an apparently simple thing. Try as he might to banish thought, memories flitted and flourished in his mind, while at the same time something was drawing him back toward the woods—something more of words than instinct, more of the human than the bird. He knew he would have to answer it.

For the moment, though, the skies were his. The dragon had passed by and was now a dwindling spot to the north, and though now Brenn could hear a chanting from the woods below, it was dim and not yet compelling. Now was the time to sport in the air, to delight in wing and movement.

To disrupt and scatter that flock of birds approaching from the north. He stirred at the prospect.

There were dozens of them, flying hundreds of feet below him in a tight chevron formation as though they were migrating geese. But the black shimmer of their feathers told the circling eagle that these were crows, or ravens . . .

There was something to remember about crows and ravens, something about moonlight and water he . . . had already forgotten . . .

Brenn banished the worry, the nagging memory. These black birds, so carefully and rigorously arranged, would make for great fun in high places. He dipped his wings, sailed above them in a thin veil of clouds where he was close enough to see the slick of their feathers.

Again the water flickered briefly in his memory; then the image fragmented and was lost.

Brenn pondered this for a moment, the path of his flight slowly bringing him closer and closer to the sailing ravens, to where he could hear the calls and the chatter that passed between them.

Closer on the left! Closer! Closer!

Keep your eyes sharp, brothers, and keep your wing away from the woods. The other She has something to say over trespassin'.

Safe enough, Brenn thought. The simple language of ravens. For a moment the clouds broke and he saw five of them, then six, directly beneath him, keeping the woods to their starboard as they spied and skirted it on their way toward the river and the grasslands beyond it.

So much for the menace, Brenn thought, as again the clouds closed around him. After all, hadn't the dragon passed by only moments ago? No wonder there was a faint whiff of danger and ash still riding on the air. It might be there for days, what with the burning that had followed in the wake of the monster.

So Brenn told himself twice, then a third time, explaining away the fears that lurked in his thoughts of words. Ravens were small, relatively harmless if one was too quick for those little tearing beaks, too strong to be held in those little talons.

If one was, after all, an eagle.

The clouds broke again, and he gathered himself and dropped with a shriek, straight into the midst of the gliding chevron.

At first they scattered, as he knew they would. Black wings danced and flitted before him like startled bats, and the air was raucous with their cries. Brenn circled tightly in the midst of them, hooked beak flashing as though he would tear apart any wing that passed too close, extinguish any eye within the reach of his outstretched talons.

Then the first of them struck his side in a sudden impact of black feather and bone.

Brenn reeled from the blow, dropping a hundred feet or so before he recovered breath and balance. Still high over the plains, his wings finally steadied and his flight level, he calmed himself and prepared to climb again.

Suddenly one, then another, of the ravens fell on him from above, talons scraping and clutching him as they passed, beaks flashing painfully into his breast and back. Bewildered, Brenn staggered in the air and looked about him wildly.

Below him, his two attackers had already passed from sight. The plains were rising rapidly to meet him, and he struggled to move his wounded wings, to keep himself from falling.

At the last moment, at the very edge of panic, something stirred in Brenn and a quick, frantic wingbeat broke his fall. Softly he settled onto the singed, hot grass of the plains and walked slowly and awkwardly toward a fence railing, half-down and aslant between two leaning posts. In a distant farmyard a dog barked and chickens burst forth with hysterical cackling. Soon the windows of the farmhouse opened, and Brenn could see into the building, from its hardened floors to its thatched eaves.

Above him now, descending slowly until they surrounded him, the ravens called menacingly to one another.

Thought he was a bravo, yes.

Thought he was a tough, a hooligan, comin' down on us. Now he's got to strain and wrestle and strangle himself just to hop a cut-limb and sit there.

A hundred glittering eyes regarded Brenn coldly as more of

the ravens settled onto branch and fence and ground until the landscape was heavy with dark wings. At times they flitted overhead, blotting out the moonlight when they passed, and for some reason Brenn remembered the dark woods and the wagon.

Now one of the birds, an old one, mangy and balding and gnarled of bill, resembling a vulture more than any raven Brenn had ever seen, stepped forth from the boiling mass of dark feathers. It hobbled closer and perched upon the fencepost closest to Brenn's rail, regarding him with dim and hostile eyes.

Y'ain't half the gallant y'fancies y'self, the old bird croaked. *Why, y'ain't even a right eagle, I can tell.* His fellows chimed agreement from their nearby perches, as the old raven lurched wickedly at Brenn, his dark bill clacking.

N-now, mind yourself and that beak of yours! warned Brenn, staggering as he backed gracelessly across the railing. But the warning sounded shrill and absurd to him, and ever so lonely here in the midst of his enemies.

He longed for the nameless old man in the wagon, for the dog that he remembered for the first time then. But no help came, and the skies above him swarmed with black wings.

Slowly and confidently, the circle of hopping ravens tightened around their quarry. Dropping from branch and paling and post, they waddled grotesquely toward Brenn, their beaks slashing and tearing the air. The song they sang was filled with death and decay and dire prophecy.

> *Ye'll sit on his white hause-bane,*
> *And I'll pike out his bonny blue een,*
> *Wi' ae lock o' his gowden hair*
> *We'll theek our nest when it grows bare . . .*

Brenn had heard enough. With a swift, shuddering wingbeat he was aloft, sailing low over the grasslands toward the light of the farmhouse, the boding sound of his pursuers close behind him, and with it a new sound—the harsh, icy laughter he had heard long ago on a lake spangled with moonlight . . .

. . . *moonlight on skin pale as teeth or tombstones.*

And yet the farmhouse drew nearer, a warm circle of light in the midst of the swirling darkness, a safety, a sanctuary . . .

. . . filled with man and his fire and weapons.

For a moment Brenn had forgotten the changed lot of things. Abruptly, he surged over the farmhouse and up on a gust of wind. He was welcome at no farmhouse with his talon and beak, with the country stories of how the eagles snatched chickens and livestock and sometimes babies.

He rose suddenly, seeking the open air where he could maneuver himself free of pursuers. Startled, his dark enemies scattered before him, and for a moment Brenn could see open sky and freedom.

Then the first of them struck his side with a resounding blow, sending him hurtling into another of them. He slowed, tumbled from his precipitous climb, and all of a sudden the ravens were upon him.

Around his face and eyes the sharp bills darted like the tails of scorpions, the claws of crabs. Wings battered against him and talons pulled him down into a smothering chorus of cries. For a moment he could not breath for the pounding, for the dark oily feathers and the hot stink of carrion. Reeling, Brenn swooped out of the frenzy of birds into a staggering glide not ten feet above the fields. They dropped on him like dark hail, razored and deadly, and twice he felt the tips of his wings brush the ground.

The grasslands stretched on endlessly ahead of him. The chase would go on forever, until he dropped, his thin, brittle bones snapping on the hard summer ground of Palerna.

They would feast on his eyes and entrails, and with his feathers they would thick their nests.

With a shriek that emerged from somewhere in him below words and reason and even below feeling, Brenn burst upward through a dense squadron of ravens, headed toward the clouds and higher still, bound straight for the bright-curtained face of the sun. The black wings parted in front of him readily, and one bird alone—a glistening, blue-black thug—stood between Brenn and the open sky, its talons outstretched, its rough voice shrill and taunting.

Brenn did not stop to make out the words. With a blunt, unstudied move toward the raven's tail, he passed by the bird in a white-hot rush, seizing it with his talons and rending it on the wing, as thoughtlessly and casually as he would wring out a wet cloth in safer surroundings. For a moment the ravens banked away, startled as their comrade seemed to explode in front of them, as the eagle seemed to pass through a black cloud of feathers and out to a great distance above them, dwindling quickly until the sky seemed to swallow him altogether.

Frantically, they launched into pursuit, croaking and yammering, but as they rose through the air the breathing became more difficult, the air more crisp and chilly on their wings, and the eagle a smaller speck in the sky above them.

Next time, one of them boded. *There's a next time in the wind, when that eagle will fall.*

But we got to tell Her now, the old bird replied gloomily, as the flight circled to the north, the younger birds falling in wearily behind the leaders. *We got to tell Her, and She ain't hungry for bad news.*

But what's an eagle to the Great Witch? still another one asked—a female, large, with an ominous bright beak. *She's prone to keep eye to the ground and Her own.*

The old bird clucked disapprovingly, the hoarse sound filling his throat and the silences of the high air as the ravens skirted the edge of Corbinwood, with Lake Teal a shimmering spot at the edge of their sight, and beyond the bulk of Maraven lay mottled and sickly.

What's an eagle, indeed? he asked. *But it warn't an eagle that slipped us. And I'll wager a bright bone 'twas the one She's fannin' for.*

Brenn could hear them whining from a great distance as they flew away from him.

When he had reached this height, he had recovered his wits. Or so he supposed. But his wits had been of little help: he could not figure how he had eluded so many ravens, nor why they had given up pursuit.

It was a curious thing, he mused. Something to ask Terrance when he saw him.

Terrance. The name struck him suddenly, as unexpected as a hurtling enemy from above.

Terrance.

Brenn heard something chanting on the air, from a distance where the words were indecipherable.

Terrance was . . . was . . .

Whatever he was, it was time to find him.

Slowly the eagle turned in the high cold wind, making his way back toward Corbinwood now, back toward his scattered memory.

>>> **IV** <<<

He sat on the porch of a lofty cabin, looking down on the assembled woodsmen.

Galliard had twined green holly in his brown hair, forming a wreath or a crown about his temples. He looked like a woodland spirit, handsome and beardless and dark-eyed, as he relaxed and held court with his cousins and followers and friends.

"What shall we do with this Terrance, Galliard?" asked the stocky, gray-eyed fellow.

"I believe you're addressing me incorrectly, Cousin Sendow," Galliard coaxed, hiding a playful smile.

Sendow looked away and shuffled his feet.

"I am waiting, Sendow."

"What shall we do with Terrance, Your Grace . . ."

"To whom . . ." the Forest Lord prompted. Ponder snorted, stifling a laugh.

"To whom I owe . . . a deep respect . . . abiding . . ."

". . . as these cedars. . . . Go on, Sendow."

"Abiding . . . as these cedars. Next to whom I am an insect . . . a . . . a—"

"Say it, Sendow!" Galliard exclaimed merrily.

"Yes, say it!" prompted a dirt-covered cousin, the one they called Jimsett.

Sendow paused and looked angrily at his hands.

"Next to whom I am an insect, a dropping. *Now* are you satisfied, Galliard?"

"Satisfied indeed," answered the Forest Lord smugly. "*That* should teach you to wager your skills against mine in archery. Next time I shall devise a form of address even more abasing and humiliating."

Jimsett and Ponder laughed out loud, and Sendow's frown finally melted. Blushing and smiling, he looked up at Galliard.

"You are the better archer, no doubt. I shall remember that before next I wager. Instead, I shall challenge you to pathfinding. Come with me over the Boniluce, to the center of the Palernan Corbinwood. We shall blindfold ourselves, spin around four times, and wait for the night to fall. The first to find his way back to the clearing wins the choice of our takings from Dragmond's next caravan!"

Sendow stepped back proudly. Galliard frowned mock-seriously, then shook his head.

"Sendow, I believe that is the most foolish challenge ever I heard!"

All of the cousins burst into laughter. The woodsmen among them fidgeted uneasily, waiting for the counsel to pass to the business at hand.

"Now," Galliard said, dangling his legs over the high porch of the cabin. "What *shall* we do with this Terrance? What do you make of him, Thomas?"

A smooth-faced man, his hair prematurely gray, stepped forth from the milling woodsmen. "His pockets, gentle coz, are a pack rat's paradise," he announced, and tossed a wild array of items before him. Three books, a peach, a thimble, some dried animal droppings, a spyglass, a sprig of parsley, a candle stub and a ball of multicolored string—all lay together at the base of the Forest Lord's cedar.

A beautiful young girl of fourteen or fifteen, her soft blonde hair tied in a snood, rushed out of the crowd and snatched up the spyglass. Jimsett stepped forward, bent down, and with a callused, grubby hand, picked up one of the dried droppings.

"Look!" he proclaimed, holding the wretched little thing in the air. " 'Tis Sendow's coat of arms!"

" 'Tis Jimsett's inheritance!" Sendow snapped back.

Galliard laughed and raised his hand for silence. When all eyes were on him, he resumed the council.

"What would *you* have us do, Lapis?" he asked the blonde girl, who regarded him intently through her newly acquired spyglass.

"Ask Jimsett," Lapis said. "He was the first to come across this wizard."

"Bury him," Jimsett suggested, wiping a smudge from his forehead. "See if he can tunnel his way to the light."

"If he's a genuine wizard," Galliard suggested with a smile, "we shouldn't put him to honest work. Wizards are no good for that. No, cousins. We must uncover whether 'tis Terrance of Maraven or some imposter. So there's the matter of Libra."

The cousins looked at one another in puzzlement. All of them knew the story of Mardonius and the legendary sword Libra, how the ancient Duke of Aquila had been betrayed by the very sword he had killed his brothers to acquire.

"If you remember," Galliard said. "The *real* Terrance was at the court in Arbor. He saw the intrigues of Mardonius come to a swift and violent end. What he remembers will prove him: let us hope he remembers clearly."

Silently and apprehensively, Terrance watched them approach. The woodsmen crossed over the soft ground of the clearing, Galliard paced over to the central tree. Setting his book aside, Ponder scrambled nimbly down the ladder. He and another man, a wild-eyed fellow Terrance had heard called Thomas, joined with the Forest Lord in a brief, intent conference as the rest of the company milled around its officers.

Terrance stood at the edge of this circle of men as all eyes fixed upon Galliard. The young man whispered something to Thomas, who nodded briskly, then passed through the circle of men and into a stand of pine at the edge of the clearing. Terrance watched the man until he lost sight of him in the woods. When he turned back, Galliard was directly in front of him, hand extended in the traditional Aquilan sign of friendship.

Bitterly, Terrance nodded toward his own bound hands.

"You have heard of the sword Libra, wizard?" Galliard asked. "The sword that rested in the rock in Arbor—the one Great-grandsire Aquila set there with a secret?"

Terrance nodded vehemently. Extending his index finger, he moved his bound hands in front of him, scratching words on the dirt of the clearing floor. Swiftly Ponder moved to his side, reading attentively lest the wizard conjure by writing alone.

"*Libra potestatis sum*, it says," the big man reported to Galliard, who stepped to Terrance's side, squinted, and read it himself.

"*Libra potestatis sum*. 'I am the balance of power.' Very good, save that a man who frequents Dragmond's throne room could read it on the sword itself as it hangs from its place on the wall of that chamber. No, Terrance. Not the slogan on the blade. Give me Aquila's legend. What was the phrase passed down from father to son and brother to brother in the governing houses of Aquila? What were the double–edged words old Aquila used to describe the double–edged power of the blade?"

"It *singled out the crown of the line*," Terrance wrote. "Now let me go," he growled, and Ponder startled and leapt, as though a bird beside him had suddenly and inexplicably chosen to talk.

"Welcome, Terrance of Maraven," Galliard said with an open smile, kneeling to cut the old man's bonds with the edge of his hunting knife. "Come to the heights of the Founding Tree and we shall talk, for I have learned by this test that your word is good."

As the two walked, Terrance leaning for support on the Forest Lord's shoulder, the younger man filled the wizard with tidings and news.

"The edge of the woods," Galliard said, "is patrolled by the Watch from the river to Lake Teal, and their patrols are not idle. Time has been that an arrow or two in their direction, a shout or a signal of birdcalls, has sent them back to a safer distance —sometimes even back to Maraven. But this morning, even before your arrival, they stepped into the woods itself, their torches uplifted and their swords drawn. Thomas brought one to earth, and I another, though I felt no delight in the matter. Only with two of their comrades felled by arrows did the Watchmen retreat from the forest. Yet they have not removed themselves entirely, but stand at the edge of bowshot, patrolling these woods by moonlight and spyglass.

"Nor do they watch unaided. The birds and wyrm of the Great Witch command the skies. All of these—the Watch and the creatures that ride with them—do not follow you to aid you, wizard: of that I am certain."

Terrance's eyes narrowed and his lip curled into a frown. He searched Galliard's eyes for truth.

"The wyrm, you say? And Ravenna's birds? Then there is no time for talk."

Galliard stared up at the canopy of limbs and frowned as Terrance stalked to the edge of the clearing, where he stood apart from the busy assembly. The wizard lifted his hands, gazed up into the obscure sky, and again raised a chant as the air about him wavered and stilled. Quietly, as though the rhythmic words summoned her as well as the eagle, the woman returned to the clearing and, standing in a faint circle of the morning's mushrooms, she folded her ruddy hands behind her and watched with interest.

"*The tersel egle*," Terrance began, closing his eyes.

> *The tersel egle, as that ye knowe wel,*
> *The foul royal, above yow in degre,*
> *The wyse and worthi, secre, trewe as stel,*
> *Which I have formed, as ye may wel se,*
> *In every part as it best liketh me—*
> *Now nedeth not his shap yow to devyse—*
> *He shal now chese and speken in his*
>   *gyse.*

The words tumbled from him gracefully, filling the clearing like the sound of a summer downpour. Most of the woodsmen, unsettled by the ancient, musical words, backed even further from the chanting wizard, regarding the scene with suspicion. Only two of them drew near: Galliard, who looked on with ducal calm, and, at his side, the huge philosopher Ponder, a pair of many-faceted spectacles fixed to the bridge of his nose, squinting at Terrance with the skeptical intent of a scientist.

The woman stepped from the circle of mushrooms, nodding and smiling.

For a while, Terrance feared that the lad had wandered past governance. The trees about the clearing seemed poised, expectant, their branches uplifted as the sky darkened toward evening.

And still no sign of Brenn. Soon a smaller bird circled the clearing—a sea eagle, Terrance recalled dimly from Archimago's fitful lessons in ornithology. Heedless of the armed men and their encampment, the bird alighted on a low limb and settled. Its green feathers mottled and ruffled, the accipiter glared at Terrance as though he had wakened it from a needful sleep.

"Is that the lad?" Ponder whispered.

"Hush!" Galliard hissed. "There is danger in words."

Swiftly, the eagle underwent its change. The air bent and shimmered about it, like heat rising from the head of a dragon. In the midst of that swimming air, the creature seemed to turn inside out, to unravel in a swirl of feathers.

Several of the woodsmen gasped, and more than one made warding signs against evil. Before them sat a slight, bearded man of about forty, naked and dusty, his face a map of bewilderment.

"Faeries," Jimsett whispered with a frown. "Faeries done that to him."

"Or enchanters," the woman added quickly. "More like it's enchanters's work."

The bearded man stared at her brightly, his dark eyes fevered and frightened. "Blort," he said, and scratched his shoulder with his nose.

Slowly the woman stepped forward, extending her hand to the man, who took it almost without hesitation. Smiling, she led him to a spot by the fire, draped a blanket over his shoulders, and set about boiling water, into which she tossed a handful of fragrant herbs.

Terrance glanced curiously at Galliard, who shrugged.

"Here when we arrived, Master Terrance," he offered, as if *that* were explanation. "Here among these shelters in lonely residence. Handy with herbs and the lore of the woods, she was, and a blessing for a handful of forest-shy cousins. 'Glory,' she calls herself, a name quite . . . exalted for a country woman, some say . . .''

He paused at Terrance's frown, searching his words for what he might have said to offend the wizard.

"Oh, by that I mean—" Galliard started to explain, but the wizard waved away the words with a gnarled hand.

"Enough of explaining and reasoning and laying of blame," he snapped. "The lad is still aloft, and the skies are a deadly place."

Again Terrance pronounced the spell, alone at the edge of the clearing.

Galliard seated himself on a stump and looked about his encampment idly, his thoughts racing over the day's strange arrivals.

This is the one who sat in the court of my father, the Forest Lord mused. *My father, who always claimed that the wizards left storms in their wake. Well, this Terrance is only hours here, and what have I seen? Dragmond's army again, a new captain at the helm who does not hesitate to send his troops into Corbinwood, into unknowable dangers. And the dragon. And as if all that weren't enough, an eagle strangely transformed into a man, or back into a man, or something, and a lad mysteriously important, trapped somewhere on the wing . . .*

His back to the encampment and to the chanting wizard, his people engrossed in magic, Galliard reached into his tunic and produced the green leathery fruit. He held it close to his chest so that none of his companions—especially not Terrance—would see it. Clutched tightly in his hands, the fruit gave off a faint, phosphorescent glow amid the green shadows of the woodland.

Like sunlight through the leaves, Galliard thought, and was filled with a sudden sadness. He leaned against a tree and smelled the warm, smoky odor of the wood.

Sunlight always descends through the leaves.

Suddenly repentant, as usual, the Forest Lord promised himself that he would restore the green claridad apple to Terrance's belongings.

Soon, he thought. *Whenever the wizard's head is turned.* But the promising seemed as timeworn and lifeless as the leathery fruit, and possessed of the same melancholy.

Terrance had almost given the lad up for lost. A third time he tried the incantation, when it became clear that the second time had not worked.

The sun was high in the morning sky by now, and the noontide fast approaching. The woodsmen were about their business, all thoughts of the wizard having been set aside as just another wonder to which there might or might not be something, like the Parthian visionary who looked out over Maraven and saw the city burning with a fire nobody else could see, a fire that he claimed *was yet unkindled* . . .

Or the fast-talking Alanyan merchant, the British forest warden, and the Irish bureaucrat, each of whom had passed through Corbinwood on his way south, carrying with him elaborate tales of enchantment and magical transformation . . .

Or now this eagle, who descended upon them at the wizard's command and, with a flurry of fireworks and feathers, was rendered suddenly and inexplicably human.

If the woodsmen dwelt upon any of those things, they did not show it, but went about gathering windfallen limbs for kindling, and sprigs of parsley and rue for some concoction Glory was brewing. Galliard alone remained at his post, soon joined by Thomas, who walked from the darkening leaves. The pair of cousins sat quietly together, watching as the wizard chanted and paused, then chanted again, until an hour had passed and the fire was burning cheerfully.

Terrance's shoulders slumped. He looked years older in the bright, bottle-green clearing. Slowly, as if it were a painful task, he pulled the wide brim of his hat down over his face. Bracken trotted over to his master, nestling his long wet snout in the wizard's hand.

Galliard waited tensely, watching the scene unfold. For he had seen the movements in the stars but a month ago—the movement of Basilius in and through the Sign of the Snake. The Duke of Aquila was no astronomer, but the nobility always kept their eyes to the heavens, where the changes that took place upon the earth were first registered and known.

Basilius was the royal star that made and unmade the kings over whom it passed. It would not pass through this part of the heavens for another hundred years. With it, perhaps, was passing the time of Dragmond.

The Forest Lord cleared his throat as Terrance turned and walked toward the fire, Bracken waddling attentively after him.

"Take heart, Terrance," Galliard began quietly, his eye intent on the wizard, "Corbinwood is large, and the trees tend to baffle the sound. Try again in an hour's time, for the wind may have turned and the sounds of the forest changed or settled."

Terrance looked at him cynically and extended his hands toward the welcome warmth of the blaze.

"Do you think for a moment, man, that I have have given up?" the wizard asked testily.

It was at that moment that the eagle came to roost in the branches of the great cedar. At arm's length from Ponder it alighted. Startled, the big man cast aside his book and scrambled from the limb. Halfway down the rope ladder his feet tangled in the rungs, and suddenly Galliard's captain and resident scientist hung by the ankles over the spinning clearing.

"Galliard! By the gods!" Ponder called out, but the Forest Lord waved him to silence.

"Hush, Ponder! You'll scare away the bird."

But despite the commotion, the eagle seemed to have no intention of flying away. Alertly it scanned the clearing until its eyes came to rest upon the wizard. It screeched triumphantly and lifted its wings, as once again Terrance repeated the chant, this time in an urgent, but scarcely audible, whisper.

Slowly, as it had done once before with the eagle-man, the spell worked its mysteries. The feathers receded, quickly and grotesquely, as though thousands of arrows were entering the body of the lad simultaneously.

For a lad it was, beneath all the flourish and light of the spell. A slight, wiry young man it was, or so Galliard remarked, and once the feathers had vanished and with them the last of the birdlike features, the fellow staggered on the branch, windmilling his arms for balance.

He seemed vulnerable, there in dirt and nakedness astraddle

the huge cedar limb, his clothes still scattered in the bed of the wizard's wagon.

"Blort!" he exclaimed weakly. Then, "Terrance! You're . . . Terrance!"

"And I am here to see to your recovery, lad," the wizard announced, stepping toward the ladder. Sensing that she would be needed, Glory left the side of the sleeping eagle-man and approached the great cedar, as Terrance climbed the first few rungs of the ladder and then, his path obstructed by the entangled Ponder, simply climbed over the protesting big man and onto the branch, where he hefted the shivering Brenn onto his shoulder and, staggering a little under the lad's weight, started his descent.

Galliard, Thomas, and several of the other woodsmen were at the foot of the ladder in an instant, each man lending a hand as the wizard lowered the boy. Ponder himself, though flushed and uncomfortably tethered, helped to steady Brenn as the wizard passed him down from the limb.

"There's sores on him!" Thomas hissed, withdrawing his hands in disgust and horror. Several of the woodsman heard his outburst, and a whisper went up through the clearing as though a wind had rushed through dry leaves.

Coldly, Galliard reached to his belt for a pair of tooled Alanyan gloves, and handed them to Thomas with an icy stare.

"Then rest your hands easy in these, my friend. Easy and clean, while the rest of us see to the lad and do what needs doing."

"B-but . . ." Thomas began, torn between fright and shame. Glory laid a rough hand on his shoulder and spoke to him swiftly, soothingly.

"He's past carrying, Master Thomas," she explained, her voice low and musical. "Past carrying but not past peril. The approaching night will decide if he weathers the Death. The night and the lad, that is."

Thomas stepped back, and Glory moved beyond him. She knelt before Brenn, who lay half-conscious and bewildered on the floor of the forest, flanked by Terrance and Galliard. Quickly the woman set a cup to the lad's lips—a cup filled with a fragrant, steaming liquid—and whispered something to him, as the wizard and the Forest Lord watched from what seemed a great and impassable distance.

Brenn nodded and closed his eyes. The woodsmen encircled him as though they could protect him from something turned sorrowful in the forest air.

And the noontide passed into afternoon, and on into evening, as the boy slept and the kingdom waited.

"Stand fast," she had said. "Remain calm. Neither take her hand nor touch her. Above all, expect the unexpected."

Brenn puzzled at the words, and thought of Faye for a moment with a smile. But it was not of Faye that this woman was speaking—this ruddy woman who smelled of rosemary and rue and yarrow. He nodded and closed his eyes, shutting out all of them—the woman, Terrance, this assemblage of rough-looking men. He would rest for just a moment, and then . . . then he would . . .

. . . what he would do he could not imagine. Instead, he wanted to sleep, to set them all aside. Beyond the lids of his eyes the whole world waited, but he was tired, he was hot, he wanted nothing to do with the lot of them.

Quickly, he passed from thinking and fatigue into a feverish sleep.

The street was hot beneath his back, and the air smelled of burning tar and thatch.

He lay on the Boulevard of Waters, on the cobblestones of Wall Town. In the rising heat, all Maraven wavered in an orange light around him, and Brenn sniffed the air urgently, hounding the source of the fire.

For of all the city dangers of that time—in Maraven or any other place in which buildings were close, cramped, and built of wood and mud and straw—it was fire that the people dreaded the most. Even at the edge of the sea, where the dryest season was still temperate and damp, they would waken to the imagined smell of smoke, the night suddenly gone hostile around them. Or the sunset would catch their eye over Ships, and, standing east of the reddening glow, their vantage obscured by buildings and evening mist, they would harbor the worst speculations, as the evening passed into night and again the sudden starts out of sleep.

No surprise it was, then, that Brenn was to his feet in an instant, the red streets spiraling beneath him. Steadying himself on the hot slick cobblestones, he looked south along the snaking Maravenian East Wall, where the buildings lay hunched and huddled—but intact, untouched by fire. Brenn sighed greatly, breathing a thanks to the assembled gods of water and wind.

It was then that he heard the army.

All of a sudden, the street rumbled faintly beneath his feet. At first Brenn thought *earthquake*, but instead of increasing in size and intensity, the tremor steadied, remaining faint and insistent like the beat of an enormous drum in the outskirts of the city.

Then he saw the first of them, though his view was clouded by smoke and the red shifting light in the city skies. Two blocks away the column marched, north on Hadrach Road, the death's-heads on their shields flickering darkly like beetle's wings as they passed quickly by the narrowing mouth of the alley—a thousand of them, bound for the beaches and for Grospoint beyond.

Brenn remained silent. Cautiously, he turned his eyes back to the Boulevard of Waters. The street had changed, suddenly and completely, into nothing that resembled the familiar surroundings of Wall Town.

"Why, it's not even *Maraven!*" Brenn exclaimed, pivoting as his eyes took in the street scenes around him—the tilted buildings and the strange white minarets that stood where shops and trade halls and market stalls had stood but a minute ago. Like a landscape from Scythia or Aegyptus it was, where the Moors had settled with their towers and their many calls to prayer.

Brenn tilted back on his heels, staring up at the icy, tear-shaped pavilions a hundred feet above him. Like crowns they were, like the promise of rest and ease and release. Around him, though, the streets were bare and lifeless and still, the cobblestones smoking, everything fevered and hushed as though it awaited yet another incredible transformation.

Brenn removed his cloak. It was oppressively hot and close here amid the looming buildings. It was as though the narrow side-streets baffled the heat and the steam, channeling it through a conduit of alleys until the whole surroundings were like one of those ancient Aquilan ovens, warmed by circling hot air.

Gasping, beginning to sweat, Brenn looked up.

The tops of the minarets were burning with bright and soundless white flame.

"Terrance! Terrance, where are you?" Brenn called into the descending smoke. Disconsolate, he sat at the curbside: Above him, a strange music toppled from the crests of the towers, minor and solitary and thin on the shimmering air.

"Making a habit of absences, that one is," Brenn muttered, and set his chin in his cupped hands.

Hot. He felt as hot as the minarets and the alleys, as the whole sweltering city itself.

"There's something I don't remember," he mused. "Something about the night air and the wagon bed."

A trio of salamanders skittered from the alley whistling merrily, their tails on fire. Brenn watch them flash from sight in the billowing smoke that approached him from all sides now. He longed for his wings back, for lofty breezes and the eagle's strength and soaring. He could rise above this smoke, into the fresh air and . . .

Something dark stirred in the smoke ahead of him. A sparse blackness among the gray, snaking tendrils, as though whatever it was had only now begun to form out of the dim recesses of heat and darkness. Gradually the darkness coalesced and solidified, and at last the lad could see the outline of black robes flickering like banners in the hot air as whoever or whatever it was approached him.

Brenn stood up painfully. There was some injury in his legs, something upon which he had not reckoned, though his limbs seemed sound enough, neither scarred nor bruised. Slowly, as though he walked through water or oil, he backed to the nearest building, setting his shoulder blades against the hot stone.

It was a woman who emerged from the surging smoke, hooded and slight—much smaller than she had seemed behind the translucent curtain of smoke. She carried a black, outsized cloak draped over her shoulder—carried it carefully, as she would a child or a precious, fragile object. Gracefully, almost vulnerably, she extended her free hand, and somewhere behind the folds of the hood her eyes glittered once; then the strange, borrowed light of their glittering faded altogether.

"Come, Brennart," she said. "There is a way out of this unbearable heat, and I am sent to guide you there."

Gratefully, Brenn stepped away from the building and stood at the curbside, the soreness passing from his body as he reached toward the woman.

But what was it she had said? The *other* woman—the one in the clearing, who had stood over him and held his hand and murmured to him as the green men gathered and Terrance frowned and the light receded?

Stand fast. Remain calm. Neither take her hand nor touch her.

He stopped, his hand only inches from that of the woman. Suddenly the space between them bristled and crackled in a strange blue light. As if he had been stung, Brenn snatched back his hand, and the woman threw back her hood.

She was pale and lean, and her black eyes wet and red-rimmed and fathomless, as though she had wept for centuries. At once she began to weep again, and the lad stepped from the curbstone, his heart reaching forth to her.

Stand fast. Remain calm.

"You remember me, don't you, lad?" she asked, her voice attuned with the minor music that descended from the pavilions. Brenn squinted curiously.

"Beggin' your pardon, ma'am, but I'm afraid I have no memory of you. In Maraven we met, perhaps? For I am a Maraven lad born and bred, and this is my first time beyond the walls of the Town."

She smiled sadly, lifted a pale hand to her face.

"Time was, when the wizard taught you, that you knew me by name and countenance. For I am Dame Sorrow, she who follows the Plague."

Brenn stepped back once more. Again the heat rose from the cobblestones around him. Even the soles of his boots were hot, and an unaccustomed dryness rose in his throat. Suspiciously, he regarded the Good Dame, who wavered and blurred before him like a mirage on a sunstruck road.

"And what, Dame Sorrow, would you have of me?" he asked.

She smiled sadly, her great eyes brimming. Wearily she shifted the cloak on her shoulder, beckoning to Brenn with a graceful, silent gesture.

"I would have you come with me," she answered softly. "Set all of this business aside, and follow. For there is a weariness about you, and despite your bravery and doggedness, that weariness rises from you like shimmering heat from the stones."

Brenn broke from the woman's gaze, and swimming through dim memory, rested his stare on the black cloak at her shoulder. Slowly, worldlessly, he found himself drawn once again into the drowning black pools of her eyes.

"Yes, it is his cloak," Dame Sorrow admitted, and Brenn shook his head, trying to recollect whom she spoke of. "His cloak, indeed. But what of it? For there are countries that welcome him, and the old and the miserable touch the hem of this cloak with something akin to gratitude, with something like a blessing. That time has come for you, Brennart."

With a patient, slow assurance, as though she moved through an air grown suddenly molten, Dame Sorrow held forth the dark cloak.

"I bring you a new dream," she said with a smile. "A coolness beyond this harsh and smoldering city." She unfurled the cloak, which flapped and fluttered like a banner in a high wind, then released her hold on the garment as the blackness at its heart swirled and steadied.

It hovered like a door in the air, like the portal above Terrance's tower.

Brenn looked back to Dame Sorrow, who had once again extended her pale hand to him.

"Come along," she urged. "Join me in this coolness and dream."

"I—I think not," Brenn replied, his hand reaching to his belt by reflex, in search of a dagger his better senses told him was useless in this phantasmal country. "Welcome you may be to the aged and sick, but I'm only a lad, and quite healthy the last—"

"The last you noticed?" Dame Sorrow interrupted. "Look at your arms, boy!"

The sores were there indeed, as black as a thousand bruises, as the heart of the wavering cloak. For a moment Brenn's spirits sank, and when he looked up, the cloak was much closer to him. Somewhere deep in its swirling folds, Brenn could make out a darkness even more profound, as though there were a place within its recesses that had passed from blackness into the complete absence of light.

Whatever that place was, he was not ready for it, regardless of fever and plague.

"No," he replied, and turned, starting up the street ahead of him, bent toward the covering clouds of smoke and whatever lay behind them—anything, as it long as it was not this counsel of despair and stillness. "Sores on my skin there may be, and plague in my bones, but I shall not rest—at least not yet. Too much remains for me to do, too many depend upon me, and . . ."

He turned, and found he was talking to nobody. Dame Sorrow had vanished into the smoke and the wavering air. A raven descended and settled on a pale fountain in front of him. Brenn shook his head, trying to remember something amid the rising heat, the fading words of the old woman. His thoughts spiraled as he turned toward the fountain, seeking coolness, moisture—anything in this landscape of desert and cinder.

The raven rose as he neared the fountain. With no outcry and scarcely the sound of a wingbeat, it lifted itself into the air, then lurched away into the glowing night. Brenn watched it sail, bank, and lose itself in an alley behind him. Then he turned and leaned over the fountain in front of him, where the water coursed and boiled in the basin, nearly scalding him with its steam.

"That's no good either," he muttered, staggering back over the cobblestones. "I expect that everywhere you look is heat and ruin, and the only place to make for is out." Taking a deep breath, coughing at the smoke, he spun about, looking for an open road, a gate, any sign of the fire's abatement—

And instead saw Faye standing in a dark doorway, extending her hand and beckoning him.

"Come on, Brenn," she urged. "It is not so bad in here. Why, some of us are waiting."

"No!" Brenn cried out, as Faye started toward the darkness. At his cry the girl turned, looking back over her shoulder, smiling winningly, mischievously at him, as she had for a dozen years.

"Come on," Faye urged. "This oven is no place for either of us."

Brenn nodded in bleak agreement. He stepped toward Faye, extended his hand . . .

. . . and withdrew it again. For the hand that reached toward him was wrinkled and spotted, and the veins pulsed dark on its fingers.

"How dare you!" Brenn hissed in rage. With a swift, angry flick of his hand, he withdrew as the aged hand clutched at him, tangling its fingers in his sleeve. The floating image of Faye whimpered and resolved itself into the old dark-eyed woman, who pulled him closer . . . closer . . .

"Away with you, damn it!" Brenn exploded, shaking the old woman from his arm. Again he reached for his dagger, again found nothing. Harshly, he raised the back of his hand, prepared to bring it down upon the white face, the brimming eyes . . .

. . . and fire rose from the streets, coursing over his damaged legs, over the doorways, climbing to the second-story windows. Brenn cried out, reeled, covered his eyes. He dropped to his knees on the cobblestones and again felt the hands at his shoulders, tugging tirelessly, insistently.

"Don't be angry," Dame Sorrow whispered. "Oh, do not be angry, child! For the anger boils the blood and deafens the ear, and I would that you came with me willingly . . . even gladly!"

Gasping, Brenn broke free of her grip. Crawling backwards over the hot stones, scuttling like a crab on Hardwater Cove—like a crab in a jar—he propped his back against the wooden threshold of the shop behind him. The door was uncommonly hot, and he smelled ash from beneath it. He breathed heavily, gathered himself . . .

. . . and the fire subsided, sank as though the stones of the street drew it in. A phoenix, her nest lodged in a balcony across the street, rose in flame, shrieking triumphantly, the light from her burning wings soon lost in the unnatural dark among the rooftops.

Brenn looked around him alertly. "So *that's* it!" he whispered. "So the fire rises and falls with my anger!"

"All the more reason that you not be angry, child," Dame Sorrow pleaded. "Oh, be *anything* but angry with me." Again, incredibly, she beckoned.

"You don't give up, do you?" Brenn asked, and the fire rose again, licking over his ankles. The absurdity struck him at last; he stepped back toward the fountain, shaking his head in disbelief. Suddenly, in the midst of impossibilities, he remembered the third instruction of the ruddy woman.

Above all, expect the unexpected.

"So if I go with you I never return?" Brenn asked. "And if I try to find my way out of this city on my own, I burn into brands and ashes?"

For the first time, Dame Sorrow smiled.

"Well, then," Brenn continued with a bitter laugh. "Well then, I expect I shall just stay here. Just stay here and wait for rain." He laughed again, a little more merrily, strangely free in having decided.

Baffled, Dame Sorrow floated onto the stoop, her hand still extended. Brenn was having none of it out there by the fountain, though she beckoned and waited for him.

And waited some more.

Finally, Brenn looked up at her, his eyes cheerful and brave.

"Go on now!" he chuckled, waving her away. "Go meddle with someone else." And suddenly, as though the lad had conjured it out of smoke and cinder, the sky opened and the rains began.

Dame Sorrow shrieked as the first drops hissed on the cobblestones. Spinning, her dark robes steaming, she rushed toward the open doorway. Brenn saw his chance: now he could follow on his own terms, not according to her dark and feverish rules. Without hesitation, he rushed after her, following the swift lurching shadows deep into the darkness of the house.

It was as if he waded through black waters.

The air was dense and warm around him, and unbearably humid. Sightless, Brenn staggered up a narrow corridor, bumping once, twice against its scorching walls. Once he cried out, sure that his clothing was burning, and choked on the moist, fetid air. He walked through abject blackness and through a strange quiet, broken only fitfully by a strange music from the heart of the house. Somewhere up the corridor, water hissed and boiled as it dripped onto the floor.

For a moment he thought about turning around, burrowing back out toward the light and the dryness and the moving air. But that was expected of him, or so something told him. It was as though the darkness and the corridors themselves awaited his turning back—as though somehow they, or something within them, fancied him daunted and untested, prone to terrible errors.

He had walked a dozen steps, perhaps more, before he even noticed that the darkness ahead of him had changed. The darkness was somehow thinner, and now he could see himself—his arms and hands and feet—in a faint red light that bathed over all things.

Brenn sighed thankfully. It was as though he was back from somewhere.

Now a stronger red light arose in the distance ahead. It was still faint, like that of a candle in a high dark tower, but enough to guide by. The lad redoubled his speed, and the walls of the corridor emerged from the darkness around him.

It was a large, cavernous room in which he found himself. He stood on a balcony, overlooking a huge rotunda in which dark shapes moved back and forth, milling over one another like thousands of insects. Brenn leaned over the parapet, looked down into the shadows.

The shapes below him were people, gathering beneath the balcony from the great room's far recesses and deeper darknesses. Their clothing was tattered—in some cases, they were naked—and they lay entangled in a landscape littered with strange and grotesque lean-tos shaped like shells, ears, the exotic pale blossoms of orchids. Oily lakes bubbled and boiled in the distance, and closer by, a ramshackle tower of sorts—all wood and bone and odd geometry—rose into the foul-smelling air, on which the shadowfolk had erected platforms, gibbets, and balconies of their own.

They had been waiting here some time, Brenn decided. Some time, as though they expected some great event.

Slowly, the pale people pushed toward the balcony on which he stood. Wedged against one another, pushing closer, gasping breathlessly, they lifted their dull eyes up to him and began to sing—a dry song that Brenn recalled faintly, in its words the smell of torch and sea air.

> *Rich men, trust not in wealth!*
> *Gold cannot buy you health;*
> *Physic himself must fade.*
> *All things to end are made.*
> *The plague full swift goes by;*
> *I am sick, I must die . . .*

Brenn looked down among the chanting people. Listlessly, joylessly, they beckoned to him, their arms entangling with one another, as pale as grubs in the fetid darkness.

There was the girl Terrance had healed that day in Wall Town, saving her for but the next day, when the Death returned.

There was the blotched, once-lovely face of Lucia, the Goniph's mistress. Brenn looked sadly into her eyes: *"Queenes have died, yong and faire,"* he whispered.

And behind her, her gaze blank and pitiless as the sea, a woman reached her dried arms toward the balcony, beckoning, beckoning, mouthing incomprehensible words.

Brenn looked even closer. Her eyes shone from somewhere in his past, from a candlelit room before he could even speak, and those arms, now gray and withered . . .

"No," he replied, firmly and calmly, his eyes fixed steadily upon them as he banished his fear and heartbreak. For a long time they stared at one another—the mourning king and his dying people—as the voices choired and echoed through the cavern.

At last, their faces began to recede, to fade into shadows, and with them the landscape through which they walked and in which they waited. Brenn could not tell whether it was he that was rising or they that were sinking, but shadow and mist passed between them, and above the lad's head yet another light blossomed—a brisk, unwavering greenness, and air fresh-smelling and less humid.

His spirits lifting as the green light spilled over him, Brenn yet yearned for the vanishing folk beneath him—for some power or gift or strong elixir by which he could raise them out of their darkness. But all of them—Brenn, Dame Sorrow, most of all the dull and tattered folk who milled on the cavern floor—knew that the power was still in the making, was years away, no doubt, still taking form and as of yet all too terribly frail.

"But it will come," Brenn whispered into the shadows below him. "And I am not with you yet because it *has* to come." He felt tears rush over his face, and the fresh light plunged to embrace him.

>>> **VI** <<<

Terrance sat in a notch between two large, exposed roots of the great spreading cedar. Bracken snored at his knees. Faintly, desolately, the wizard repeated the spell of the eagle, reversing and entangling the words until one bird, then another, alighted in the fragrant branches of the tree above him.

"Go home. The one I wanted has come," Terrance murmured, frowning at Bertilak, the bright-eyed eagle man who peered at him dazedly through a cluster of dark needles. "And I have no time to reckon further with you."

The man whistled faintly, and the wizard inclined his head to the sound.

"You say that you saw him, though? Saw him above, in the daylight?"

Bertilak scrambled to a higher branch, whistled again. Bracken awoke beside his master to what must have seemed a curious sight: the old man with his nose in the air, his white beard disheveled, arguing with a naked man in the branches above him.

"I *know* he was clumsy, damn it!" Terrance snapped, "and not strong of wing! He was only a bird for a day, mind you!"

He stretched and creaked and stood up slowly. Out of one of his boots a squirrel darted, rousted from its sleep by the old man's sudden movement. Bracken stirred, then settled again. Suddenly alert, Bertilak watched the skittering rodent intently, but at a brief warning stare from the wizard, he receded into the green shadows until Terrance saw only the brilliant and amber glow of his eyes. Then the eagle-man slipped from the branch, and the lights went out with a crash.

"There," Terrance proclaimed with a whisper, shuffling wearily over to the pile of belongings Galliard's men had brought from the wagon and dumped unceremoniously on a thick carpet of evergreen needles. He reached into the pile of blankets and disheveled clothing and produced a shawl—neither his own nor Brenn's, not belonging to anyone as far as he could recall—and wrapped it around his shoulders, quietly thanking the gods of discarded and forgotten things. Spreading one of the blankets on the ground, he lowered himself upon it and, reaching into the bottomless storehouse in his sleeve, drew forth a small ceramic flask.

"That's better," he said aloud, then looked around, startled and a bit embarrassed by how he had forgotten his captivity and even the fact that he wasn't alone. Sure enough, men in green and brown and gray, armed with bow and spear, seemed to glide through the clearing around him like so many strands of fog, so many wraiths.

"Now it's waiting for the boy to waken," Terrance sighed, uncorked the flask. The juniper smell of its contents rose and mingled with the odor of fresher evergreen in the air. The wizard took a quick, moderate sip of the Zephyrian gin and lay back on the blanket, gazing up through entanglements of branch and needle and leaf into a starry patch of sky. For a moment he thought he saw the celestial Forest Lord—the star the ancients called Basilius—drift through the dark patch of air above him. But Basilius had moved from this sky by now, adrift on the northeast horizon.

Calling Brennart back had been, in many ways, the last thing Terrance wanted to do. Here among this band of woodsmen the plague could spread like fire, like nightgrown mushrooms made fertile by the deep and rotting roots of oaks and hackberries. But Glory, whoever she was, swore that the lad was past carrying.

The wizard took another sip from his flask, continued to ponder.

Even if the lad was past contagious, was well on recovery's path, these were not the safest of surroundings. Galliard, in Terrance's brief acquaintance with him, had been cordial and soft-spoken and downright unfathomable—just the kind of man the wizard avoided by instinct. It was that combination of quiet aristocratic bearing, that sense of being somehow out of place within all this wildness, that seemed to mark not only Galliard but a goodly number of his followers.

Terrance looked suspiciously at the big woodsman Ponder, who, having been left in charge during Galliard's vigil over the lad, had simply climbed back atop a low-hanging, thick branch of the giant cedar and, propping his feet amid cones and greenery, settled into a volume of *Mira Parthae*, the ancient and disreputable encyclopedia of Parthian wonders, dismissed by most scholars as a book for the young and the gullible. On occasion Ponder would look up from its pages, and with a straight face describe one of the listed wonders to his hostage.

"They say, wizard," he called down, shifting his enormous feet in the cedar branches, "that in Partha there is an animal known as the camelis, who lives sometimes the span of a hundred years. It is said that this creature can go for a hundred days without water, for it keeps moisture in a hump on its back, and that if its drover sells it to another owner, the camelis itself will bicker over the price." He blinked and smiled amiably. "What think you of this wonder, Master Terrance?"

The wizard shrugged and propped himself on his elbow. "I've seen stranger," he replied, marveling at the big man's innocence.

Camelis, indeed!

"I've seen," Terrance intoned mock-seriously, his eyes fixed on his captor, "a kind of man whose mouth is in his belly, who lowers his food to eat instead of raising it—"

"I don't believe you," Ponder declared flatly, his eyes fixed again on the *Mira Parthia*.

It was then that the first set of amber eyes glowed and flickered over the shoulder of the big man. It did not seem that Ponder noticed them, or indeed any of the eyes that joined them, spangling the clearing with a thick yellow light. They were like a thousand fireflies in the branches, and yet the light was steady, cold, a bit menacing.

Terrance sat up, sure that five hundred birds had returned to the clearing, drawn by the words he had hoped would fetch Brenn home. It was only a second, though, until he saw that the lights were disembodied, borne on a thin mist that hung amid dense and innumerable branches.

"So . . ." Terrance whispered with a half-smile, "Galliard and his troop are not alone in these parts. But it takes the gin to bring out the neighbors."

Quickly he waved the flask through the air, and the shadowy clearing was aglow with eyes: eyes under rocks and roots, eyes amid needles and cones, even eyes glittering amid the strewn belongings of the wizard and his apprentice. Terrance looked around, but found he was the only one who was startled by the occurrence. Indeed, he seemed to be the only one who had noticed. The woman was gone now from her place by the fire, but the woodsmen who had attended her continued about their tasks, some gathering wood, it seemed, for an enormous supper, while the amber eyes bristled like firelight around them.

"*Also in Partha,*" Ponder intoned, several pairs of the omnipresent eyes at his shoulder as he read the text aloud to the wizard, "*is a beast called the manticora. It is red-eyed, bearing the face of a man, the body of a lion, the tail of a scorpion . . .*"

"Yet another wonder, I should wager," Terrance observed, but the big man above him shook his head disgustedly.

"Lion," he pronounced. "Or catamount. Seen, no doubt, under the influence of gin." He glanced down disapprovingly, and after a long look at the big man Terrance smiled and toasted nothing in particular with another swallow of the clear, fiery liquor.

"The credulous," Ponder lectured, "see monsters in the everyday, see bears in bushes. A trick of light striking a waxy leaf—a magnolia, say, or a mountain laurel. Strikes it just right, and it's faery time."

"A scientist, I see," Terrance observed, as the eyes winked out suddenly in all parts of the clearing. No doubt the conversation would have passed on from there, ranging over animals and marvels and exotic lands and climates, had not Galliard called him to the center of the clearing with an urgent and jubilant cry.

"Hush! he awakes at last!"

There were shadows outlined in green sunlight above him, shifting and wavering and blocking out the sun then and again. Brenn tried to speak and gave up, settling instead for a weak and painful swallow.

A cup was at his lips, smelling of sage and oranges and rue. He drank and closed his eyes, sinking back to the ground away from the clean, pungent smell.

"Thank the gods," murmured a voice at his shoulder . . . Terrance's voice . . .

"Thank the gods of the weak and injured that the lad is alive."

"Take your oaths and gratitudes to the fireside, magician," a gruff female voice murmured. "This celebrated lad is mine for the moment. To me he belongs, and to my herbs, and mostly to Dame Nature and her restoring kindness."

Then the woman set the cup to Brenn's lips again, her voice more quiet, considerably kinder.

"Drink up, Brennart of Maraven. For though you are safe here, by no means shall you be idle."

She laughed softly, and in her laugh lay birdsong and the rustle of leaves. Brenn opened his eyes and sipped once more at the strange concoction. He swallowed, this time savoring the sharp tea, tasting a hint of angelica on the back of his tongue.

Angelica. Warder of evil spirits. Antidote to poisons and the sorrows.

Brenn smiled as the woman's hand passed over his face. His herblore failed him after an inkling or two, but it was enough. The hands into which he had tumbled were safe and benign.

Slowly the woman began to massage his hands, cramped with the memory of heat and flight and continual clenching. And slowly the muscles loosened, grace and dexterity passing once more into the tips of his fingers, then back into his arms and shoulders.

She touched the sword-shaped scar on his left hand, its pommel the tip of his index finger, its blade pointing toward his palm, his wrist, his heart. "It itches when it rains," Brenn said quietly, knowing he had confessed this before. His thoughts floated aimlessly.

She rested her hand upon that scar, and a feeling of warmth and peace passed through the lad, of delight and rightness in the body, of trust in the things around him and above all a gratitude for the hands that held and tended him. Tears rushed to his eyes, and with them a great serenity.

"Wh—what was that?" he rasped.

"Hush, child," she whispered. " 'Tis the Whelming. The surpassing peace, the Old Folk call it."

Brenn nodded stupidly, no wiser for his new knowledge. Then he settled back into sleep, and the forest bent over him, sheltering and watchful.

"At last the boy is safe, Terrance," Galliard pronounced, flicking his sharp knife over the dried branch of a maple, as a clever, finger-sized canoe took shape in his hand.

Terrance frowned. The Forest Lord, it seemed, was an expert in whittling—not a talent the wizard liked to see in a young man, whose skills should be employed in more active pursuits. And yet, this Galliard was a puzzler—a notorious guerrilla fighter with a scholarly bent.

Well, contradictions ran in the family. The wizard nodded absently, his eyes still on the woodsman's hands. A handful of peasants, armed with staves and with sharpened sticks that passed for spears in a beleaguered countryside where Dragmond had outlawed metal weaponry, plodded by the fire, nodding reverently to the Forest Lord. They escorted a cautious drover, his leather tunic gleaming and loud with ornamental bells, behind him a pair of heavily laden mules.

Terrance looked up into the honest face of one of the creatures, its big eyes rolling with uneasiness. Secretly the wizard pushed his thoughts toward the beast, who calmed instantly and, with a grateful snort, followed the peasants and the jingling drover out of the clearing.

"Safe, though to what purpose and for what greater good I have yet to ascertain," Galliard continued, his eyes lifting from the toy boat and fixing candidly upon Terrance, who turned his attention back to the words at hand. "And since I cannot ascertain these things without you, Terrance, the time approaches when you must help me."

The wizard nodded. Despite his formalities and roundabout manners of speech, the Forest Lord was in ways a blunt sort, given to cutting quickly to the issue at hand. With a man this direct, it was best to be direct in turn. Terrance leaned forward, his face now scarcely a foot from the Duke's.

"Within your camp, Galliard," he whispered, "sleeping and recovering from the Death, is the rightful King of Maraven and Palerna. He is your cousin, and two hundred years of Aquilan tradition enjoin you to support him in both his need and his ambitions."

"I see," Galliard replied, his eyes averted. Slowly, pensively, he turned the boat over and over; then, with a great sigh, he tossed the thing into the fire in front of him. "It is as I suspected, then. The stars were in commotion, you know, and Cousin Ponder saw portents in the flight of birds."

Both men smiled at each other.

"When the birds are ravens, it's every man a prophet in Palerna," Terrance observed.

Galliard laughed and stood warming his hands uneasily at the fire's edge. He looked over Terrance's shoulder to the spot beneath the solitary olive tree that stood inexplicably at the edge of the clearing, dwarfed by huge evergreens yet strangely resilient, struggling each year to bear a handful of black, bitter fruit. How it had grown there, with its love of heat and light and dry weather, none could altogether know.

There Glory leaned over the boy, murmuring something sooth-ing and inaudible.

"So he is the one," Galliard mused, and Terrance saw a look of great disquiet pass over the Forest Lord's face. "Would he had come in a year's time, or two. But such is the way with history: it unfolds neither neatly nor predictably."

"I do not understand, Your Grace," Terrance said, rising creakily to his feet as Galliard reached over and helped him up. "Why would a year from now have been better?"

" 'Tis a tale that must wait in the telling until the lad . . . until my cousin is ready to hear it," Galliard explained, his archer's eye on the sleeping boy at the edge of the clearing.

Terrance nodded skeptically, his years in the court having schooled him in awaiting the royal pronouncements. "That time may come, sire," he observed, "before yet another evening passes. For the woman's touch is a blessed one, and the boy's color is already returning.

"Reminds me . . ." the wizard continued, his thoughts on a rusty old story as he turned back to the exiled duke. But Galliard was gone, already halfway across the clearing toward Thomas and Bertilak and two other green-clad woodsmen.

"Curious sort, that Galliard," Terrance muttered. "Out of story's range before a man gets a chance to spin the yarn, and all of it without a fare-thee-well."

Wearily, the wizard seated himself by the fire again, and stretching out his spindly legs, removed his mud-crusted boots with a sigh of pleasure and relief so loud that the owls, only now wakening as the evening approached, rustled and called from the shade just beyond the clearing.

"So the scritch-howls beckon to each other," Terrance said to no one in particular, smiling as he tossed his boots near the fire to keep them warm. " 'Tis time, then, as Archimago always said, that a gentleman can tip a glass without consequence."

He looked around him a bit cautiously. This was a disgustingly clean-living lot—no doubt a legion of waterdrinkers. Furtively, he reached into the folds of his robe for the flask. He produced a set of gold compasses, a crossbow bolt, two lemons, a marmot, and a bone button.

"Somewhere in here," he muttered angrily, his fingers groping through fold after fold until they came out through a pocket
he had abandoned long ago for its multitude of holes.

"Damn!" the wizard exclaimed, disentangling himself from
his garments with a wrestle and wrench. "Must've dropped it
in the clearing somewhere."

Above him, on a high, overhanging branch, an early owl called
to its mate on the wing in the depths of the wood.

The boy was on his feet after the second night. In late afternoon,
having rested and fed and bolstered himself with another of
Glory's concoctions, Brennart walked through the camp, rubbing
his eyes, gathering his bearings. Propped against the great cedar,
a cup of ginseng tea steaming by his hand, Galliard watched
him with curiosity and not a little concern.

Transparent. That was the word that came to mind, though of
course you could not *read* through the lad, or any such foolishness. But his skin was pale, passing pale, and when he walked
through the sunlit edges of the clearing, his skin shone with a
light from somewhere above and behind him, as though the rays
of the sun passed cleanly through him.

Galliard stayed his distance. Brennart had seen sights—of that
he was sure. Something had come to pass during the plaguestruck
hours that the Forest Lord could not comprehend, much less put
words around. So he waited until the third night, when Brenn
walked out of the darkness and, his face and arms like veined
marble in the dappling fire, sat lightly beside Galliard and Terrance.

He was out of breath, and strangely abstracted. Galliard
frowned, but Terrance winked reassuringly.

"They tell me," Brenn began, "that you are my cousin."

"They tell me the same," Galliard replied. "If by 'they' you
mean Terrance."

Brenn smiled wanly, his eyes fixed on the firelight. "Oh, by
this time they're all saying it," he murmured. "Not just the
master here."

Terrance snorted and turned to the lad, waving the words away
with a flicker of his gnarled hand.

" 'Master' indeed!" the wizard exclaimed. "Eighteen months

of apprenticeship and nothing but stubbornness and sulking and trouble; then all of a sudden you're released from indenture and *then* decide it's time to call me 'Master'!"

The old man's frown softened. He even smiled a little through the gray beard tangled with dried grass and burrs.

"Like it or not, Brennart," the wizard proclaimed, "you're the closest to 'Master' among all of us."

"I know, I know," Brenn muttered. "This king business again. I can't say as I'm all that ready for crown and scepter and throne, Terrance. After all, I'm just six seasons away from sleeping regular in tunnels on stolen blankets. What's more, I can't say as I've seen anyone who wants me kinged outside of you."

The wizard and the Forest Lord exchanged a quick, piercing glance.

"You may count me among that number . . . sire," Galliard said, his voice quiet and distant.

"Well, don't *injure* yourself jumping to the lad's aid, Galliard!" Terrance snapped, and, startled by the wizard's outburst, a squirrel rushed out from under the skirt of his robe and barrelled toward a nearby pine. Bracken, who had been curled beside one of the roots of the cedar, his ample backside warmed by the fire, was on his feet in a breath, lumbering after the squirrel and closing his jaws an inch from the tail of the terrified creature as it sprang to the bole of the tree and rocketed into the lower branches with a crash of cone and needle. Bracken sat beneath the pine tree, looked up, and belched.

"Perish that I should sound reluctant," the Forest Lord protested, oblivious to the racket of squirrel and dog behind him. " 'Tis only that I do not know what help I can offer, though in my heart I would gladly offer all."

"I see," Terrance grumbled, folding his arms and flopping straight back onto the ground. Dust and dried needles floated about his head, then settled on his hat and in his hair. "These fair-weather offers are as good as . . . as *Dragmond's*, if the truth be told."

Galliard rose slowly to his feet and walked toward the fire, his calm features and elegant bearing scarcely masking a smoldering anger.

"I should thank you, conjuror, to remember whose woods this is. Whose camp it is within which you are a welcome guest."

In the distance, Terrance heard Glory laugh merrily, and the air around him whined, as if with a thousand mosquitoes. Again, dim lights spangled the clearing. Alertly, the wizard drew his thoughts back to the shadowy clearing, to the young man walking toward him, bow slung over his shoulder.

"Very well, Galliard," he replied, relenting, and after a pause at the edge of the firelight, the woodsman crouched.

"For all hesitancy there is a reason, Master Terrance," Galliard began properly, his eyes on the flickering fire in front of him. "Nor is this a different story on that account."

He lowered himself and sat in the dried leaves, the sparse grass, and the story rose from him as the sunlight faded and the pale lights shone all around him as though, shielded by darkness and the shadow of leaves, a thousand eyes were fixed on the tale and the teller.

"Aquila was home to me, and home among homes was the summer palace at Arbor. North of Orgo and closer to seaside. Close also to the cool waters of the Corrante as they descend from even more northern climes down along the coast and, as every Palernan knows, into the Gray Sea. I remember it from earliest childhood: the black beaches, the salt smell of the air, and the palace itself aglitter with dark obsidian.

"It was all beautiful—palace and beach and peaceful little town. All, that is, except the garden, planted years before by old Danton and neglected ever since. It was walled and shadowy and overgrown. I was loth to enter there, for to my young eyes and young imaginings it seemed like a wilderness. But it was the one dark spot in bright memory, and I thought that surely I could live with its presence.

"For my cousins were there, also—all five of them, clambering over ramparts and walls like five hundred monkeys. Ponder was a year my elder, and rhyming Thomas scarcely a season older. Sendow was my age to the day, and the only one among us with a fondness for old Danton's tangle of a garden. Jimsett, six months my junior, bored and tunneled in the porous volcanic rock along the beachside, twice burrowing up through the floor of the summer palace. And Jimsett's unlikely twin, little Lapis? Well, the evening would see her perched on the battlements like some strange, multi-colored bird, reading the shape of the darkening clouds, testing the winds for omens.

"Six of us in all. A half dozen ways to bother and perplex the great household at Arbor. Together we would clamber to the top of old Danton's tower, look out over the Corrante where the wizard was swept away on the eve of Julian's marriage, dance with lanterns in the high chambers, leaping from bed to bed and shouting and wrestling and yodeling until Grandmother's guards—or sometimes Grandmother Malina herself—would storm up the stairwell promising dire punishment. We would blame all misdeeds on Lapis, who confessed them with a straight face, fully knowing that nothing short of murder would draw down Malina's wrath upon her only granddaughter. We escaped unscathed—always—though nobody in the tower ever believed our stories."

Galliard smiled and lay back, his hands behind his head. As the Forest Lord mused and remembered, Brenn caught himself smiling also, thinking of how innocent these "crimes" were, recounted by the odd young man who seemed scarcely more than innocent himself, as if the years between the tower in Arbor and the cedars of Corbinwood had not touched him at all. Indeed, as the story unfolded the woodsman became less formal, more lively, and the lights about him winked and fluttered.

Terrance glanced cautiously at Brenn, but the lad was oblivious to the strange luminescence, his gaze fixed on the firelight, his attention on the words of the Forest Lord.

"Ponder was the first to suffer . . . the Mishap," Galliard continued, his voice strangely distant now, and abstract, as though he were talking about something that took place centuries ago. "It was a week or so following his tenth birthday.

"I suppose that his cousins were the last to know. For three nights he was gone, and there was rustling and uneasiness in the topmost rooms of the tower where we were quartered. Then the word came up to us that Father and Uncle Edgar and Grandmother Malina had held counsel over the misdeeds of my cousin and were now debating his punishment. He had, it seemed . . ."

"Stolen a map," the soft voice interrupted, and Terrance and Brenn turned quickly to see the mild-mannered blond giant amble into the firelight, clutching what appeared to be a thin silk scarf. "*This* map, to be precise," Ponder said, "though to this day, only the gods know why I chose this one."

Amiably, he tossed the cloth in front of Terrance, who crouched over it, squinting at the lines and charactry upon it.

"Alanyan caravan routes," the wizard pronounced with a frown, tracing a long blue line at the edge of the map.

"Nor have I used it in the twelve years since the lifting," Ponder admitted with a blush. "It was . . . the glamor of the place. Its distances."

"It was the sickness," Galliard interrupted. "Whatever the map relates, it was only one of many lifts."

"Lifts?" Brenn asked, looking at Terrance in amusement. The wizard shook his head sternly, his gaze returning at once to Galliard.

"Lifts," the Forest Lord repeated uncomfortably. "Lifts caused by the curse and the sickness.

"For Father and a fuming Uncle Edgar rifled through Ponder's quarters, finding . . . what was it, Cousin?"

Ponder blushed. "Two rings," he confessed quietly. "And a pair of Grandmother's shoes. A Venetian merchant's knife, six Parthian coins, a bird cage, a shovel, four tulip bulbs, a dancer's mask—"

"Tell our guests the best one, Ponder," Galliard said with a smile. "The thing that made Uncle Edgar draw sword and offer to kill his firstborn, there in the tower at Arbor."

Scarcely hiding his laughter, Brenn turned back toward the big man. Ponder traced a circle in the dirt with his toe and, his eyes downcast, murmured a single word so quietly that Brenn had to strain to hear.

"Boat."

"What did he say, Brennart?" Terrance shouted, cupping his ear and craning in the direction of the giant woodsman.

"*Boat*, Terrance," Galliard replied with a chuckle. "It seems that our cousin Ponder had stolen a boat, hauled it up the tower steps, and hid it in his quarters."

"It was a small boat," Ponder protested, and Brenn tumbled backwards, hooting with laughter. At the edge of the darkness something short and wide stirred, and Bracken waddled into the firelight, his large liquid eyes fixed on the laughing boy. Quickly he rushed to Brenn's side and nudged him, his short tail wagging.

"It . . . it is scarcely that amusing, sire," Galliard protested, masking a smile of his own.

"Nor was it to me," yet another voice interrupted, and a young man, dirt-covered and spade in hand, appeared from behind the wide bole of the big cedar, "for the shovel they found there was my own, and had been missing for days."

"Your cousin Jimsett, Brennart," Galliard announced, and the unkept man bowed at the introduction, soil raining from his smudged red hair. Bracken trotted over and sniffed the intruder curiously, then, apparently liking what he smelled, lumbered back to the fire and rested his chin on Terrance's knee. Slowly the dog's eyes closed, as Galliard motioned his burrowing cousin closer to the fire.

"Thomas was next, cornered about the time Father decided that Ponder was unmanageable," the Forest Lord continued. "And after the other, less likely things—the crockery and the diamond, the Alanyan playing cards and the eyeglasses that rendered those cards transparent—came the Parthian bard to the palace in outrage. Thomas had stolen one of his melodies, it seems, overhearing it as the singer rehearsed it on a lute in the vision tent, then whistling it note for note to Sendow and Lapis up in the chambers as they dodged light and grandmothers."

"Of course, it made the song useless," Terrance explained to Brenn. "The Parthians guard their tunes jealously, and the last verse of the lyrics is always a retext—a chant to induce forgetfulness, so that the song remains the singer's and what the listener recalls is a gist of the words and the melody only."

"Needless to say," Ponder chimed in, running his fingers through his tight blond curls, "the bard had not added the lyrics yet, much less the retext, for this was rehearsal only. And Cousin Thomas had not bothered to ask about it. It was only after the Parthian threatened a plague of sandcrabs in the tower that Duke Edmund took him altogether seriously and made Thomas swear never to sing the song again. Poor Tom swore and swore, but he found himself confined with me shortly, the two of us placed in a well lit, locked room on the ground floor of the tower.''

"Cousin by cousin, we each found our way into that same locked room,'' Jimsett continued. "Sendow stole a dozen nuts from the rune tree of an Umbrian alchemist and was nearly turned into a squinch fly in the process. And I tunneled beneath that same garden, coming up beneath the one store of serpentine root in all of Aquila. Which, of course, I brought home with me. The smell was fascinating.''

Brenn glanced briefly at Terrance, whose eyebrow arched.

"Is . . . is there any still growing there?'' the wizard asked, but Jimset shook his head gleefully.

"Last of the lot,'' he boasted, and would have gone on about it, had not Galliard interrupted.

"As was Lapis,'' the Forest Lord said. "The last of the cousins to fall to the curse. They say that girls resist it longer. Or perhaps she was better than the rest of us—kinder, and more honest.''

A whistle sounded deep within the woods to the east, answered by another whistle. Galliard's eyes flickered briefly in that direction, but he continued with the story.

"She took a perfume bottle from the Alanyan duchess. That, more than anything, brought us here. For the Lady Mercuria blustered and whined and wheedled, then threatened breaks in diplomacy. Threatened war was as a last resort. Father stood his ground for awhile, granting her audience after audience until he could stand it no longer, then maintaining correspondence by carrier pigeon for yet another month. All the while he maintained that none of us knew anything of her damned perfume, and he questioned the boys and threatened each of them, but we all were as baffled as he.

"That is, until he caught a strange scent wafting from the battlements, descending through the windows of the tower and making the guards dream of spice routes as they slept at their posts. It smelled, Father said, *like a Rabian cathouse*, though where an Aquilan duke had encountered those grounds for comparison I suppose we shall never know. Whatever the case, the smell drew him upwards, over the last stairs to the landing, where he found that Lapis had drawn up the rope ladder to preserve her privacy. Finally, boosted to the roof by two of his taller guards, my father found his niece, the dearest and most favored of cousins, asleep atop a bartizan. She had nodded off while reading the winds, she claimed.

" *'Those very winds have done you in, niece,'* my father replied angrily. For the circumstances had passed beyond his control. He looked out over the battlements down into Arbor, where a Parthian bard, an Umbrian alchemist, and an Alanyan noblewoman all blustered and fumed against his throne. Who knew but that further thefts would alter foreign policy even more direly?"

A silence settled upon the company around the fire. The Forest Lord smiled and drew an arrow from his quiver. He turned it idly in his hand, lifted it to the firelight, then deftly replaced it as though he had examined something from a great distance and decided to set it aside. The whistles sounded again, this time nearer, and Bracken stirred at the feet of the wizard.

"So that is why you were set here, Galliard," Terrance mused. "To keep you from . . . stealing your father's throne, in a way. Stealing it by stealing from others."

Galliard nodded. "It was frightening here at first," he continued quietly. "But we were not the first. After all, didn't the Romans expose their unwanted children?"

The clearing was silent except for the rustle of leaves in a high night wind.

"Though that is harsh, and scarcely fair," the Forest Lord maintained. "For after all, Glory was here when we arrived. Had been here all along—and all alone, for that matter. Were it not for her guidance, I hesitate to think . . . why, only Sendow among us knew one plant from another when we came south over the Gray Strand!"

Galliard frowned, leaned back on his elbows.

"Yes," he continued, after a long pause. "I expect we owe a good deal to Glory, though who she is still eludes and perplexes me. Natheless, we have been here since those days—ten years since Lapis's theft was uncovered. Thrice I have tried to leave Corbinwood, and have returned heavy laden with Alanyan spices, with Zephyrian leatherwork and Umbrian silver, with whatever the caravans carried on the road to Maraven."

He looked at Brenn sadly, and the firelight shadowed his dark countenance and mood.

"The curse remains with us, and in turn we must stay in Corbinwood. Far from innocent folks, whose hard-earned belongings we might steal as readily as the perfume from a spoiled Alanyan noblewoman, though we would sorrow for it as we stole.

"So you see, Cousin Brennart, 'tis as I said before this long telling began. I do not know what help I can offer, here in my forest fastness. For I am bound to Corbinwood as surely as the cedar underneath which we sit. In my heart I would gladly offer all, but all, it seems, is confined to the wood and the wilderness. Though I would restore you to Maraven, I cannot travel there for the restoring."

Brenn leaned forward into the warmth of the fire. It was all perplexing to him, how his return to Maraven and the awful king business had become such an issue of a sudden. He had hoped that his life as Pretender to the Throne was over as soon as it had begun, and that what remained was getting as far away from Dragmond and Ravenna as possible. And yet here they were— Terrance and Galliard and even the woman Glory—still talking pretenders and kings, though the wood was fast around them and Maraven far away.

So he would have mused for hours had not the whistles sounded again. The woods to his right bristled with commotion, with the sound of shouting and sword slapped against leather. Bracken rose barking, and Galliard was to his feet in the instant afterwards, eyes turned alertly to where a squadron of weathered men broke into the clearing.

'Tis the Watch! Brenn thought for a moment, preparing to scramble and hide and lose himself in the depths of the woods. But there was little or no alarm in Galliard's stance, nor in that of the two cousins or Terrance's, for that matter. The men were familiar, were the Forest Lord's, and Brenn sank back to the ground, his legs heavy with the memory of plague and fever.

It was then, as he nodded dizzily by the fire, that he saw Dirk in the midst of those arriving.

Dirk seemed a dozen years older.

When Brenn had last seen him, straddling a cornice on the old Hall of the Poisoners, his cloak lifted against the tumbling rain, Dirk had looked almost childlike, thin and small under layers of oil cloth. Scrambling to a purchase above them, the little fellow had waved merrily to his comrades below—to Faye and the Goniph and to Brenn himself—before vanishing into the Maravenian dark.

That was only a week ago, ten days at the most.

Or could it have been a fortnight?

Brenn closed his eyes and shook his head, remembering not Maraven, but the red streets and minarets through which he had passed in his fevered dreams. Meanwhile the woodsmen, Sendow at the head of them, led Dirk across the clearing to those assembled by the fire.

Again, Brenn tried to stand. His head swam, thousands of tiny bright lights burst in front of him, and he could see nothing beyond them. At his side he felt a strong hand sustaining him.

"Easily at first, lad," Glory's voice whispered behind his ear. "The plague is like a tide that returns and recedes. 'Twill be a while before you gather your sea legs."

When his head cleared of stars, Brenn stepped forward to greet his old friend. For a moment the clearing rocked again, and amid the thick branches of cedar Brenn thought he saw dozens, hundreds, of amber lights, spangling the shadows, winking on and off. But they lingered after his balance caught, and, thinking he was ready to faint, he reached back, grabbed Glory's arm, and with the help of the forest woman, shuffled across the clearing.

* * *

"Thanks to the gods what look after thieves and miscreants that ye're here!" Dirk exclaimed for the fourth or fifth time. He rolled back his tattered sleeves and leaned into the fire to warm his hands. He smelled of smoke and rain and muddy roads. "Else I am sure I'd be eaten alive by something . . ."

He gazed harshly at Sendow.

"By something or *someone*," the little thief muttered, and Sendow smirked, his eyes flickering alertly around the clearing.

"That'll be enough, Dirk," Brenn scolded, surprised at how pompous he sounded. "You are, after all, a guest in his country, and he would expect the same courtesy were he your guest in Maraven."

Brenn cleared his throat and swallowed. There was a long silence in which Terrance and Dirk both looked at him curiously, frowning as though they had just noticed a precious stone in the brow of a toad.

"Well, Brenn," Dirk replied finally, his voice high and thin and bitter. "if he expects *that*, he is a bigger fool than I fashion him. For Maraven welcomes nobody, and the people claw at one another like . . . what was it that the Goniph always said?"

"Like crabs in a jar, Dirk."

The little thief nodded. "Like crabs in a jar."

On the night they were all betrayed by the Goniph, Dirk had seen it coming from the rooftop. A squadron of the Watch descended on Light Street like a dozen scavenging raposa, and yet another crept by torchlight through Starboard Alley, swords at the ready.

Dirk saw them all. Saw the Goniph's glittering hand motion them to the Hall of the Poisoners, where they set up station outside the doors and the windows.

"I thought quickly then," Dirk recalled, a hint of pride in his voice. "on account of I knew at once the Goniph had betrayed us. Indeed, if I'd of had Faye's brains or even yours, I'd of seen it coming like I seen the Watch convergin' on the Hall."

Brenn blushed, and Terrance snorted mischievously.

"I confess we never saw it coming ourselves, Dirk," Brenn replied quietly.

"I should say not!" his little friend exclaimed. "On account of when all was said and done there was the three of you in there—you and Faye and Marco—who did not know what was going to come about. So I says to myself, says, 'Dirk, it is up to you to let the Goniph see that he trained you well and make him kick himself for it.' "

He winked at Brenn, his dirty face creasing with a smile. There was another broken tooth in it. Brenn nodded, encouraged the rest of the story, though his memory darted back to the dark hour in the basement of the hall.

Marco, he thought. *For a moment I had almost forgotten Marco.*

"It wan't for nothing that the Goniph made me always the lookout," Dirk continued merrily. "So I think of the bird calls, of all the warning signals we had between us, and most of them are day birds, and I think, if just one of those Watchmen has any sense he will know a day bird when he hears one and he will wonder what a lark is doing singing in the dead of night on Light Street in the middle of the rain . . ."

"Dirk," Terrance urged. "Dirk. Less strategy and more story, if you will." Drawn in by the little thief's tale, Galliard and Sendow stood behind the wizard, and Ponder, who had been at the edge of the fire when the stories began, opened his book now and pretended to read, all the time listening alertly.

"Very well, very well . . . Your Wizardry," Dirk conceded with a short wave of his hand. "But what I done was this: I lean over the gargle on the cornice . . ."

"Gargle?" Ponder asked, and blushed deeply when all eyes turned to him.

" 'Gargoyle,' Cousin," Brenn explained amiably. And seeing a look of embarrassment pass over Dirk's face, added quickly, "The Maraven accent is different from the accent in these parts, and what's a gargoyle to Aquilans is a gargle to us."

He turned to Dirk and nodded for the story to continue, not noticing the proud smile on the face of the wizard at his side.

"At any rate," Dirk continued, "I lean athwart the gargle and 'Up here!' I says. 'They's one of them on the cornices!' Then I done the esquilo down the side o' the building."

Brenn turned to Galliard. "Esquilo's a trick jump," he said. "Old as larceny."

Dirk smiled, still marvelling at his own cleverness.

"So up the walls three of them come, clutchin' at brick and puffin' under their own weight and under the bumbles. 'Cause, you see, they warn't wall climbers as much as soldiers . . ."

"Dirk—" Terrance interrupted, his irritation growing the further the thief's story rambled. Brenn glanced at the wizard with a curious half-smile.

"I'll bet you led them a merry chase, Dirk," he prodded, looking straight into Terrance's eyes.

And Dirk was off on a story of rooftop adventures, of lofty flights and escapades, reeling over the streets of the city with Dragmond's army at his heels. Slowly the numbers of pursuers increased in the telling from three to seven to twelve to twenty, decreasing once to eleven under Terrance's icy stare, but doubling to twenty-two once it was apparent that the wizard was calling no numbers into question. Dirk led these multitudes merrily indeed, if you were fool enough to believe his story. Nonetheless, he enthralled Brenn's wide-eyed country cousins with a tale of acrobatic leaps from rooftop to rooftop. He told of his sword fight with two of the Watchmen atop a blood-slick widow's walk, and of a last desperate scramble through a torrent of arrows to the crest of the East Wall and over, where he lost his pursuers in the shadows of the black maple groves south of Terrance's tower.

"Now you might call me a hero for all my doings," Dirk observed, fixing his audience intently with his most noble stare. "But I wouldn't call myself that. No, for you see, when a man has to wade through over a hundred well-armed and battle-blooded swordsmen . . ."

Brenn smiled. Dirk was at least a league or two past the facts by now.

"Well, when the odds are that bleak is when a man must wade through them, is what *I* always say," Dirk concluded proudly, as Jimsett, who had been absent from the circle for some time, returned with a bowl of venison stew, setting it quietly beside the storyteller. Having lied his way over half of Maraven and through a hundred fictional soldiers, Dirk had worked up a sizable appetite and wasted no time in getting to his supper.

"Tell us, if you would, how you left Maraven," Terrance asked, and Dirk looked up from the bowl, another story brewing in his ample imagination. Dramatically, he pointed his spoon, still dripping with the thick stew, at the listening wizard, and dramatically he opened his mouth as if his next words would be oracles.

Then a shadow crossed his face and he stopped. In a quieter voice, a voice more humble and shaken with anger and fear, he told another story, briefly and without ornament.

" 'Tis a sight, Master Wizard. 'Tis a horror and abomination. For on the morrow after Brenn left, the city gave up its dead."

"Gave up its dead?" Galliard asked, frowning when he saw Brenn shudder. Dirk nodded slowly and continued, all the drama fled from his voice as he closed his eyes and spoke haltingly, the memory overwhelming him.

"The streets was choked with them. Must of been a thousand in Wall Town alone. And not a dozen sword-wounded or arrow-riddled, so they weren't no military dead, mind you."

Galliard cleared his throat. "Then . . . then what . . ."

"The Death, most of them. But not overnight. These had been dead for weeks, for months. Some of them was bones only—no telling how long *they* was there. By the morning the scavengers had come. The streets was filled with rats, and ravens perching on each of the bodies like big black flies . . ."

Dirk shook his head as though he was trying to banish the recollection. Around the fire they all waited respectfully—wizard and would-be king and bandit cousins—as the thief wrestled with the terror of memory. Then Bracken, having napped too long at the edge of the clearing and now smelling food beside the visitor, waddled over to the thief and sat inelegantly on his leg. The little man opened his eyes and smiled, petting the serene, silly dog, who stretched himself to his full length and buried his nose in the half-empty stew bowl.

"Thanks be to dogs," Ponder breathed, "who teach us the folly of too much thought."

"A prayer I have said myself a thousand times," Terrance added, "in the fifty years I have known this beast,"

All eyes flashed curiously at the wizard, who stared and mused at Bracken's great dome of a head. The dog was snoring now, having fallen asleep with his face in the empty bowl.

Dirk recovered himself and continued.

"Well, it was a nightmare on the Maravenian streets. That's the long and short of it. The Great Witch come from the castle in that black coach—or so I hear, for *I* was hiding in the shadows all the while."

"Stay, Dirk," Terrance ordered, a soft urgency in his voice. "You mean to say that Ravenna was on the streets in daylight?"

"Mind you, Master Wizard, I said I only heard tell, on account of I was hiding in the shadows when the coach in question come through Wall Town." The little thief stared directly into the firelight, his brown eyes haunted. "I heard tell that Himself was out, overseeing the Watchmen while they disposed of the dead, and the Pale Man, too, at the head of a marching column."

"The Pale Man?" Terrance asked. "I know of no Pale Man."

"I do," Brenn said with a shudder, and the eyes of his cousins and the wizard turned to him once more. "Go on, Dirk. What of the king and the Pale Man?"

"They was there and mingling with the army," Dirk said. "Silk masks over their faces and the smell of garlic and rue about them."

"Dragmond down in the city," Terrance remarked with a mischievous smile. "Well, well, Brennart. It seems we've put the scare into your uncle."

"And changed the city for the worse, if to the worse it could go," Dirk snapped. "For that very night they set a sunset curfew for all but the Watch, and they give orders to kill them what broke it. And if that wan't enough, they're prisoning everyone of questionable age . . ."

Brenn and Terrance winced. *Of questionable age. That phrase again.*

"And the next night the fires was burning all through Maraven," Dirk continued, his small voice hushed and wary. "Burning the dead, was Himself, and the smoke was all about Wall Town like a black fog. They tell me folks in the upper stories could barely breathe, but they didn't dare go outside. On account of the curfew and all."

Dirk paused and coughed nervously.

"They tell me other things, too. How the living was mingled with the dead, the plague getting worse and all, and how the Watch made no reckoning 'twixt them as they stoked the pyres in Wall Town."

Angrily, Brenn started to his feet, but Terrance's strong hand restrained him. Back he sat on the hard ground of the clearing, flushed and coughing. Dirk paused again, and continued.

"It was then," he announced, "that the ravens come back to light on the sills."

"I beg your pardon?" Terrance asked, leaning forward.

"Ravens. Flotillas of 'em," Dirk said. He smiled, repeated *flotillas* under his breath, savoring the word. "They lighted on the sills and the steeples, on the bastions and the gargles. It was ravens wherever you looked, it was, thick as they were on the corpses the morning after you left, Master Wizard. You could lean out a doorway and hear wingbeats all through the city, and what with the *galho* sound and all, a fellow couldn't tell whether they was afront or aside or somewhere up a tower or alongside the beaches."

Brenn nodded. He knew the tricks of sound in the city well.

"And you *needed* to know where they was, because by the gods of plugs and shackles, they was watching, gentlemen. Watching the indoors of the city, looking through the windows and the doorways, the portholes and the skylights. Looking from atop the gibbets, too."

"You mean along the Causeway," Brenn said. For years Dragmond had disposed of dissenters, of the suspicious and the politically dangerous, on the gallows that lined the narrow wooden bridge stretching from the northernmost point of Ships all the way across the Needle's Eye to the south shore of Aquila and the foot of Kestrel Tower. No doubt, the gibbets would be full there.

"The Causeway for certain, Brenn," the little thief answered. "But also in other places. Has him a regular bridle path from Teal Front all the way to the cove. Hadrach Road is lined with 'em. He must of strung up two hundred afore I left. And I was only three nights after you."

Dirk leaned forward dramatically.

"Took a chunk out of the Guild, too, he did. Our numbers was halved by the time I left. Randall they got, and little Theodor."

Brenn closed his eyes wearily, and for the first time since he fled Maraven, sorrow overwhelmed him. *Randall is bad enough*, he thought. *A goodly sort. But the boy. No more than ten years old.*

A rough hand rested on his shoulder. Through the tear-blurred light Brenn looked up into the face of Galliard.

"Whoever these people are, Cousin," proclaimed the Forest Lord, "the time will come when Dragmond will answer for each of them. The time will come, I promise you!"

"That time would come more swiftly, Galliard, were you inclined to leave Corbinwood," Terrance declared coldly, his eyes fixed on the center of the fire.

"But you know why, wizard!" Galliard snapped, and walked to the edge of the firelight.

"There are some who twist and wave above Hadrach Road who would give you all their belongings for time to breathe," Terrance pronounced dramatically, staring directly at the young man.

"And what's more, Master Galliard," Dirk added, "There's not too many in Maraven what are easy to steal from. Take it from one who has found himself caught on the rooftops or without a penny to bless himself on many a moonheavy night."

Though shaken, Brenn could not help but smile. Standing slowly, braced on one side by Terrance and on the other by Galliard, he swayed a little as he stepped around the fire to where Dirk sat with his clothes nearly dried, covered with dust and dog hair. With no fanfare, no formality, but a gentle quietude, the rightful King of Palerna laid his hand softly on the oily hair of his old comrade and smiled again, his eyes still brimming.

"It's welcome you are among us, old Dirk," he said, "though the news you bring is far from pleasant."

"Stay as long as you like," Galliard added. "There's food aplenty and a warm place by the fire."

Dirk nodded a curt thanks to the Forest Lord, then looked up at Brenn. In the moonlight his old friend looked changed, wearied, as though he had passed through a dark country and only barely returned.

It's like the light is passing through him, the little thief observed in wonder. *Like it's passing through him . . . or out of him; a body can't tell amidst all these fireglows and shadows.*

"I wish I had more to tell ye, Master Brennart," Dirk said softly, surprising himself that he would ever address so formally a lad whose cloak he had stolen and whom, after a half-forgotten disagreement of a decade past, he had wrapped in sailcloth and beaten with a broom.

It wasn't the kind of history a Wall Town boy could respect. And yet, there in the clearing, deep in the midst of Corbinwood, little Dirk swore a silent allegiance to the old friend who stood above him, all the while wondering why.

>>> VIII <<<

That night, as the little thief huddled into the clearing just beyond the Boniluce, reunited at last with one of his old comrades, the city of Maraven began to glow with a fierce, unnaturally red light. Slowly a mist rose orange and then yellow from the walled interiors of the city, like flame from the inside of an oven. Lightning flickered and lazed over the turret of Kestrel Tower.

It could be seen for miles. By instinct the kestrels and gulls, sailing homewards when the night began to fall, saw the mist entangle the towers and steeples and, thinking it was dawn again, reeled wearily back out to sea. The captain of an English ship, racing west along the coast of Palerna, saw the light from a distance and, fearing plague or the outbreak of war, turned up the Aquilan coast and back toward the Mare Atlanticum.

This glowing was the third decree of King Dragmond. "I shall have seven," he whispered to the witch Ravenna after she had ceased her raving and descended the steps, when her candles were cold and her augury was still.

The next morning, the two of them lay in the king's chamber. Ravenna had not closed her eyes all night.

"Seven," Dragmond repeated. "Like in the stories."

Ravenna nodded, her pale limbs entwined in the black silk sheets, her dark hair cascading over the king's bare thigh.

"Seven," she said absently, trailing a black fingernail across Dragmond's white chest, and resting it over his heart. Her thoughts were racing still, from road to road out of the city, remembering a branching path on the Gray Strand that led to a copse of evergreen, the two ancient forks in Hadrach road, the leeward caverns along Stormpoint.

The wizard *was* findable—he and the miserable boy. Headed for Hadrach, or Rabia, or even perhaps into Zephyr where the Athelings waited and the armies mustered.

"Seven, I said," Dragmond murmured tediously as he sank into sleep. "And each one more dire than the first."

Ravenna nodded again. Her gray eyes lifted to the window and grew suddenly black. There, framed by the glow of the city across the straits and the cleaner light of the sun rising over the Sea of Shadows, the first of the ravens alighted. The bird stared wickedly at her, shaking its dirty feathers.

No. Not yet for the boy, it seemed to say.

Over the wood? she asked in her thoughts, her eyes narrowing at the news.

Eagles and hawks, the bird announced. *The folk of the air alone*.

Suddenly, another raven appeared on the sill, landing heavily with an ominous murmur. Another followed soon after, as the Great Witch looked on dreamily. Slowly the rising sun blanched the redness of the light behind the birds, and their shadows grew out of the darkness of the room as they watched her, their feathers patchy and tattered.

"Tis the third time already, loves," Ravenna whispered to the birds. "I shall call on you again and yet again. 'Tis the King's decree."

Stupidly the ravens stared back at her.

"Get to sleep now," she scolded playfully. "Your wings must

be strong and your eyes sharp. The war is shifting to far-off countries, as wars often do, and we must travel to find it.''

The Great Witch laughed quietly, and rolled over. Her first sleep in days was restless—haunted by a landscape of winds and ice, wherein she dreamed of shattering crystal.

Five floors below the drowsing Ravenna, in a hard cot on the ground floor of the tower, Faye's sleep was even more restless. She could no longer distinguish between sleep and waking: Her dreams were of endless floors and towering woodwork, through which she walked with a small, ineffective mop.

Faye awoke from these dreams angry, already tired, facing the real floors and the real walls as though already she had worked a full and tiring day. A voice stirred faintly in her thoughts, like the distant humming of bees, when Ravenna passed her in the hallways, appeared on the stairwell or stood framed in moonlight on a balcony. *Danger, danger, there is danger in this*, the voice urged, and the witch's shadow seemed to grow and bristle like an ominous, untended plant.

Because of that voice, Faye could not love the Mistress. Though there was another voice, stronger and with her always —a smokey, high whine repeating and repeating. ''Why fearest thou?'' it asked . . .

> *Why fearest thou, that canst not hope for thing,*
> *And fearest not, that more thee hurten might,*
> *Now in the powre of euerlasting Night?*

When Faye stood over her broom, over tarnished rows of candelabra, over the floor littered with dry wax and ash and other, unspeakable things, she heard the soothing voice more loudly, more musically, and there were times in which it almost drowned out the nagging sense she had of being ill at ease, of misgiving and of sleeplessness.

After all, she was lucky to be safe in the tower, was she not? For she had heard the stories of what had come to pass in the town. Of the plaguestruck bodies littering the streets and the Death that followed, in which a third of the town had died, they told her. Then there was the army of ravens descending onto the city, settling like a dreadful black rain.

Faye stirred restlessly on her little cot, pulling the thin blanket tightly about her shoulders.

Plague and ravens, she thought. Those were the first two sicknesses. So the servants were saying, at least. And all of them were grateful to be here, the water and the Causeway between them and the dying, between them and the scavenging birds. They told her she should be thankful, too. And yet there was that other voice, quiet and insistent, lying somewhere deep within the being of the young woman, from where it told her that all things were unsafe in the Tower.

There was the voice, and there was the Pale Man.

He rode up the Causeway nightly, upon a pale horse. In his wake the air seemed to burn, and the hot smell of rue and cinnamon ruffled the air. Faye had watched him from the window, taken into account his cold handsomeness, the immaculate white cape and hood he wore, and the scarf he wrapped over his face like a shroud as he left hours later, his business with the king concluded.

Lightborn, the servants called him. Said he was a duke or something, though none of them could name his homeland. Though her memories of the Wall Town streets had faded considerably, Faye's instinct for danger remained. And this Lightborn was dangerous. Though she could not put words around it, could not even name what it was that told her so, Faye knew that the man was completely and thoroughly evil.

She sat up in the bed. Above her, Ravenna's pacing had ceased almost an hour ago. Faye had heard the footsteps as the witch descended the stairwell, bound for the king's chamber, no doubt, where Dragmond would dismiss Lightborn and admit his mistress. Now it would not be long before the servants would be stirring and the day beginning.

These things were like clockwork at the Tower, as regular as the seasons. Faye sighed, and outside her window, hoofbeats clattered across the stones of the Causeway. The girl rose, crossed to the window, and leaned out.

Lightborn looked back once, then passed between the rising shadows of gibbets, south toward the slanting streets of Ships.

Faye watched until the horseman lost himself in the shadows and then, with a long disconsolate sigh, turned back to the spare barracks of a room and wearily picked up the mop again.

"I can't remember," she whispered to herself, padding barefooted toward the door, the hallway, and the labyrinth of dusty corridors and stairwells. "I can't remember at all. But there's someplace else I'm supposed to be."

He had seen her, too, as she gazed out her ground floor window, framed in candlelight and soft brown hair, the gray eyes ringed and hollowed from sleeplessness. She did not know that he had seen her, any more than she knew how she figured in the history of things.

Lightborn tightened the scarf over his nose as he rode over the Causeway, past the gibbets where the latest array of bodies swayed and dried. In his nostrils now was the acrid odor of bittersweet and camphor, scarcely masked by the thick Aquitainian perfume.

The girl was important. That much he knew. Beyond that was cloudy, as cloudy as the streets ahead of him. The Great Witch knew, as did the King himself, how that brown-haired wisp of a girl fit with the lad in the cellar of the Poisoner's Hall.

How she fit further, into some intricate, far-reaching plan.

Lightborn would have to find out these things.

Slowly his horse passed between the rows of guttering torches at the middle of the Causeway. Faintly he heard the Corrante boiling around him, below him, on its dangerous passage through Needle's Eye into the Bay of Ashes. Occasionally, in the dark waters where the bay widened far off to his right, something white would bob on the surface, tossed and buffeted by the dark waves. For the Watch had yet to clear the ashen waters: still the cwalu floated in the murk and the distance.

But he was safe from that, here on the Causeway. Lightborn sighed as his thoughts turned to a warmer province.

For he could guess how the girl fit with the lad.

He leered beneath the white silk of the mask.

Where young girls such as this always fit in, it was the fitting that broke them, that tossed them finally from monarch to monarch, from potentate to atheling until they became fierce and hardened.

Like the Witch back there.

The Pale Man flicked the reins of his horse, who stepped from the Causeway onto the northernmost point of Ships, where the Street of the Chemists ended at a makeshift scaffold encircled by carts and booths, the platform of last spring's execution of Blue-eyed Duval, Second Master of the Thieves' Guild. Slowly the white horse walked past the scaffolding, already rain-darkened and salt-rimed.

Lightborn scarcely noticed his surroundings. His thoughts circled in narrowing spirals around the Witch, like hunting birds around an elusive, hidden quarry.

She keeps the girl for some intricate reason, he thought. *Some reason beyond luring the Pretender back here. Oh, the girl will do that soon enough, but that is too easy to be the whole story. Ravenna must have other things in mind for her, things darker than the boy and his wizard can imagine.*

Darker than the King can imagine, too, the Pale Man noted, his cruel smile widening. *The time will come when he rues bedding her.*

With a steady gloved hand, he guided the white horse east onto Cove Road, his pale eyes shifting and calculating, all the while seeing nothing.

When that time comes, he promised, *I shall not make the same mistake.*

Down Cove Road the Pale Man rode, singing softly to himself.

> *Je veux te raconter, o molle enchanteresse!*
> *Les diverses beautés qui parent ta jeunesse;*
> *Je veux te peindre ta beauté*
> *Où l'enfance s'allie à la maturité.*

Toward the stockyards and the abbatoirs he rode, singing a song his mother had taught him. Ahead of him the gulls reeled and parted, and the last stars of the night sky winked over the Sea of Shadows.

He crossed out of Grospoint and the odor of the yards reached him, the smell of offal and a slick, coppery whiff of blood filtering through the scented handkerchief to his nose. Free of the shadows of the buildings for a moment, Lightborn looked up into the sky, where the green star flickered faintly in the rising sunlight.

Pytho had passed entirely through the Forest Lord. Through Draco and the Chariot, too, and the Great Hay Rake. The constellations came quickly to him, as they did to all who studied in the Aquitaine.

"It is now," he announced to himself with the same tuneless baritone murmur in which he had been singing only minutes before. "Only a little time now, Mother and Father and Father."

He clicked his tongue at the horse, which broke from a walk into a trot. The rest of his thoughts were lost in the daylight, as west he rode into the dark circle of the stockyards.

The Watchmen stationed near the stockyards saluted as the captain approached on his pale horse. His white robes and white armor glittered, almost silver with the light of a seaside dawn. He returned the salute, passed by them, and again the guards breathed.

They had been taught to salute their superiors, schooled well in the barracks and in the great training fields along the southern coast of Aquila. But they were Teal Front boys for the most part, the sons of wealthy merchants and accustomed to giving place to no man—not even the King himself. Other commanders, even the revered General Helmar, complained of the looseness of discipline, of insubordination and plunder and even the occasional lieutenant found floating in with the tide or stuffed in a barrel back down some Wall Town alley, a gilt knife in his back.

The Watch knew better, however, than to trouble Captain Lightborn. Aside from all the rumors—of rebellion, of assassinations, even of infanticide—there was something about the man that none of them could put words or even thoughts around, something deep and cold that repelled them, that made the very horses restless.

The white stallion beneath him shivered and rolled its eyes when he mounted, they said.

One of the Watchmen, a round-faced boy of seventeen named Danjel, looked wonderingly at his lieutenant after the captain had passed.

"Amiens?" he asked, a flurry of frightened questions rising to his thoughts as the uneasiness and heat of the air faded back into the morning briskness.

"I have no idea, Danjel," Lieutenant Amiens responded, his eye on the large central building of the stockyards, where Lightborn was dismounting, was handing the reins of his stallion to another Watchman. "Whatever your question, I have no answer for it."

"Indeed," he continued, facing the soldier with an unsettled smile, "even if I knew the answer I would not know the answer."

Danjel nodded. He had grown up on Teal Front and was used to the cloudy dance of explanations.

"We have been reassigned," the Pale Man announced to his assembled lieutenants.

They sat together in the large, bare room, cleared out in September by orders of the king, and washed as thoroughly as stockmen and carters and butchers and the odd patrol of Watchmen fancied to wash a place. For commerce in the slaughterhouses declined as suspicion grew that the Death rode in from the countryside in the eyes of the cattle bound for the abbatoirs and butcheries. Indeed, what animals were left were confined in the outer buildings. At night the Watchmen heard them, lowing with their unsettling, almost human, cries, and the sound was desolate, disorienting.

It was one reason why the troops were eager to move. Lightborn knew the other reasons, too. That no cleansing, not even with lye and smoke, could take the smell of dying from the district—that the stockyards would probably smell of death when the buildings and even the city were no more. There were also the *symbola*, the faint marks of the guild scratched in the ceilings, in the dark corners and outside on the cornices, on the foundations: the signs of Zeus and of Mithra, older signs such as that of Melkart and strange Assyrian scrawlings that baffled even the visionaries. It was a house marked for death in a dozen languages and by a dozen dead gods, and the Watch who waited therein could not help but feel its dying and its memories of death.

There in the dark and vaulted room all eyes fixed suddenly and hopefully upon Lightborn; the wine he had poured lay untouched in their cups, and none of them turned when Amiens, the fifth and last of the lieutenants to arrive, opened the door and slipped into the room.

"Reassigned, sir?" asked Lieutenant Elrach, the boldest of the five. Lightborn stared directly at the lad, his pale eyes expressionless.

"Reassigned. To Kestrel Tower."

The cup was shaking in Amiens's hand as he lifted it and drank. The others followed suit, some with caution and others more confidently. Elrach drank last, his hand firm and his eyes never lifting from the white-robed man in front of him. Lightborn nodded, smiled, and seated himself upon a spare mahogany stool that seemed to rise out of the darkness. Slowly, and to himself, he began to count.

His lieutenants stood before him like a group of recruits assembled for review. They coughed, shuffled, and glanced furtively at one another.

Lightborn waited. One of them would speak, and soon. He believed it would be Elrach.

Indeed, he was sure it would be Elrach.

"We had assumed, sir," Elrach began, as a faint smile flickered at the edge of the Pale Man's mouth, "that we would be sent south, to Corbinwood to scout out the movements of Duke Galliard."

"Of *Galliard*," Lightborn corrected. "Galliard is no duke."

Elrach nodded. "Natheless. We expected to be sent to the edge of his forest—"

" 'Tis the *King's* forest, Elrach," interrupted Lightborn. "Galliard is trespassing there."

"As you say, Captain. Natheless, we were given to believe, by our daylight ventures down Hadrach Road, and by coming yesterday to within the eye's distance of the forest, where with but the scant aid of a spyglass, a sharp-eyed man might see the birds circling . . ."

Birds? Lightborn frowned and steepled his long, pale fingers. What was the man suggesting under all this courtly phrasing?

Nothing, he concluded. *There is no subtlety in Elrach.*

All the while the Pale Man counted silently, his numbers at fifty now. One hundred, it was, if the Alanyan had told him rightly.

"Plans change, Elrach," he answered quietly, his thoughts back on the shadowy room, on his arranged lieutenants. "You know this well from your time in the King's service."

"Aye, sir," the young man agreed. "But we took on the uniform for venture and travel and for gold, perhaps, but not to shepherd some cowering king in a tower."

" 'Tis a part of the duties of the Watch, Elrach," Lightborn answered cautiously, his mind racing over what he knew of the men in front of him, whether any of his lieutenants had those elaborate, unspoken connections with the king that the rich often did with the royal, especially in Maraven. If it were so, what he said could draw him murkily toward treason.

Again, and again reluctantly, the captain decided to play at loyalty. He leaned forward, scowled at Elrach, for the first time letting the white silken mask drop from his face.

"Whether you imagined it or no, lieutenant, it is your duty."

Something fluttered high up in the darkened rafters. A swallow, perhaps, or a bat. Nervously, the lieutenants averted their eyes, glancing above them, then quickly returning their gaze to the Pale Man.

Good, Lightborn thought. *Indeed, better than I had hoped. All are frightened of me, and yet all stand fast. Brave men . . . or too frightened to run away.*

And now . . . what remains?

"Castle duty it is," the Pale Man announced hoarsely, his eyes expectant upon Elrach, as he silently counted *seventy* in the vaulted silence. For the moment depended on the young man's movement, on the rebellion Lightborn had seen coming for a week or more. He knew the lad would have to be dealt with, and through guesswork and logic and auguries of his own, he had seen when the moment would come: this night, this place, and in this company of men.

*Do not let me down, Elrach. Speak up. Do not let me seem
. . . cruel.*

"What we are, then," the young man pronounced angrily,
"is Dragmond's bodyguard. No more than a squadron of thugs
about the anointed presence."

Lightborn leaned back in his chair. Masterfully, he feigned a
lazy unconcern, but intensely his eyes sought the eyes of each
lieutenant—of Amiens, too scared to protest, of Florian and
Rowland and the others.

No swords would be lifted. Good, for the moment approached.
His counting had reached ninety.

"I detect a note of treason in your complaining, Lieutenant
Elrach," Lightborn declared coldly, his eyes fixed on the angry
lad. Almost at once, Elrach's anger faded. He took an uncertain
step backward, as though he were trying to remember something.
Ninety-five.

"I . . . I . . ." Elrach began, then suddenly clutched his
stomach. His eyes rolled upward, then fixed frantically on the
cup in his hand. Slowly, in consternation, he turned his gaze to
Lightborn, who shrugged and nodded, as though what was happening to the lad in front of him was a minor inconvenience—
say, a sudden, unfortunate change in the weather.

"*Agonia*," Florian breathed, and Lightborn smiled readily,
his blue eyes twinkling with an eerie merriment.

"Found me out, Lieutenant Florian!" he conceded cheerfully,
as Elrach dropped to his knees, groaning. Lieutenant Rowland
took one step toward the dying man, extended his hand briefly,
almost undetectably, then stopped, turning back to the captain,
his eyes cold and expressionless.

Natheless, Lightborn thought. *I shall have to watch Rowland,
too.*

"Your . . . your foresight is remarkable, sir," young Rowland
observed. "To have known beforehand the cup that . . . that the
traitor would take. And then to have known that it would be on
this night that . . . his treason would be made manifest."

Elrach lay on the floor now, his insides boiling.

No wonder the Alanyans prefer agonia, mused the Pale Man.
*Next to it, the charms of aconite and nightshade seem childish,
unsubtle.*

"My foresight," he observed, "takes into account many things, Lieutenant Rowland. All the more reason that the King wants me by his side in Kestrel Tower. There is peril to our beloved city, lads, and the King has appointed us to attend his presence until the peril is turned away. It is a great honor, I assure you."

And a greater chance, he thought, as his lieutenants filed silently from the room, bearing the instructions to muster their squadrons and convene on the south end of the Causeway. Alone in the abandoned slaughterhouse, Captain Lightborn reclined in his chair, his eyes fixed on the white silk handkerchief in his lap, but looking through it, actually, focused on nothing but a strange, unnatural darkness and upon his own thoughts.

A greater chance, to be seized by a greater gambler. For Elrach was foreseeable and easy, a foolish lad with a temper and a dimwitted sense of pride.

But now I am bound for the Witch's country. Up in the tower, where the rules shift daily, and the windows have eyes.

He stood, fixing the silk mask back upon his face, uncovering a small glass phial he had wrapped in the handkerchief as he addressed his lieutenants. Carefully he placed the phial up his sleeve.

He could not use it now. Indeed, to use it would be unthinkable . . .

. . . and yet they are only months from turning, he thought. *Dragmond and Ravenna, that is. Only months away from a time in which all things may avail—whether wolfsbane or agonia or even more poisonous words. And in the meantime, the castle will bear watching, and bear it well from this closer distance. For soon the Witch and the King will begin to wrangle, if I know intrigue and unrest. For I shall be there. I and those who travel with me.*

For I shall be the balance of power.

With a brief, high-pitched chuckle, the Pale Man opened the door of the slaughterhouse. The blinding light of mid-morning caught him off guard, and he startled at the boy standing there, holding the reins of his white horse. Quickly he mounted, and quickly goaded the horse into a trot west on Cove Road, unsettled by the sunlight and the sudden freshness of sea air.

Behind him, the boy glanced once into the slaughterhouse before closing the door. There was something in the rafters, fluttering back and forth, but such was often the case in a large, high-ceilinged building, especially one that lay idle for so long.

Thinking no further, the lad closed the door. In the foul-smelling, windowless dark, the fluttering shape descended and perched on the high back of Lightborn's chair. It sat there for a moment, croaking and boding, its dark eyes glittering and its feathers black and sleek.

➤➤➤ **IX** ◄◄◄

The King leaned over the balcony until Lightborn passed through the gates beneath him, his white armor shining like bleached bones in the mid-morning sun.

Now seal off the doors to the tower, Dragmond thought bitterly, *and we shall swarm and menace like hornets in the nest.*

Or elks battering themselves for a solitary doe.

I am the King of Palerna, and somewhere out there lives a boy who is free, untrammelled, no doubt in open and plague-free country, with a counselor he can trust. That boy is youthful and rested, abroad with all things possible . . .

. . . and he would trade all of that for my crown.

He turned from the window wearily, staring into the shadowy chamber draped in dark tapestries. The dark canopy over his bed drooped with the numberless finger bones hung upon it as wardings, through which the night wind whistled and clacked when the sea was high and stormy, keeping him awake as everything kept him awake, with sounds like voices at the edge of his understanding. On the bed was a useless litter of maps and globes, geographies of Zephyr and Umbria, notes freshly delivered from spies and scouts and informers throughout Palerna, all assembled in the king's attempt to locate the wizard and the lad.

Dragmond breathed deeply, and prepared for the darker lessons.

Ravenna had left but an hour ago, and in her place the visionaries had assembled—a Parthian astrologer, a retemancer from northernmost Aquila, and the woman from Provence, new to the court, who needed neither stars nor nets, but simply closed her eyes and waited for the future to show itself.

There were the others, also: the Rabian *cadaverii* who looked into the eyes of the drowned, the Byzantine haruspex who read the entrails of birds. There were a dozen in all, penniless and ambitious, called from their hovels in Grospoint and Wall Town, and expected in the presence of the King within minutes. They came only when Ravenna was not there, when she was safely away, asleep or at augury. For the Great Witch laughed at them and at their prophecies and especially at the king who called them, all the while serenely convinced that the future rode nowhere else but in the flames of her candles.

It had grown old. The day was here in which Dragmond could no longer abide her laughter.

So he assembled them in her absence, and in her absence received instruction.

"As the last thing, look to the smallest leavings, Your Grace," the Aquilan warned, his northern voice thick with the burr that made Dragmond shudder with thoughts of Galliard. "To the smallest leavings last, for they'll tell ye what happens the furthest from ye. The conch shell and the drowned gull tell ye about yesterday or today. Indeed, what they have to tell may already have happened. It's in the cowries and the periwinkles and the weed that you look, to gather the times to come afore they gather ye."

"What do the cowries say, Master Hubert?" the King asked, craning over the Aquilan's shoulder and frowning.

The old retemancer looked up at him.

"War, Your Highness. The cowries say war."

Dragmond stepped back, clutching his chair. Slowly, breathlessly, he seated himself. The Aquilan turned to him and cackled, his face split with a wide, toothless grin.

"But never ye mind, sir. What's war to the likes of a shell may not be war to the likes of ye and me."

"Then . . . then what of the conch? Of the gull?'' Dragmond asked, his gaze intent on the old man as he leaned forward.

"Well, the gull is plain enough, being daunger in high places,'' the old Alanyan explained, and again the king thought of Galliard, wondered if he was that *daunger*. Wondered if the old man before him had been planted by the Forest Lord to feed the king with lies, to create in him a great and crippling suspicion, that would have him looking for wizard's boys while the real threat grew down in Corbinwood.

Perhaps Galliard was more subtle. Perhaps all the visionaries were his spies, his emissaries, knowing whatever future the Forest Lord wanted them to know, and giving the King lethal, partial answers like the oracles in the old stories.

"And the conch,'' the old fellow continued serenely. "Well, owing to her position in the nets and to the presence of the gull, I'd be looking for that daunger nearby me and under the shell, if you understand. For 'tis already here and right in your closest circle.''

Dragmond closed his eyes. He longed for the time in which he knew enough to read all augury himself, a time in which he would need to consult no diviners, whose spoken prophecies poisoned the air, shaded the future to their own bias and purpose.

But what if the old man was not lying? If what lay in the bottom of those nets was pure and unshaded truth?

The King sat back, entwined his gloved fingers, and brooded as the retemancer went on about weather and tides, about shipping routes and harvests. In his thoughts he thumbed through the dangers, and the dangers were many.

Lightborn came first to mind, of course. Nobody could trust Lightborn, with his past obscure as morning fog and nearly as treacherous. Only minutes ago he had entered the tower grounds, a hundred men at his command and his the select assignment of guarding the King's Person. No matter that he was ruthless and cold, Dragmond had thought. The better to frighten away spies and assassins, for whether by stealth or by force, who would willingly enter a room filled with adders?

But indeed, who would bring the adders in and dwell among them?

He mulled over second thoughts. Let Lightborn and his company be sent to Corbinwood, joining with the southern ranks of Helmar's regions. Let the Pale Man and the Forest Lord wrangle until the end of time, far from Maraven and the Tower.

Far from Ravenna.

Dragmond smiled at his own foresight. He turned his thoughts back to the circle of diviners, where the old Aquilan was finishing his litany of weather and season. The Rabian *cadaverii* spoke next, and the King was glad that the man did not bring into the royal presence the instruments of his murky graveyard trade.

"The plague clouds things over, Your Grace," the Rabian explained timidly, reaching into his robes for a small scroll of impeccably clean linen and neat letters. "Not that the signs leave the body, mind you, but that the plague refuses to leave. Hours, it will be, or sometimes days, until it is safe enough to send my boys out to the gathering of evidence."

Not that you would risk that duty yourself, the King thought with a dry irony. *Little Rabian, the most surpassing wisdom that you have for me is in the way you gather your knowledge.*

"By the time it gets back to me," the Rabian continued, his eyes bright as he opened the little scroll, "it is sometimes deceptive, for I must understand the eyes, the twelve pallors and the seventeen angles of the jaw, all from what my prentices tell me, knowing full well there are signs that they might misread, marks and telling gestures that they might pass over. For you know full well, that visions bend and sully as they are passed from hand to hand."

Dragmond winced at the prospects. It was as though the second sight was a huge, distorting glass, through which the things to come would sparkle, slant, and disappear before the baffled eyes of the visionary. Whether nets or stars, whether entrail or tea leaves or the strange, colorful gallery of the Italian *tarrochia* cards, it seemed like dice play to the Palernan king—that no matter how you divined or augured or prophesied, the future was still obscure, elusive.

But only a floor above him, where the candles flickered and gutted and speckled the old inlaid map of the subcontinent with yellow, the Great Witch paced amid chants and oracles, and despite his doubts, Dragmond knew that she brought things back over distances and time, if only enough to vex them both. Slowly, in the last few weeks leading up to the Night of the Cwalu and the Pretender's unforeseen escape, Ravenna's augury had become more secretive, more disturbing.

Now the chanting lasted until midday, sometimes into the following evening. Dragmond knew that she slept only fitfully, of late going two, three nights without closing her eyes.

Soon the candles were joined by the ravens and orbs.

The birds, of course, patrolled the countryside as far east as the outskirts of Rabia and west into the grassy Zephyrian heartland. So the King's visionaries told him, and the leaders of caravans confirmed when the Watch dragged them to the Tower for inquiry. You would see flocks of them, black wing to black wing, settling and boding in blasted oaks, atop Alanyan gravestones, sometimes surprisingly on the riggings of ships skirting the Shallows around the Ruthic Islands, but mostly circling overhead, spying you out and seeing who rode with you. At all times, day or night, they dove and banked through the windows at the top of Kestrel Tower, circling the parapets and crying loudly in a thin, unintelligible language that Dragmond knew was no longer only the language of ravens.

On occasion, if you stood in the overgrown garden, untended since the days of King Albright, and if you asked the Watchmen to extinguish the torches around you so that the light of the flames would not war with the thinner light of the moon and the lamplight in the upper stories . . . why, then, you could see it all. The ravens swarming like flies, like hornets, and Ravenna standing at the balcony as they reeled overhead, raising her pale arms and chanting something, something that tumbled toward you, toward you, only to be drowned in the raucous outcry of the birds she had summoned.

It would all be different, reassuring, somehow, if he could believe that the birds had been summoned with his safety and best interest at heart. But now, seated in a hard mahogany chair, his eyes fixed on the chamber window, his thoughts far away from the chatter and outcry of the visionaries who gestured and prophesied there in the same room, Dragmond was no longer sure of the Great Witch's loyalty.

Not *that* loyalty, mind you. He had never trusted Ravenna

when it came to matters of power. She was with him as long as it served her interests and not a moment longer. He had played by those rules since his boyhood.

But now he could not trust her in a tower full of young, vital guardsmen. And Lightborn's presence—his cold and ruthless handsomeness—was a menace the king had yet to consider.

Darker still, Dragmond was unsure of the Great Witch's judgment.

After all, she had summoned the cwalu.

It had seemed a plausible plan when first he heard it. If the dead were sent through the streets in search of the wizard's brat, there was no fear at which they would balk, no need for rest or sustenance until they found the boy. They would provoke great respect in the ranks of the Watch, and make them fear for their value to the King. They had, after all, failed him miserably.

The next morning, when the bodies were cleared from Ships and Grospoint, the Watch captains had reckoned a thousand in all. They had climbed out of the graves and mausoleums lining the southern coast of Aquila, had swum across the narrows of the Needle's Eye or crawled and staggered across the gibbet-lined causeway, their nooses left dangling above. The King had watched from his chamber windows, and Ravenna's coach, black and spangled with silver ravens, had wheeled among them through the city, growing smaller and smaller in the orange moonlight until he had lost it altogether somewhere in Ships, in an alley off Mizzen.

Then he had waited, as she told him to wait. The waiting swelled the limits of his courage.

The next morning there were bodies littering the dirty back streets of Wall Town, sprawled over booths in Gaunt and fences in the stockyards, over half-finished pinnace hulls on Tar Street. One was discovered outside the huge oaken doors of a Teal Front estate, its two inch nails, continuing to grow in the dark of a cheap coffin, having scored the hard wood of the door in foot-long, inch-deep grooves.

From a certain distance, a nervous Watch sergeant had said, and from a certain angle, at an hour or so before sunset when the light struck the center stiles of the door just so, the scars across it looked like writing.

Hearing this, and ever the student of omens, Dragmond had gone there himself, curiously at first, but more and more eagerly as he travelled through the modest residential districts south of Grospoint. Past shops and chapels and guild halls he rode, the windows of his coach closed tightly and the handkerchief about his face, his eyes half-closed and the sweet smell of camphor in his nostrils from the Causeway to Teal Front and the notorious oaken door.

There he disembarked, and, with a handful of visionaries, he had inspected the scars, looked at them desperately from a step away, two steps, ten, trying to read their rough, indecipherable language. He squinted at sunset, and then through the night, as the Watchmen stood at various distances, various heights, raising and lowering the torches so that the light of the flame struck the marred wood at every angle imaginable.

He had gone home unanswered.

The future is like that, Dragmond thought now, as he stood near the hearth, stirring the cold cinders with a rusty iron log fork, despite himself reading the swirl of the ashes for portents and omens.

The future is like a thick door. It is scarred and mysterious, its scoring a map of something, if you only had the sense or the foresight to read it. But for me, for my visionaries with their guts and planets and the flotsam of fisherman's nets, it is finally a door and a door only—a barrier, bolted and locked unto a time when it opens of its own accord.

The Great Witch, on the other hand, has the key to that door. She may never sleep again for the having, may pace the room filled with mirrors and candles, a dark form moving through tilting light.

Nonetheless, she has the key, and I do not.

But when I find it I shall be rid of her.

The King of Palerna stirred the ashes quickly, angrily, the smallest of murderous plans forming dimly in his mind. He dwelt on Ravenna through most of the afternoon, crouched by the outer hearth, seated in the tall mahogany chair from which he received petitioners and augurers, then crossed to the bed, where he lay napping fitfully, waking to the same oppressive thoughts.

Black. It was the color she rendered. At night, exhausted from his bouts with her, as they lay intertwined and sweating on this very bed, Dragmond could think only of black. He would see black only, whether his eyes were closed or open.

And he would want her again, like a wounded man longed for lethe or morphia. Like Tantalus, cursed with a hunger magnified by the feeding.

He stirred beneath the thin sheets, his thoughts playing nervously over various matters.

Over the matter of Faye. What Ravenna planned to do with the girl was beyond him.

Of course, she would make a good hostage, this . . . Faye. Terrance's brat had something for the girl, obviously. After all, she had been in the cellar with the lad, or so Lightborn had told him. The Watch could have killed her there, too, down in the belly of the Hall of the Poisoners. But then, they could have captured the lad there, too, and had they done so, this Faye would have been of no consequence.

Still, it was Faye they had, while the wizard and boy were loose in Zephyr or the gods knew where. And if Faye had been brought here as a hostage, Ravenna had a funny way of keeping her—hiding the girl, secreting her away instead of making her presence known so that word of her capture would return to the wizard.

Whatever her plan, Dragmond decided, Ravenna had her reasons. Of that he was sure, and sure that in those reasons lay a poison for Terrance. For the King was not as thick as his mistress supposed, and he heard her voice glaze at the wizard's name. So there: it was more complicated than simple ransom. He was sure, and from the moment Faye had fallen into their hands, he had been trying to outguess the Great Witch, to figure her larger plan.

Still her thoughts were opaque, impassable.

Ravenna had brought the girl to the tower even before the Watch had begun dragging the cwalu out of the streets, out of the tunnels and houses and onto the pyres prepared for them in the wider squares of Wall Town. When the black coach arrived, its driver slumped in the seat, whip hand dangling as the vehicle moved slowly like a stately ship up the Causeway, the king had watched from the balcony. He squinted, hoping to catch a glimpse of the Great Witch, of her black hair and black eyes through the darkened moving window. And from that glimpse to fathom her plans.

Instead, he had seen the girl, her face strangely placid, almost unreadable.

The king caught his breath, sat up in the bed. After a moment his shoulders sagged. With a low rumble in his throat, he settled back upon the bed.

Ravenna, he recalled, had brought the girl in under guard and hidden her away at once. Since that time Dragmond had seen Faye only fleetingly, traveling quietly through the halls in the swirling wake of her mistress, and once at a somber, candle-lit meal he shared with Ravenna, when the girl slipped in and poured dark burgundy into their glasses.

Then there was the time when he stood in the overgrown garden, watching Ravenna's window from a distance, as he always did. Unexpectedly, the girl stepped out upon the balcony and the constant flow of ravens about the window scattered for once, and Dragmond could see her clearly, her brown robe awash in the burnished light of the moon.

It was a thinner garment than she would like, no doubt, given the brisk turn in the nights of late as summer declined into fall. Much thinner . . . why, if you moved to the cluster of acacia on the west side of the balcony, where your view of the girl was framed in the amber moonlight, you could see through it, see the curved shadow of her breasts and the graceful incline toward her narrow waist as the rest of her was lost in shadow, blocked by the stones of the parapet . . .

Dragmond shivered as he inhaled, pushed the sheet away. Quickly he rose from the bed, padded to the wash basin by the hearth, and splashed water on his face. Slowly he picked up the copper mirror by the basin. His face wavered in it for a moment, then his gaze settled.

What Ravenna had in mind for the girl was a mystery, but

whatever it was, it would not bode well for the lad and somehow, Dragmond was certain, even worse for Terrance.

He was not sure it boded well for him.

Uneasily, the king set the mirror by the basin. Outside the window the evening was falling with a raucous, expectant outcry of birds.

Dragmond did not want the throne, she thought.

Or did not want it enough to grapple and intrigue and fight for it.

Sooner or later, that reluctance would cost him.

A floor above the King, Ravenna lit the candles, one after another, as the dark map of the subcontinent glittered with life at her feet. Umbria glowed beneath her, then the southern plains of Palerna. Northwards across the black floor glided the Witch, and at her touch each candle burst into flame, illuminating yet another province, another fork in a river, another city or bay or passage through mountains.

Since he would not keep the throne, she would keep it through him.

Ravenna stopped, knelt over the westernmost spot on the map, there at the edge of the carving where the ancient artisan had inlaid the white, triangular images of Zephyrian tents, inscribing the symbol with its mysterious, obscure title.

"Agilis," Ravenna breathed, touching the white tent with one black, enameled fingernail. "Castra Agilis."

The Light Camp, they called it, the chief Zephyrian settlement. The oldest legends claimed that Agilis rode the back of the wind, eluding the enemies of Zephyr by vanishing from their maps overnight. Even today, most of the countryfolk claimed that it was a city borne on the backs of horses, shifting its geography with the changing seasons and the changing pasturelands.

Indeed, not thirty years ago, in the midst of one of the continual conflicts between Zephyr and its northern neighbor Partha, an entire Parthian legion, five thousand men strong, cavalry, dragoons, and dromedarians included, had vanished in pursuit of the elusive city. Messengers had returned three times to the Parthian King's palace, each time saying that Agilis was only a day's march off.

Then no more messengers came back, and the Parthian king withdrew his other legions into the desert fastness, and it was said that the domes and pendentives of his temples there were draped in black silk for a year.

Ravenna smiled. Her science was better than the Parthians's. She knew that the city moved indeed, but that the price it paid for elusiveness was permanence. Agilis was a city of tents, constantly traveling according to the judgment or whim of the Council of Athelings, who could simply order it packed up and taken elsewhere.

It was easily explained, but not so easily found.

Quickly, the Great Witch set her hand to the cold marble and closed her eyes. Around her, the flames of the candles tilted and rocked, and outside on the balcony, a dozen ravens croaked and boded. In her mind's eye, the far Zephyrian plains appeared, the endless and featureless brown grasslands which, having weathered the last heat of the late September sun, had settled into an autumn dryness, awaiting the November rains.

Those rains were still weeks away. Quietly, Ravenna breathed the cantrip that set her Zephyrian vision in motion.

> *And yonder all before us lye*
> *Desarts of vast Eternity.*

She opened her eyes and saw the image of the grasslands reflected in the marble's soft glow beside her hand. Suddenly the image shifted. The wavering, envisioned trees vanished, only to be replaced by others, thin and bare within the wide expanse of savannah.

Ravenna's vision was moving. Alertly, like a circling predator, the Great Witch's gaze flashed over landscapes she saw deep in her own imaginings as though she remembered them well from a recent past, though in fact Ravenna had never traveled west of the Gray Strand. One by one she rejected those images, moving on her knees around the glowing spot on the map as she did so. As Ravenna circled the vision, one candle, then another in the ring behind her cast its light on the map and the scene changed.

The twelfth candle found Agilis.

At first it seemed like a cloud of dust at the farthermost edge of the vision. Ravenna squinted, breathed deeply, then recited the chant that would bring her closer yet.

> *Follow still, since so thy fates ordained!*
> *The sun must have his shade,*
> *Till both at once do fade.*
> *The sun still proved, the shadow still disdained.*

And she saw them riding the plains ahead of her, a company of five hundred horse, the cavalry armed and dressed in hides, in occasional bronze mail that glinted in the declining sun. The young man at the head of the column she recognized from rumors.

It was Namid, the Baron of West Aldor and Viscount Campestris of the Assembled Horsemen. Topmost of the Zephyrian Council of Athelings, and son of the late Baron Macaire, who came as close as any of the Zephyrian bandits to taking Maraven outright. Namid was smarter than his father, saner and colder.

She knew him by the patch over his left eye. Blinded when he was only sixteen by a stray, remarkable shot from a Maravenian archer, he was lean, bearded, and no larger than Ravenna herself. The Zephyrian commander rode quickly over the waving grass astride a long-haired Zephyrian pony that was visible only from the withers up, the rest of the animal lost in high grass. Namid carried two swords, crossed and sheathed in leather scabbards, over his back; it was said that he made no difference between the left hand and the right, and fought on horseback, with the reins clutched in his teeth.

Ravenna shuddered, then remembered he was miles away. Her gaze flashed down the column behind him, searching for

Terrance's green robes and wide-brimmed hat and gray beard, searching for the lad who had caused all the trouble.

But behind Namid rode a line of Zephyrians only, the shoulders of their horses breaking through the swirl of high grass, gray and black on a wavering wash of brown, like dolphins coursing through the waters of a muddy river.

"Not in Zephyr," the Great Witch proclaimed. "At least, not with Namid."

So the west was safe for now. Namid might menace, might raid a caravan or two, might waylay a company of Watch. But the real danger was with the lad.

"Corbinwood," Ravenna whispered. "Though the birds have scoured it, and the Green Man cannot move."

With a swirl of her dark robes she stood, turning toward the southern realms of the map. Passing through a bright gauntlet of candles scented with bayberry and cinnamon, dripping red wax onto their tall brass sockets, to the green swath in the glowing map the Great Witch walked, then stopped, raised her hands, and called forth a vision of Corbinwood.

> *Mean while the Mind, from pleasures less*
> *Withdraws into its happiness:*
> *The Mind, that Ocean where each kind*
> *Does streight its own resemblance find;*
> *Yet it creates, transcending these,*
> *Far other Worlds, and other Seas;*
> *Annihilating all that's made*
> *To a green Thought in a green Shade.*

A dark, flitting shadow passed over the green light of the map, and the floor seemed to open, and she stepped again into a long dream.

The coach had bogged heavily in the red earth. Clay-spattered and wet and angry, the Watchmen pushed at the thoroughbrace and at the back wheels, trying to turn them by hand and shoulder.

It was no use. Try as they might, the vehicle would not move. Finally, angrily, a rough hand reached out the window and yanked the door open. Into mud up to his shins General Helmar stepped, as briskly and as casually as if he were walking the grounds of his estate along the Eastmark River.

From her view on high, her head aching and a great dizziness filling her, Ravenna recognized this man. "Self-important old bag of medals," she murmured.

The old man had been a commander under Albright and then under Aurum, serving them with distinction in the Second Zephyrian War and again in Macaire's Incursion. Helmar's loyalty to Palerna had kept him at the head of the armies when Dragmond ascended the throne, despite the general's cordial dislike for the new king and his outright scorn for Ravenna. Had he not been so loyal, and had not his brilliant tactical victories on the battlefield been the stuff of military textbooks for the last half century, Dragmond would likely have replaced him, as Ravenna had plotted. Finally the Witch had persuaded the king to send the old bastard south, where he might have a chance to get himself killed by a stray arrow.

Ravenna smiled and narrowed her eyes. Perhaps this was the chance. Perhaps the arrow had been nocked and drawn, and she would be lucky enough to see it fly.

"By the arses of these mares and all the fools staring into them," General Helmar swore in disgust, "you'll never unmire this thing by elbow grease alone. Why, look at the depth of the mud here! 'Tis as though . . ."

The general paused, sinking further into the mire of the roadway, then lifted his hood in puzzlement. Ravenna watched him closely, the white bushes of his moustache and eyebrows turning up almost comically. Something in his countenance passed rapidly from anger to vigilance, and the pale, heavy-lidded eyes scanned the clearing alertly.

"I am a bigger fool than the King himself," he declared flatly, and drew his sword. His troops watched him in bafflement, thinking that at last the General had passed into dotage and foolishness.

Then the tattered men emerged from the woods to his left.

Lightly armored, their bows and javelins at the ready, they approached out of the darkening shadows in a trained, intelligent silence, efficient as hunting wolves. Within a breath they had surrounded the coach, their numbers twice that of Helmar's Watchmen, most of whom huddled against the doors and panels of the vehicle, dropping their weapons as the bandits encircled them.

"Good!" Ravenna hissed, her pale hands framing the unfolding scene in the maplight. She settled back into the vision, watched, and awaited the slaughter.

"Please, sirs!" one of the Watchmen began, falling to his knees in the mud. "Oh, please! I've a . . ."

"Compose yourself, sergeant!" the general snapped angrily, attempting a kick at the kneeling man and nearly losing his balance in the process. "You Teal Front boys haul out the wives and offspring when you're at sword point, then put them away again on leave!" he exclaimed, leaning on the back wheel of the coach. "By the gods, I'm tired of the convenience!"

The commander of the woodsmen stifled a laugh.

"I haven't seen a mud trap since I fought Macaire up on the strand," Helmar observed, looking down toward his vanished feet, then up again, meeting the gaze of the woodsman commander.

"It's . . . Baron Sendow, isn't it?" the general asked the gray-eyed, rough-featured man who stood smiling in front of him. "I recall you from Aldor, from the Summer Palace. Edgar's second son, if I'm not mistaken. The one who tangled himself in Danton's wreck of a garden?"

"No doubt you even held me on your knee, sir," the young man jested politely, obviously flattered that the general remembered.

"Oh, I doubt it," Helmar snorted. "They aren't much good to me until they can hold a sword." He stared in dismay at his empty-headed, cowering troops. "How's your cousin Galliard and the rest of them? Still plotting sedition?"

"Twelve kinds of outrage and subversion, sir," Sendow replied cheerily, lowering his bow. "Only we prefer to call it dissent, sir. Rightful and thorough-going dissent, I think the Duke calls it. I shall tender your regards when next I see him."

"I suppose I can do that myself, now that I've waded into

your trap,'' Helmar remarked, slogging to the front of the coach and, in a movement surprisingly athletic for his years, pulling himself from the mud and mounting the footboard.

"I'm afraid that won't be possible, sir,'' Sendow replied, and Ravenna smiled wolfishly as she watched, her gray eyes turning black in the shifting candlelight of the tower.

"Now . . .'' she whispered, almost afraid to believe what she suspected, "now they'll . . . dispose of him."

Sendow stepped heedlessly into the mud and approached the front wheels of the coach. He propped his hand on an axle and leaned forward, his voice quiet and assuring.

"No, sir, we've no earthly use for a hostage or prisoner the likes of you in the heart of Corbinwood. You'd eat our food and drink our ale. You'd probably take over and march our men to exhaustion. At the best, we'd have to post incessant guard on you, and we both know that the King would shrug away your capture gladly, and the Witch up in the Tower would declare a national holiday at your taking."

Sendow turned and opened the door to the coach. "No, General Helmar,'' he continued. "We have only one choice, and that's to steal from you, then . . .''

He paused, and the words hung in absolute silence. One of the Watchmen whimpered, and several others joined the sergeant on his knees in the mud. Only Helmar was steady, looking at the young bandit as if he were about to receive news of the weather.

Ravenna knelt and leaned forward, bent over the green map as if in some strange, intense devotion. A large raven, its old head balding and a strange, intelligent look in its eye, settled on the chamber floor and hopped to the far eastern corner of the marble map.

"Then let you go, I suppose,'' Sendow concluded, and around him the Watchmen sagged, sighed, and murmured prayers of gratitude. The sergeant and the other kneelers climbed laboriously back to their feet; standing beside the coach, they looked as though some mischievous sorcerer had formed them out of mud and suddenly, on a whim, breathed life into each of them.

"No!'' Ravenna thundered, leaping to her feet, toppling four candlesticks as she reeled angrily through the chamber, bracing herself against the door of the balcony. The old raven fluttered to the north wall, where he perched on an ornamental pair of crossed swords and looked down on the tirading witch, his little black eyes glittering.

"No . . ." Ravenna repeated, this time more quietly, more uncertainly. She closed her eyes, breathed rhythmically, regularly, and gathered herself into an icy calmness.

For after all, she thought, *we are no worse off than we were before. I shall tell myself and tell myself, for my quarrel is not with Helmar but with the wizard and his brat.*

"Are you sure," she heard Helmar say, his voice still rising out of the green glow of the floor, "that you don't want to have at some of the cowards in my ranks?"

It was yet the wizard and his brat she searched for. Done with distractions, she repeated the chant, then gazed into the shifting wall of leaf and branch in front of her. Despite every effort, she could not see past them.

With growing suspicion Ravenna regarded the unyielding woods. It was the last place left that might harbor the lad, and after all, it had sheltered generations of rebels before him. Zephyrian rebels had sought refuge here, and so had exiled mages and deposed kings. They were long dead and vanished, these insurrectionists, but others had come to replace them, and a strange sort still peopled the dark banks of the Boniluce as it flowed through the wilderness, all dwelling forever in green thought and green shade. Indeed, Galliard was but a newcomer to the fastness of Corbinwood, and though his curse would ever keep him from returning . . .

Ravenna smiled, thinking of the curse . . .

Nonetheless, his presence made the woods impassable to Watch and Maravenian merchant alike. But not even the Duke of Aquila could stop the sharp, visionary eye of the witch.

"Here at the Fountain's sliding foot," Ravenna continued,

> *Or at some Fruit-trees mossy root,*
> *Casting the Bodies Vest aside,*
> *My Soul into the boughs does glide:*
> *There like a Bird it sits, and sings,*

> *Then whets, and combs its silver Wings;*
> *And, till prepar'd for longer flight,*
> *Waves in its Plumes the various Light.*

And the leaves and the branches, the thick entanglements of Corbinwood, still rushed forward to meet her.

Ravenna lay against the cold floor, staring deeply into the rippling map. She repeated the chant and waited, but her vision went no farther, stopping at the edge of the woods, smothered in a wall of leaves. She squinted, following the paths of moonlight into the woods, where they lodged against the gnarled and wrinkled boles of oak and water maple. Rapidly, with increasing urgency and anger, she rushed through two, three, a half dozen chants, but the woods remained closed to her—a thick network of green thought and green shade.

"*She's* at the bottom of this!" Ravenna hissed, her eyes going gray, then black, then gray again as she reached for the vials about her neck, fumbling with the green vial, opening it, lifting it to her lips . . . then suddenly changing her mind. For the depths of Corbinwood were not her country, no matter how she chanted or brewed or augured.

The wizard had sought refuge there, and with him the boy. Ravenna could guess as much, for the simple reason that they were not elsewhere. She sat back, her long black robe fanned across the floor, and slowly, deliberately, she resealed the green vial.

The ancient raven at her shoulder rasped and groaned.

"Th'art true in thy bodings, as always," she replied soothingly, slipping naturally into the old formal tongue, the "thees" and "thous" with which enchantress had greeted raven since the old Egyptian days of ornithomancy, when the Ptolomies scanned the skies for their omens. "Th'art a prescience, my dear," she continued almost affectionately, stroking the bird's balding head with one black-nailed finger.

"And what if Terrance is hiding there? Better there than in Agilis, or in the court of Hadrach or Rabia, for that matter. For there is no help for him *beyond* the borders of Corbinwood. Let his urchin rule in exile from a forest fastness—it will not harm us here.

"And if I cannot enter, I shall see to it that they cannot leave."

The old raven hopped to her shoulder, once more rumbling as it settled and tucked its head beneath its wing.

"Th'art wise beyond even thine hundred years, old bird," the Witch soothed, stroking the mottled, glossy back of the raven. "For it is a time of sleep. Of sleep in this very tower, and the lady would do well to look beneath her own wings, would she not? For it is said that vermin visit feathers left too long unattended."

With a new energy she sprang to her feet, as agile as a girl of fourteen. The raven fluttered from shoulder and sailed with angry whistle to the rafters. He perched there, cocked his head, and regarded Ravenna with a blear and skeptical eye as she turned, cupped the flame of a solitary candle in her pale hands, and breathed the chant of the dream-reader.

> *By each spot the most unholy,*
> *In each nook most melancholy*
> *There the traveler meets, aghast,*
> *Sheeted Memories of the Past:*
> *Shrouded forms that start and sigh*
> *As they pass the wanderer by.*

And into the dreams of the castle she plunged, through swirling darkness and many-faceted, blinding light.

Now and again the image of a room flickered once, twice, in the flame. Ravenna saw the inside of the Tower pantry, an eerie, desolate landscape that reminded her of central Alanya where the dragons lay, an alley that could be in Hadrach, or Florence, or scarcely a mile away in Grospoint. She paced through these dreams—the dreams of the staff and servants—like a winged shadow, or a faint whining sound like a fly in a jar, or only a cold wind at the edge of their fancy.

Of all who slept in Kestrel Tower that night, only two recalled their dreams the next morning. One was a Palernan falconer named Walton, freshly hired as Dragmond's keeper of the mews. The young man woke from a melancholy remembrance of his homeland. Instead of sighing and turning back to sleep, as he had done the night before and the night before that, Walton rehearsed the dream in his memory, recalling something faintly disturbing about it, as though his village—a hamlet of less than a hundred people just north of the Notches—was suddenly bathed in a strange, unholy light, the dear familiar hill to the south of the village dimpling and pulsing like the belly of a spider.

Walton shook his head, folded his hands on his chest, and vowed to return home before winter.

He sat up. Lying on a cot beside the window was the new captain of the guards—the Pale Man, the moonlight cascading over his unnaturally white features. Captain Lightborn was smiling faintly, menacingly, and Walton added that smile to the growing list of reasons that a village in southern Palerna, no matter how desolate and unpromising, looked better all the time. The young man climbed out of bed and, wrapping a blanket about his shoulders, walked out through the brisk night and into the mews, where he fell back to sleep beneath the perches of kestrels and gyrfalcons.

Lightborn turned over in his cot, his face drifting from the moonlight. He, too, remembered his dream.

Walking the dream, marking her path to avoid immersion and *croglath*, that ancient and dreaded condition in which the enchanter is lost forever in the dreams of the victim, Ravenna found herself in a moonlit garden, the pale form of Captain Lightborn weaving itself out of the silvered branches of the trees. Out of the ash tree he rose like a specter, his body white and knotted and hardened, and from the tangled darkness of the brier a woman rose to greet him, dark-haired and dressed in a sheer black tunic that danced and rose above her knees as she walked, unveiling thighs as cool and white as spindrift.

Ravenna noticed that the face and the body of the woman were her own. She caught her breath and peered more closely as the dark, phantasmal witch wrapped her arms around the Captain's neck and drew him closer. Ravenna felt her own hands shake as the two forms embraced.

Ravenna smiled, the flame of the candle playing lazily against her palms. At the worst, it promised a pleasurable night.

Quickly, she breathed the second of the chants, and waited for the change to come.

> *But yet, O dream, if thou wilt not depart*
> *In this rare subject from thy common right,*
> *But wilt thyself in such a seat delight*
> *Then take my shape, and play a lover's part.*

It happened almost instantly. Ravenna moved forward and extended her arms, merging rapidly into the white insubstantiality of the phantom witch. Quickly, as though she were putting on a robe, she slid into Lightborn's embrace, and it was her arms now that snaked about his neck, her fingers coiling in his short, blonde hair.

Slowly, with scarcely a movement of his hand, Lightborn untied the thin string about the neck of the Great Witch. The tunic slipped over her shoulders, tumbled to her ankles, and out of it she stepped, naked and warm in the dreaming light of the moon.

She lay on the marble map as dawn approached. The candles were snuffed in their own wax and the room was cold. She had slept for an hour, perhaps two, risking *croglath* to stay in the dreams of the Captain. Now she propped herself on one elbow, tracing the coastline of Palerna lazily with her long, black nail.

He may be dangerous, she thought. No doubt he is ruthless. She could tell such things by the way a man handled her, by the way his hand moved as it coursed up the inside of her thigh. Dangerous and ruthless, but she could have him if she wanted him.

He would see black in his dreams now, black for seven nights, until he would wonder if he had been left dreamless. And then he would want her again and again, and soon in the waking world outside of this safe little garden of dreams, whether in his chambers or this room or in Dragmond's bed itself. If she could have him long enough, could draw him to her again and again, the addiction would set in. For the spell was an easy one she had learned from a Parthian courtesan when the restless king a floor below her was only a lad of seven.

She had waited nine years to use it, and the King had gone

from dreams of games and village girls to black upon black and dreamless sleep, and nightly visits to the black silks of the Witch's bed.

Now, after many years, she would try the spell again, on a new man. For Dragmond had never been very interesting, and now grew less and less necessary.

Ravenna lifted her finger to her lips, fluttered her tongue lightly against it. Now Lightborn would be hers, as surely as morphia or madness or death claimed their men after brief flirtation. She smiled at the thought, rolled over on her back, and stared into the rafters, where the boding, shaggy raven hopped from beam to beam.

Below her, with a smile that would have chilled young Walton, chilled Amiens or Danjel though they wrapped themselves in fur and red armor, Captain Lightborn opened his eyes and turned to the window, where the moon was a deepening orange over the Bay of Ashes.

She had come, as he knew she would, in malice and espionage. He had been ready for her, dosed with Alanyan *cupiditas* so that his dreaming would be perfumed and warm and peopled with women. And he had thought of her as he tumbled to sleep, saying her name again and again until he said it in his dreams and she came to him, first out of the dream vision and then with heat and energy so that he knew the Great Witch had entered the figure he had dreamed.

She had stayed there for an hour, and when she left he dreamed of a windswept coast not far from here, of a deep southerly current and a long two-handed sword and of voices, hundreds of voices converging like the creaking of gulls out on the distant waters.

But already the dance was beginning.

The Pale Man smiled and fingered the dagger in his belt— the dagger he slept with, because even sleep was dangerous.

Despite the dangers of sleep, Faye would have suffered it gladly that night. Through midnight and through the first ringing of bells across Needle's Eye over in Maraven, the girl lay awake on her cot, anxious for something she could not quite name. It was less than an hour before she was supposed to be up and about, strewing the rushes and raising the fire in the various elegant rooms above her.

Rubbing her hard and reddening hands, Faye tried to remember where she had been before she came to Kestrel Tower. Sometimes there was a flash of darkness in her dreams, and she would smell the sea air and hear the tolling of those bells closer and closer until the noise of them wakened her and she lay on the cot in a cold sweat. The memory always lay just beyond the waking moment.

The blisters on her fingers were only now hardening to calluses, the hard shoes hurt her feet, and her long skirt tangled and tripped her until she felt as though she were constantly wading in water. Worst of all was the light—the constant glare of day hurting her eyes until she longed for night, when only the stars and an amber moon guided her thoughts and wanderings, and she felt hidden and safe. All of this spoke of another time —a time of soothing darkness and a loud carillon of bells and of others whose faces she could not yet recall, who danced at the edge of her memory like foxfire or sprites.

So the night passed, and so passed the hard and bright summer days into a darker autumn.

$$\text{\textbf{>>> XI <<<}}$$

"Pennyroyal, again, please you?" she asked him.

Brenn sat on the stump, his eyes averted, not at all pleased. In the distance he saw Thomas and Sendow emerge into the clearing, bearing between them a buck trussed to their spearshafts. Beneath the huge spreading cedar, Galliard and Terrance and Ponder argued and speculated over a map-covered stump. Lapis sat on the lowest branch of the big evergreen, looking at its needles through a faceted piece of glass while Jimsett tunnelled at the far edge of the clearing, dirt leaping from his spade.

Bertilak, in a strange fit of melancholy, had climbed onto a branch of the cedar, where he perched and crouched and stared down upon the bustling clearing. He still could not speak.

It seemed everyone had more interesting work, more entertainment, than his lessons in Glory's herb lore.

"Pennyroyal . . ." Brenn repeated dully, "for discouragement of fleas and body lice. Mixed with wormwood, good for seasickness. Good also for the head cold and the problems feminine."

"Excellent!" Glory exclaimed. "Now comfrey. Tell me about comfrey."

So passed Brenn's days in Corbinwood. Terrance had insisted that herbs and berries were the new course of his resumed study, and Brenn had followed dutifully, if reluctantly. All around him the forest settled into deep fall, the oak leaves turning red, then brown, then a deep violet black over the passage of days, and the maples flared red and orange and bright, fiery yellow.

It was all beautiful, and for a boy reared on the gray Maravenian streets, it was a brilliant October. The breeze smelled of pine and woodsmoke rather than garbage and seaweed, and Brenn relaxed in the new surroundings, savoring the change in the brisk air.

He wished Faye were there to share it with him. Wished it daily, in his wanderings over the leaf-strewn paths of Corbinwood. And yet, though there was a melancholy in missing the girl, he rather enjoyed most other aspects of his stay.

Indeed, the whole season would have been near holiday, had it not been for Glory.

From the first, when her care had drawn him from the outskirts of Dame Sorrow's burning city, Brenn had taken a liking to the industrious and cheerful Glory. She had tended him for a week with soft touches and herbs, with the smells of exotic flowers and teas and strange songs.

Then she had vanished, and nobody would tell him where she was. When she returned after a fortnight, the first frost had rimed the grass and needles on the forest floor, and the smell of boiling verjuice and roasting nuts hovered around the fires in the clearing.

It was then her instruction began in earnest. In the brisk weeks of November, Glory guided the lad through the network of trails and footpaths that encircled the central clearing. On these forced walks, Brenn learned about rosemary, which brought forth remembrance, and yarrow, which banished melancholy. He gathered more of the rue that had helped save him from the Death, and learned to avoid the monk's hood and the foxglove.

Nonetheless, he drifted into frequent melancholy and distraction.

Oh, it wasn't that the herbs were that dull nor Glory's instruction too dry. Quite the opposite. Brenn had heard of some of the herbs, and seen some of them hanging dried and bound in the shops of apothecaries in Grospoint. The Hall of the Poisoners did an unhealthy traffic in leaf and stem, too, as far as the lad remembered. But here, where you could see them rooted in the ground, could smell their green odors that would linger only a few days before the hard frosts arrived, you could see them . . . in their places. It was interesting stuff, when you came right down to it, but Brenn was having a rough time keeping his mind on these fleeting mysteries.

"If it's weathering the winter you're after," Glory whispered, interrupting his thoughts in the uncanny way she had with thoughts and interruptions, "there's none of these that will last a fortnight more, so listen and learn while you can."

Brenn turned quickly to the woman, his eyes wide. Glory smiled and pointed with a thick finger at the hard ground under Brenn's feet.

"What is that you are almost standing on, Brenn?" she asked.

Brenn jumped, imagining snakes or scorpions. Beneath him instead was a humble vine, its leaves already turning a light muddy red.

"Raspberry?" the lad asked, rifling his thin herbal memory.

"A good guess, Brennart, for a guess it was," Glory pronounced briskly. "Look more closely."

Brenn crouched, squinted, and cradled a single leaf in his hand.

"Raspberry it is, to my way of thinking. I don't suppose that, being king in waiting and all, I can *decree* it to be raspberry and escape the lecture that you are no doubt brewing up."

Glory laughed, and crouched down beside him. Brenn heard

her joints crackle and creak like the cedar branches in a high wind.

"Petrial," she whispered. "Dig for its root there." She scrawled a mark in the hard soil, and dutifully the lad set knife to it, digging up a bright yellow root that lay only a couple of inches from the surface. Gently the woman took the knife from Brenn's hand, and setting the blade against the root, muttered a brief incantation before slicing a coin-sized piece from it.

"Here," she said, offering the piece of root to Brenn. "Eat this, then look at the leaves again."

Skeptically, Brenn brushed off the morsel and dropped it into his mouth. It was bitter, tasting of the heart of the plant and of old and fertile soil. He swallowed, and at once the leaves of the vine took on a subtly different shape and color.

"Why, it's not raspberry at all!"

"Petrial, as I said," Glory repeated softly, bracing herself against the lad's shoulder as she rose to her feet. "It's a primary ingredient in acumen, which is, as I understand, a favorite of your aunt in Kestrel Tower."

"She's no aunt of mine," Brenn protested without anger. Somehow, despite the damage Ravenna and her charges had worked, the misery and sorrow they had caused in his life and in the lives of those dear to him, the Great Witch was still abstract to Brenn, a distant force like bad luck or the plague that had touched regrettably, but not personally.

"You still have the anger to pass through, don't you?" Glory asked, plucking his thoughts from the darkness as readily as she drew roots from the shadowy ground. "You're a long way from home, Master Brennart, and not yet on the road back."

He thought about those words as he sat alone later, whittling at the edge of the clearing as Jimsett tunneled furiously, like a bee-stung badger, scarcely a dozen yards away.

"Of course, I'm far from home," Brenn muttered, the piece of cedar turning in his hand, transformed by the knife into a ship whose keel was broken by a clumsy tilt of the blade, then into a snake botched by inattention, then finally into a small, shapeless sliver. "But no farther from home than Terrance or Galliard, or even Jimsett who's trying to dig back there the best I can see it.''

He gave the wood a savage swipe, nicking the side of his thumb in the process. Quickly, painfully, he slipped the cut into his mouth, and sat angrily alone in the clearing, in a silence broken only by the rhythmic scrape of Jimsett's shovel.

He was being busy-worked. Or so he decided, the prospects of further herb lore staring at him in the weeks ahead. All around him, his cousins set to tasks far more glamorous and useful than his own.

Sendow and Thomas were gone most of the time. To Brenn they remained serious green presences at the edge of his thoughts, intruding now and then with a pheasant, a deer, news of troop movements, or the occasional strongbox filled with Alanyan coins or Parthian jewelry, bright items promptly stolen by the other cousins, or by Bertilak, who spirited the things away to his bed made of twigs, dried grass, mud and feathers, high in the spreading cedar.

Once, on a remarkable occasion, they brought home a dress uniform and gold pendant said to belong to the legendary General Helmar of Maraven.

Theirs was a business adventuresome and certainly dangerous. Brenn longed for the excitement that Sendow and Thomas must have deeper in the woods or out on the Gray Strand—the encounters with beasts and with wonders, the endless pursuit and eluding of General Helmar and his notorious legion. It sounded like marvelous fun.

Ponder, on the other hand, was quite accessible and quite stationary. The big man had set himself in the lower branches of the cedar, flanked by almanacs and herbals and bestiaries and books of lore. Through the night those branches were aglow with his lantern, and yet by morning Ponder seemed fully rested, sustained by his long and difficult study. Brenn watched him enviously from the forest floor, but he knew that the books would baffle and bore him after only an hour's perusal.

Jimsett and Lapis, the twins, involved themselves in strange and opposite searches. Brenn could hear Jimsett puffing and grunting in the ground below him, hear the resolute *whick* of the spade against hard earth, breaking through rock and ground as down among mole and taproot his cousin labored to underlay all of Corbinwood with a hivelike series of tunnels and combs. It struck Brenn as absurd, this digging, but nevertheless it had purpose and energy. Jimsett would continue for days, sleeping in his tunnels and waking shortly to continue, bent on completing the tunnels by some mysterious deadline nobody understood. But at the end and at least, Cousin Jimsett would have something to show for his efforts.

Meanwhile, somewhere above all of them, Lapis lay back in the topmost branches of an ancient hackberry. The tree had shed its leaves early, and the girl could lean back with nothing between the clouds and her examining eye. For it was shapes that Lapis regarded—the shapes of clouds and arrangements of stars, whether with naked eye or by the aid of one of her many glass lenses. She descended from those heights with the only prophecies that Terrance gave credence—simple, accurate forecasts of the weather.

Through the lot of them marched Galliard, dressed in dark greens and browns, the black bow always readied at his shoulder. Brenn thought he recalled something about how a perpetually taut string could ruin a bow, but Galliard laughed it off. The Forest Lord put no stock, it seemed, in the tales of old archers. To illustrate his point, he would point out a distant target— sometimes uncomfortably small, like a cluster of cones near the top of a hundred-year-old pine or a solitary knot at the heart of a slim young water maple. Then he would turn and pace away from the target, sometimes out of the clearing altogether, so that Brenn saw only shadows moving on shadow where he believed his cousin had stopped and nocked his arrow.

Then the arrow sung by and the target, which Brenn generally had to squint to see in the first place, shivered or split or flew apart. For his arrow never missed. It was that easy for him.

Next to all these skills and relatives, Brenn felt clumsy, ignorant and green. Terrance at least set great store by potions and poultices and healing, but the flashier, far more regal talents of his cousins made herb lore look like a sort of country midwifery that the lad found unbecoming and too quiet. He didn't like the wizard's insistence that he spend his spare time scouring the forest for roots and leaves, but aside from that, Brenn was unsettled more because he didn't actually despise the gathering as much as he made out.

He could imagine Faye sneaking up on him, laughing behind her hand at his new pursuits.

"It's just . . . just not *kingly*," he pronounced to himself, sheathing his knife and standing. Jimsett had stopped and the clearing was silent except for the occasional scolding of birds, the crackling of the great central fire . . .

And Glory approaching, calling his name.

Instinctively, as he had done so many times before on the Maravenian streets when faced with unwelcome curiosity, Brenn looked toward the shadows. Quietly he slipped behind a huge bending alder, and circled the edge of the clearing, catching an occasional glimpse of Glory's red hair and blue robe as he snaked through the drying vines and the soft undergrowth.

"My apologies, ma'am," Brenn murmured to himself with mock politeness, "but as they say in Wall Town, I'm about foundered on the business at hand."

He chuckled and slipped into deeper shadows, taking care to keep the clearing within view and earshot.

Only minutes passed before he was entirely lost.

Corbinwood was an elaborate maze of vine and bramble and bush that fractured the sunlight and made it seem as though you walked through a hall of green mirrors, doorless and endless and thicker the farther you traveled. Brenn circled for a while, his unease growing into fear as the evening quickly approached. Three times he shouted, but his voice seemed to fall back against the dense network of leaves and branches, until he feared that it carried no farther than he could see.

"Well," he said finally, leaning against a knotted old maple as the sun passed into the Aldor Mountains. "Well, I expect the safest thing to do is to settle here for the evening, or until Galliard sends the cousins for me, whichever comes first. After all, how dangerous could it be?"

As though in answer, the woods around him became suddenly loud with the snuffling and cries of strange animals. Something lurched through the underbrush far to his right and called in an eerie, fluting voice. Brenn swallowed nervously, thinking of an old song the Goniph used to sing. He would look askance at the younger thieves as he sang it, delighting in their trembling and deep alarm.

> *The leopardes savage,*
> *The lyons in theyr rage,*
> *Myghte catche the in theyr pawes,*
> *And gnawe the in theyr jawes!*
> *The serpentes of Lybany*
> *Myght stynge the venymously!*
> *The dragones with their tonges*
> *Myght poyson thy lyver and longes!*
> *The mantycors of the montaynes*
> *Myght fede them on thy braynes!*

The song faded weakly into the dark forest air. With a sigh, Brenn grabbed onto the lowest branch of the maple, intending to climb up to a higher vantage point.

"But wait!" he said, dangling thoughtfully from the branch, his feet swaying back and forth like those of a hanged man on the Causeway. "If I climb too high and get trapped, there's no way down but a nasty fall. Who's to say that it's any safer above than it is below? After all, the last time I was airborne the ravens nearly killed me, and to hear Galliard and Sendow talk they're still over the Corbinwood, circling and boding and keeping a lookout."

Pensively, he kicked up onto the branch, as the woods around him fell entirely dark.

"I expect, then," he pronounced finally, "that when you're in danger, it's best to have your feet on solid ground."

With that bit of philosophy and a fleeting memory of how far up he was, the rightful king of Palerna let himself drop from the maple branch . . .

. . . and crash through through a thin shelf of ground into a ten-foot-deep pit, the dead end of one of Jimsett's less successful tunnels. Loose earth scattered above him and tumbled into the crevice he had made, and he tried to speak, but his breath had fled entirely. Almost at once, the deepening dark of the forest was replaced by an opaque and absolute black, as the boy lost consciousness.

Sometime later, Brenn awoke and stirred at the bottom of the pit, startling a pair of screech owls who perched on the lowest branch of the deceptive maple. With a shrill, scraping cry, the birds lurched off into the dark, the intermittent moonlight flashing on their wings as they passed over the mouth of the pit. A great silence followed the receding sound of their wingbeats.

Slowly Brenn stood up, but the pain in his ankle was excruciating.

"I expect I've broken it," Brenn muttered through clenched teeth, inspecting the walls of the pit for some kind of foothold. The tunnel was deep and smoothly fashioned. He scooted disconsolately to the ground.

"No choice, then," he said, rolling the dirty fragments of root in his hand. "Can't get up to the surface, don't want to hop through the tunnel and risk getting buried alive. I expect I'm here until morning."

He looked above him, straining to catch any light, the outline of anything in the dark of the woods. But the moon had sunk behind a wall of leaf and branch, and soon he could not even see the mouth of the pit above him.

"I'm hungry," he murmured irritably. "If I have to keep watch against manticores and lions, the least I could do is have something to eat."

As he did, a familiar odor struck him—a freshness rising out of the mottled stench of the dirt around him. Sniffing like Bracken on the trail of a squirrel, Brenn thrust his hands into his pockets.

"The roots!" he growled. "They're . . . they're . . . comfrey or petrial or *something*! Glory showed them to me—I remember that much, and whatever it was didn't taste that bad."

Fumbling and sniffing in the dark, Brenn finally groped into a handful of the roots.

"Just hope it wasn't a purgative," he muttered, as he bit into another of the thin, bitter tubers.

It was only minutes before he saw the lights. Slowly, as though it grew from the darkness, the wall of the tunnel took on shape and definition. For a moment Brenn thought the moon had broken through the foliage again, but he looked up uncertainly into a shadowy ceiling of leaves lit by . . . by something he could not place for the life of him.

Floating on the maple branch were six faint, yellow globes of light, paired like luminescent eyes amid the shadows. Brenn held his breath and reached slowly for his knife, though something in the lights told him they were not dangerous—that, if anything, they meant him far more good than ill.

As he watched, the lights tumbled from the branch onto the floor of the forest. He lost them for a moment as they passed somewhere beyond his line of sight, and then the tunnel he lay in glowed with a white, unearthly light, as they appeared at a great distance in the darkness, blinking and remote, like six distant beacons. Brenn gazed at them stupidly, then looked down into his hand.

Petrial. The yellow heart of acumen. Then what he was seeing was neither spell nor hallucination, but clearly there and usually veiled from human eyes.

His curiosity roused, Brenn stared back at them. It was not long—a minute at the most—before he knew they wanted him to follow.

"Nonsense!" he muttered. "It's the last thing I want to do, alone in a dangerous woods and lamed and addled by the fall . . ."

Still, against all argument, they seemed to beckon. Behind them he could see small, human-shaped shadows, as though the lights were indeed the eyes of little creatures, or the lamps they used in the place of eyes.

Poised and prepared for trouble, Brenn drew his knife. Still the lights hovered at the end of the tunnel, moving neither toward him nor away from him. Finally, as though surrendering something in this long exchange of stares, they turned from him and fled down the dark passage of Jimsett's old tunnel. Squinting to follow their retreat, Brenn lost them almost at once. And yet, from somewhere in the blackness a song returned to him:

> *Who hath the upright heart, the single eye,*
> *The clean, pure hand, which never medled pitch?*

Who sees Invisibles, *and doth comply*
With hidden treasures that make truly rich?

Baffled, Brenn took another bite of the petrial, blinked, and stared intently at the darkness ahead of him. Faintly he could make out four, six points of light, but he was not sure that he saw what he saw or whether his eyes, deprived so long in the darkness, had fashioned a light of their own.

"They can't be evil and sing like that," he told himself, conveniently forgetting all the horror stories of siren and lorelei told by the sailors in Maraven. As he hobbled up the tunnel in the direction of the song, he forgot other things, his common sense and fears among them.

"I know they mean no harm," he told himself, "but don't ask how." It was an instinct, like he had known in Maraven when someone was thoroughly evil and not to be trusted. He couldn't put words around the feeling now, just as he couldn't when he was younger in Wall Town, but one thing stood out: If the eyes and the things behind them had meant him harm, there had been no better time for it than when he lay at the bottom of the pit, stunned and injured and unable to see them.

They had let that time pass, and he was still alive. They meant him no harm.

Of all the stories that he could believe at that moment, it was this one Brenn chose to believe as he hobbled through the tunnels in pursuit of the lights. They hovered just ahead of him like will-o'-the-wisps, turning each corner and leaving him stumbling behind in the darkness. He shouted at them then and flung oaths at them, but he passed through the darkness quickly, the pain in his ankle growing less and less until it was nearly forgotten.

Gradually the tunnel before him lightened. Although by now the effects of the petrial had faded, it no longer mattered: Ahead of him was moonlight, or firelight, and on his face he felt a breath of crisp forest air.

Never stopping to mistrust his headlong pursuit of the lights, barreling on with neither caution nor misgiving, Brenn burst into the open air, stumbled, and fell on his face. Quickly, he scrambled to his knees and looked about him for the yellow, elusive eyes.

Instead he saw Galliard. And Terrance and Sendow. He saw Lapis, startled in the midst of pouring hot water into a bathtub for her grimy brother Jimsett.

And finally he saw Glory. She was standing where he had left her when he plunged into the forest, as though she had not moved for what had surely been hours.

"Angelica," she said with a curious smile, as a pair of owls descended from the trees and settled quizzically on her shoulders. "Tell me the virtues of angelica, Brennart."

⋙ XII ⋘

"Put your hands on your ankle once more," Glory urged.

"But I've done this a score of times already," he protested.

"Natheless."

Brenn did as she asked, and then closed his eyes. Glory hovered over him, her wide face placid and alert.

"Now," she whispered. "What do you see?"

"Purple," Brenn replied. "I see purple."

"Fabling again, Your Highness," Glory scolded merrily. "What do you see?"

"Six white points of light, faint in darkness," he answered, opening an eye to look at his teacher. She smiled.

"Close your eyes."

It had been three weeks since his fall and injury—weeks in which, stationary at first, then confined to crutches, then a cane, Brenn had been easy to locate, easy to overtake when there was another lesson in the offing—whether of herbs or touch or of incantation. Brenn was fascinated with herbs now that the yellow petrial had availed him in his night lost in Corbinwood. For the others—for hands and incantation—he was less skilled, less ready.

Touch was the worst. To Brenn, it seemed like a guessing

game. Glory would have him close his eyes and place his hands on a ''wounded or ailing part.'' Yet for the life of him, Brenn had yet to see any good from this kneading and handling and imagining of colors. It was like an impossible guessing game, where Glory dangled the answers just out of his reach.

He first laid hands on Dirk's nose, bloodied in disagreement with one of Sendow's men, a burly peasant lad named Meles. The nose continued to bleed afterwards, and the pain stayed just where it was. Glory said it was because he was new at it, that the skill and the insight would come with time.

Next was a bump on Ponder's head, the result of reading while walking beneath a low-hanging branch. Then Bertilak, who rolled over in his sleep and fell screeching out of his makeshift nest. Then Dirk's nose again, when the little thief resumed his acquaintance with Meles. Then the sore foot of one of Thomas's men who had stepped on nettles in the darkness, followed by Dirk's nose yet a third time.

In all of these episodes, Brenn healed no one. He saw no colors, could not clear his mind and concentrate. Other things came to him—homesickness, thoughts of Faye, the dangerous world outside—but nothing of a healing sort.

As he sat in the clearing, clutching his own ankle, he rehearsed his failures in his memory, sighed, and opened his eyes once more.

''I see . . . I see nothing but the inside of my eyelids, Glory. Don't you reckon we'd better give up on this? I think you're wasting your time and all on a useless student.''

Brenn lay back, propping himself on his elbows, and looked around the clearing. The cousins were gone, bound on separate businesses. Of his friends, only Terrance and Dirk remained, crouched beneath stand of willow, rooting through the undergrowth for the gods knew what.

For Glory's faeries, perhaps.

'' 'Tis faeries in the farthest branches,'' she said. ''Nought more than the Invisible Folk themselves.''

Of course, Brenn leaped upon her words, plying her with a thousand questions, but she had said little more after that, and what she *did* say was brief and guarded and mysterious.

He learned the rest from Terrance. Corbinwood, it seemed, and all of Palerna, for that matter, had housed a nation of faeries back in the times of the Romans.

"At that time," the wizard explained, his spindly legs astraddle a stump and his flask glittering in the light of the rising moon, "our homeland was known by other names. Andoria it was called, and Lantis, and men dreaded it because the faeries dwelt there. You know the story, how the old romance goes."

Brenn nodded foolishly, having no idea what Terrance was talking about. Leaning back, rapt in lore and memory and fueled by a little Zephyrian gin, the wizard raised one bony finger and intoned.

> *Al was this land fulfild of fairye.*
> *The elf-queene with hir joly compaignye*
> *Daunced ful ofte in many a grene mede.*
> *This was the olde opinion, as I rede—*
> *I speke of manye hundred yeres ago.*
> *But now kan no man so none elves mo . . .*

"Driven to the forest fastness," Terrance said, an odd note of sadness lingering after his words, "and now beyond our sight and understanding, visible only when they will it so."

"So . . . what are they like, Terrance?" Brenn asked, seating himself and hugging his knees against the brisk November cold. Dirk, wrapped in a horse blanket, his nose reddened by the cold and by constant encounters with Meles, dropped down by Brenn and stared up at the wizard eagerly.

"Yes, Master Terrance," he intoned, his voice flat and nasal, like the honking of a goose. "If I ain't intrudin' on something private, I'd sure appreciate you tellin' the both of us."

Terrance smiled at Brennart and his rough little friend. "Do you remember the elves, lad?" he asked.

Brenn snorted.

"I wouldn't express such opinions so loudly," Terrance cautioned, his eyes on the leaves and bushes around them. "For the faeries, you see, are close cousins to the elves, only untouched by city living."

Dirk nodded thoughtfully and blew his nose into the blanket.

"They're not what I should call fond of humankind," Terrance continued, "though by no means are they our enemies. They are what the country folk call 'possessed of a distant turn,' shy and remote, having little or nothing to do with the likes of us. And for good reason, I might add."

"We have done them harm, then?" Brenn asked, and the wizard nodded.

"Indeed, most grievous harm. It is nigh unto a miracle that they do not snatch our children more often than they do, nor train their bows on us of a night, leaving us elf-shot, scatter-brained and abstracted and walking through life like the cwalu."

"So it's true, then, Master Terrance?" Dirk asked. "What they say about 'em?"

"Hush, boy," Terrance warned, his gray brows fierce above his glittering, stern eyes. "Hush, and think upon whether it's true what they say about *us*."

Brenn and Dirk leaned forward, rapt as Terrance explained the great injury done to the faeries by the kings of old. Once, it seemed, the elf-queen's people had been plentiful and wide-spread, known from the mountains of Bavaria to the far-off reaches of Umbria. Some of them had set up *specula*, schools of instruction in Hadrach, where apt young men and women could go to learn a makeshift magic involving mirrors and lights and something ancient and probably druidic that had to do with trees.

"I wish I knew more of such arts," Terrance sighed, "but the last *specula* burned two centuries ago, under orders of the Councils of Hadrach, and even an old codger such as I wasn't around in those times."

He winked soberly at Dirk and continued.

"In the worst of times, across the Eastmark they came, in caravans and upon white ponies the size of small dogs. They traveled by night, trailing a milky stream of lights behind them like a shower of comets, carrying with them their wounded. In the heart of their caravans, sometimes you could see a solitary light grow dim and wink out, as another died from the beatings and burnings in Hadrach, in Jaleel . . ."

He paused, stared significantly at Brenn.

"And in Maraven. Where even King Albright saw them as 'corrupters of the young.' Corrupters, because they outhealed the surgeons and laughed the augurers to scorn. Corrupters, because they preserved forgotten texts of poetry while the scholars of Maraven turned to retemancy and textual commentary on textual commentary . . ."

The wizard snorted angrily and lifted the flask to his lips.

"My grandfather, Terrance?" Brenn asked in horror. "My *grandfather* helped do this?"

"*Great*-grandfather," Terrance corrected. "And a half century ago, when even good men mistrusted the faerie knowledge. Natheless, we have much to account for, much to answer. But as to the journeys. I am old enough to remember them. We watched them pass when I was a lad . . ."

The wizard's eyes focused somewhere in the treetops, sad and wistful. Brenn wondered who had watched the faerie caravans with Terrance.

"Nor did they find the countryside any more hospitable," Terrance continued. "Alanyans, Zephyrians, Aquilan mercenaries—everybody hunted them, while everyone in power turned their powerful heads away. Your grandfather Albright included."

Terrance sighed, held the flask up to the moonlight in a way that reminded Brenn of Lapis and her numberless bottles and lenses.

"Hunted them?" Brenn asked. "Why?"

"Because there were rumors, started by hateful, fearful people, that the faeries stole babies and livestock and drove people mad."

"But you just said they done that, sir," Dirk interrupted, his brow wrinkling. Brenn frowned, too, and Bracken, seeing the dismay and puzzlement of the young men, trotted forward, planted his wide backside between them and, looking deeply and seriously into Brenn's ear, began to lick the side of his face. Brenn snorted, then laughed, then hugged the dog at his feet. With a satisfied grumble, Bracken curled up on the pooled robes of the wizard.

"Bracken knows," Terrance said soothingly, stroking the

dog's back. "Bracken knows well those faerie caravans. Barked at more than a few of them, he did."

A hard crust of bread tumbled from the wizard's sleeve into the dog's opened mouth. Terrance cleared his throat.

"Yes, the faeries do those kinds of things now, Dirk. They steal babies, though I'll be switched if I know what they do with the things once they steal them. And in each village there's some poor elf-shot soul who babbles about circuses and squirrels and marbles, and we all know it was the faeries who did it to him."

Terrance pushed his broad-brimmed hat back on his head. Slyly he peered over the flask at Brenn, smiling that maddeningly cloudy smile his apprentice remembered from misfired lessons.

"They do these things now," Terrance repeated, "because our fear has put them up to it."

Dirk glanced in bafflement at Brenn, who shrugged amiably.

"He's always got some proverb at hand, Dirk," Brenn explained, "and damned if I can follow any of them."

"It weren't that I was puzzlin' over, Brenn," Dirk said cautiously. "It's about that dog down there. How Master Terrance seen the faeries pass when he was a lad. Beggin' your pardon, sir, but that would be . . ."

"Over fifty years," Terrance conceded, and Dirk whistled in wonderment, looking down at Bracken with a new respect. The dog rolled over in his sleep, kicked against the stump, and belched.

"Then why didn't they shoot me?" Brenn asked. "Or spirit me off to wherever they take the babies they steal?"

"I hear that you have to *see* them before they'll spirit or shoot you," Terrance explained. "They do that, or they replace your eyes with wooden ones. That's how the song goes, isn't it?

> *I wad taen out thy twa grey een,*
> *Put in twa een of tree.*

At least, that's what I hear."

"But I *did* see them!" Brenn protested. "Six points of light racing away from me down Jimsett's abandoned tunnel! Jimsett himself said he hadn't thought of that passage in years . . ."

"Which proves absolutely nothing," Terrance interrupted. "Those lights could be fireflies, or foxfire, or whatever you like or believe."

"But I heard them singing, Terrance! Something about upright hearts and seeing invisibles . . ."

"You . . . fell quite a way into that pit, didn't you, Brenn?" Terrance asked teasingly, and his apprentice stared off angrily into the forest.

"By the four winds and the hairs in your beard, Terrance," Brenn swore, as Dirk shuddered at the subdued, dangerous tone in his old friend's voice, "you have dismissed me in this matter long enough."

Terrance arched a bemused eyebrow, but Brenn was hardly finished.

"And I will not rest until I have combed these woods and brought a handful of them back to you!"

"Watch how you're swearin', Brenn!" Dirk urged in dismay. "They're dangerous folk, them faeries. You heard about the snatchin' and the shootin'."

But Brenn was on his feet and hobbling across the clearing in search of Glory. Twice he stopped, crouching to rub his injured ankle. "Not well yet," he murmured. "Not yet."

He closed his eyes and looked for colors, but saw nothing but blackness.

"Glory!" he called out angrily, and limped toward the central fire, Dirk following dutifully after him.

Alone by the cypress knee, Terrance chuckled and stroked Bracken again.

"Speaking like a king, he is, with all those commands and all that bluster. Good. Ah, good it is, Bracken."

Hearing his name, the dog looked up wisely and awaited another sleeve to open, another crust of bread to tumble out.

"And now he's about the king's business," Terrance pronounced. "For it's time the old wounds mended—time the new king found the Invisible Folk."

The wizard smiled mysteriously, as a pair of screech owls

dove toward him out of the wooded night and nestled like doves in the folds of his long green robe.

So began Brenn's fruitless hunt for the faeries. Accompanied always by Dirk and Bracken, the rightful king scoured the undergrowth, chewed petrial root and kept watch from the clearing edge and from treetops, waiting for floating lights that never came.

For a month the search lasted, as November passed into December, and the last of the leaves fell. The herbs boiled and set aside to dry, the incantations left to the dead of winter, the study now was almost all of hands, when the nights would be spent by the side of the large central fire and instruction would dwindle to words alone.

No matter what Brenn was *supposed* to be learning, his attentions had turned almost entirely to the pursuit of the faeries. Terrance, now fearing that his stories had created a monster, began to stew and fidget as he watched his apprentice set snares in the creeping juniper and post the pliable Bracken on guard amid a tangle of dry vines.

"Find them," Terrance whispered urgently in the direction of the boy. "Oh, let them be found, so that we can get on with this."

"This one works in accordance with the tilt of the moonlight," Lapis pronounced importantly, handing the prism to Brenn.

He took the beveled glass from his little cousin and stared into it. The outline of the cedar fractured into a dozen waves of color, and the January sunlight passing through its needles was cold and red and yellow and blue.

" 'Tis not much more than a plaything by day," Lapis explained, "good for the sorting of colors and nothing else."

"Where did you get this, cousin?" Brenn asked idly, training the prism on the black feathers of a raven perched a hundred feet above them, on the bare branches of a tall poplar. The bird wavered and dilated in the glass, indigo and purple and a darker color yet at the edges of its wings, and the lad shuddered, thinking of the Tower back home and the eyes that watched there.

"By night it spangles the moonlight's silver," Lapis replied, clearly avoiding her cousin's question. "Then a new world comes into the making."

"A new world?"

"Oh, yes, Cousin Brennart!" Lapis exclaimed, relieved that the subject had changed. Brenn smiled. Perhaps this was the very glass in question—the one she had stolen in accordance with the curse.

"You . . . you would be surprised, Cousin," she continued, shaking her white-blonde curls and gazing directly at him with those brilliant amber eyes that sorted and unsettled. "Surprised altogether at the . . . depth of things."

"The . . . depth of things?" Brenn asked despondently, dreading the explanations that would surely follow.

Except that Bracken burst through the undergrowth at that very moment, hauling behind him a rather unkempt little Dirk, clinging at the end of a leash. Puffing and coughing they both were, and when Bracken sat down in the midst of the clearing to sneeze, Dirk leapt to his feet and staggered toward Brenn and Lapis, pine needles dangling from him as though he were some grimy, moving pin cushion.

Lapis stifled a laugh and held up the prism, looking again at the big black bird. Distracted from his puffing, leash-entangled comrade, Brenn turned in puzzlement to his cousin while fumbling through the folds and pockets of his robes.

Sure enough, the prism was gone.

"Lapis—" Brenn began in exasperation, but Dirk broke in.

"Come quickly, Brenn! And you, too, Miss Lapis, though the goin' mought be dangerous down at the edge of the woods. The Watch is tryin' to cross over the Boniluce south of here, and Master Galliard's got a welcome for them!"

Brenn and Lapis were up and moving quickly. Guided by the sniffing, waddling Bracken, whose heavy winter coat and layer of fat were beginning to show in these January days, the three of them left the clearing, heading down one of the few familiar trails. As usual, Brenn was amazed by the dog's assurance. Though it was hard to believe, Terrance maintained he had grown up with Bracken not far from these parts, and sure enough, the dog moved through the woods without indecision or even pause until, nosing aside a curtain of juniper and blue taxus, he slid down the riverbank, nearly dragging Dirk along with him.

Contentedly, the dog lapped water from the margins of the Boniluce, as his three companions stood winded above him.

"Like as not, it'll be a great show, Brenn!" Dirk marveled, his voice hushed and urgent.

"Like as not," Brenn replied absently, his eye suddenly drawn to the bare branch of a thorn tree over on the river's east bank.

There, a raven perched and cocked its glittering, blue-black head.

"Well, come on then!" Dirk goaded, tugging at his friend's sleeve and at the dog's leash at the same time. Lapis handed Brenn the prism with a winning smile as Bracken scrambled up the bank. Together the four of them raced south over the winding trail, hushing the sound of birdsong as they passed.

Before he lost the river bank in the foliage behind him, Brenn turned and looked over his shoulder, back toward the thorn tree that drooped over the blue, flowing Boniluce.

The raven was gone, as somehow he knew it would be.

As Dirk had said, it promised to be a great show.

The three of them stood at the wood's edge, safely hidden behind a spreading taxus bush. Below them the ground sloped out of the forest onto the plains of Palerna, and they could see the smoke from campfires not a half mile away—campfires strung to the north as far as they could see.

"Cousin Galliard was right," Lapis breathed ever so softly. "They've put us under siege."

She pointed to the south, where glowing bivouacs lay in a line all the way to the banks of the Boniluce. She drew another looking-glass—thumb-sized and green—out of her hair, like a magician produces coins from a handkerchief. Brenn had no time to gape before the girl set the glass to her eye.

"Dirk is right," she whispered. "It's the Watch, and they're coming this way."

"Where's . . . where's Galliard, then?" Brenn asked uneasily. "Where's the rest of them?"

"He's close enough to hear you breathing," Lapis assured.

Brenn looked uneasily around him at the brown and green and the intermittent grays of the winter forest. He searched for any sign of Galliard and his followers, but Corbinwood was as quiet and unmoving as the necropolis along the shores of Aquila.

"See that?" Lapis asked, turning Brenn's attention back to the approaching Watch. "What you see is the steam of their breathing. Soon enough you'll see the red armor. Then it won't be long."

Brenn nodded and drew up even closer to the tree trunk. And so they waited, half an hour at the most, while the Watchmen left camp and approached across the plains, shields strapped to their backs and spears at the ready. There were a score of them at least, perhaps two. Among them Brenn saw familiar faces—faces he had glimpsed in Ships and amid the market stalls of Grospoint.

"Maravenian," he whispered to Lapis. "These boys are as fresh from the city as I am."

Lapis glared at the loudness of his voice and cupped her hand tightly over his ear. "Even fresher. Alley fighters, not used to long bows. See how close they're skirting the woods? Might as well draw targets on their breastplates and stand still."

Brenn frowned in puzzlement. It was then that the forest began to move around him.

The scattered evergreens seemed to have found words, or the wind sighing through the bare branches of the elder and thorn had taken the shape of whispers. With a smile, Brenn recognized Galliard's voice.

"The battle is at hand," the Forest Lord whispered.

The command seemed to come from all sides of him. Brenn craned his neck, looked about in the brush and the layers of leaves. It was like the galho-sound at home, and for a moment the lad feared that Galliard was actually miles away, his voice audible through a baffling series of echoes.

Brenn started to rise, but Lapis caught his arm hard. Her eyes warned him to be still.

Brenn settled back, drew a breath, and suddenly the bare forest erupted around him.

The air filled with the humming of bowstrings and the whistle of arrows. Out in the sunlit fringes of the wood a Watchman fell, a black barbed arrow jutting from his neck, another striking him as he dropped to his knees and fell face first to the ground. Yards behind the fallen soldier, an older man—a sergeant, Brenn guessed—spun about on a knoll, spear leveled, searching for the enemy. The first arrow struck him in the leg and two more shivered into the ground inches away as he fell and dragged himself back toward the troops, who were turning, retreating, fumbling for their shields and crying out like children. A lieutenant wheeled at the front of the column, sword raised, shouting orders that went unheeded as the Watchmen stumbled into each other and fell, dropping weapon and shield, and then scattered in a frenzied run toward the smoldering remnants of their campfires.

Brenn recognized the accent of the officer. He thought of home and shuddered.

The lieutenant, brave beyond all common sense, stood his ground for a long moment in a rain of arrows. Then, with a show of reluctance, he backed away from the woods, his sword raised defiantly. He stooped, lifted the wounded sergeant to his shoulder, and continued his measured retreat as a shout rang out through the vaulted trees and the volley of arrows stopped as quickly as it had begun.

Lapis handed Brenn the green glass. Nervously, he looked through the lens into the surrounding foliage. Three archers sat in the branches of a large blue spruce, shrouded in shadow and needles, arrows nocked and eyes trained on the gray-white column forming off by the fires. Beyond the three, two others rose from a squat stand of juniper, and beyond them still, at the edge of clear eyesight, Brenn could see Galliard and Thomas approaching, carefully stepping and dropping to roll or crawl through the dappled greens and browns of the woods.

"That's . . . that's . . ." Brenn began, and Lapis smiled, her eyes on the approaching woodsmen.

"That's it, Cousin," she replied, still in a hushed tone. "It's over for today. No doubt for the morrow. Though they'll camp out there until Ravenna says 'Move.' "

Brenn looked at her, forming a question.

"No, Brennart," Lapis replied. "It was *not* like this before you and the wizard came."

"I feared as much," Brenn replied, looking up as the three archers descended from the branches of the spruce and all of the woodsmen formed a tight, protective circle around Galliard, who spoke to them quietly, his face austere and kind. Briefly, briskly, he laid a gloved hand on one archer's shoulder and then walked out of the midst of them, his path directly toward the spot where Lapis and Brenn were sitting.

"Lapis," Brenn said, his eyes on the battlefield. "That boy out there . . ."

"Suffered the fate of a boy in war, who strays across the arrow's path," his little cousin declared flatly, motioning to Galliard, who waved back in response and signalled back toward the clearing and home. Suddenly, as quickly as they had emerged from the trees, the woodsmen vanished.

Brenn looked at Lapis in alarm. She seemed unchanged—the same round and innocent face, the same golden halo of curls and flawless, wide amber eyes. Yet in her voice was the absoluteness of the wilderness and the coldness of a child schooled in long guerrilla war.

"We have much to account for," Brenn said, his eyes on the red-armored form sprawled in the sunlight. "We have much to account for and much to answer."

>>> XIII <<<

January passed into February and the bitterest cold of Palernan winter. The besieging Watchmen threatened less, confined to their camps on the other side of the Boniluce. Great chunks of ice slid down the blue river. There were spots, especially to the south where it emerged from the shelter of Corbinwood, that the river iced over entirely, its currents passing deep beneath the frozen surface, swelling and diving further still, until those who lived along its bank were apprehensive, fearing the spring thaw and the heavy floods it would no doubt bring.

Meanwhile, Galliard's camp filled with visitors. Most of them were country folk, fleeing the inclement weather and the even harsher presence of Dragmond's pillaging army.

Galliard welcomed them all, but a troubled gaze took up residence on his dark face. For the winter brought with it not only the cold but a dearth of provisions.

In late January, old Archimago came to visit. The gods alone knew how he crossed through Dragmond's lines, but the guesses ranged from enchantment to bribery to lethe in the water. Brenn had always wanted to meet Terrance's master, but he was disappointed; the ancient mage was half-addled and thoroughly, unflinchingly corrupt. He gambled day and night with the woodsmen, stealing tidy sums from the younger men through the aid of carefully weighted dice, and none of the women in the encampment fancied themselves safe. Finally, at Galliard's heated request, Terrance took his old master aside and asked him to leave.

"I shall visit you in the spring," Terrance promised, his gray eyes bright with embarrassment.

"And bring young Lapis with ye?" the old fellow asked, spittle freezing at the ends of his beard.

"I shall visit you then," Terrance repeated, boosting Archimago into the saddle. The old mage dwindled into the forest, speaking bits of spells and cantrips to the passing trees.

"A shadow of how I remember him," the wizard proclaimed, a little sadly. He turned to Brenn and smiled.

"Then again, he was *always* a shadow of how I remembered him."

Laughing, the two of them walked together back to the fire, where Bertilak scratched for seeds and worms in the warmer ground. There, seated on furs and blankets, Brenn bored Terrance with yet another elaborate plan to uncover the faeries.

Snares had failed to uncover the faeries, of course, as had the saucers of gin that worked so effectively on the elves at home. So had the rakes and brooms which Brenn had leaned against each other in the center of the clearing, in the vain hope that the faeries were as fanatically clean as legends made them out to be and that morning would catch them intent in the midst of groundskeeping.

Each time another of Brenn's strategies failed, the faeries seemed farther and farther away. Dirk watched his old friend try out legend after legend, incantations and traps and snares, all of which came up empty. Soon the little thief began to believe that Brenn had fashioned them all out of thin air and fancy— the faeries, for sure, and perhaps even the elves and sprites he spoke of from his days in Maraven.

Glory was not much help either. She knew the forest better than anyone, and unlike Brenn's cousins, took the idea of faeries altogether seriously. Nonetheless, she offered no advice as to how he might find the Invisible Folk. Brenn suspected she knew far more than she was telling, so he made it clear constantly that his intentions were nothing but good.

"You see, Glory," he explained importantly, dangling his feet from a low cedar branch. "You see, I wish to right the wrongs of five generations. Humans should live in *harmony* with the Invisible Folk, and I want to see that it's done."

Having announced that, he thumbed through Ponder's volumes of lore for yet another spell or device to draw the faeries near.

"That's a noble undertaking, Brennart," Glory observed, setting a kettle of water upon an open fire. From a pouch at her belt she drew some dried leaves, then stood above the kettle, waiting for the water to boil.

"Too long have we visited outrage on the faeries," Brenn pronounced, then cleared his throat when it became apparent that Glory wasn't listening to him. "Too long, I said. Did you know that in Hadrach . . ."

"They burned the *specula*," Glory said with a faint smile. "Yes, Brennart, I have heard that they did such things. And worse." She looked up from the kettle, regarding the lad serenely. "And you will rescue them from that, I am sure," she observed, and dropped the leaves into the water.

So it continued through February. Doggedly, Brenn and Dirk searched for the faeries, from the edge of the clearing to the banks of the Boniluce, north once to the foot of the Aldor Mountains and south as far as the Zephyrian plains, where they saw a squadron of Namid's famous cavalry, bundled in furs against the cold, riding like a harsh, heralding March wind.

All the while, Glory was beside them. Or most of the time, at least; it troubled Brenn that there were occasions when he sought her knowledge that the herb woman went missing. She had vanished as surely as the faeries themselves, and his cousins, as used to her coming and going as they were to soft rains or changes in season, had no idea where she had taken herself.

And yet she was there when he absolutely *needed* her presence, teaching him simple things, such as how to tell time by the sun's movement, and things more difficult, such as the strange heel-and-toe walk the forest people use to imitate the sound of four-footed creatures.

She taught him more of healing and herbs, of course, and of the Inlustral Touch made famous by Edward of Anglia, in which the hand felt out the spirit's malady in the chambers of the back.

"Here," she would say, touching Brenn's lower back. "Here is where the fears lie. Above them are the griefs. Then the angers, above them the worries, and finally, about the shoulders rests the dark acquaintance with the world."

"The dark acquaintance?" Brenn asked sleepily. Her hands felt good as she rubbed his middle back, his shoulders. He remembered the whelming—the healing rush of warmth into his hands and through his damaged body.

"The anguish for no clear reason," Glory explained, her strong fingers massaging the lad. "The dance on the edge of the canyon. It is growing in you, Brennart. Perhaps it was the doing of the plague, or perhaps it is all those promised burdens accompanying this newfound kingship. But I fear it will be your companion for some time."

Brenn opened his eyes, watching Dirk and Bracken wrestle beneath the great cedar. Lapis was with them, teasingly cheering on the dog. "When will it be like that again?" he asked Glory, pointing at his cousin and friend.

"Not for a while, I fear," Glory replied, and there was neither sorrow nor pity in her voice. "Perhaps never again."

Brenn looked out over the wide clearing to where Dirk and Bracken rolled on a carpet of soft evergreen needles. The little thief had a grip on the big dog's head, and Bracken strained, his black tongue lolling, to lick the face of his playful captor.

Glory's grip tightened on Brenn's shoulders.

"Yarrow," she pronounced. "Yarrow tea. Good for the royal melancholy and Your Highness's dark acquaintance."

February was indeed a time for arrivals. Not all of them were as harmless as Archimago's.

By the end of the month the winter had begun to break. The mourning doves had returned, and the swallows, and woodwise folk such as Sendow and Glory maintained that the ospreys and nighthawks were not far behind. Then, on the first of March, three weeks before the year turned, the still bare branches of the elder and the buckthorn suddenly seemed to blossom with ravens.

First there was one, not far from the clearing itself. Thomas reported it to the assembled cousins. He had actually seen it alight on the ground, dip its beak into the puddles formed by the thawing snow, and drink menacingly, its beak thrown back to swallow the icy water.

"Then it will not be long," Galliard maintained, casting an apprehensive glance at Brenn, who sat with Ponder, their noses deep in a book of faerie lore. "For surely she knows the Pretender is here among us, and it is only a matter of time before Helmar breaks his winter camp and comes after us again."

"You don't think Dragmond would try to enter Corbinwood, do you?" Terrance asked, leaning forward and steepling his fingers.

"Let him try," Thomas declared fiercely, his hand moving dramatically to his sword.

Galliard smiled, his gaze circling over each of his cousins. "Indeed, let him try," he agreed. "But do not forget, Thomas, that it is the forest, not our swords and bows, that turns him back."

In the distance, Glory called for Brenn, holding up a sprig of dried leaves.

Wearily, Brenn glanced toward Terrance, who gestured toward Glory. The lad ambled over to attend the herb woman, followed by Dirk, Bracken, and the cautious glances of his cousins.

"Not yet, Galliard," Terrance warned, craning over the fire to warm his pale hands. "The boy has enough of a burden in recovering from the Death. Enough to learn he is the prisoner of kingship, which is a hard lesson after the enormous freedoms of thievery. So whatever you have to say, touching strategy or the way things wag in Maraven, it is better put in my ears than in those of a melancholy boy.''

Galliard nodded grimly and continued. ''There is something in Corbinwood,'' he maintained, ''that baffles trespassers. It would almost make one incline to Brennart's account of faeries.''

''I see,'' Terrance replied, hiding a smile.

''I could swear that the forest accepts or rejects its visitors,'' Galliard maintained intensely. ''If you are welcome in its midst, why, it opens itself to you, showing you pathways and fords . . .''

He gestured around him.

''Showing you clearings such as this. But if you are unwelcome, the trails shift and dodge and vanish. The light drifts at impossible angles, so it appears from inside the woods that the sun is rising in the west or sometimes that the moon herself is a second sun.''

The Forest Lord settled back, folded his arms, and shook his head.

''It's as though the forest is a living thing, giving and taking as it pleases,'' Jimsett added, and his cousins' eyes flashed ironically to him.

''You've been under the ground amid tuber and bulb too long, coz,'' Galliard scolded. ''Yet even there you should have learned that the soil itself is a fiercely living thing, choosing to shift and open before your spade, to allow some things to flourish and grow while others die in the seed. And why shouldn't a forest be the same?''

''And why,'' Terrance asked quietly, ''should there be no faeries in that forest?''

Galliard regarded the wizard cooly.

''For no reason,'' he replied, ''save that I have lived here for fifteen years without seeing one.''

''They are called the Invisible Folk, after all,'' Terrance observed mischievously, his eye on the Forest Lord. It was a capable young man he saw before him. Galliard took the pulse of the forest brilliantly, readily. There were spots he had found in Corbinwood—isolated glades and grottos—in which he could stand and listen, and because of the strange lifting and baffling of sound as it echoed through the trees, he could know what was moving, who was speaking, and for the most part, what was happening from the foothills of the Aldor Mountains all the way to where the Boniluce broke from the edge of the forest on its way south toward the Notches.

All this, Terrance thought, and yet if it is not within sight or smell or hearing, it does not exist for him.

"Leaving aside the faeries," said the Forest Lord, as he watched intently the king he served, who crouched over billowing steam as Glory boiled whatever herbs she was teaching at the moment, "we are safe from Ravenna's magic here. Something in the forest frustrates and deflects her most powerful conjury."

The cousins agreed eagerly. Terrance, on the other hand, remained silent. There was a long pause in which the only sound was the high wind in the treetops and the distant trumpet of arriving geese, flying over Corbinwood from their winter home in Umbria on their way to the Gray Strand and the Bay of Ashes.

"Well, then," Terrance pronounced finally, folding his arms and staring apprehensively at Galliard, "we are at a standstill. For though Ravenna cannot come into the forest, you cannot leave it."

He looked long and hard at Brenn, dutifully carrying a bucket of water into the clearing toward Glory's cheerful fire.

"That is to Ravenna's advantage. For all she has to do is protect the throne, which is, of course, in Maraven. It will be a long Spring, Galliard, as we sit and wait for something she will not let happen. The news will be bad for us, or there will be no news. But tidings will not be good unless Ravenna falters."

The wizard stalked to the big stump and seated himself. Wistfully, sadly, he watched the boy assist the herb woman in her quiet, everyday business.

Not all the news was unwelcome, nor were all arrivals embarrassing or threatening. Sometime in late March, when the first buds were appearing on the trees and, for the first time, the more delicate songbirds alighted in the branches, Corbinwood had yet more visitors.

Brenn was seated above Terrance on the stump. His large, nimble thief's hands rubbed the wizard's shoulders, and he felt the old man knotted and tight beneath his kneading fingers.

"You're like an old tree yourself, Terrance," he observed. "All gnarled and twisted. 'Tis a dark acquaintance with the world you have."

The wizard snorted, his eyes following Bracken, who paraded through the clearing and stopped, sniffing the air once, twice. Suddenly the old dog began to leap and gambol and frolic, as Sendow entered the clearing, escorting two familiar visitors.

"Ricardo!" Brenn cried out. "Delia!" And Galliard's encampment erupted with greetings and introductions.

It had been almost two years since Brenn had seen them, when Ricardo had turned and smiled and waved goodbye and the two of them waded into the milling crowds of Grospoint. Brenn had known he would see them again, though why he had known this he would have been hard-pressed to tell had someone forced him into explanations. It was just that Ricardo was perpetual. He seemed like the sort who always danced on the edge of disaster but always kept dancing.

Yet now, amid the changing light of the clearing, the Alanyan looked older, tired. There was a faint frosting of gray at his temples and in the long black braid down his back.

On the other hand, Delia had blossomed. From a pretty girl she had become a beautiful woman, her black skin flawless and gleaming and a hint of sadness in her amber eyes that did nothing if it did not deepen the beauty. Brenn was thunderstruck, and all the male cousins were scrambling over each other, offering the young alchemist's apprentice dried fruit, water, ale, tea, and even a pair of slippers Jimsett had produced from nowhere. Politely, a little wearily, Delia deflected all the offers and stood by Ricardo as he seated himself before wizard, Forest Lord, and uncrowned king.

"How did you get through the lines, old friend?" Terrance asked.

"Bribery," Ricardo answered casually. "First of all, even the most foolish Watch lieutenant is not going to harrass Alanyans. We're officially neutral, you know, and Dragmond has enough trouble with the Zephyrians to begin with. I told them I had family business in the forest, slipped the lieutenant a dozen coins, and the man went blind on the spot.''

"Welcome to Corbinwood, Ricardo," Galliard said with a laugh, his eyes constantly flickering to the exquisite woman before him. "Your friends here speak highly of you, and that is surety enough in our eyes and presence.''

Ricardo smiled. Everyone, intent on Delia, failed to notice how that smile creased the Alanyan's face with new and deeper lines.

" 'Tis an honor, Your Grace, that I shall do my utmost to deserve," Ricardo replied deftly, and from beneath his braid two glittering eyes peered. Out of the alchemist's hair fluttered the reciting owl. Ponder, leaning forward to hand Delia a thin volume of Italian verses, leapt back at the sudden movement of the bird.

There, perched on Ricardo's shoulder, as it was trained so that travelers might learn texts or be lulled by stories in the long miles, the reciting owl began to chant:

> If thou beest borne to strange sights
>   Things invisible to see,
> Ride ten thousand daies and nights,
>   Till age snow white haires on thee,
> Thou, when thou retorn'st, wilt tell me
>   All strange wonders that befell thee . . .

The bird stopped, and Jimsett and Ponder applauded. Perched above them, Bertilak cocked his head scornfully. Thomas removed himself, drawing out a quill as he strode away.

"The same song," Terrance observed. "I remember that from Grospoint. And though it has not been ten thousand days and nights, it has been aplenty, Ricardo.''

The Alanyan nodded and removed his gloves. Glory approached, rake in hand, and stood a stone's throw away, her soft eyes first on Brenn, then on the visitors.

"But then," Terrance conceded, his gaze and his thoughts elsewhere, "the song may change though the words and the tune are the same, for the ears that hear it may differ from what they were."

"There are wonders enough in the great world beyond the forest, Master Terrance," Ricardo announced, a darkness crossing his face, "and I, for one, breathe more easily in this woodland."

Galliard and Terrance exchanged puzzled glances.

"You must," the Forest Lord offered, "have been to Maraven of late."

"Indeed, I have," Ricardo admitted. "The Great Witch governs, and things have passed from bad to worse."

He went on to explain that passage. How not only the plague but starvation worked its damage in the city, and slowly but lethally, permanently, the poor were erased from the streets of Wall Town and Ships. Whole blocks of Maraven, he claimed, were abandoned now, left to the wandering wild *raposa* who yapped and whined and foraged at night.

Strange as it seemed, Ricardo claimed, Ravenna did not care. Not that anyone expected her to be an advocate of the poor or the helpless. Still, it would seem that her neglect had primed the town for a great and violent unrest.

"But she knows the workings of power," the Alanyan observed bitterly. "She feeds the army and the rich, and your old guild, Brennart, is tied to her by the purse strings. Indeed, an old acquaintance of yours is now first master."

"Squab," Brenn declared flatly. "Or 'Master Squab,' I reckon."

All eyes turned to him curiously.

"It don't take a prophet to figure that one," explained Dirk, who was now standing at the fringe of a gathering circle of Aquilans and woodsmen.

"Between the Guild," Ricardo continued, "which is now nothing more than a circle of spies, and the presence of Captain Lightborn in the Tower—"

"That name again," Terrance interrupted.

"—'tis an armed camp, is Maraven, and the ships dock, unload, and sail away, their sailors forbidden shore leave. And where that cargo ends up, we can only guess, but everyone's guess is Kestrel Tower and the barracks of the Watch."

Throughout Ricardo's story, Delia stared at her hands. Brenn looked at her, tried to catch her eye. From his days at Terrance's tower, he was sure the girl knew more than she was telling, but now her face was obscured, unreadable, like the clay tablets found in Umbrian tombs or like the veiled pronouncements from the oracle at the Notches.

"The gibbets on the Causeway droop," Ricardo proclaimed. "The Great Witch still rounds up those of dangerous age, and by now all Maraven is free of them. Even most of Palerna."

"Most of Palerna?" Terrance asked, a greater alarm rising into his voice.

"Why, of course, wizard," Ricardo replied, ironically and bitterly. "Did you expect that evil to stop at the city walls?"

"Of course not," Terrance answered, his voice scarcely a whisper. "At least if you had asked me, pressed me into predictions. But here in the woods . . ."

Brenn sat back. He watched Glory glide across the clearing serenely, intent on herbs, no doubt, or on the elusive language of trees, the first words of which she was only now teaching him. But his thoughts were elsewhere, past Glory, past Delia, resting in the dangerous streets of his old city.

"Ricardo," he asked, steadying his voice, "you've heard something of the Guild? . . ."

"Faye is in Kestrel Tower," Delia interrupted. Her normally musical voice sounded harsh in the silence and in the news that it bore.

Brenn gasped. His eyes on the Ruthic girl, he did not notice as Terrance turned away.

"But what that means, nobody knows," Ricardo was quick to explain. "Some think she's the Great Witch's prisoner. But others—and, mind you, nobody knows for sure—others think that she is more . . . guest than hostage."

Brenn stared across the clearing. It was like swimming in deep water, where there is nothing but darkness below you and your mind fastens on what inhabits that huge and yawning blackness. Suddenly the closeness and safety of the clearing, the companionship he had enjoyed with his new-found family—with Dirk and Terrance and Glory—seemed uncertain, almost menacing.

He stood, he paced through the reeling clearing and into the woods. Lapis turned, reached out for him, but he was suddenly past her and losing himself amid the green dappling of old needles and new leaves.

$$\succ\succ\succ \text{ XIV } \prec\prec\prec$$

He did not notice where he was going. The woods seemed to close behind him, and all around him was darkness and shadow and the muffled, chittering sounds of animals he could not name.

Brenn tripped over vines, over exposed roots. Twice he crossed forest trails, racing past them as he hurried through the heart of the forest toward what he thought was the sound of rushing water. For the Boniluce lay nearby—somewhere amid this maze of leaf and undergrowth—and he was bound to find it. Water could help him think, a known steady current within this heaped and loud confusion.

So he kept on running, away from the clearing and the truth that Ricardo and Delia had brought with them. His thoughts were as tangled as the woodlands around him: He did not know whether to fear for Faye or to be angry at her.

Every instinct told Brenn that if Faye was in Kestrel Tower, she was there as a prisoner. It simply could not be otherwise. He thought of her in the darkened doorway of a hovel in Wall Town, passing stolen food into a widow and her three ailing children. He thought of her teaching letters to a handful of the younger guild urchins, Marco and Theodor among them. To serve Ravenna, or worse, to serve her willingly, would go against everything that Faye believed.

Or said she believed.

For now, wearied and circled about in the labyrinth of the forest, Brenn began to imagine himself into smaller and tighter circles, closing fast on a thought that lay in the center of his darkness. Who could know, he asked himself, how Faye had changed since last he saw her? Who was to say that she couldn't be bought, as the Goniph was bought, or Squab?

He leaned against the trunk of an alder, breathing heavily. The whole unmanageable largeness of things seemed to close around him, and he thought of how little he could do—how little, really, when compared to the enormous world of injury and intrigue beyond the borders of this woods. Slowly he slipped to the ground, where he sat and pondered and doubted until he could ponder and doubt no more, and his eyes closed and sleep rushed up to swallow him.

They looked for Brenn until well after dark, scouring the woods, peering down obscure, moss-covered trails and through the drooping tunnels made by the overhanging branches of willows. Desperately, with fading hope, they shouted and called his name into the widening shadows. Terrance was at the head of the party, a blue light glowing from his fingertips and small creatures rushing from the folds of his robe in brief and fruitless searches. Galliard and Sendow were there for guidance, while Jimsett and Ponder were nosing through the tunnels beneath the forest. Thomas and Ricardo and Delia had taken a canoe and floated down the Boniluce, their eyes on the banks and the dark, folding current ahead of them. Lapis had climbed to Galliard's quarters, the small cottage high in the branches of the cedar, from which she had a hawk's-eye view, aided by a dozen crystals and lenses.

All in all, though, it was the wizard who took command of the search. There was something beyond urgency about him, Lapis noticed from the cabin window. There she stood, a peculiar circular red lens at her eye, watching the forest below for signs of movement. Twice she saw the wizard moving between the trees, and twice he stopped, looking around him for any sign of his apprentice.

" 'Tis not mere concern that drives him," Lapis whispered to nobody, squinting into the red lens. "There's something of remorse in that face, and of deep mourning, I'd wager." Only the owls and a pair of quarreling squirrels were close enough to hear her. Meanwhile, Terrance moved farther and farther away, until he was a green, dodging shade at the edge of her sight.

* * *

"Come," Galliard said, as the moonlight tangled in the branches around him. "Come, Terrance. 'Tis the dangerous part of the night, when even the light is treacherous."

He set his hand on the wizard's shoulder. Terrance startled, drawn from a long, elaborate worry. He turned angrily to the Forest Lord, brushing away his grasp.

"What would you have me do?" the wizard snapped. "Simply give up and go back to that clearing of yours, seat myself by the fire and go to sleep?"

"Indeed, Master Terrance, that is precisely what I would have you do," Galliard insisted, taking the wizard by the arms and lifting him over a hollow log, setting him softly on a well-worn trail that snaked off into the shadows. Nimbly, Galliard leapt over the log, and Terrance caught himself marvelling at the young man, the strange admixture of gentleness and coldness, of wisdom and innocence.

If something has happened to Brenn, the wizard thought, and caught himself before he thought anymore.

Something, indeed, *had* happened.

Brenn awoke, and the clearing around him was spangled with a hundred lights. The lad reached for the knife at his belt and found it missing. Breathing a time-honored thieves' curse, he scrambled around the alder, trying to place hard wood between himself and his glowing visitors, but it was no good: on the other side of the tree, a hundred more lights shimmered.

It was a strange glow they gave off, illuminating nothing more than the lights themselves, so that they shone like strange, phosphorescent gems on a black velvet cloth.

It took Brenn a moment to remember. Often, when you search for something long enough and hard enough, what you are searching for is dimmed so by desire and expectation that when you find it, it is almost impossible to recognize.

"At last!" he exclaimed finally, extending his hand. "I have searched long for your company."

The faeries did not move, but continued to stare and blink impassively. Brenn rose cautiously to his feet and stepped toward the nearest light. Still nothing moved, nothing wavered.

Now, closer still, he could see the creature's outline against the darkness. It was a small thing, and gangling, almost monkey-like in its long arms and squat little legs. Brenn caught his breath and extended his hand again, but suddenly the faery was not where he had seen it, and suddenly the lights seemed more distant, flickering in the high branches of the evergreens and deep within the mesh of undergrowth, wavering as though he saw them at some great distance, as though they were the reflection of stars upon the water.

Brenn seated himself uncomfortably on the damp, loamy floor of the forest. "Very well, then," he conceded. "I await your wishes. What would you have me do?"

Slowly and reluctantly, the cousins returned to the clearing. Jimsett and Ponder were covered with mud and dirt, muttering angrily at the foolhardiness of Town boys. Ricardo, his dark eyes haunted, listened intently to Sendow's plan for the morning—how each of them, with a band of men, would file through the woods' complexity until every brake and hollow and clearing had been searched and the lad turned up.

" 'Tis only hours," Sendow had said, his voice consoling and soothing. "We shall find him by midday tomorrow." Ricardo and Delia nodded soberly, though neither of them believed him.

Brenn was not the only one missing. Terrance sent Bracken on a winding search through the near woods, and the dog came back panting and thirsty, all hope of finding Brenn given up entirely to the woodland's strong smells and distractions.

Finally Lapis tried every lens and glass she owned, starting with a new and fancy monocle that drew all color from the air. Delia had planted the thing in her own belongings, knowing that Lapis would rummage through them when she thought nobody was looking. Since the girl would steal no matter what, Delia had concluded it was best to arrange things so she would steal something she would enjoy and use.

Enjoyable it was, but useless, as were the rest of the glasses, from the best—a living lens that showed the viewer all sides of an object at once—down to the oldest, the faceted perfume bottle that simply separated red light from green. Lapis set down the last of them, carefully placing it among the more expensive, less-valued pieces in a little blue velvet bag. Sighing, she turned to her cousins.

"Nor does that work, either," she concluded. "Cousin Galliard, I expect we have no choice but to follow Sendow's plan for the morrow. Cousin Brennart is safe from our sight and from our dogs and burrowing, and no doubt far from the reach of our magic."

"May the powers protect him from other magics," Ponder breathed, and Thomas and Lapis—the more devout of the cousins—joined the big Aquilan in a quiet sign of warding.

All eyes turned to Terrance, who coughed and shot back a grim stare to each of the assembled woodsmen. They had all given up, he concluded. Though they could have searched through the night, combing the foliage and the river banks. They could have dragged the river on the off-chance that the faeries among them were kelpie or malevolent sprites.

They could have done anything short of magic. But now they had given up, and Glory, the wisest one of the bunch, had lost herself in the green darkness, and all that was left, it seemed, was the wizard's conjury, whatever good that would do.

One thing for sure, Terrance concluded. *At the moment the ether wavers in this desolate place and chants or auguries go forth, there will be eyes upon us that we do not want. Faerie eyes, for one, but as far away as Kestrel Tower folks will be stirred into watchfulness.*

If Ravenna does not know yet, she will know by sunrise.

He sighed deeply and nodded.

"You are right, Galliard," he said mysteriously, his eyelids drooping. "It is time to rest, to sleep, perhaps. Tomorrow will be soon enough to find the lad. Yes . . . Sendow's plan . . . is the best of policies . . . and the one we shall take up . . . tomorrow."

Weaving on his feet, the wizard began to snore. Ricardo and Sendow were to his side at once, lifting him onto a bed of straw by the stump, setting him comfortably on his back.

Terrance smiled a little as his gray head nestled into the soft straw. Ricardo smiled in return to see his old friend so at peace. *It must be well with him*, the Alanyan thought. *It must be*

better than I had imagined. For now he sleeps readily and rest-
fully.

And no longer is there need of the lethe.

Their instruction had been simple. Brenn had marvelled at its
brevity and depth, once he had passed through the strange and
elusive web of the faerie language.

When he first heard the words, he had tried to locate them
among the languages he had known. Palernan they were not,
nor thieves's cant, nor certainly the harsher tones of Zephyrian
or Parthian he had learned long ago at the Goniph's knee. Brenn
had heard Umbrian before, and Latin and Italian, and though he
understood none of them, he had schooled himself in their sounds
enough to know that this exotic faerie talk was no language he
had ever heard, filled with music and bizarre changes in pitch
and inflection.

It was like strange, open vowels riding in the songs of whales
or the chattering of dolphins. For a time Brenn heard only the
sounds, mournful and remote, as he had once or twice heard the
sounds of the big sea mammals somewhere off in the dark beyond
Palern Reef. He fumbled with the calling and crying, trying to
find the words in the midst of it, but he could make no sense of
what the faeries spoke.

He listened intently for a long time, until he wearied and his
s stopped reaching for words. He settled back into the sounds,
and suddenly, as though it had been waiting for him all along
if he would only relax and pay attention, the strange singing
blossomed into words, though Brenn could not tell if the words
took shape in the air or in his imagining.

> *Heart of the alder*   *holy and hidden,*
> *Guided and gardened*   *grown in the wilderness,*
> *Sown beyond seed*   *and soil, what bring you?*
> *What in the wilderness*   *waits for your tending?*

Baffled by the obscure questions, Brenn stammered and blushed
and grew silent.

"What . . . what waits for *my* tending?" he asked. Then he
paused, looking about him at the dim array of lights.

He was afraid even to guess.

Still singing, the faeries formed a circle around him. Brenn's fears magnified in the ring of glowing lights. After all, what was a faerie round but the beginnings of spellcraft—a brief and powerful dance where the creatures linked hands and spirited away whoever or whatever had crossed into their midst?

Again the faeries sang, as if in answer to his unspoken question.

> *The nests of nightingales* *new in the springtide:*
> *How do you help* *the hovering fledglings*
> *Mount and master* *the maintaining wind?*

This time, it was clearer. Brenn closed his eyes and ventured an answer.

"I . . . I guess I don't," he said. "Time does that for them. Time and the high summer and . . . and something in their nature."

The eyes around him glimmered brightly, casting light on the woods around them. Suddenly, Brenn saw where he was—in a clearing almost overgrown, given way to neglect and vines and burgeoning ivy. For a moment he thought he had given the wrong answer, and again reached instinctively for his missing knife. It seemed that the faeries had drawn nearer. Once more his thoughts reeled with visions of abduction—of eternal sleep on a moonlit hillside in a circle of mushrooms, or long years locked in the musty heart of a hollow alder.

Then, as quickly as they had brightened, the lights grew dim. The faeries were where they had always been, their green, attentive gaze spangling the new leaves and the evergreen branches.

Brenn took heart.

"That's . . . that's the answer, isn't it?" he asked the encircling lights. "That I can't do much about . . . well, about *most* of the things I *want* to do something about?"

He took their silence as agreement.

Smiling, Brenn leaned back against the alder. He sighed deeply and shook his head. "Even faeries don't know how true *that* is," he said, sketching a circle in the dirt with his finger. "I've been here nigh on four months, and I've yet to do *anything* that has in it a spark of purpose or good or even usefulness."

He stopped and his face flushed deeply, as he realized he was confessing to a dim array of lights.

"Well, what of it?" he asked out loud, and barreled on.

"It seems . . . it seems like I'm always being *prepared* and never get beyond the preparing. Schooled and instructed and set to tasks I can do no better than I could the magic Terrance tried to train me in."

The lights did not move from the midst of the foliage. Brenn sighed again.

"Nor does any of this healing craft settle all that well with me either. Glory says that a king can lay hands without harming himself—can draw the Death away without suffering the boils and lesions and fevers, can take away blindness though his own sight remains whole. Makes me wonder if I'm the king at all, from what she's saying. For I can learn the herbs all right, and the angers and the worries and the dark acquaintance. All those things a body can know and study about healing, just like they were set down and waiting to be memorized."

He paused and rolled his eyes in frustration, surprising himself when he looked up to find two faeries perched in the lower branches of the alder, staring intently at him, blinking and sober as a brace of owls.

"Oh, yes, I can learn all of those *things*," he confessed to the pair above him. "But it's the doing that baffles me. The spells backfire, I boil elves and set curtains afire, and here in the woods all I've done is call down a passel of ravens instead of bringing a rain. And as for the healing . . . well, I can't see the colors and my hands have gloves on them, it seems, on account of I can't feel the darkness in a body so as to draw it out like Edward of Anglia or Carolus Magnus or the other good kings."

Brenn lay back and linked his hands behind his head.

"I confess," he admitted with a rueful laugh, "that I'm not cut out for heroics. My father wasn't either, to hear the stories. Now my grandfather was, and his father before him, but the only trouble with that was the kind of things they did to folks such as you, all as a matter of course while they were sitting on that throne in Maraven.''

He looked up. The lights were still there—intent, expectant.

"I don't want this kingship near as much as other folks want it *for* me, if you understand," Brenn concluded. "Still, some of them will listen to me a little because they look down the years a way and expect to see me crowned and all, and they think that listening is wise and politic and good for what ails the country.

"So tell me, because if I can do it, by the gods and the four winds I shall . . . tell me what I can do for you."

The eyes of the faeries brightened, dimmed, and brightened again, and all of a sudden Brenn heard the singing again—a haunting arrangement of whistles and drones that rustled the leaves like a fresh spring wind. He closed his eyes and listened, smelling comfrey and juniper in that song, while green light splashed in a downpour onto the insides of his eyelids.

"I am the enemy," the faeries sang,

I am the enemy	*inside the forest*
Rootless the wreaker	*of ruthless knowledge*
Iron my arrogance	*my insight fire*
And the hard heft	*of my hand is sunlight.*

Brenn pondered the riddle for a moment, his chin cradled in his hands. It was too obvious. All of the clues pointed to the simple answer—"man." He had always imagined that faeries were more subtle than that.

And yet, each of the verses pulled him back to Galliard, to the cousins and the deer blinds and the building of camp fires, to the harvest of mushrooms and the long, continual hunt from season to season. None of them belonged there. Not even Sendow, who knew the forest as well as anyone. They were tenants, with their axes and fires and their cabins in clearings, and the real inhabitants of the wilderness—the faeries and the animals, the birds and even the trees—would always regard them with mistrust.

"And no wonder," Brenn whispered to himself, and the green owlish eyes around him glimmered alertly.

"Very well," he said, climbing to his feet. "Human things there are that lie within my power. Though I can see little else that I can do for the likes of you, I shall see to it that the trespassers—both my friends and my enemies—cease their trespassing and leave you entirely alone."

His words rang in the air with a power beyond normal speech and he gasped at the boldness of his own promise. He could no more force Galliard to leave Corbinwood than he could uproot every single faerie. Nonetheless, he had said the words. Deep within himself, Brenn resolved that this was a promise he would keep.

The lights flashed brightly, like distant meteors over the ocean. At once the circle of faeries opened, and a dimly lit pathway wound off into the forest. Brenn had no need to question: he knew that it led back to the clearing, to his cousins and friends and the heavy duties of the large world outside Corbinwood.

He shivered as he left the little clearing, the circle of lights dwindling into the foliage behind him. It was as though he had taken on too many promises—to Terrance, to Faye, to Galliard, to Glory. Finally there was this grandfather of vows to the assembled Invisible Folk. Brenn feared he had just assured the snatching of his future children and the curdling of all the milk ever brought to his house.

"I'll be elf-shot for sure if that one fails," he whispered with a chuckle, parting the leaves in front of him and following the trail as it wound through the slanting trees toward a distant, bright destination.

>>> XV <<<

Galliard stood by the fire, bow in hand. Terrance was asleep now, as were the rest of the visitors and cousins, and the late watch was left to the Forest Lord and a handful of his ill-equipped woodsmen.

How quiet the sleepers are, he mused. Only an hour ago they were all hustle and commotion, each of them unraveling in vain attempts to find young Brennart. Ponder and Sendow strewed maps of the forest over the clearing in a frenzy of tactics, only to realize that the search parties had covered all of the woods west of the Boniluce to no avail. Thomas and the alchemists argued as to who should take command of the search, the bardic cousin duelling words with the eloquent Ricardo until close-mouthed Sendow pointed out that neither of them could find his way from one edge of the clearing to another, much less around the whole of Corbinwood.

Bertilak had scrambled from branch to branch, calling out for Brenn, never alighting on the ground in the midst of his urgent, acrobatic search. Finally, he too was at rest; pulling his cape over his head, he snored peacefully in the sweet-smelling branches of the cedar.

Jimsett, of course, had been ready to dig to Cathay, convinced that Brennart had fallen into another pit. The Forest Lord smiled to remember his tunneling cousin, perhaps the most absurd of the whole company.

Only Lapis and Terrance, it seemed, had remained altogether calm and sensible. Through her many lenses, Galliard's youngest cousin had surveyed the growing darkness around them until the light left the woods and she could see no more. And as for the wizard . . .

The wizard had been the first to fall asleep.

Galliard looked down at the gray-haired, bearded puzzle of a sorcerer stretched out beside the fire. Only an hour ago, Terrance had been the most worried of them all, ready to run himself to death in search of the boy. Then suddenly, unexplainably, he settled himself on a tattered Zephyrian horse blanket, pulled his wide-brimmed hat down over his eyes and, taking Bracken under the crook of his arm, was dozing in a matter of minutes.

For the first time in Galliard's memory, the wizard had set aside the lethe he drank before retiring.

"What I can do now is best done in a dream," he intoned, and winked solemnly at the Forest Lord. Then he closed his eyes.

It was as though he had willed himself to sleep.

Galliard drew an arrow from his quiver, pointing it toward the fire as he checked the shaft for worthiness. It was straight and true, the way he liked all things. This magic and wizardly folderol left him baffled and weary, as though he had been caught in a labyrinth.

Idly, he fitted the arrow to the string. He drew the bow, then pointed it toward a low point in the spring sky, scarcely visible through the canopy of leaves, where the green star descended on its way out of reckoning for another three years. Through Horologe, the last of the constellations it would pass, gliding to the other side of the heavens, where it would emerge in what was called the Sign of the Ram. Or so Portuguese traders had told him.

Lapis and Thomas had marvelled at the prospect—a sky entirely different from this one—but then Lapis was a dreamer and astronomer and cloud-reader, and Thomas was a poet.

Galliard replaced the arrow carefully. Though drawn to visionaries of all sorts, he mistrusted the lot of them. Cloud-readers and poets, for all their glamor, were little better than Portuguese traders. It was safer to treat with visible things. When Pytho vanished on the western horizons, who was to say that the green star rising some three years hence in the Sign of Gallus was the same one? Out of sight, gone forever, he liked to say. And who could prove him wrong?

It was safer to treat with visible things.

Hence the curse—the uncontrollable urge to thievery. Galliard stood and walked closer to the fire, holding out his hands for warmth against the brisk spring night. Every single one of them. Who could prove that this Brennart was any different? After all, the story was that Terrance had caught him in mid-burglary . . .

The wizard frowned and stirred in the firelight. Galliard craned over him, longing briefly and fancifully for the power of the old Philokalian seers Thomas babbled about—the red-haired mystics who, after they died, dwelt in the dreams of others, where they continued to shape the world through influence and suggestion.

"Not that," he snorted quietly, embarrassed at his own playfulness. "Better a fly on the wall of his dreams."

At that moment, the clearing erupted in unearthly shrieking.

✳ ✳ ✳

They were all to their feet at once—the alchemists and the cousins, the woodsmen and Dirk and the dog. Through the clearing they all reeled dazedly, stumbling over bedding and each other, rubbing their eyes, shielding their heads against the outcry that echoed all around them. From the underbrush to the highest branches and even to the crown of the enormous cedar itself, the forest was loud with the menacing shrieks.

Galliard pointed his bow at first one tree, then another. The sound raced and circled shrilly above him like dark fireworks, and he followed it from tree to tree by guesswork.

"Hold still . . ." he muttered through clenched teeth, aiming at the top of the cypress. But the sound was gone again, cascading through the branches and onto the floor of the forest, where it thrashed and screeched through the high grass like a maddened boar.

By now Sendow had drawn his sword and was walking slowly toward the center of the loudest noise. He moved gracefully, in a half-crouch, the blade held low in front of him.

"Where is it?" Dirk hissed beside him, but Sendow pushed him back with a strong and gentle gloved hand. Covering his cousin's movement, Galliard leveled his bow at the churning undergrowth.

Suddenly, like a startled quail, a black thing soared out of the darkness with an explosion of leaf and twig and dried grasses, its call exploding into a blood-curdling cry that sounded like tearing metal, like an animal on fire. It brushed past Galliard like a dark *alienado*, sending him sprawling out of the firelight, the heat of madness on its wings and in its wake.

The needles of the cedar browned and blistered as the creature rocketed under them on its path to the far edge of the clearing. Scrambling to his feet, the Forest Lord gathered his bow, raised it, and aimed at the dark heart of the dodging, receding shape.

Here, at last, was something he could see.

It was not the best of shots, but the arrow was true and its path was straight. Its shaft flashed once in the brindled moonlight, and then, with a shriek that surpassed all of the ones before it, the creature plummeted into the drooping branches of a willow.

Galliard drew his knife and raced across the clearing to the spot where the thing writhed and coiled, churning the grass and the sod in its agonies. Sendow was close behind the Forest Lord, all caution abandoned now, and Dirk to the right of him, armed with a wicked little dagger. To the right of Dirk, drawing his curved Alanyan cutlass, the alchemist Ramiro closed bravely in support.

Galliard smiled grimly. Whatever it was—bird or reptile or wizard's invention—it would find no hospitality in Corbinwood.

Bird or reptile or wizard's invention. It was all of these.

It was a raven at first, or at least it seemed to be a raven. Quickly, as its enemies approached, the thing wrapped its growing tail about the bole of the willow and continued its fierce transformation. The black feathers fell away from it like cinders from a burning log, and the scales that took their place glowed an angry, incandescent red from the back of the creature to the end of its long, snakelike tail and the twin fangs that sprouted from it like some hideous, fast-growing plant. At the same time the beak receded, twisting and mottling before the startled eyes of the woodsmen until it had become a squat, reptilian maw, bristling with six rows of angular teeth. The creature looked up at Galliard and hissed, gnashing the wicked array of fang and incisor.

Despite himself, the Forest Lord stepped back. It was a wyvern, no doubt: he had heard the fanciful stories. Behind him and far to his right, Ramiro and Sendow slowed their pace, bravado replaced by a new caution and respect. Only Dirk barrelled on. Heedlessly, the lad continued his rush, raising his dagger and coming to a halt only when he saw that he had outstripped his comrades, that he was alone and scarcely ten feet from the wyvern.

It was then that the wyvern lashed out, its tail uncoiling with the speed and the precision of a fencing master's foil. Dirk raised his arm at the last moment as the unsheathed double fangs of the sting, aimed no doubt for his neck, hooked into his arm and lodged there for a terrifying moment. The scales of the monster rippled and yellowed, turning a bright orange as the poison coursed through them. Then slowly, almost gently, the thing pulled away, and with the mildest of outcries—a brief, almost matter-of-fact *Oh*—the little thief fell to the ground.

With an angry bellow, Sendow lurched at the wyvern, and the beast raised its tail, preparing to strike once again. Ricardo saw the chance, moving silently and gracefully to the creature's flank, and when Sendow had its complete attention the big Alanyan leaped onto its neck and raised his cutlass, his face scarcely a foot from the wyvern's jaws. He brought the blade down quickly, and again and again. The beast's eyes grew distant, almost soft. With Ramiro astride it like a rider, it staggered toward the center of the clearing, then hissed and fell, its great wings smothering a camp fire and scattering the ashes before the wyvern turned, heaved, and lay still.

Ricardo stood over the dead beast, surprised by his own quickness and fury. Slowly he sheathed his sword, the grim smile fading from his face as he realized, beyond his darkest imagining, that he was smiling.

It had been an exhiliarating moment—there on the back of the wyvern, the monster thrashing and stabbing with its tail, and his own sword descending once, twice, a third time into that sinuous scaled neck. It had been doubtsome for a moment, the Alanyan thought . . .

And he was stunned that he enjoyed the danger of it.

Now Lapis cried out—could not help but cry out. Breaking away from her brothers, she rushed toward the astonished Alanyan, then caught herself and regained her composure. All around her woodsmen and cousins were rushing toward the fallen thief. Delia, either the quickest or the most level-headed of the lot, reached his side first.

Taking Dirk's hand, she examined the color of his skin, passed her fingers over his cold face, and turned to Lapis.

"Quickly, girl!" she ordered brusquely. "Bring one of those lenses here!"

"Wh—which one?" Lapis asked, folding her hands awkwardly in front of her. Delia shook her head and beckoned with rising urgency.

"*Any* of them, by the gods!" she exclaimed. "Don't stand there like . . . like *a damned Aquilan princess*!"

Stung, Lapis stepped back. Then suddenly, reaching into the

pouch at her belt she rushed toward the Ruthic girl, who extended her dark hand to receive a dozen glittering lenses. Without ceremony, Delia dropped all but one of them, and taking the one she had kept, a shiny red oval, placed it against Dirk's lips.

Delia held up the lens, showing it to Ricardo and Galliard. "There's a mist," she said urgently. "He still lives! Now who among us can heal . . ."

All eyes raced around the clearing. Neither Glory nor Brenn was there, and Terrance lay in the same spot by the fire, having slept unexplainably through all the shouts and commotion.

With long, determined strides, Galliard crossed the clearing to the slumbering wizard. Twice he shook Terrance, once he even kicked him, but the wizard snored deeply and did not stir. Galliard stood over him and stared, baffled by the invisible country of magic.

Terrance knew full well where he was.

The streets resembled those of Maraven. They were bathed in a deep red light as Brenn had said they would be. Above the closely set buildings rose the domes and cupolas of minarets that had troubled the lad when he saw them, foreign as they were to his familiar streets and architecture.

Terrance smiled. The old Philokalian temples, they were. Built in the landscapes of dreams when the priests and seers could not return to the waking world. Terrance knew them from legends, had seen one or two of them before in especially vivid sleep, but that had been long ago, before the lad came and he had been forced to drink the lethe every night.

Gliding through the alleys like a wraith, the wizard marveled at the brilliant shifts of color and light, at the smell of ale and pastry and ordure and sea, how the rushing sound of the waves reached him this far inland deep in the bowels of the city.

It was Maraven, all right. A Maraven of memory and desire and vision—like the glittering version he had seen from atop the open stairway that jutted from the roof of his tower. For a moment Terrance was breathless, caught up in the lurid beauty of the dream town.

Then he remembered where he was.

"Steady," he cautioned himself. "Look around you, old boy. Like as not, there's a witch in the wings." She had to be there, or else this wandering in dreams was all for nothing.

For Terrance knew that they had reached an impasse. Galliard could not leave Corbinwood, because his sense of honor would not allow him to venture out among innocent people from whom he might steal something, and Ravenna, for mysterious reasons, could not enter the forest. The Watch was there, too, of course, encircling the forest like a great red serpent. They all could stay there for years—for centuries, provided they lived that long— and nothing would change, nothing would better itself, and half a continent would suffer in the bargain.

So he prepared himself to meet Ravenna. It would be between him and the Great Witch, before she had time to marshal forces, or worse, to find the boy.

Instead, Ravenna would find him. She would not be able to resist the possibilities. Her old enemy, gliding through a cityscape of dreams, unarmed except for his own wiles and ingenuity. No, she would not be long in acting.

The dream streets blazed with uncanny light, as the wizard stepped into a square that was almost familiar. Several tall buildings faced inward, toward a tranquil, windless courtyard, in the center of which lay an elaborate, dry fountain.

Terrance looked about him, folded his hands, and said the first of the incantations.

> *By each spot the most unholy,*
> *In each nook most melancholy*
> *There the traveler meets, aghast,*
> *Sheeted Memories of the Past:*
> *Shrouded forms that start and sigh*
> *As they pass the wanderer by.*

Dark, winged creatures, as swift and black as flies, scattered at the last word of the chant, fluttering into the windows of the buildings. Terrance caught his breath and looked beyond the fountain to the mouth of an alleyway opposite.

Sure enough, almost where he had expected her, a faint column of black smoke arose, rippling like heat shimmers off the dark surface of the alley. Terrance turned and watched on the sly, tilting his head so that he could see the apparition at the very corner of his gaze.

Soon it became apparent. It was woman-shaped, drifting from building to building, from stoop to sill, now twisting itself about a white, marble dolphin arched above a dried fountain. Terrance stood motionless. He tried to recall the old incantations.

"Something about . . . *shades*," he murmured. And then it returned to him, as though Archimago had spoken it in his ear from some great and unfathomable distance.

> *Follow still, since so thy fates ordained!*
> *The sun must have his shade,*
> *Till both at once do fade,*
> *The sun still proved, the shadow still disdained.*

"Now, Brennart!" Terrance murmured, with a last fond thought of the lad, who wandered the gods knew where. "May what you told me about this world be prophecy."

The wizard turned to face the woman-shaped shadow nestled in the heart of the fountain. Calmly he leveled his gaze upon her as a fresh wind, hot as an *alienado*, coursed through the alley behind him, buoying his robes, the red curtains of the red windows, the pennants on the Philokalian minarets that towered over the buildings themselves. The breeze swirled past the fountain, and the smokey shadow lifted itself out the basin and over the arching dolphins. For a moment it hung like a thick storm cloud above the fountain, and then it was off, afloat on the breeze, moving swiftly back toward the dark alley out of which it had risen.

Boldly, even recklessly, the wizard followed. Passing over the wide square with several long strides, Terrance looked ahead of him as the shadow darted out of the alley and into another patch of light, this time flickering and yellow and far brighter than the light out of which the wizard had come. The familiar smell of grass and sun and clean places rose out of the shifting light.

"Fresh . . ." Terrance whispered. "It is the country. It is home on the plains of Palerna, clean and unruffled by the stench and the evils of cities. Or so she would have me think."

With a deep breath the old man readied himself, preparing for last-minute sorcery, for ambush or illusion or treachery. He stepped from the alley.

Ravenna was not there.

Instead, the wizard found himself in a wide and featureless field. Grass gave way unto grass, and as far as Terrance could see there was no landmark, no sign of witch or city or shadow.

Uneasily, he looked behind him. The same fathomless grasslands stretched on into eternity.

It was the country, but it was not home.

Nervously, the wizard folded his arms and pondered this mapless landscape. He had heard of *croglath*, in which the dreamwalker is lost forever in the dream. But that, he had also heard, was only when you trespassed on the dreams of others.

To be lost in your own dream was. . . .

Terrance closed his eyes and thought of the seacoast. Thought of the black, porous rock that lined Hardwater Cove, of Palern Reef beyond a short stretch of gray waters. The sudden, flourishing smell of grass raced into his nostrils, and the wizard coughed and opened his eyes.

Grasslands all around him still.

"But it is my own dream," he told himself, and closed his eyes again. The rocks rose out of memory, and the faint, reeling shadows of gulls on the black sand he saw in his mind's eye. Slowly, surprisingly, the smell of the grass subsided, and in its place the wizard smelled salt, the rank and fishy smell of high tide.

He breathed deeply. The air was moist and bracing.

Gratefully, Terrance opened his eyes.

He was alone in a rowboat on gray water. Alone, and yet the boat moved swiftly, silently, as though strong arms manned the oars. Behind him in the darkness, the city glowed red upon yellow upon red. Its tall minarets glimmered like low stars on the horizon.

Terrance wrapped his robe tightly around him and looked to

the prow. Ahead of him, forming out of the mist, the gravestones lined the approaching coast like jagged teeth.

"Aquila," the wizard murmured, and as he said the word, he found himself aground.

"The seacoast," he mused. "But not my seacoast."

Slowly he looked up the rising rocks, into the foothills that marked the southern coastline of the Aquilan province. Stones and markers lined the footpaths up the hills, tiers upon tiers of gravesites and sepulchres stood unadorned, untended, and abandoned to the cold winds off the Bay of Ashes.

There, dodging among the whites of marble and granite, gray against the black of obsidian and pumice, the shadow he had followed from the red streets flitted and wavered.

She was waiting for him, up there.

As alone as she was when their paths had parted last.

Forty years ago? Or was it fifty?

"In her sepulchre down by the sea," Terrance sang softly, his voice thin and melancholy as he climbed one of the footpaths toward the shadow. *"In her tomb by the sounding sea."* It was a song they had sung together as children, caught up in its strange notes of sorrow and gloom.

It was on the first of the larger tiers, indeed by a white marble sepulchre that housed the earthly remains of the Family Gauderic—the old corrupt merchant himself and his daughter Myrra, who died young—that Terrance found her where he had expected to find her from the moment he had begun the climb. She stood against the white marble, waiting for him, her gray eyes turning to deep, expressionless black when they rested upon the climbing form of the wizard.

"You haven't changed, Ravenna," Terrance observed with a bleak smile. "The years have been kind."

In a cold fury the witch stared down at him, and the white marble of the wall behind her began to boil and swirl and change.

➤➤➤ XVI ◄◄◄

"This has nothing to do with the lad," Terrance pronounced warily. He stood amid the tombstones and looked up toward the sepulchre, the white walls of which were ablaze with swirling lights. The Great Witch stood before the marble tomb, casting no shadow in the dreamlight, her long dark hair loosened and her robe lifting and dancing on the breath of the *alienado*.

The alienado is the madman's wind, Terrance told himself uneasily. *Beware*.

"Nothing to do with the lad?" Ravenna asked coldly, incredulously. "When placing the crown on his head would destroy my Dragmond? Would destroy *me*?"

"Not you," Terrance assured her, raising his hand. Ravenna flashed a dark warding sign with her left hand, and the air crackled.

But Terrance had meant no aggression by the gesture. "Or at least," he continued with a wan smile, "it does not have to destroy you. After all, your powers are such that they can shape themselves from king to king, from heart to change of heart." He stared at Ravenna hopefully.

He does not want a struggle, the Great Witch thought. *Good. He will be the weaker for his reluctance*.

"Look behind me, Terrance," she hissed, "and tell me how my powers have changed."

The wall of the sepulchre began to mottle and blister. Terrance gaped, as before him, as though in an ancient, shadowy mural, a painted array of shabby streets rose from the white of the marble, taking shape in reds and violets and deep ochres.

"Wall Town," Ravenna announced triumphantly. "Wall Town, where neither my Dragmond nor your bastard brat can govern the Death!"

The mural began to move. Slowly and mournfully, the

171

becchini—the masked handlers of the dead, dragged bodies into the red streets. Ravenna stepped away from the sepulchre wall so that Terrance could see it all—the dead, the swelling and boils, the dance and twitch of the mortally ill.

"You have brought the plague here, Master Terrance," the witch said cruelly. "More than the vaporous air or the rats or the sailors from Venice or Avignon, the Death is your doing, Master Terrance—your doing and that of your hideous boy."

Terrance frowned. "I . . . I don't—"

"Oh, but you never did!" Ravenna exclaimed triumphantly, seeing that her words had wounded and perplexed the wizard. "You were right all along, and you so love to be right, don't you? Right when you suspected that I carried the plague with me on that long coach ride from Rabia to Maraven, the night that Aurum was born. After all, what else can one purchase in Rabia but disease?

"*I* cannot be blamed, though. Not for your negligence, not for your cruelty. It came to me in the coach that night. I could feel the Death traveling with me, feel the fever in my throat and arms when all I was thinking of was *bring this to the baby, bring this to the newborn child* . . ."

Terrance shuddered as the walls of the sepulchre began to change, swirling in blackness like an enormous dark maelstrom out in the Sea of Shadows.

"But I relented," Ravenna said mockingly, gesturing gracefully at the walls as they roiled and turned. "You had made yourself safe against the pestilence, there in the chambers of Kestrel Tower. So instead, I set loose the Death upon your city. If it could not infect your bodies, far better that it infect your souls through the suffering stares of the poor and their children."

Terrance flinched as his arms began to burn, to blossom in boils and hard, black discolorations. For a moment he reeled and staggered, and Ravenna seemed somehow larger, more solid.

Her black fingernails clicked together like the wings of beetles.

I am not beaten, the wizard told himself. *Not yet not yet there is something something* . . .

Myrra.

Anger raced through him like a tonic, a balm.

"How did you feel when your sister was the first to die?" he asked fiercely. The boils faded from his arms, and for a moment the apparition of the witch became translucent, as though she had tried to escape the dream and found herself trapped and cornered.

"It is like you to rejoice in such cruelties, Terrance," she replied, but the wizard was not finished.

"It was your doing, Ravenna. Pure and simple, the plague was your gift to Maraven. You have done great damage to us, and what I can do to mend that damage seems small next to the suffering. But Brennart will come forth. The lad will come forth and heal thousands, for we both know that the king's touch lifts all pestilence, and as they will say of Edward in Anglia they will say of Brennart in Maraven and Palerna and along the Aquilan coast

> *that strangely-visited people,*
> *all swoll'n and ulcerous, pitiful to the eye,*
> *the mere despair of surgery, he cures,*
> *and to the succeeding royalty he leaves*
> *the healing benediction . . .*

"Poetry again!" spat Ravenna, interrupting the wizard. "Cipher and sing all you will, mountebank! Your verses will not avail you long."

A strange, fresh light that had begun to silver the landscape faded suddenly, as the wall of the tomb resolved itself into dusty, forbidding grasslands. "Perhaps you will enjoy this scenery instead," the Great Witch taunted.

It was Palerna, the southern plains of his dear and forsaken homeland. Keedwater, nestled on the banks of the Boniluce where the river bends east toward the fabled oracles of the Notches.

"Home," Terrance breathed, almost with reverence, as he recognized the thatched cottages, the old stone chapel and the hedgerows of the village in which he had spent his boyhood before he hired out as apprentice to Archimago. At once Terrance became even more cautious and wary: he was sure Ravenna showed him this out of no kindness.

"You are correct as usual, Terrance, for aren't you *always* correct?'' the witch asked, her voice sugary with venom. ''There is no kindness in the showing. Indeed, there is no kindness in your home. Look closer.''

Terrance paused, stared directly into the scene that assembled itself against the white wall of the tomb, and suddenly felt himself being drawn toward it, drawned into its parched and windy midst.

The windows of the cottages were thrown open. Somewhere behind the chapel, a wooden shutter slammed aimlessly against a frame, and throughout the narrow streets of Keedwater a harsh wind coursed and whistled.

''Oh, you are right again!'' Ravenna exclaimed to the dumb-struck wizard. ''Abandoned. Abandoned for a year now. When the droughts and the *alienados* came from the south, the handful of peasants still fools enough to live here gave up and came north into the city. Where were you then, wizard? You and your poetry and healing? Where were you when your own blood starved and suffered?''

Terrance tried to speak. His throat was as dry as the parched alleys of the deserted town.

''They are forgetting the village already, Terrance,'' Ravenna continued exultantly. ''Those whom the plague has not taken will scarcely recall it two years from now. In a decade these abandoned houses will fall into ruin, and a hundred years from now, all that will remain of your beloved village will be a moss-covered square of stones and rubble that marks where the chapel once stood. How does it feel when your past vanishes, wizard?''

Terrance stared long at the faded image of Keedwater on the side of the tomb. Slowly he began to remember: there, by the chapel, the fencepost was down again, victim of the cleric's complete inability with shovel and hammer. There, too, was the fruit tree by the smithy, subject of many a boyhood raid, and the statue buried face first by the doorstep of Philip, the Man of Law and Anna, Seeress of Lady Justice—an ancient Umbrian superstition the young couple had tried in a vain attempt to sell their house and leave the village for good. Gradually, as though they were appearing one by one in this strange shifting image of the village, things odd and broken and familiar appeared in the picture, and the desolate place became Keedwater once more—Terrance's Keedwater.

The wizard watched and remembered and smiled. "How does it feel?" he asked Ravenna. "It could be worse. The town is alive in my memory, no matter what the years and the famine and the drought and your most poisonous curse can do to thatch and brick and stone. It feels the same as it does to everyone . . . only perhaps a little less so."

Nonetheless, it moved the Great Witch. She shrank against the tomb wall as the image of Keedwater melted into moonlight and marble. Against all that whiteness she looked dark and diminished, as though like the moon above her, the first moon of the year, she was somehow waning.

"Look, then, at something you *can* change, wizard!" she cried, her pale hands flickering in silver light and black shadow. "Behold what may come of this fever for thrones and crowns!"

It was a red field that the wizard saw on the wall of the tomb. Red, and littered with broken pike and spear, with shattered armor and with smoke and blood. Bodies lay strewn over the field, waylaid by sword and by a murderous hail of arrows. Through the silence and the stillness grotesque scavenger birds hopped and crouched and bent—condors, their heads naked and red, vultures, and bright black ravens.

"Have you seen enough, Terrance?" Ravenna asked, sympathy false and sugary in her voice. "After all, one field of battle is much like another, except this is *your* doing, yours and that regal brat's. For it is one of many battles that will be fought so that he can ascend the throne, and in each of those battles, thousands of men—as old as you or even younger than Brennart himself—will fall to axe and lance and oil, and you can thank your ambitions for each of their deaths."

She gestured at the stones around them.

"Why, your work could overflow these very grounds!" she exclaimed, and let forth a thin, high-pitched laugh that echoed over the tiered cemeteries. In the distance a pack of wild dogs yammered and howled in response.

Terrance shivered and looked deeply into the red field, the iron and bronze and broken flesh. For a long time he stared at the hand of a young soldier, its fingers motionless and stretched toward the sky as though with the lad's last breath he was reaching for air and sunlight. Slowly under the tearful eye of the wizard, the hand became a branch, a bush, a tree. Slowly the tree blossomed and bloomed, and the air of the graveyard sweetened with the smell of dogwood and jasmine and magnolia. Eagerly breathing in the fragrances, the wizard broke his gaze away from the blossoming tree.

The red field had changed. Indeed it had vanished altogether. The Great Witch gasped in dismay, and Terrance gasped, too, a little surprised at his own victory. All before them, in luxuriant green light on the face of the marble, lay the image of an orchard filled with flowering trees and shrubbery, a resplendent garden in the shadow of an enormous stone tower. And in its midst was a circle of evergreens, and in the center of that circle a lowly olive tree, green and burgeoning and beautiful.

"If it is war, Ravenna," Terrance said hoarsely, "then war it must be. Men will die in our service, as they will in yours. But see what will come of it. For we shall war against Dragmond, against you, and against the things you stand for. And what do you offer but plague, poverty, and famine?"

"And what do you leave behind but worse?" Ravenna asked, her eyes black and glittering with anger. "You would kill them all to have your way—Galliard and his followers, even Brennart himself!"

Calmly, Terrance faced down her stare. The Great Witch fell to her knees and, bowing her head, looked up at the wizard through a curtain of black, cascading hair.

"See what you left behind, Terrance," she said quietly. "You left her behind with Archimago, alone with the *claridad* and the memory and the long, terrible river . . ."

There on the tomb wall, in a final cloudy light, Terrance saw the form of a girl, framed in the silver light and in the green glow of the *claridad* fruit. Seated on the broad branch of the tree, she shielded her eyes and looked across a large expanse of water, toward a dwindling shape on horseback. Though Terrance could not see them, he knew those eyes were gray, were turning black in sorrow and rage and thoughts of abandonment.

"You made *me* into what I am when you left me, Terrance," Ravenna said bitterly, "and the famine and plague and war that I bring, I bring in your name."

Terrance tore his eyes from the scene on the sepulchre and

turned angrily to Ravenna. On his lips were harsh, accusing words. *How dare you blame me for your evil! You who courted the dark from infancy, whose every choice was a black and baneful venture because you willed it so!*

But the words faded when he looked deep into her peerless eyes. They flickered black to gray, then black again. And then they filled with tears.

"I owe *this* to you, Terrance," the witch proclaimed, her voice shaking. A warm southern wind streamed through her hair, and for a moment the wizard thought of how delicate she was —indeed, how delicate they all were, despite their posturing and magic.

She is still that girl by the Boniluce, he thought, his hand reaching for the dark crown of her swirling hair. He would touch her with the touch of healing, would draw all sorrow and bleakness from her.

Terrance closed his eyes and thought of the song of birds. Of nightingale and lark choiring in the gray of dawn, and of the mockingbird and the faint, chipping song of the cardinal. He felt her hair twining between his fingers, and he saw nothing but black. He thought on the wings of the marten, and slowly the black bristled with blue and purple as though a bright, violet star had emerged from a bank of clouds.

Be still, the wizard thought, *and abide in peace.*

But Ravenna shrieked, recoiling at the wizard's touch. A long purple scar snaked over her neck as though her skin was opening, and steam rose from her burning flesh. Stunned, she fell back against the sepulchre.

"Poison!" she screamed. "As though you have not harmed me enough!"

Baffled, Terrance reached for her again. Ravenna shrank against the marble wall, waving her hands at him helplessly.

"What do you want?" she asked, her voice faint and weak and hopeless. "Name what you want, and I shall give it to you. Only do not mark me with that searing, violet touch!"

Terrance paused above her. He drew back the hand he had extended in compassion, and despite himself, there in the dream necropolis, his thoughts turned dark and speculative.

"Nothing, Ravenna. I want nothing. Only—"

The Great Witch lowered her hands, her black eyes narrowing.

"Only your word not to harm the lad Brennart," Terrance continued, watching her face carefully, lest she should display some outward sign of deceit—some crooked half-smile or shift of those ebony eyes that were drawing him . . . drawing him . . .

"You have my word, Terrance," Ravenna said quietly and innocently. "And whatever you think of my doings, I have never given you occasion to doubt my promise."

Terrance folded his arm. He heard the pack of dogs baying nearer and nearer, and reminded himself that he was dreaming.

"Very well," he said, having no choice but to trust her. But he trusted her only so far.

"One thing more, Ravenna," he said, lifting his hand ever so slightly. The Great Witch cringed at the movement. "One thing more: I must know how Galliard's curse is lifted."

Ravenna looked at him suspiciously through the web of her long black hair. "Why?" she asked. "Why *that* secret of all secrets? I have given my promise not to harm your brat. What need have you of Galliard's protection now?"

Coldly, propelled by a fury he did not understand himself, Terrance raised his hand as if to heal her again.

"Very well," she said, her voice frightened and broken. "You must lose the curse in the Bag of Ladra."

"The bottomless bag of a thief?" Terrance asked. "I have heard the legends, but I thought it had been lost or destroyed."

"I know nothing more," Ravenna protested, rubbing her fingers delicately over the long wound on her neck. Nonetheless, she teased him with fragments of a long-forgotten story. And there, in the shifting landscape of his own dreams the wizard crouched, listened, and remembered.

The sound of the dogs passed into the distance, and Terrance lost himself in Ravenna's words.

Glory met Brenn at the edge of the clearing, an urgent, grave look on her pink face. Taking him by the hand, she ushered him into the light, where the woodsmen stood, knelt, and sat in a hushed circle about a blanket-covered form.

"*There* you are!" snapped Galliard, rising from his spot in the circle. "By the four winds, if you *are* too late . . ."

"By the four winds, what will you do?" Glory snapped, her green eyes instantly cold and her broad back rigid. "Stand back, Your Grace. Think you to punish this boy without my consent, when you cannot pilfer the least button without my knowing?"

Chastened, Galliard stepped away, and Glory slipped by with a puzzled Brenn in tow. Quickly, almost instinctively, the circle tightened around them, as the herb woman knelt over the bunched little form and quietly lifted the blanket.

"Dirk!" Brenn cried. For a moment the air seemed to thin and sparkle around him. His old friend was ashen and still.

"But Brennart is *not* too late," Glory said, her voice soft and urgent. "And soon all ye of regal blood shall see how the touch of his hand can mend even lethal wounds, can call back the heart from forgetful kingdoms, the mind from a lasting sleep."

As she spoke those words, Glory seemed to rise above the assembled woodsmen, her face half-lost in a dazzling green light. Later on, when Terrance had left and Brenn after him, and the cousins had gathered to talk about what they had seen and heard, the mystics and poets among them—Thomas and Ponder and little Lapis—each thought for a moment that he or she would tell all the others assembled how the herb woman floated in light above them as though she were aloft on a forest breeze. Yet all of them held their peace and let the moment pass, each thinking that the practical ones in the clearing—Galliard and Sendow and burrowing Jimsett—would laugh at them and call them foolish.

Nonetheless, everyone agreed on what happened next. Glory leaned over Brenn's shoulders, and in a soft, level voice that somehow carried to all parts of the clearing, she told him to place his hands on Dirk's swollen arm.

"Glory!" Brenn protested, his eyes widening with fright. "I . . . can't! 'Tis far beyond me yet!"

"And why is that?" Glory asked, leaning even closer to him. Her breath smelled of rosemary and mint. "You *are* the king after all," she said. "And only the king can lay hands on the ailing without carrying away some of their darkness with him. This wound is mortal: none other can touch it."

"So you have told me," Brenn muttered. "But my hands

haven't the power. At least not yet. And this is Dirk, Glory! This is my friend for ten years—more than half my life! What if my hands should fail my friend?"

"There will come a time," Glory said, resting her ruddy hand on Brenn's shoulder, "when you will ask that question with every wound you touch, unless you answer it now. The time is coming when every plague-ravaged face is lifted to you in hope and yearning. You will love them all then, as much as you love this lad before you."

"I cannot believe that," Brenn replied, his voice breaking as he removed his gloves. "People just aren't made that way."

"Natheless, it is true," Glory stated. "Whether you believe or no. Now lay hands to that arm of his and trust in the four winds and the company around you. Then tell me what colors come to you when your eyes are closed and your heart is open."

Brenn set his hand on the blackening wound, lightly at first and then with increasing pressure. There was no warmth in Dirk's arm. Nor was there a pulse through the veins or a surge of that strange, magnetic energy across his skin, as Glory's teaching had said you would find in a healthy, vibrant body.

"Why, Glory . . . he's . . . Dirk is—"

"Do not think that," the herb woman urged. "And above all, do not say it. Instead, close your eyes again, and tell me the color that comes to you."

Brenn did as she asked. At first it was as though he lay in complete darkness—in the Maravenian sewers, perhaps, or in one of Jimsett's tunnels.

"Black," he said, his voice thick with despair. "No colors. Black is all I see."

"Good," Glory said. "Now open yourself to the spectrum. Open yourself and wait."

Galliard watched in great puzzlement as the herb woman's hand hovered over the lad's shoulder. Glory reached out, almost touching Brenn, and then slowly, unexplainably, drew her hand away.

Ponder and Thomas nodded in unison, as though somewhere below words they understood what was going on. Lapis raised the special lens—the live one—to her eye, and looked at the shifting air above her royal cousin's head.

"Green," she said. "I see green."

It was the first of the colors Brenn saw.

>>> **XVII** <<<

Lying in an outer darkness, the cold creeping over his legs and thighs, Dirk felt a sudden freshness, an alertness pass through him. He breathed in short, shivering gulps.

He was in Maraven, in the dark hot streets where the dead walked.

"No," he said. "Not back here. I come to the woods to get away from ye."

From the deeper dark of an alley a pale hand beckoned. It was the hand of a woman. Her solemn, tearful eyes shone in the dodging city moonlight.

"Come with me," she urged, her voice mournful and strange.

"No!" Dirk protested, this time more strongly. He felt the street tilt below him on a steep incline, felt himself sliding down toward the alley, quickly and inevitably. He called for Faye, and suddenly the lightning flashed and he was atop the buildings in Grospoint, scrambling from roof to roof in a squirrel's path toward Wall Town.

The lightning flashed again, cold white with a hint of green in its forking tines, and the landscape below him was shoreline, Cove Road snaking out of the darkness of shambles and a slim, familiar shape running east along it toward the boundary wall.

In Brennart's cloak, but not Brennart.

Dirk squinted, and the sky wheeled violently, the dream image swirling upwards into a nebula of green light.

" 'Twas Faye!" he said aloud, and smiled. " 'Twas Faye on Cove Road, that very night. I seen her from the parapets!"

"God speed ye, girl," he murmured, and the green light above him swelled and pulsed. It was as though the night had broken over a broad expanse of leaves. Instantly the little thief began to dream again, in images shot through with brilliant green light.

He dreamed he was a leaf, freshly budding from a dark branch. But the dream changed suddenly, and he was a cloud awash in a blue and lofty sky, and then the glint of light in the rising sun, first pink, then fluttering red, then purple, and gold finally, a rich and mellow gold, as again he was the leaf and falling, falling into wakefulness. . . .

He turned onto his side, opened his eyes, gasped and began to weep. Black tears coursed down his face, steaming as they spattered onto the ground of the clearing.

That evening he sat propped on soft rush mattresses, wool blankets spread over him like the robes of a Parthian king. He blushed as the women attended him—Glory with her broth and tea, Lapis with her soft beauty and entertaining lenses, and the dark and lovely Delia, who set medicines before him and spoke in a melodious Ruthic accent that sounded like distant bells at sea. Dirk wanted little to do with the hushed conversation between Brenn and a newly wakened Terrance—all this talk of faeries and dragons and curses and thieves' bags.

The wizard had slept through it all: through the killing of the wyvern, through Dirk's wounding and the laying on of hands. Ricardo had jostled him awake, and Terrance arose with some far-fetched story of a battle in his dreams—a battle he maintained was every bit as important as the one Dirk had fought himself with that poisonous monster of a lizard.

Then again, wizards were always stuck on themselves. Dirk snorted in disgust and looked impatiently for Glory, who was at the kettle mixing another of those unsavory wormwood potions concocted to undo the poison of serpents.

"Here, so the malady stays away," she had whispered, and it tasted bitter as he swallowed it.

"Can't much see how poison's any worse than *that*," Dirk muttered. "Give me the brandy any day. And that sassafras tea, and the leek soup. But if it don't work this time, she can keep her old wormwood till the next stinging."

He looked over at Brenn, who sat in conference with the

wizard and Ricardo and the Forest Lord. Their heads were close together, and occasionally one of their voices raised and drifted across the clearing.

It did not sound as though Brenn was in the best of moods. He had been angry with Terrance when the hubbub was over, while Dirk sat up, vomited, wept more black tears, and while the cousins first wrapped him in blankets and hastened to arrange his bedding. Brenn had asked for Terrance then, had looked around, and to his great surprise found the wizard snoring blissfully by the fireside, Bracken murmuring beside him. Beside himself, Brenn had stomped into the peaceful scene and planted a solid kick upon the wizard's backside, shouting something about how the old coot was never around when you needed him.

Terrance continued to sleep through the shouting and kicking. Gradually Brenn had grown alarmed when the wizard did not waken; then he was downright furious when Ricardo shook the old man softly, and Terrance opened his eyes, smiled and stretched, and asked if something were wrong.

Only now, it seemed to Dirk, were things beginning to calm and settle. Now they all talked in high counsel with the Forest Lord, something about dragons and bags and curses. For now the grudges were set aside, and everyone's thoughts were on faraway prospects and journeys and magic.

"Oh, it's rich to lord it among dukes and chymists and wizards!" Dirk exclaimed, swirling medicinal brandy in a battered pewter cup, while thoughts of the poison faded and Delia and Lapis looked lovelier and lovelier.

"Amalek," Terrance repeated, his finger poised over a crumpled map. "His name is Amalek. Lives due east of Hadrach, in a thicket of briar and thorn the Alanyans call the Aralu."

"Dense and terrible and nearly impassable," Ricardo added.

"Impassable, indeed," the wizard agreed, "And more so because the lair itself lies in the vent of a small, dormant volcano, rising like a glittering island out of that sea of brambles. And no, I don't know exactly what it is that the Bag of Ladra is supposed to do to the dragon, or to the curse, for that matter . . . Brenn? You aren't listening."

"What?" Brenn asked, his gaze returning to the intent stare of the wizard. "Oh . . . so *that's* all you know about the dragon?"

Terrance shrugged. "'Tis all Ravenna told, for that matter. You're to find the bag in his hoard. Perhaps you're to place within it the first item stolen by each of your cousins. Perhaps the bag will devour those things—after all, they say it is bottomless and is always hungry."

"And what does that mean?" Ricardo asked. He looked eagerly at Brenn, his dark eyes intent, hoping that the glamor of dragons and magic had drawn the lad's interest.

Brenn looked idly back toward Dirk, no more interested in the conversation than if the subject were philosophy. Ricardo sighed, gestured resignedly at the wizard.

"I don't know," Terrance replied. He reached over and tugged at Brenn's sleeve to recapture the lad's attention. "I said I don't know. And the best I can tell, neither does Ravenna. The things vanish, I suppose."

"And with them goes the curse?" Galliard asked hopefully.

Terrance nodded. "'Tis all a guess, of course. A groping in the dark. But never mind that the road of the next few weeks is unmapped and uncertain, nor that the dragon is an enemy whose strengths we have yet to sound. When the time comes, there are a hundred magics that can untangle *that* puzzle."

He smiled confidently, a little smugly.

"You can rest assured that my old friend Ravenna didn't want to give me *that* news," he boasted to the men about him.

The Forest Lord frowned at Ricardo, who lifted one eyebrow and shrugged.

"She didn't know the all of it, I'll grant you," Terrance continued. "But she *did* know that the bag was the key to the curse, and she held that knowledge from me until . . . well, until I displayed a greater power than hers."

It was Ricardo's turn to frown. The Terrance who blustered and boasted in front of him was not the wizard he remembered. He looked at the old man closely. Yes, the same the same eyes and tangling beard, and the same broad-brimmed hat.

Perhaps he had been mistaken.

"No. I do not know the powers of the Bag of Ladra," the

wizard admitted. "But even that is part of the sport, gentlemen. It makes for great adventure, for yet another embarking into the unknown."

He tugged at Brenn again.

"You know, Brenn, that Galliard's curse must be lifted for his forces to take the field," Terrance said. "We must free him from Corbinwood for our fortunes to prosper."

"And when that day comes," Galliard said, leaning forward eagerly, his gaze honest and level upon the abstracted lad in front of him, "I shall bring a thousand well-armed partisans to you banner."

"How about it, lad?" Ricardo urged. "Let's go to Alanya and find the dragon."

"A thousand partisans," Galliard repeated. "And my life, if it comes to that."

All three of the men stared at Brenn expectantly, but the lad's thoughts were elsewhere again.

"That . . . healing, Terrance," Brenn said softly.

The wizard leaned forward to catch his words.

"When I laid the hands on Dirk and the poison came out of him."

Terrance nodded. "You were the only one who could, Brennart. It would have killed me outright, drawing that poison. But what of it?"

Brenn was not listening. He was to his feet and stalking toward Dirk across the wide clearing. Terrance snorted, struggled to his feet, and followed.

The two younger men looked at one another in bafflement.

"Wizards," the Forest Lord explained tersely. "Give me a man of the sword any day. When you dwell for a year with wizards, it takes a lifetime to clear the cobwebs from your musings."

"Not with this one, Your Grace," the Alanyan replied. "He's a rare and suspecting sort, this Brennart, and he doesn't take to conjury. The stuff in him is good, noble as gold, though it is a ore that needs much refinement."

"Spoken like an alchemist," Galliard growled.

Ricardo smiled curiously, and placed his gloved hand on the Forest Lord's shoulder.

"Let us eavesdrop, then, on the dealings of kings and wizards," the Alanyan suggested. "Perhaps in the course of all their high language, someone will welcome a sensible word."

Together, the two of them hastened after the wizard, who hastened after his apprentice and king.

Dirk was half asleep on the rush mattresses, dreaming of brandies and lenses, when Brenn shook him gently. For a moment the little thief thought he was back in Maraven, when he heard his name called softly and awoke to find his old friend crouched above him.

"Y—yes? 'Sit you, Brenn?" he asked.

"You were talking, Dirk. Babbling when I healed you. Something about Faye, was it?"

Dirk closed his eyes and searched his memory.

"Seems like I recollect it, Brenn. Night of the Cwalu, it was, when you and the wizard left town and I was runnin' from rooftop to rooftop with the Watch behind and below me."

Brenn nodded impatiently, hoping his old friend was not off on a long swashbuckling account of his own heroics. But Dirk was intent, his eyes focused somewhere beyond the dark curtain of leaves, on a time he only now remembered.

"Then I seen her," the little thief continued, his eyes still distant, as if he were calling up the memory as he spoke. "Seen her on Cove Road. Traveling west. Toward your tower, Master Wizard."

He turned and stared at Terrance, who looked away.

"Of course, she never . . ." Brenn began, then saw the wizard's averted gaze.

At once he understood. He glared at Terrance, anger warring with disbelief. Sensing the storm at hand, Dirk struggled quickly to his feet and staggered out of earshot, scattering blankets and teacups behind him. Galliard and Ricardo stopped in their progress toward the central tree. In all corners of the clearing, the other cousins and the woodsmen turned toward the central cedar, where the Pretender and his wizard faced one another, bristling like swordsmen.

"I had my reasons, Brenn," Terrance said quietly. "As you know, all of Palerna lay in the balance."

"And what's the life of a girl next to a kingdom, eh?" Brenn asked scornfully. "No matter that she's . . . she's . . ."

"Too much," Terrance explained. "She was unforeseen and unforeseeable. She would have kept you in Maraven, and by now Ravenna would have you. It's that simple: you would have been in Kestrel Tower in the clutches of the Great Witch."

Angrily, the wizard turned away. Grannars rushed chittering from his robes, and phials and scrolls scattered among the roots of the cedar as he waved his arms frantically.

"By the four winds, boy! D'you think I *put* the girl in the tower? Do you think I *handed* her to Ravenna?"

"I don't know, Terrance," Brenn answered coldly. "Whether you meant to or not, no matter what you did or didn't do—she's there now. It's all the same, isn't it? And you never once told me anything."

Terrance looked scornfully at the lad. Somewhere within him a blackness rose and swelled, and for a moment the clearing itself seemed to spin. The wizard felt ill, and a dark song whined in his ears. All of a sudden he hated the petty little wretch in front of him—his whining, puling boy who thought an accident of birth had given him the right to . . .

But what was he thinking? Terrance gasped, clutching his head. How could he think such . . .

The dream. And Ravenna.

He had tried to heal her, had touched her, and had carried back her darkness.

Owls trilled and danced in the trees beyond him. Ricardo stepped toward the wizard and caught him by the shoulders, bracing and holding him up.

Suddenly Terrance felt the weight of his years. He was old, surpassing old, and he had been found out. Despite all the knowledge he had wrested from Ravenna in a grave-littered landscape of dreams, she had taken as much from him. Something deep within him was wounded, was poisoned, and if he stayed with Brenn . . .

He looked at the lad, and felt the same unaccountable black anger rising.

"Leave me alone, Brennart," he said. "Leave me for but a

while.'' Shrugging off Ricardo's steadying hand, he walked toward the stump, reeled, and then collected himself. Galliard took a step toward him, then thought better of it.

Obscured by the bubbling kettle, nearly forgotten in the quarrels and outbursts, Glory lifted her eyes from her concoctions and regarded the wizard curiously.

Terrance seated himself on the stump. Despite his anger, Brenn felt halfway sorry for the old man. The old man propped himself against the bole of the tree and fumbled in his robes in a long, exasperated search. "My flask!" he shouted, and spat out a searing oath. Two squirrels dropped from the branches, stunned by the sound of the words, and lay motionless for a moment before they recovered their senses and scurried off into the darkness.

Her eyes averted, Lapis sidled over to the wizard and handed him the flask.

"Glass, sir," she explained. "Passing lovely to look through, it is."

Terrance snorted, but as he regarded the girl, a softness returned to his face. His shoulders slumped a bit as he gently took the flask and opened it. Brenn caught the faint smell of juniper on the forest air, and deep in the recesses of Corbinwood an array of lights danced closer and closer, as the faeries smelled the liquor, too.

The wizard leaned back, drew from the flask, and regarded the moonlit sky above him.

"There's something about the color of the moon that prophesies," he said aloud, and the cousins, pretending to be busy stopped to regard him. "D'you know what it is, Ricardo?"

The Alanyan shook his head.

"I'm a city lad born and bred, Master Terrance," he said. "I've learned the stars for navigation alone—for the seas and most featureless plains. They tell me nothing of the future."

Terrance sighed. "They are telling *her* something even as we sit here and wonder at their silence," he said bitterly. "D'you know, Ricardo, that they *sing*? The stars, I mean. Archimago says that their music alone is a kind of augury, nestling along the nerves and in the deepness of dreams so that even the least prophetic of us can feel invisible change a second before it happens, and be forewarned even if we can do nothing about it. I could've learned the whole bloody business from him sixty years ago, when I was sharper and in my prenticeship. Augury and divination, entrail and star—the whole lot of it. Would've stood me a sight better in these troublous times, when poetry fails and a wizard's healing infects the healer.''

Ricardo stood silently by the wizard. "What would you have done otherwise, Terrance?" he asked finally. "You who are as born to healing and poetry as that lad over there is to the crown of Palerna."

"Not so, Ricardo," the wizard argued. "I could set it aside. Even now, and after all of these adventures and years, I could abandon wizardry and do something else entirely—something of scholarship, perhaps. Perhaps even alchemy."

Terrance looked slyly at his old friend.

"Aye, wizard," Ricardo replied ironically, a slow smile spreading over his face. "Scholarship and alchemy. *Those* feed the poet and the healer in you. Would it be so horrible to do what you're born to do?" As the Alanyan looked off toward Brenn, who stood fuming beneath the cedar, talking angrily to Galliard and Delia, a strange look of sadness crossed his face.

"I am afraid I have bad news for the lad over there," Terrance said, interrupting Ricardo's reveries. "Despite myself, Ricardo, I have taken a wound."

The words fell into a sharp silence. Intently, the Alanyan examined the face and the eyes of the wizard.

He seems the same, Ricardo concluded. *Neither scar nor burn nor sign of a deeper hurt. And yet . . .*

"I must go away for a while," Terrance said. His words seemed final and forlorn, and he searched himself to see if they rose from the dark wound. He closed his eyes and found them, waiting in a globe of purple light at the point of dark acquaintance.

So it is mine, then, he thought. *Good*. Satisfied, he repeated himself aloud.

"Yes. I must go away."

For a moment the two men sat in silence. Above them the

squirrels, recovered from the wizard's outburst, began to brawl and quarrel in the green maze of the cedar.

"Go away, Terrance?" Ricardo asked. "But what of this . . . Amalek? The curse and the legendary bag . . ."

"The Bag of Ladra will be waiting whether I go or not," Terrance said. "And whether I go or not, the lad must recover it to lift the curse."

Ricardo let out a low whistle. "That boy against a dragon?"

"How else to prove himself a king?" the wizard asked, his eyes still uplifted toward the wheeling stars. "How else to earn the thousand partisans Duke Galliard has promised?"

"King though he may be," Ricardo objected, "he is still a lad of . . . sixteen? Seventeen?"

"Which is where you come into the story, Ricardo," Terrance said somberly, and beckoned him closer. "You and Delia, of course."

Ricardo rolled his eyes as the wizard's meaning dawned on him. "A rare trio we shall make in Alanya," he exclaimed. "An alchemist and two prentices . . ."

"And none of you what you wish or seem to be," Terrance teased. "Go with him, Ricardo," he asked, more seriously now, and the Alanyan nodded before even thinking. "Go with him. But only as far as your heart will take you. The time is coming when we all shall turn to the things we love. Indeed, we *must* do it, or *they* will triumph." He gestured vaguely to the north, towards Maraven and Kestrel Tower.

"It is up to you, Ricardo, to get the lad as far as the Eastmark. The last steps of the way he must make alone, else there will always be rumors that your hand guided his, that Delia planned his strategies."

Ricardo nodded uneasily. The wizard was right: the minds and the hands of others would avail a young king in all but a few of his ventures. And those ventures were all of a kind— lonely and in desolate lands, where a man must master himself to master the beast that confronted him.

"I believe I know what you mean," Ricardo said. "Those last steps have something to do with . . . with . . ."

"With being a king," Terrance said. "Indeed, Ricardo. It has everything to do with just that."

>>> **XVIII** <<<

The week that followed was a time of strains and departures. The merriness and the odd behavior of Corbinwood settled into a brief, unnatural gloom, and the rains of late March came.

In the clearing the woodsmen huddled under blankets and cursed the West Wind, whom it is said that all rains call their father. Fires smouldered and went out entirely, and Galliard's camp was fogged with a low, abiding smoke that even the continual drizzle and shower could not seem to drive away.

It was in this sogginess, this mist and mud, that Terrance packed for a trip south.

"For a month," he told the dumbstruck Brenn. "Perhaps more. Archimago is neither young nor healthy. It may be my last chance to attend to him."

"But Terrance!" the lad exclaimed. "What about the dragon? The curse?"

"As I see it," the wizard replied brightly, slinging a dry blanket over his drenched and thoroughly miserable horse, "that is now your concern, and yours alone."

The wizard recovered his widespread belongings from the various hoards of the cousins, then immersed himself for a long hour in hushed conversation with Ricardo and Galliard under the spreading cedar. Brenn looked on bleakly, water coursing over his soggy hair. In the days following Dirk's healing and Terrance's revelations, he had almost forgiven the old man. After all, Terrance had been right: rushing back into Maraven while Ravenna unleashed her powers and the dead walked through Wall Town would have been foolish, perhaps suicidal. Add to that the fever and weakness of that night, the onset of the plague, and Brenn should be thanking Terrance rather than blaming him.

Nonetheless, he thought of Faye alone in Kestrel Tower, beset by unnamable dangers, and he felt his anger rise again. Terrance had lied to him, Brenn figured, and now he was set to abandon him.

It was the Goniph writ all over, and the same affections warred within the lad as he shuffled through the rain back toward the ladder and climbed up to Galliard's cottage, aloft in the lowest branches of the cedar.

He could see the top of Terrance's hat from the window. Water cascaded off its green and broken brim as the wizard gathered provisions and oddities into a huge rucksack.

"Bless you anyway, Master," Brenn murmured sadly. "Bless you anyway, you meddling old goat."

Dirk, cracking the last of the winter walnuts by the warmth of the cabin fire, turned toward his old comrade.

"You'll fuss and fidget 'til he's gone, and then you'll say your regrets to the rain and the rest of us," the little thief prophesied. "And Master Terrance will be out of earshot to the south somewhere, and nothing you say will touch him or reach him or smooth him over."

"Since when did *you* become my counselor?" Brenn grumbled, still staring out the window. In the midst of the dark rain the forest glittered intermittently. Perhaps the moonlight reflected off leaf and water, or perhaps the faeries had gathered to see off the wizard.

"Since you got rid of Master Terrance," Dirk replied tersely, turning back to the fire. "And it's a fine mess to come all the way from Maraven, passing through Watch and raven, and end up watching the two of you spit at each other like cats."

"He's going," Brenn said disconsolately. "He's going, Dirk, and I think I'm driving him off."

"Call 'im back then," Dirk said, his mouth half full with walnut meat.

Brenn shook his head. "Trouble is . . . I'm beginning to suspect he's right."

Dirk swallowed. "So you mean you want him gone?"

"Yes. No. It's more like . . . a season has passed. And it is best for me to go east with Ricardo and Delia, as we planned. Together the three of us will find what to do with this Amalek, I'll warrant. After all, Ricardo's handy with the sword and an excellent alchemist to hear him tell of it, and Delia . . . well, she's calm and smart, and more resourceful than the two of us together, and . . .''

"Oh, you'll have a fine time of it. Traipsin' through Palerna and Hadrach and all points east like a regular caravan," Dirk said, his gaze on the shifting light of the fire. "All fine and full of heroics, 'cept it leaves me here in the woods, waiting for the wondrous to happen."

Brenn smiled despite himself. *If you only knew*, he thought, *how wondrous it is right under your nose, with faeries and herbs and all kinds of colors. You don't have to go searching for wonders, Master Dirk . . .*

"And yet it's a hard thing to learn," he said aloud, and blushed slightly as Dirk turned a curious eye on him.

"Dirk," Brenn asked, after a moment of embarrassed silence, "how about your going *with* Terrance to Archimago's? And to wherever else his wanderings take him, for take him they assuredly will."

"I—I don't understand, Brennart," Dirk stuttered, pausing with a walnut in each hand.

"Simple, Dirk. If I know old Terrance, he's going to need some anchoring—someone to keep him on the road and out of accidents. And if I ask you to go along, even a furious wizard will know that I harbor no lasting ill thought. Else why should I trust my oldest friend to his magical care?"

It was Dirk's turn to blush, and Brenn watched him crouch by the fire, and stand, and crouch again, his thoughts racing over the options. Finally, the little thief smiled and stuffed the nuts into his pockets.

"Why not, Brenn?" he asked, his voice excited and a little triumphant. "Since everyone else is bound for adventure, why not me?"

So that was how Dirk the Reiver rode out of Corbinwood at the side of Terrance the Mage, and once again in the recent history of Palerna, thief joined with wizard in a time most uncertain and dark.

It did not take Terrance long to see the little thief for what he was—a companion rough-hewn but promising, whose presence was a peace offering from the apprentice king.

They left in the rain that very afternoon, huddled atop two docile horses. Gaunt wizard and little thief, their shapes as ill-matched as their origins, both weaved unsteadily on horseback. The big dog Bracken, grown fat and lazy from the attentions of Glory and Lapis, waddled merrily behind them, nose to the trail.

"How do you plan to magick us past the Watch, Terrance?" Dirk asked.

The wizard did not answer; but looked behind him. Solemnly he dismounted. He knelt beside Bracken and hugged the old dog.

"No," he said. "I need you to stay with Lapis."

Then just as solemnly, he mounted again. Merrily the dog trotted back to the girl as Dirk and Terrance faded into the rain and mist. Watching from Galliard's cabin, Brenn lost them finally behind a stand of evergreen.

"Godspeed," he whispered. "Safe journeys to both of you. May the reef bow its head as your boat passes over."

He smiled sadly. He had almost forgotten the old Maravenian blessing and farewell.

Terrance, too, looked back once, as the evergreens rose above him and swallowed the last sight of the cedar and the Forest Lord's cabin, of the pale face that watched them mournfully from the window.

"Godspeed, lad," he whispered in return, as the woods around him grew loud with birdsong. Dirk, struggling manfully to stay atop his horse, turned in the saddle and stared impatiently at the wizard. "Godspeed, and forfend it that my last attempt to keep from hurting you be the very thing that hurts you the most."

"'Tis up in the day for philosophy, Master Terrance," the little thief urged. Reluctantly, the wizard flicked the reins against the withers of his horse, and the beast broke into a canter.

An even more somber departure took place the next morning, when Brenn started east with Ricardo and Delia, their destination Alanya and the lair of the dragon Amalek.

The rain let up a bit for their riding forth. The air in the clearing was heavy and damp, with the deep, loamy smell of drowned woods. All around him Brenn saw the faint faerie lights in the distance, as though the Invisible Folk had gathered to see him off.

Delia sat on the rickety seat of Terrance's old wagon, the reins in her hands. She was intent on a silk cloak Ponder had given her, tracing its bright decorations with her finger, her lips moving as she committed drawing and lettering to memory. Perched on her shoulder was a small sea eagle who regarded Brenn with a curious but strangely familiar gaze.

Meanwhile, Ricardo and Brenn loaded the vehicle for the trip across the plains. Plenty of blankets they spread over the wagon bed, and dried fruit and bread for a week's journey. Then the two of them stood and faced each other, waiting for Galliard to gather the cousins and for the goodbyes to begin.

At once, they all assembled in the clearing, from enormous Ponder down to Lapis. All but Thomas carried odd items, wrapped in sailcloth and parchment and, in Lapis' case, in silk.

"Make room in the wagon bed for whatever it is they have brought us," Brenn told Ricardo. "It will all stand us in good stead, if we are to believe the bodings of wizards."

As Terrance had instructed them, the cousins brought forth the first things they had ever stolen. Two small branches Sendow carried, intricately marked with strange designs.

"Rune tree branches," Sendow explained. " 'Twas but a nut when I first took it from an alchemist's garden."

Brenn nodded soberly, trying not to laugh at the notion of stern, gray-eyed Sendow stealing nuts like a squirrel.

Thomas was next, whispering the song he had stolen into Brenn's ear. The lad's training in poetry and incantation served him in good stead at last, for he mastered it on only the third repetition, committing the tune to memory.

" 'Tis a good song for the road, Thomas," he said bravely.

The poet shook his head. " 'Tis no song for bellowing abroad," he cautioned. "Save it until you need it. I trust it will tell you when," he added darkly.

Nodding, Brenn breathed the song to himself in silence as he accepted Jimsett's serpentine roots, Ponder's map, and the red perfume bottle from little Lapis, which reflected the light merrily as she lifted it to Ricardo's hands.

Galliard was the last to step forward. Slowly, most reluctantly of all, he set his black shortbow and the quiver of arrows in the wagon bed.

"Surely not, Galliard!" Brenn exclaimed. "Of all the things you have!"

"It was the first of all too many lifts," the Forest Lord admitted. "And the wizard said that the first fruit of our arts should ride with you into Alanya."

"But there must be a *way*," Brenn protested. "Something else besides the bow. You're *known* by it, after all. It's like . . . like setting aside your name."

"The time has come," Galliard said quietly, his eyes still resting on the black bow in the wagon bed, "when names are set aside. Principalities and powers, might and dominion—none are important if the curse is not lifted. I have waited for you to free me, King Brennart of Palerna, and when you have done so I shall be bound to you forever."

"May the laces that bind you be light, Galliard," Brenn said, resting his hand on his cousin's shoulder. "And if it is at all possible, I shall return the bow to you when the dragon is defeated and the curse is lifted."

It felt odd to reassure the Forest Lord himself. Brenn felt as though he was dressed in borrowed clothes. All of this talk of exotic creatures and distant evils seemed strange and unbelievable, and stranger still was the prospect that he was about to embark on a journey to another country, where he would set himself against real dragons and real curses, his only companions a ragtag pair of alchemists.

Still, Galliard didn't laugh at the promise, and the assembled cousins treated him soberly, with dignity and respectful silence. They stood behind the wagon as Delia clicked her tongue and the horses began to move, and seated in the bed of the wagon among branches and blankets and bottles and roots, Brenn wondered aloud when he would see any of them again.

"Oh, soon enough," Ricardo replied with a laugh, stretching his legs as he seated himself beside Brenn. "It's three days to Hadrach and three days returning. I don't expect you to stay long. You'll have the dragon dancing to your tune before you know it."

"Especially with you two there to help me," Brenn said.

The Alanyan smiled and shook his head.

"I think you know that will be impossible, Master Brennart.

We are escorts only, Delia and I. We shall accompany you as far as we can—perhaps into the Aralu itself, though something within me tells me you will find that thicket alone. Wherever we part, though, whether it is at the mouth of Amalek's lair or only a mile up the road, the longest part of the journey is in your heart, and there a simple step may be a thousand miles or only the step that it is. When the time comes, it will depend on you.''

Sullenly, Brenn propped himself against the side of the wagon and pulled his hood over his face, regarding the eagle sullenly from beneath the dark folds of the cloth. He felt betrayed on all accounts, betrayed and herded into this adventure, no matter how brave and willing he tried to be.

And yet Ricardo was right. Somewhere within him, Brenn had already known that he would face Amalek by himself when the time came.

But there is still time to change minds, he thought hopefully, as the wagon jostled through thick roots and underbrush. *Three days to Hadrach is a long time for convincing.*

The Alanyan lay back and watched the dappled leaves pass over him. He had hitched his horse to the back of the wagon, but for now he was content to ride in luxury with his two companions, to pass the time with listening and lore. Lazily, he steepled his hands behind his head and gave forth a brief, sharp whistle. The reciting owl flashed out of the tree and alighted on his shoulder. Ricardo reached into a pouch at his belt and, drawing forth a strip of dried meat, dangled it in front of the bird.

"Sing us a warding against melancholia, bird!" he exclaimed, closing his eyes.

The owl gulped the jerky, rolled its square, tufted head, and burst forth in a clear alto voice.

> *Ha ha! Ha ha! This world doth pass*
> *Most merrily I'll be sworn,*
> *For many an honest Indian ass*
> *Goes for a unicorn.*

> *Fara diddle dyno,*
> *This is idle fyno.*

> *Tie hie! Tie hie! O sweet delight!*
> *He tickles this age that can*
> *Call Tullia's ape a marmasyte*
> *And Leda's goose a swan.*

> > *Fara diddle dyno,*
> > *This is idle fyno.*

Brenn smiled, though he didn't find the jests especially funny.

"I've never had a family," he confided quietly to Ricardo, after the owl had finished singing and the clearing was lost behind them. "At least, not that I really remembered. And though I *like* Galliard and the rest of them, I expect I don't know how to be cousinly to the likes of the landed gentry in exile."

"Well, you *are* landed gentry in exile," Delia called back to him, "and you'd best learn to live with the family you're given."

Ricardo laughed softly, and the reciting owl, taking the noise as applause, leapt into the air and circled the moving wagon, hooting his final chorus.

> *So so! So so! Fine English days!*
> *For false play is no reproach,*
> *For he that doth the coachman praise*
> *May safely use the coach.*

> > *Fara diddle dyno,*
> > *This is idle fyno.*

With a "fara diddle" and a "dyno," the unusual lot of them—thief and alchemist, reciting owl and charger and mournful-faced wagon horses—passed through the hanging branches of Corbinwood and forded the Boniluce at a spot both shallow and safe.

It was there that the owl hushed in the midst of an "idle fyno," and they saw the woodsmen at a distance. Lean, rough-looking folk they were, dressed in green and slipping from tree to tree like wild animals or hamadryads. Ricardo sat up and set his hand on Delia's shoulder, and the girl reined in the horses. Still and apprehensive, the three travelers watched the column of partisans cross the path ahead of them and vanish into the woods again.

Before they were completely out of sight, the last of the woodsmen turned toward the wagon. With a long, direct stare he regarded the lad in the wagon bed. Then the man bowed—not a Parthian gesture full of kneelings and dippings of the head and shows of sugary respect, but the bow of a man unaccustomed to bowing to anyone or anything. Then, just as briskly, the woodsman turned and followed his companions into obscurity.

Brenn fidgeted and fingered Lapis' perfume bottle, his eyes on the empty path. This bowing and respect would take getting used to.

From the corner of his eye, the Alanyan regarded the lad seated in the wagon bed.

A curious mixture, this would-be Brennart, Ricardo thought. *Nothing of the kingly in him, it would seem—and to hear Terrance tell, there was little of sorcerer or thief, either.*

Oh, well. He lay back again and closed his eyes. *Perhaps it's a long apprenticeship. After all, such things are familiar in my trade.*

He smiled and opened his eyes yet again. The trees above him thinned rapidly, then suddenly seemed to fall away altogether as the old wagon cleared the forest and rolled into the Palernan grasslands. Ricardo lay back and dozed, dreaming of adventures on horseback, of charges and musters.

Delia, her golden eyes on the plains ahead of her, clicked her tongue at the horses and let her thoughts ramble and race.

Serpentine root. She could smell it in the wagon behind her. That, at least, was good. As for the lifts of the other cousins . . . well, time and circumstance would see to that. Something told her that all the ingredients were there, that the substances and the mixtures were right.

The world was alembic and retort. She believed that thoroughly. From serpentine root and thieves, from an unready king and an old wagon, from the Aralu and the labyrinth of thorns Brenn must pass through, only to find the dragon at its heart . . .

It was dismal to think upon it. Something in that of the wizard's dark acquaintance. But the world was alembic and retort. She had been taught the six ways of remembering in the earliest lessons. Mathematics showed it, and geometry and astronomy, in their rhythm and regularity.

There was also an old song that said so, that brought music to the heart's memory. From Ruthic or Random it had come. She could not remember which, though she recalled the melody and the first consoling verse. Quietly, her hands light on the reins, Delia began to sing.

> *Truth is the triall of it selfe*
> *And needs no other touch,*
> *And purer then the purest Gold,*
> *Refine it ne'ere so much.*

"Well," she whispered, after a long, deep breath, "I suspect that the worst is yet to come, and that we will pass through it, too."

They reached the Maravenian lines within an hour. The troops were spread thinly across the plains from north to south, but all in all there were a good five thousand of them, each man with orders to stop and inspect any vehicle passing into or out of Corbinwood.

Brenn peered out from under the blankets. Ricardo sat beside him in the bed of the wagon, a silk mask drawn over his face. He looked like a bandit from the ballads.

"Careful, Brenn!" he whispered. "Stay under cover. Be still."

Delia turned on the seat and glanced at them. The eagle whistled on her shoulder. A black kerchief fluttered on a stick she held.

" 'Tis, the arranged place?" she asked, and Ricardo nodded. "And his arm is speckled with lampblack and woad?"

The Alanyan nodded again.

"Haven't you something for the young master?" Delia goaded. "And some words to accompany it?"

As though he were following the orders of his own apprentice,

Ricardo produced a vial from his pocket. Quickly, he slipped it beneath the blanket, as the owl at his shoulder recited yet again.

> *This distilling liquor drink thou off,*
> *When presently through all thy veins shall run*
> *A cold and drowsy humor; for no pulse*
> *Shall keep his native progress, but surcease;*
> *No warmth, no breath shall testify thou livest;*
> *And in this borrowed likeness of shrunk death*
> *Thou shalt continue two and forty hours,*
> *And then awake as from a pleasant sleep.*

Brenn looked at the vial, held his nose, and swallowed the contents.

"By the winds, I hope it works!" Ricardo swore.

"What do you mean—you said . . ." Brenn began in alarm, but the drowsiness was already upon him. Sinking into a deep and pleasant sleep, then deeper still, the last he saw was the dark of the blanket above him, the last he heard was the brief outcry of the Ruthic girl in the wagon.

"Then *now*, brother eagle!" Delia said. "Now, and godspeed!"

Slumbering in unnatural stillness, Brenn did not see the eagle launch from her shoulder and speed toward the red-armored men in the distance. With a shriek it passed over them, and with an outcry and flurry of bows, the Watchmen filled the air with arrows around it.

Their attack was too little too late. The bird soared to a great height, wheeled above them, and sailed serenely toward the west. Helpless, the Watchmen milled about their campsite. Then six of them, armed and flushed with anger, rode out to meet the wagon, but stopped several feet in front of it.

" 'Tis you again, Alanyan," their lieutenant said, his face obscured by the silk mask used as protection against the plague. "Your family business is concluded, is it not? Why do you fly the plague flag? You are both well, it seems."

Several of the Watchmen eyed their leader curiously.

"He passed this way but a week ago," the lieutenant explained, leaning forward in the saddle.

"I return to Alanya, with the body of my brother, who has met the Death" Ricardo said.

"Our condolences, sir," the lieutenant responded mechanically, but his sergeant was more insistent.

"Let me be the first to pay my respects to the dead," the man offered. "There are carrion birds about, and we must assure that all is secure."

"That bird overhead?" Ricardo asked innocently. "Merely an eagle given to me by a wizard. I have let him go, for he was most unhappy to live among humans."

Ricardo smiled oddly. It was curious to tell the complete truth.

"Natheless," the sergeant said, and moved toward the wagon bed.

Compliantly, Ricardo reached back and, lifting the blanket, exposed the pale, black-spotted arm of the body beneath it. Gasping, the sergeant raised handkerchief to his face and backed away rapidly.

"We have seen enough," the lieutenant said, waving the wagon through the Maravenian line. "and may the gods spare the lot of you. Keep to the road and out of the villages."

It was an hour before the raven settled in the camp and in a hoarse voice told them they had failed.

"The eagle is not the one at all," it boded from a tent post, wagging its bald head. The Watchmen looked at each other in consternation.

"And the Great Witch is not pleased."

"Then the Pretender was magicked and in the bed of the wagon!" the sergeant shouted, preparing to sound the alarum along the lines.

"Wait!" the lieutenant ordered, extending his gloved hands. "This were best done silently, and by a few. They are only an hour ahead of us, their progress slow, our horses fast. I shall take one man and follow them."

He pointed to another masked Watchman—a short man, who nodded and mounted at once.

"There is still time to make amends," the lieutenant said, his foot in the stirrup as the sergeant held the reins of his chestnut horse, ''and since it will be my head bobbing atop the noose, I must be the one to redress the wrong.''

They rode from the camp as swiftly as eagles, the long strides of their horses swallowing the plains. Soon they vanished on the eastern horizon, and shaken, the sergeant and the rest of the encampment returned to the long business of siege, watch, and waiting.

>>> **XIX** <<<

Her cries brought Dragmond running. To the Chamber of Candles, to the topmost room of the tower he raced, sword drawn and three burly Watchmen behind him. He took three, four, of the stairs at a stride, losing his balance once, then again, until the men behind him feared he would break his neck. And yet the king raced on, imagining poison and knives, Ravenna trapped forever in croglath.

Imagining things new risen from dark incantations, smelling of fire and ordure.

At the top of the stairwell he paused and gathered himself, his breath clipped and shallow. The dire thoughts left him then, and he discovered he was alone by Ravenna's door, his bodyguards crouched apprehensively behind him, their shields raised, their faces uncertain in the nodding torchlight.

He set his hand to the latch and paused once more. Only now did he consider that the knife or the creature might still be in the room beyond, waiting for him to enter.

For who knew and what guaranteed that he would not burst in upon death or danger?

''Oh, help!'' the witch exclaimed from the other side of the door. Her voice was weaker now, a strange whistling sound in its midst as though her throat had been slit.

''Danjel,'' the King ordered. ''Into the chamber.''

The young swordsman behind him wavered, looking at his two companions.

"We'll be behind ye, lad," the sergeant soothed, his accent rough in the street brogue of Gaunt. Reluctantly Danjel stepped forward, drawing his sword. Dragmond stepped aside and behind the young man, keeping Danjel between him and whatever lay in the room ahead.

Behind them footsteps echoed on the bare stone of the stairwell, and an eerie, melodic whistling rose from the darkness below. Then the high thin tenor voice rose after it, as they knew it would.

> *Tes nobles jambes, sous les volants qu'elles chassent,*
> *Tourmentent les désirs obscurs et les agacent,*
>   *Comme deux sorcières qui font*
> *Tourner un philtre noir dans un vase profond.*

"Think about it, lad," the sergeant warned harshly through clenched teeth. "Would ye rather face what's loomin' ahind the door or what's in back of ye?"

Danjel listened for no more than a second. Then, catching his breath, he burst into the Chamber of Candles.

The Great Witch lay on the marble map, in the midst of guttering flames. In her nightmare it seemed she had risen from the hard little cot by the balcony and walked to the center of the room, overturning candelabrum and lamp in her staggering, senseless attempt to flee whatever haunted her dream.

Immediately the King was at her side, cursing himself for his cowardice but a moment before. *Wake her*, he told himself, *just wake her, and thank the four winds that Lightborn did not* . . .

The scar on her neck was a livid purple and burned at the touch. She caught his gaze, her eyes fathomless and black and empty beyond the worst he could imagine.

"Oh help me, Dragmond," she murmured. "He has killed me again."

The King cradled her in his arms and murmured hollow, angry

words. He was reluctant to touch her, but when he did marvelled at how cold she felt, as though all the heat from her body had rushed to the pocked and coruscated skin of the scar.

Something in him rejoiced at her wounds, her weakness. He was surprised at his own elation.

The Watchmen stood awkwardly behind him, their eyes on the ceiling, on the blackened candles, on their boots.

"I shall kill him, Ravenna," Dragmond swore softly, half guiltily. "And the boy I shall draw and quarter, and oh I shall scatter to the raposa all the noble houses of Aquila, and all for that scar, that terrible scar . . ."

A shadow passed over his shoulder, and behind him the Watchmen caught their breath sharply. Dragmond turned, and saw Lightborn standing in the doorway.

Suddenly he felt foolish and helpless as the cold eye of his captain appraised him from the higher position.

"The wizard did it," Dragmond said, and cursed himself for whining. The Pale Man frowned and nodded slowly.

"I know," he said softly, almost compassionately. "The wizard is a monster. All wizards are."

The Watchmen glanced at Lightborn uneasily. Danjel slipped over between the sergeant and the third man, a hefty merchant's son from Stormpoint. The three of them watched, fearful and fascinated, as though from a great height and distance, they watched a leopard stalking its prey.

"Help me," Ravenna repeated, even more desperately, more pathetically than before, her gray eyes wavering and unsettled.

"Indeed we shall, m'lady," Lightborn said, his voice oddly consoling. "Heal her, Your Grace."

"Heal her?"

"The King's Touch, sire." He was insinuating, convincing. "The hands. The healing." He smiled.

The Watchmen's gaze passed suddenly from the Pale Man to the kneeling king. Dragmond swallowed, looked at Ravenna's scar.

"But—"

" 'Tis in the lore, Dragmond," Ravenna rasped. "You must do this for me."

Uncertain, the king turned to Lightborn, who nodded.

"You are the anointed, sire. You are the crowned. Your hands restore where surgery despairs."

Nervously, Dragmond looked to the Watchmen, who averted their eyes.

"Heal me," whispered Ravenna. "Lay your hands at my throat and do what I say."

Dutifully the king complied. Her throat was hot beneath his fingers. He closed his eyes at her bidding, and while the soldiers watched, Lightborn slipped behind them and stood in the doorway, his hand on the pommel of his sword.

"Now think of green," Ravenna urged. "Of green shade. Of light on a cedar."

Dragmond closed his eyes, and the room whined and hushed. He thought of the garden at the foot of the tower, of wild liana and elder, of thorn and black maple. He thought of them green for a moment, the gold with the wind of autumn passing through them into . . .

Suddenly, unexplainably, the Great Witch cried out. White fire coursed up the king's arms into his shoulder, and yellow he saw, then red, then violet, then colors he could not name.

For a moment he remembered this same room, twenty years ago. Or was it thirty? He thought how little it had changed— the same angle of the noonday sun on the candles, the same smell of feathers and burnt wax, the Great Witch standing . . . standing . . .

He shifted as he lay on the floor, but his legs failed him. His hands were white-hot, blistered, but slowly the pain was receding, and he was back in that room twenty years ago . . .

Or was it thirty?

Nothing had changed. Nothing since he began.

The room sank into a deep and abiding black, and he saw no more.

"By the four winds, it worked," Lightborn observed, as casually as though he were remarking upon an unusual shape in the clouds.

The Watchmen startled at the voice behind them. The Pale Man had moved again—moved while their eyes and thoughts were riveted to the king lying in the midst of the candles on the marbled map, to the Great Witch rising to her feet, the scar on her neck vanished entirely.

"Worked?" she said in horror, staring at Dragmond sprawled at her feet.

Lightborn was silent, and three ravens settled on the balcony railing, boding in low, rattling voices.

Ravenna leaned over and placed her fingers at the neck of the King. "Dead!" she hissed, with a baleful stare at Lightborn. Her eyes flashed black, then gray, then black again.

Do not show fear, the Pale Man told himself. *Above all, show no fear now.*

"Oh, but see to your own neck, m'lady," he said with a smile, and even the Great Witch shuddered.

"We're ruined," she announced bleakly, and with a swirl of black garments, turned toward the balcony.

"Oh no," Lightborn whispered after her. "Not yet, m'lady." *Now!* his instincts said to him. *Now the balance shifts and it shifts forever.*

He drew his sword from the scabbard.

Now now now . . .

The sergeant fell before the other two noticed, his cry cut off by the swift stroke of the sword. The big lad from Stormpoint turned quickly, but the captain's blade whistled under his ear and blood sprayed across the chamber, startling the Ravens.

Danjel was slower still, his sword half-drawn when Lightborn turned to him. Confused, the lad saw the Great Witch turn at the sound, saw the surprise passing over her face, and tried to defend himself quickly, pitifully, as the hot sword passed beneath his guard, toward the unarmored spot just below the red leather breastplate, where cloth and skin alone stood in the path of the glittering steel point . . .

. . . and where the sword stopped short. Lightborn eyed him over the blade, his stare cool and regarding.

"Begone with you, lad," he hissed, and nodded toward the door.

For a moment Danjel was stunned, motionless. His jaw dropped and his knees wavered.

"Before I change my mind," Lightborn threatened, and nodded again.

Danjel was no fool. He turned one last time at the door and saw was them standing over the king—Great Witch and Pale Man. They seemed more distant, their words more cluttered and clouded, until, as he descended the stairwell, he thought he had dreamed this all, that soon he would awake, alive and untouched, in the barracks at the border of Grospoint or even in his bed at home, the days in the Watch a pointless nightmare he would soon cease to remember.

"Ruined," Ravenna said again. "No matter how many of the Watchmen you waste, no matter how many you spare. We are ruined, Captain Lightborn."

The ravens, startled by the sudden flurry of violence in the chamber, still fluttered about, calling boisterously to each other. Ravenna raised her voice above the shrieking and wingbeat of the birds, but Lightborn seemed to notice none of this, his gaze calm and reflective as he looked upon the dead king.

One of the birds alighted on the chamber floor and hopped across marbled Parthia, the dark stone that represented the Bay of Ashes. It cocked its head brightly at the king's pale hand. Ravenna, sensing its intentions, brushed it away with her foot.

"Why ruined?" Lightborn asked finally. Ravenna was suddenly alert.

"Why, because . . . regardless of our powers, we are nothing without a king on the throne," she replied cautiously, in her voice almost a question. "When Namid and Galliard and the peasant brotherhoods in the countryside hear of Dragmond's death, they will assume—"

"Nothing," Lightborn interrupted. "They will assume nothing."

His gaze met that of the Great Witch.

"Why are these Watchmen not . . . 'wasted,' as you say?" he asked her, as though he were asking a child a simple question of grammar or geometry.

"The cwalu," she breathed in response, her black eyes fixed upon the Pale Man. "The walking dead."

Suddenly it dawned on her. Ravenna smiled slowly—a lazy, wicked smile. "What is good enough for the common soldier . . ." she said.

Lightborn rejoiced inwardly.

Good. She will do anything.

"But the third Watchman," she protested. "The one you let go."

"I have plans for him," Lightborn explained cryptically. "Trust me."

And though she did not trust him, though she would trust a snake or wyvern before she would trust this man before her, his white armor spattered with a spray of drying blood, Ravenna nodded, and walked to the center of the room.

"But what of you?" she asked, as the captain set right the candelabra and circled around her, lighting the tapers. "How do I know that you will remain silent?"

"Trust me," he said again.

"Trust me in return," she replied. "For I promise you enough gold to fill your heart and assure your silence."

The Pale Man smiled and bowed gracefully. Ravenna raised her hands, rocked back on her heels, and began the chant, the words cascaded readily back to her.

> *At the round earth's imagin'd corners, blow*
> *Your trumpets, and arise, arise*
> *From death, your numberlesse infinities*
> *Of soules, and to your scattered bodies goe . . .*
> *All whom the flood did, and fire shall o'erthrow,*
> *All whom warre, dearth, age, agues, tyrannies*
> *Despaire, law, chance, hath slaine . . .*

And lying sprawled across the map of Palerna, Dragmond's body began to stir. Below the enchantments, by candlelight in the maid's quarters, Faye also stirred on her cot.

The cry of her mistress had wakened her. For an hour Faye had sat there, wide awake, hearing the sound of footsteps in the corridor. She did not know why she had not gone to see after Ravenna, except that she was tired and that she knew others would come to the mistress's aid, if aid were truly needed.

From her quarters, late at night, Ravenna seemed less powerful, less compelling.

Faye sighed, turned again on the cot. She had dreamed the

same dream. The young man appeared in it again, disheveled, dressed once more in the cloak she had worn when she came to Kestrel Tower. She still could not see his face, but there was something about him knew she should remember.

Faye reached beneath her pillow and drew forth the book. It was a thin volume, thin enough to escape notice on the shelves in the library, where it had been wedged between volumes on agriculture and theology for some time, judging from the dust it had collected. Faye had taken it down, wiped it with a cloth, and started to set it back on the shelf, when the front cover fell open and she saw the curious markings on the frontispiece.

They were not letters she knew, and she prided herself on knowing letters. Of all the maids in the tower, she was the one who could read beyond a few simple words. She had no idea how that knowledge had come to her, but there was another knowledge, even deeper and more cloudy in its origins, that told her to tell no one about her reading.

That reading had done her no good, for the frontispiece was marked with letters upon letters upon letters, as though one scribe after another had tried his hand—sometimes in the Roman alphabet, sometimes in Greek or Cyrilic or Umbrian runes. The result was a mish-mash—indecipherable scratchings on the thin vellum page.

Curiously, Faye had looked at the spine of the book. She looked at it again by candlelight, alone now in her room.

"*The Leaves of Morrigan*," she whispered, then laughed quietly at her own thick-headedness.

"You ninny!" she whispered to herself, hiding the book deep in her bedding with a silent vow to replace it on the morrow. "Next time you steal a book, make sure it's one you can read to while away the midnights!"

The Watch lieutenant reined in his horse.

In the distance the wagon rocked over the rough plains. It was in sight now, and the Maravenian lines lost in the distance behind him.

The lieutenant turned to his companion—the small cavalryman on a black pony—and chuckled slowly.

"Looks as though they're safe enough for the moment, Dirk," he said.

Dirk swore loudly and flicked the reins against the neck of the pony beneath him; it was all the stalwart little creature could do, evidently, to keep up with the longer strides of Terrance's horse. And yet the pony showed more spirit, more bottom, as it quickly closed ground with the wizard, just in time for Dirk to discover that Terrance was beginning a lecture, spinning some yarn or theory into the waterladen air.

". . . not as momentous, say, as a meteor storm or the tidings of war. Perhaps not even a season's change, but more than a change in the weather, it is, and damned if it doesn't come at the start of my exile, when I am most useless and most away!"

"Beg pardon, sir?" Dirk asked, tossing aside his Watch helmet, doing his best to stay on horse. His right foot slipped from the stirrup and suddenly, dangerously, the saddle shifted beneath him. Perfunctorily, the wizard turned in the saddle, his thin, gristly arm snaking out quickly to catch the falling lad and set him aright.

"I was saying, Dirk, something of moment has come to pass. Something large and northerly, and I don't mean just that we've sprung Brenn out of the siege. No, there's something astir in Maraven, I'll wager, and no doubt it deals with the fate of the throne."

"No doubt?" Dirk asked, his curiosity sudden and fierce. The wizard wrestled off his red lieutenant's breastplate and dropped it unceremoniously from the saddle. Then with a click of his tongue he turned his horse south, away from the trail Ricardo and Delia had followed, back toward the banks of the Boniluce.

Balancing precariously, Dirk turned his mount and followed.

"How do you know for sure, sir? Divining? Augury?"

Terrance sighed and regarded the slip of a boy beside him struggling bravely with the unruly horse.

"Do they always believe in sleight of hand?" the wizard asked quietly. And it occurred to him that a strange new freedom lay ahead of him. Though his botched attempt to heal the Great Witch had returned harshly, wounding him in a silent and secret way so that even a thought of Brenn ran him the danger of anger, of resentment and even of jealousies, there might well be some good to what they called the dark acquaintance.

For now, the business at the enemy lines over, Terrance was off on his own again. Perhaps to Archimago's. Perhaps to Umbria, or Aegypt, or even beyond to Constantinople. What was it that held him now?

After all, Brenn would never be far away; indeed, the wizard had sent a lookout, aloft and sharp of talon and eye.

Bertilak had jumped at the chance. Somewhere, north of the wizard, a translated eagle was on the wing, changed and delighted by the same spell Terrance had rushed Brenn into that frightening morning in the wagon. Freed of his human form, Bertilak's only instinct was to guard the untried lad who traveled east toward the Aralu and the dragon who lived there.

Terrance sighed, at home again in the great uncertainties.

Now was time for a new apprentice. A genuine sort, with aptitudes. Groomed for the wizardry and not for a throne.

"For when a man drops out of a story," he murmured, as Dirk leaned forward in the saddle, straining to listen, "it is not like a book, where he walks off the pages into nothing, his tale no longer of import or interest. No, he begins a new story elsewhere.

"And who is to say that the new story is not the one intended all along?"

Terrance spun about in the saddle triumphantly, catching the toppling Dirk by the back of his tunic. With one muscular movement, he hauled the lad up behind him in the saddle. Together the two of them rode out of the morning mist, the pony following merrily behind them, a small thief lighter.

"No. Not augury. Simple cause and effect. And balances. The old girl wounded me, Dirk. There's something within me all dark and boding now, and it's her doing. Or rather mine, for laying hands upon her in attempt to heal . . . well, a wound I gave her long ago."

Dirk looked at the wizard curiously, and Terrance saw a sly smile cross the lad's face.

"They don't heal easily from them wounds, do they, Master Terrance?" the little thief asked, and winked knowingly.

So he's figured it already, Terrance thought. *He's ten years older on the streets than the other. Older than I am, for that matter. It's the kind of calculation she had when she was young.*

He whistled, and Bracken emerged from the underbrush some fifty yards ahead of them, dripping with mud and river water. The dog regarded them curiously, then belched and padded along behind them, his tail wagging peacefully.

Alone? the wizard thought with an ironic smile. *There's enough to do while I'm mending, and maybe beyond that. By the four winds, it does begin again. It always does.*

"Not augury, Dirk. The first thing you must know is the limits of augury. The second is verse, and the third is alchemy. The fourth and fifth will come later. In the meantime, there is a simple writ somewhere here in my robes . . . just a moment, I'm certain it's here somewhere amid the inkwells and the grammars . . ."

Brenn had not been awake long when Delia stopped the wagon at the crest of a hill. Below the Palernan plain rolled to the east, its farthermost reaches lost in the shadows of oncoming night.

Ricardo had urged that they stop. Dragons and curses were urgent matters, he maintained, but travel in these regions was downright dangerous by night. The Plains of Sh'Ryll were somewhere about, though after a long consultation over Ponder's silk map, neither he nor Delia was altogether sure just where they were.

" 'Tis a perilous spot by day," Ricardo cautioned. "The old Umbrians sent their boys into the midst of it with a day's supply of food. Those who came back claimed to have been gone but a day, and indeed they were still young and fresh, the bread they had carried away with them not even stale. But as the Umbrians measured time, it had been years since the boys were last seen. The infants who had waved goodbye to them were grandparents now, or gone to their fathers. Danger or no, it is said that the Plains of Sh'Ryll grant you visions, if you choose to see them.''

"And you believe this?" Brenn asked, and the Alanyan was silent. The lad snorted and squinted toward the darkening east in hopes of a glimpse of the twice-named river. The Eastmark, the Palernans called it, but from Ricardo he had learned that the Alanyans called it the Xanthus.

Names of rivers were not the only things he had learned from his fellow travelers over the last two days. Alanya was a place of a thousand legends, it seemed, and the Ruthic Islands a place of curious sciences—of opticks and anatomy, of chemistry and alchemy. Brenn had learned from both Ricardo and Delia eagerly at first. But the days were long and windswept, the plains looking roughly the same no matter where you turned. And night was no real respite, for the bedding was hard and the fires low or absent to escape detection.

Brenn groaned and stood up in the wagon bed. Above him yet another eagle whirled and sped to the east. It was as though the bird Delia had brought from Corbinwood continued to follow them at a distance, but given the nature of the creature, Brenn thought it more likely that the wagon was simply an object of curiosity for creatures in this bare, wild land.

Far on the purple horizon, Brenn saw pinpoints of light winking and bobbing. Caravan wagons, Ricardo had told him. Bound from Jaleel across the Eastmark and north to Stormpoint, where they would follow the Palernan coast up to Maraven, their beds laden with saffron and salt, with clove-spiced and Auvergne wines, with bolts of silk and rare cotton cloth, and occasionally with exotic animals for the bestiaries along Teal Front: monkeys and century-old talking parrots and boofers—long little dogs that danced for bread and cheeses.

"April is the trader's month," Ricardo explained, slipping from the wagon bed onto the back of the proud black stallion he had brought with him. Naranja was the horse's name, and a finer specimen of animal Brenn had never seen—there was no telling where the Alanyan had purchased it, if he had not acquired it by less respectable means.

Early on, Brenn had decided *not* to ask where the horse had come from. Stamping and impatient for level ground, Naranja danced and snorted, yearning no doubt for a long gallop and the sound of the wind.

"The trader's month," Ricardo repeated, settling into the saddle. "The first time since the end of fall that hot-blooded things such as spice and coniures can make the northern trip to temperate climes. 'Tis Alanyans that drive the distant wagonry. Alanyans, or Umbrians, or the coblyns, the little people from southernmost Auster, where the ice crazes still waters until March."

As the Alanyan pointed at the distant caravan, Brenn noticed an array of wagons approaching even closer, scarcely a hundred yards from where the three of them stood watching. He tugged at Ricardo's tunic, but the big alchemist ignored him, his eyes still fixed on the far horizon.

"Ricardo . . . Delia . . ." Brenn insisted. "What of . . . of *these* approaching?"

The three of them watched the caravan pass by, as though they were spectators at a silent, exotic parade.

For the caravan in the foreground moved without a sound, no hoofbeat of horses or creaking of wheels or cry from driver to drover. The last light of day flickered crazily off the bronze ornaments on the wagons, off the red billowing sails hoisted in the midst of the wagon beds. Little men drove the vehicles, no larger than five-year-old children, their long beards tied like scarves about their necks and shoulders.

At the back of each wagon, the wrights had sculptured the faces of the four winds. Brenn had seen it before on the sterns of ships; sailors said that the carvings were intended to bring wind into the sails, and some of the older men claimed that the Stern Winds actually worked.

But this was a different version. The faces of icy Gogleth and hot Dehevol, of young Durain and ancient Gorlewin—all were swollen and cross-eyed and clownish, as though the winds had set about to blow into a bottle. A sea urchin from his earliest days in Maraven, Brenn found the carvings irreverent, unsettling.

On the other hand, he liked the figureheads. For the front of each wagon had been crafted to resemble the face of a monster. Wooden leviathans staggered past, and wyverns and dragons and manticoras. Brenn marveled at the intricacy of each creature, and took his mind away from the disrespectful images at the back of the vehicles.

"I've never seen them," he confessed to Ricardo. "At least none of them save the wyvern, but I'll wager if I was out on the plains a ways from here, and I saw these wagons coming . . ."

"Hush," the Alanyan whispered, laying a gloved hand on Brenn's shoulder. " 'Tis but an eidolon before you. The ones in the distance—the real ones—must be wary of something."

"Eidolons?" Brenn asked. "And what's this of *real ones*? Is this something other than wagons before me? Will somebody please explain . . ."

"As for now," the Alanyan cautioned, "all ye need to know is that there is no doubt trouble afoot, if the caravans are wielding the mirrors."

Perplexed, Brenn looked first at Ricardo, then at Delia.

"And if there's danger on the plains," Ricardo observed, "we're better off in numbers." He looked at Delia. "Even if the numbers are shadow and smoke."

"Sit back in the wagon, Your Grace," Delia said to Brenn with a smile, "and I'll explain more of this Alanyan foolishness than you care to know." Then, at a motion from Ricardo, the Ruthic girl steered the wagon into the midst of the eidolons. From a closer perspective, Brenn could see that the shapes of horse and wagon and drover were insubstantial, translucent, as though crafted of manycolored smoke and tinted glass. Ricardo rode ahead of the wagon, and on occasion outriders and even a wagon or two passed through him harmlessly, as the legends say that ghosts may pass through walls.

"Diversion," Delia explained to a slack-jawed Brenn, as they pulled up beside a covered wagon, its blue canopy ornately adorned with hundreds of green stars. Up close Brenn could see the grass wave through the sides of the wagon, the darkening eastern horizon through the canopy. "A diversion for the open plains, where bandits and Zephyrian raiding parties are all too eager to surround and strip a solitary caravan."

"If they see two from a great distance . . ." Brenn began, the idea dawning quickly on him.

"Two," Delia said with a nod, "or three. Depending on the power of the wagonmaster's mirrors."

And she went on to explain how the wagon of each Alanyan caravan master is painted on the inside with murals of other caravans, with clever likenesses of wagons and horses and drovers. It is the lens they carry with them—the *speculum vivandem*, as they call it in the Ruthic islands, that reflects the design, layer after layer of embroidery and paint, through enormous magnifying lenses into a three-dimensional shape somewhere at the fringes of sight.

"It's like a mirage," the girl concluded, her eyes on the plains ahead of her. "But a controlled mirage, if you understand. A projected, living image of something faraway."

Brenn whistled quietly, unsure he understood the science of it all. "Wouldn't Cousin Lapis love to see *this* arrangement?" he marveled, thinking of the girl aloft in the cedar branches, regarding the constellations through smoked and faceted glass. Then he thought of Lapis's prized possession, how the lens moved and shifted, its surface constantly expanding and contracting, wrinkling and inflating.

"By the four winds, I believe she *has* one already!" he exclaimed. "And so *this* is its purpose." Ricardo turned in the saddle to say something, but Brenn, carried away by the prospects of these strange and wonderful optics, pointed over the Alanyan's shoulder to a spot far to the North.

"And the lens in *this* particular caravan must be a mighty one. Look! 'Tis another eidolon coming our way!"

Ricardo turned toward the distant approaching shapes and frowned. Quickly he pulled a glass of his own from the bright green sleeve of his doublet—a collapsible spyglass that he extended quickly and brought to his eye.

"No, Your Majesty," he said apprehensively. " 'Tis the easternmost wing of General Helmar's cavalry. Two hundred strong. Not the best of Dragmond's army, but two hundred of the worst outnumber the three of us."

Ricardo sat back in the saddle and loosened his sword in the scabbard. "Stay within the eidolon, Delia," he ordered. "No matter where it goes. We can only hope that their eyes are bad and their orders elsewhere."

"But the Plains of Sh'Ryll. What if . . ." Delia began. Then she looked to the north and counted the banners.

Two . . . three . . . four companies.

"You're right, Ricardo," she said softly. "There is no choice but to go where the eidolons lead us."

As always, the caravan was a baffling sight for Captain Lubin.

Do not fear, he had told the men, as the wagons approached, their monstrous faces leering and grinning. *They are apparitions only . . . some Alanyan trick of mirrors and conjury.*

And so the faces were. So they always were. But sometimes the caravan itself would shift and ripple and vanish altogether, and he would look at the men and they at him, and all would wonder if they had seen it in the first place or whether they had been too long on duty and in the saddle.

Twice the captain had followed a long string of wagons bound across the plains of Palerna into Zephyr. He had followed to make sure that they carried no instruments of war, though he was damned if he knew what weaponry a quarreling little second-rate power like Alanya could offer to the peerless Zephyrian cavalry. He followed nonetheless, but at a distance, as General Helmar had ordered. For the word was caution with the caravans of Alanya: one hostile border was enough for Dragmond.

Both times as he followed, each caravan had passed before him and vanished, leaving him at the head of his baffled cavalry, chasing air and light across the plains.

The second time, someone had snickered behind him.

Angry at the memory, Captain Lubin squinted into the midst of the passing vehicles, disregarding the passing colors, the mocking sculpture, the coblyn drivers, searching for boys of dangerous age. For still the orders issued from Kestrel Tower: someone was loose in the countryside, it seemed, who had designs against the welfare of the state.

Guerrillas were younger and younger, Lubin mused grimly. Yesterday, at the edge of Corbinwood, his troops had overtaken a young peasant—nine years old at the most. The captain would have let him go, let him sink back into the woods, into whatever rathole housed him, had the boy not drawn a knife and slashed at the horses. It was quick, what followed. Quick and merciless.

The caravan passed before him, not a hundred yards to his east. The men looked to him for a sign, the sergeants leaning forward in the saddle and the archers gathering behind him, ready to rain arrows into the midst of the colorful wagons.

There was a boy in the bed of one cart. A boy of dangerous age. Lubin raised his hand, then paused, his eyes coursing over the array of horse and sail and canopy passing at a distance.

What if the lad is some . . . Alanyan dignitary? The captain thought. *Or what if he is smoke and light only?*

Lubin was a simple man, baffled by choices. Again he looked at the caravan, and again, as if some evidence of sight could bring him a truth that only insight could offer him. His troops were poised around him, his hand still raised.

There. Had he not seen the green sleeve of the tall rider's doublet, seen it through the transparent flank of a horse that stood between the two of them? Captain Lubin blinked, looked again, but the chance was gone.

For the caravan reached a spot on the plains where the wind rose and whined and the grass whirled about them. In a moment they all vanished—all except the big man in the green doublet, the boy and his wagon and driver. Lubin had only time enough to see that the driver was a girl, her skin a fathomless black against the dusky grass of the plains.

Then they, too, vanished, and the plains spread vacant and silent before the dumbfounded cavalry.

"Now what, by old Gorlewin's beard, was *that*?" the sergeant asked, settling back into the saddle.

Lubin smiled bleakly and turned his horse about with a deft twist of the reins.

"Alanyan foolishness, I believe," he told the sergeant. "Light and enchantment, and hundred-year illusions. Natheless, no man is to venture onto that caravan path, nor onto the spot where the wagons vanished."

The sergeant nodded, turning his own horse a little more roughly. It was an order he would obey gladly.

"Damn!" Ricardo exclaimed, as the wind buckled and cavorted around him. He had been careless—had set aside his traveler's sense and followed the eidolons, even when the ground before them was suddenly translucent, the landscape around him suddenly bright with hanging crystal, and it looked as though they were about to enter a cavern of glass.

The Plains of Sh'Ryll. The Alanyan knew the signs and some of the legends.

"Soon the music," he murmured, and looked back with concern at Brenn and Delia. The girl had leaned forward over the horses, her dark hands steady on the reins and her eyes on the path ahead of her. He did not need to worry over her.

The lad, on the other hand, had spent no time in countries of visions. He startled when the music began, and dove underneath one of the blankets. There, swaddled in dusty wool, Brenn peered out in alarm, unnerved by the clear whistling of wind over crystal, the faint, melodic chiming that sounded like a distant carillon.

Ricardo took a deep breath and looked about him. The reciting owl at his shoulder piped one of the songs of Felix, the Coblyn bard, who was said to be at home in the heart of these plains.

> *Sometimes a thousand twangling instruments*
> *Will hum about mine ears, and sometimes voices,*
> *That, if I then had wak'd after long sleep*
> *Will make me sleep again: and then, in dreaming,*
> *The clouds methought would open and show riches*
> *Ready to drop upon me; that, when I wak'd,*
> *I cried to dream again.*

And the dream will come soon enough, Ricardo thought, as the crystals fractured and distorted the light in front of him. *And soon enough the voices.*

It was simple, the vision that came to Ricardo—far simpler than he had imagined it would be. For after all, he was an Alanyan, schooled in double-talk, in the ambiguous and complicated. But when the simple vision came, he was strangely relieved.

He saw himself in the heart of a hanging crystal, on horseback riding up a black beach. The horse surged and raced beneath him like a powerful dark wind, and the long strides of the beast swallowed the shoreline, the waters rising in its wake as though he was drawing the tide behind him.

Suddenly, Ricardo was no longer watching. The air crackled about him, and somehow he entered the heart of the crystal. Along the beach he rode, the big stallion beneath him, at such a speed that the conifers along the opposite coastline seemed to bend and blur at his passing.

Rock and sea, he told himself. *Rock and sea and black glassy sand. As I am a traveler and know my coasts and waters it is Aquila across that arm of sea.*

The reciting owl piped dreamily at his shoulder.

Instantly, with the apt illogic of vision or poetry, the sword rested in his hand. It was a formidable blade, a good four feet from hilt to point, and yet it was uncommonly light, weighing no more than a dagger, perhaps a foil. In mid-gallop, marvelling, Ricardo turned the sword in the slanting sunlight.

Libra potestatis sum, it said on the blade, in letters so ancient they hovered between printing and rune.

"I am the balance of power," Ricardo whispered, and together, he and the horse froze in midstride, encased in glass or in crystal.

Brenn blinked nervously in the wagon bed. Ricardo had vanished into the bright, reflecting slivers of ice and light. He and Delia continued, the wagon navigating the dangerously narrow passages between crystal and crystal. The backs of the horses steamed in front of them, and the air was crisp and uncommonly cold. It was as though, here in late April, Delia had turned the wagon about and driven back into winter.

"So these are the Plains of Sh'Ryll," Brenn said to Delia, his voice too high, too jovial. "I reckon that the visions come on us next."

Silently, her back to him, the girl drove the horses. He knew that her thoughts were elsewhere, and somehow that was true loneliness, far deeper and more desolate than the departures of Terrance and vanishments of Ricardo. Brenn reached out to touch Delia, his hand extended and hovering a foot, six inches, an inch above her shoulder.

It was then that the plains closed in. All around him the crystal surged forth like hard, inevitable waves. It encircled him, bathing him in fire and freezing and light incredibly green. He breathed in the odor of mown grass and of juniper, and he tried vainly to recall where first he had smelled them together.

Suddenly he was alone in a bare garden. The trees were stripped and black, the evergreens among them brown and dried, scarcely the memory of spring in their twisted branches. Somewhere above him, though he could not turn his head to follow the sound, the cry of a raven burst through the wintry air.

All of this was important, he knew. He longed for Terrance to read the signs, to explain the vision. But the wizard was far from here on a southerly road, and for the first time in matters divinatory, Brenn was left to his own resources.

Such as they are, he thought sourly. *I don't know what to make of sere winter trees and bird calls and ice.*

He smiled and squinted. *Natheless, I shall remember it all*, he thought triumphantly. *I shall pay attention.*

And instantly, as though he were at rest in a prism, the garden around him burst into light of many colors. Green danced on the bare branches, blue on the towering stone walls that enclosed them. All around him the air dappled red and purple, and he saw in this oddly fashioned light that each of the trees was different. There was a small but hale plane tree, its bark greenish-brown in the altered light; and from it lobed, waxy leaves began to sprout, as though spring was rising out of a garden of ice.

Cedar and cypress suddenly burgeoned in wild aquamarine and darker, lovely emerald, and between them a tiny acacia sent forth its feathery leaves. Brenn held his breath and marveled, marveling still more that he, a Town boy and serenely indifferent to plant life, either remembered the names of the trees from some cloudy early teaching or learned them on the spot, as he lay among them, encased in crystal or ice.

"By the breath of Durain, 'tis a spring in the midst of winter!" he whispered, overwhelmed by the sight.

And he was on the plains again. The wagon creaked along steadily as though it had never stopped, and it occurred to Brenn that no doubt it had kept on moving through the trees and the ice and the bird cries and the many-colored lights.

Serenely, Delia held to the reins, her gold eyes fixed and fathomless. If she had a vision passing through that strange maze of crystal, it was one she never shared with her companions. Alongside her, pensive on his black stallion, Ricardo rode silently, a look of trouble and of deep turmoil upon his face.

That was all it was. Brenn lay back in the wagon bed and looked into the night sky. The constellations reeled above him, and it seemed that Pytho, even greener in its last months in the sky, had passed all the way through the Sign of Horologue without his notice. He would notice it all, heaven and earth, with greater care from this time forth.

Or so he promised himself, fearing it was another promise he could not keep. And beside him, as the wagon rolled steadily toward the Eastmark and the Alanyan border, his companions dreamed and remembered and dwelt on the light in the crystals.

≻≻≻ XXI ≺≺≺

The Eastmark was not as wide as Brenn had feared, but it was wide enough.

Flowing oddly north, sluggishly and muddily out of the high ground of the Notches, born of the confluence of the Boniluce and the Umbre, the big river split the plains in two, dividing Palerna from Alanya as neatly and as definitely as the most exacting geographer or territorial warlord could ask. For five centuries the river had served as a border between the two countries, undisputed except for the issue of its name. Though Brenn had always heard it called the Eastmark, he discovered that most Alanyans—Ricardo included—called it the Xanthus, for the yellow mud that swirled turgidly along its banks.

Again, though in a different and entirely unexpected way, the Eastmark served as a boundary that divided Palernan from Alanyan. For it was there on the banks of the big river that Ricardo announced his departure.

"It is here that our ways part, Your Majesty," the big Alanyan said gravely, bending over in the saddle and drawing a folded blanket from the wagon bed. "This covering is almost all that I'll ask of ye, for 'tis a long and cold ride back to Corbinwood through the night."

Astonished, Brenn seated himself heavily in the wagon. Straw and dust motes rose about him, and though he felt betrayed and longed for angry, commanding words, all that reached his lips was a sudden, violent sneeze.

"Bless you, Brennart," Ricardo said solemnly, his own eyes watering. "I am sorry that I must leave you so soon. But I was honest from the first with you that you would travel the last part of the journey alone."

"But I didn't expect the last part of the journey to begin . . . before the first part had ended!" Brenn protested with a sniff. Delia smiled distantly behind him, her hands playing with the reins of the wagon.

"I suppose this goes for you, too, Delia," Brenn said huffily. "I suppose you'll be off with Ricardo on his cross-country jaunt to . . . did you say *Corbinwood*?"

Ricardo laughed. "It seems as though I've been traveling in circles, Master Brennart, only to return to Galliard and your assembled cousins. For I learned from passing through the plains behind us that my future and my mystery have something to do with Aquila. I cannot say more. Indeed, I am unsure what to say."

Brenn sneezed again. Disconsolately, he looked out over the river.

"As for me," Delia said softly. "I shall stay by you yet a while."

"Which brings me to the second and final thing I shall ask of ye, Brennart," the Alanyan said, draping the blanket about his shoulders. "See that the girl has safe passage to the Ruthic Island. Take her into Hadrach, if you will, and launch her aboard the ferry to Random. She knows the way better than I, and once among the islands she'll find her way home like a navigator. But there are traps and snares for an unwary girl from here to Hadrach, and I'd rather she travel by the side of an enterpriser like yourself than try those roads alone."

Despite himself, Brenn was flattered. He knew, of course, that Ricardo was peddling, but the request was fair and earnest. The reciting owl cocked its head on the big Alanyan's shoulder, and Brenn realized he had been won over without a struggle.

"Then I shall travel with her, Ricardo," Brenn declared, "for no other reason than to show the both of you how Palernans stick to their loyalties."

Brenn regretted it at once, would have given anything to call back the hurtful words. But Ricardo laughed and sat back in the saddle.

"Then it will be the right thing you do, Master Brennart, though for the wrong reasons," he maintained. "For my loyalty does not show in always doing what you'd like me to do."

He waved and turned the big stallion westward, and thundering toward the sunset they went, like the predictable ending of some creaky and belabored old romance. Brenn stood in the wagon bed and watched them until he could see them no longer, until they had dwindled to a speck on the horizon, then to nothing.

"Delia? What did *you* see on the plains?" Brenn asked, his eyes still fixed on an empty spot in the distant west.

The girl did not answer. Quietly she climbed from the wagon and set about to make a small fire.

"Waters crest at night," she explained. "The perpetual draw of the moon. We had best wait until the morrow before fording a river like the Xanthus."

Through moonlight and cloud, Ricardo rode the black horse west toward Corbinwood. He skirted the edge of the Plains of Sh'Ryll, having seen enough visions to last him. In the moonlight he could see the air sparkle south of him as he passed by the plains and onward into the steady night.

Twice Palernan cavalry spotted him and gave pursuit. The Maravenian horsemen he outdistanced readily, the long strides of the stallion leaving the horsemen agape and their horses winded and lathered in the waving grass behind him. The second group, a crack southern squadron of country boys, was not so easily shaken. Ricardo took them north, through an orchard and into the pasturage of a large manor farm, vaulting four fences and sliding recklessly down one bank of a creek and up the other side, his horse breasting the swollen waters like a galley. Then, at a full gallop across the open grasslands, his boots wet against the oily flanks of the horse and smelling of wet wool, wet leather, wet animal, the Alanyan reached the crest of a hill and, looking down and behind him onto the level lands of the farm, saw the troopers milling about, lost amid fencerows and hayricks.

"Even their best are not good enough," he whispered quietly, and gathering his bearings from the late spring stars, rushed toward Corbinwood at the head of an easterly wind.

Alchemy is over at last, he thought, as the night grew darker and the owl at his shoulder rustled to wakefulness. *All the nostrums and the snake oils, the mirrors and the dodges and the doubletalk are over. I am changed from base to noble, from lead to gold. The sky is changed—a May sky, perhaps even June by the paths of the planets, when the best I remember, it is still April. But what does it matter? I am riding as I know I was born and meant to ride. There is no longer dishonesty in my hands, and the wind is behind and under me.*

The visions are true at least in this—that I have dreamed this moment and I am going to do this from now on.

So blissfully he rode until the sun rose behind him and the woods loomed gray and green in the brightening distance ahead.

The next morning they arose and followed the river north, looking for a shallow place to ford.

It was scarcely an hour before Brenn became impatient. The river beside him seemed changeless, featureless, as though somehow they had circled the wagon again and again so that the same stretch of water rolled yellow and sluggish and wide not a hundred feet to the right of them.

When she saw that the lad beside her had begun to fidget, Delia started the stories. Brenn was surprised as the long silence of the girl broke in a rich downpouring of myth and of legend and of song.

How the four winds quarreled over where the river would run, and how Gogleth had frozen the others in crystal and thereby won the argument, so that to this day the waters flow north, like those of the great Nilus in far-off Aegyptus.

She told of the Ten Prophecies of the Notches, four of which had come to pass, and the fifth having something to do with the green star Pytho resting in the constellation of the Forest Lord. Brenn reminded her that the time had passed, that the star had ushered through the Forest Lord, through Horologue, and out to the other side of the world.

"And nothing has happened," he teased, looking sideways at her from his new perch beside her on the driver's seat of the wagon.

"Nothing you have seen," Delia answered briskly. "Natheless, the prophecies have stopped your grumbling."

Brenn snorted in annoyance, but Delia was talking again before he could think of a sharp and proper response. On she went about the last great border dispute, when a company of Alanyan bandits had dug an enormous ditch just north of the Notches where Painter Falls tumbled eccentrically into the source of the Eastmark. There in a feat of mad engineering, the soldiers prepared to redirect the river so that acres of hilly Palernan land would become part of Alanya with one new rush of the current.

Brenn smiled, his impatience forgotten. These were the stories he liked, of ingenuity and roundabout skullduggery, as a smaller, more clever hero outwitted an enormous and powerful foe. What matter that the powerful foe had been his great-grandfather Albright the First? The story went that the old king blustered and raged and ordered his troops about, only to find that when he reached the spot in question, the redirected river had overflowed its new banks and flooded the disputed land, rendering it a mosquito-infested bog that nobody wanted anymore.

But it had been worth the venture. Brenn leaned forward, closed his eyes and propped his chin on his hands, admiring those Alanyans—the sheer ambition and brass and cleverness of the whole enterprise. So he dwelt in the story until his companion broke through the revery.

"Here," Delia said. "The river is fordable here."

Brenn opened his eyes and looked down into the swirling current. Indeed, the waters broke over rocks and shallows, wrinkling and cresting and doubling back upon themselves before they tumbled into a deeper channel and rushed north again, their strength renewed, toward a dim gray smoke on the horizon that Delia claimed was Hadrach.

On the edge of the smoke, barely visible even to the lad's sharp eyes, a hawk turned on the warm air.

Without ceremony, Delia turned the wagon straight into the water. It was as though she had a map of the currents: the wagon sank no farther than its thorobraces into the water, and the horses were on steady footing as they passed to midriver.

But the river was wide and strong. At the point where you might say that the Eastmark left off and the Xanthus began, the horses dropped suddenly into mud or a declivity of rock. The water now rushed against their shoulders.

"Delia!" Brenn exclaimed, clutching the girl's arm uneasily. "Don't you think you'd better . . ."

"I'd better hold to the reins now, Your Majesty," Delia replied plainly, wresting her arm away from him. Brenn sat back, grasped the driver's seat beneath him, and took a deep breath.

"By Gogleth and all the winds of water," he muttered, "I never imagined I'd have to come inland to be drowned!"

Of course, they were nowhere near drowning. In a moment, after brief uncertainty, the horses found their footing. Slowly, through the churning yellow waters, they drew the wagon, and Brenn, who had gathered his cousins's belongings into the silk map and tied them there, sat down in the wagon bed and watched the current glide around him.

"I suppose . . . I've *seethed* a bit too much," he confessed to Delia, who smiled, her eyes intent on the waters ahead of them. "For that I am sorry. It's just that . . . we seem so *vulnerable* here."

Delia turned to him and started to speak. Whether she intended to soothe or to scold, Brenn never found out. For it was at that moment that the sky darkened above them, and the horses bucked and panicked in the driving waters.

Amalek shifted his wings into the warm spring wind and circled the river. The wagon in its midst, the creatures in the wagon and even their horses seemed small and insignificant from this great height, like insects drowning in a trickle of muddy water.

Deeply the dragon breathed, and the smells of the plains came to him. The watery fragrance of grass and mud, the faint smoke from Hadrach and the washed, celestial smell of the crystal plains off to the west.

There it was, in the midst of familiar odors, the hot, coppery smell of blood. He banked in an eddy of high wind, the green iridescent scales dropping from his eyes, unhooding them as his ancient, uncanny eyesight collapsed the great distance between him and the wagon, as he saw them up close . . .

In a panic of fumbling, Brenn rifled the silk for the bow and arrows. Delia steadied the horses, wrestled to keep them all from being swept away into the downstream current. Above them the dragon circled, its green armor glittering and seamless, its enormous dark batwings green, then red, then a deep violet in the brilliant sunlight.

He had seen the creature before. On the wing somewhere, in the skies of a late afternoon, but he could remember no more than this. Distractedly, almost lazily, he combed his memories of Maraven, of his stay in Corbinwood.

Nothing came to him.

At last he dragged the bow from the midst of branches and silk and blankets, puffed and grappled over the string and the nock, only to find he lacked the strength to draw the weapon. Angrily he dropped to the bed of the wagon, again stirring straw and dust. Serpentine root skittered into the corners of the vehicle, and the thick, unwieldy branches of Sendow's tree rustled and snapped, their green smell rising over the smell of the water, the sharp, sweaty smell of the horses.

With all of her strength, Delia steadied the animals. Desperately, she looked across the river to the Alanyan banks, where a flock of ravens had settled expectantly in the overhanging branches of osier and poplar. ''Damn!'' she swore through clenched teeth, and wrestled the horses again.

Whickering, their eyes rolling, the big beasts thrashed in the water. And then from aloft, tumbling down upon them like a thick and fetid rain, the dragonscent reached Delia, too, and she reeled, scarcely holding to the wrenching, twisting reins in her hands.

It was infamous, this hot overpowering odor, smelling of

smoke and standing water and old, unspeakable death. Powerful as the venom of the wyvern, as the narcotic breath of the panther, the scent of the dragon struck panic from miles away. The legends said it was how the great beast hunted, its scent strong enough to stun buffalo, horses, to paralyze coblyns and human children—for dragons were known to prefer two-legged prey to heavier beasts.

Amalek was no exception. His was a history of plundering caravans for children and small, tender women, and for the occasional coblyn or two, though he found the little people tough and gristly. And yet of all two-legged prey, Amalek had strayed farthest from his lair in pursuit of the one in the wagon.

For every evening the ravens had settled in the Alaru and sang of the arrival of this one, boding hoarsely from the entanglements of thorns from sunset until midnight, when their black feathers were no longer distinguishable from the fallen night.

And their song, again and again, told him that the King was coming and the King must die.

He had smiled when they sang their instructions. Nothing bound him to the Great Witch in Maraven—neither fear nor duty nor enchantment. But she asked so insistently.

He would do her this favor, would hand her this little death.

Amalek folded his wings and dropped toward the surface of the water, as the horses shied and burst through the traces below him, as for the first time the ones in the wagon looked up in wonder and awe and fear, the King and the other, as the monster plummeted toward them and opened his jaws that could swallow a cottage, could swallow a minaret or a tower, as he fixed his eye on the male one, on the King, as she had said he should . . .

And suddenly, amazingly, the waters burst into song. The monster careened, dazzled by a light so bright, so golden, that he feared its sheer purity and heat. With a groan that shattered windows in Hadrach, that rang harbor bells in Random, the dragon lurched from the dive so abruptly that the air roared around his wings. The waters of the river churned and roiled, and the ravens scattered from the trees on the Alanyan side of the river, flashing raucously off in all directions.

Amalek wheeled upward angrily, shrieking like a large predatory bird. The trees on the riverbanks bent and swayed, and yet the song persisted, rising from the southern waters upstream where a purple light spread softly at the edge of his sight, drowning his cries and the thunder of his wings. Sullenly the dragon rose to an even greater height, scattering starlings and sparrows, frightening one swiftly moving sea eagle. In rage the monster looked southward, his lidless eye erasing the miles, his long sight burning through mist and distance until . . .

. . . he saw the barge, like a burnished throne, flaming on the water in a violet light. A rumble rose in his throat, and his anger gave way to fear. Circling north away from the wagon, away from the menacing light on the water, he dipped his wings over the outskirts of Hadrach then streaked toward the east, toward the thorny maze of the Aralu at a speed that raised fire on the tips of his wings.

She could not follow him there—the bright She that stood against the one in the Tower and the ravens. Amalek was no fool: his allegiance to the Great Witch was easily broken. The dragon would retire from the field, would let the queens fight it out between themselves like in some far-flung game of chess across the continent. As they conjured and enchanted and spun their webs of light, he would keep jaw and scale and wing safely away from the swirl and clash of their powers.

Let them destroy one another. He did not care.

Mired in the midst of the river, neither Brenn nor Delia could figure out what had happened. The dragon, it seemed, had swooped upon them, with the intent to destroy them or to carry them off. And then the air had bristled and exploded with a hundred flashes of light, gold and purple, and when their sight had cleared and they looked again, old Amalek was gone.

"Do you reckon something . . . *vanished* him, or reduced him to dust?" Brenn whispered to Delia.

"Where *do* you get your magical notions?" she scolded. "Look upstream. No, not toward Hadrach, you . . . Your Majesty. To the south. Toward the Notches, and toward that light on the water."

Brenn turned and squinted toward the purple glow, and it was then that they first heard the singing, for a dragon's ears are hunter-keen, and all animals know that human folk walk through the world with muffled senses.

"What—" Brenn began, but Delia, tired of his questioning and continual mistakes, dropped all protocol and slapped her hand to his mouth.

"Hist!" she whispered. "Stop guessing and jumping to every conclusion, and in a moment we'll know!"

It was only a moment until the barge loomed into sight, shining like a huge amethyst in the yellow waters of the Eastmark. Draped with pennants of white and forest green, curtained with forest scenes embroidered in the same colors on broad rich tapestries, the ship approached the stranded wagon.

From its midst arose the choir of voices soprano and alto and contralto, weaving in harmony with the strings of psaltery and lute. The singers themselves fluttered and flashed in golden light about the festooned masts of the ship.

Brenn gaped in wonderment, then laughed aloud.

The barge was manned by faeries.

Winged and graceful, the creatures held the sails aloft, singing a clear and lovely descant over the choiring elves on deck, who scurried about comically, manning the rudders and oars. It was foolish, incongruous, but both the winds and the strong little backs of the rowers propelled the boat harmoniously, so that the barge moved with unnatural speed, and sometimes seemed to rise above the waters, to skim the surface of the river as though it might soar aloft at any time.

Soon the ship was close enough that Brenn could catch the words to the song the faeries sang.

> *You spotted snakes with double tongue,*
> *Thorny hedgehogs, be not seen,*
> *Newts and blindworms, do no wrong,*
> *Come not near our fairy queen.*
>
> *Weaving spiders, come not here;*
> *Hence you long-legg'd spinners, hence!*
> *Beetles black, approach not near;*
> *Worm nor snail, do no offense.*

As the words of the second verse faded into the strumming of the lute, a square canopy amidship opened, as the coblyn guards, squat and hairy but nonetheless kind-faced and gentle in their movements, drew the purple curtains aside. The queen stepped out onto the deck and waved at the two companions who stood in the wagon, wide-eyed and gaping.

"Glory!" Brenn exclaimed. "By the beard of the West Wind, the Faerie Queen is Glory!"

Indeed it was Glory. It seemed so right, so fitting, that Brenn was surprised that he had not known all along, or that something had not given her away during his long lessons in Corbinwood.

"Too busy searching for faeries to find them, I was," Brenn allowed, as Glory smiled at him and walked to the edge of the barge.

The coblyns anchored her ship by Brenn and Delia's wagon, in midstream where it hovered and rocked lazily on the slow waters. Brenn watched the unkempt, hairy little creatures curiously, marvelling that from such an unlikely stock had come great mystics, great bards.

But then, the humble herb woman he had known in Corbinwood had turned out to be queen of them all.

There was no accounting for appearances or prospects, Brenn decided, and stepped from the bed of the wagon onto the deck of the barge. Glory took the hand of the future king, and the air about them chimed with the music of sprites.

Remember this well, my friend, Delia thought, as the coblyns busied themselves with dislodging the wagon and setting it back upon its path toward the Alanyan shore. *Remember that powers greater than you could imagine have traveled great distances and suffered great danger to aid you on your journey*.

Two coblyns scrambled up on the driver's seat beside her. They smelled of fish and, oddly, of chocolate and marigolds.

Remember these well, too, Brennart, she thought, her dark hand resting on the shoulder of one grizzled little creature as, with a movement both graceful and gentlemanly, he took the reins from her hands and guided them on the next short steps toward Alanya, toward the Aralu and toward Amalek.

Remember both great and small, Your Majesty, she thought, as she stepped onto the barge herself, where Brenn, with a movement both graceful and gentlemanly, stood and offered his arm as she approached the throne of the Faerie Queen. *For remembering that the great have ventured much, risked much, on your behalf will give you faith in the hours to come.*

And remembering the small will remind you why.

Behind them, the spokes of its wheels heavy with algae and mud, the wagon tilted and rattled as it rolled into Alanya. The coblyns on the driver's seat chattered to one another in a language as old as the river itself.

>>> **XXII** <<<

Their audience with the Faerie Queen was brief, and conducted entirely from the barge. Glory—or Gloriana, as the Invisible Folk on the barge called her—refused to enter Alanya, insisting that to do so would dishonor the dragon her magic had turned away only moments ago.

"'Tis an agreement we struck before the Romans or the Umbrians," she explained to Brenn. "Before even the Philokalians built their minarets in the dreams of each other and fashioned the moonharps which played continually at night, changing their melodies as the moon waxed and waned. It dates to a time in which the world was portioned between the dragons and the Invisible Folk."

"Old, indeed, is that agreement, m'lady," Delia observed.

"And of all agreements forged in that time, Delia, the one that remains is between Amalek and me," Glory said. "An alchemist of your skill and stature should know that queen and dragon make a volatile mixture."

Brenn stared at Delia suspiciously. *Alchemist? But surely Glory . . . Gloriana is mistaken. Surely Delia is only Ricardo's apprentice, as she claimed to be from the first time I met her in*

Terrance's tower. And yet Gloriana motioned to a seat beside her and politely the girl took it.

Brenn, for all his kingly expectations, stood before the two women like a petitioner.

"We agreed even then that we would never cross into each other's country."

"But what of his flights above Corbinwood, Glory?" Brenn asked aggressively. "He was there as Ravenna's scout, regardless of the pact you made in centuries past."

"Indeed he was," Glory said with a smile. "And the breaking of his word is no reason that I should break mine. As far east as I will venture is the middle of this river."

"Couldn't you . . . make exception, Glory?" Brenn asked. "These are extraordinary times, after all."

"And 'twas, in turn, an extraordinary oath," Glory argued. "If I were unfaithful in the extraordinary, Brennart, how could I be trusted in the daily things? And if you cannot trust me daily, what good am I as queen or faerie, or indeed as your teacher?"

" 'Tis all too philosophical for me," Brenn dodged. "I know that my cousins are trapped in the woods back there, and that something to do with this dragon will spring *them*, and that you stand to benefit as well as I, for the Invisible Folk want their woods back free of human disruption and human fires and heavy human feet."

"But the woods would not return to us if I broke this oath," Glory explained. "To break this oath would be to break our hold on the forest itself. I cannot tell you how or why I know this, but the rule is a simple one. To treat with a thing of evil you must fly above it, not beside it."

She looked at Brenn softly, almost maternally, and the lad felt a surprising tenderness for her. Oh, he knew that the faeries were indifferent, more or less, to human problems and human desires and ambitions. But Glory had taught him herbs and lore and the laying of hands toward a purpose, and he could not imagine that she had done so altogether without affection.

"But you are right, Brennart," she said, and though she meant that she stood to benefit from his success against Amalek, Brenn felt that the answer lay deeper—that she was answering his thoughts aloud. "It is in the interest of my people that you prosper, but to prosper you must find the victory. Instruction is over; I can tell you only that you carry with you all that you need to defeat the dragon, and that when you are finally victorious you will lie in greatest danger of defeat.''

Brenn wrinkled his brow. "An oracle, m'lady, and I fear that your words are veiled and too complicated for the likes of me."

"I am, after all, the Queen of the Faeries," Glory replied with a laugh, and suddenly, they were all gone—queen and coblyn, sprite and faerie and barge. Delia and Brenn sat dazed in the wagon bed, not a hundred yards into the country of Alanya. Behind them the river flowed unperturbed, swelling its banks as the day waned.

"I have a bone to pick with you, too . . . *alchemist*," Brenn grumbled, and Delia averted her gaze.

"Could we have done it otherwise?" she asked, reaching down for the reins, and with a quick and practiced movement, jostling the horses to life and motion. "When we came to Terrance's tower two years ago, and you sat on the roof and watched us approach, would you have believed me then had I said, 'I am the one, Brennart. I am the alchemist, and this gaudy man before me protects me from the eyes of the world so that I can be about my business'?"

"Is there a one of you who has not lied? First the Goniph, then Terrance and Ricardo, then you, and Glory's season-long masquerade as a root-doctor . . ."

So he continued on the road to Hadrach, belaboring her with her injustices, his hardships, as they followed the Xanthus north toward the Random Shallows, where the river emptied into the Sea of Shadows and the city rose on the right bank, brown and red and streaked with bright yellows, for much of it was carved out of the cliffs along the Shallows.

They smelled the incense from a mile away, and then the city loomed into view. Their first sight, as it was for all travelers from points south, was the rugged rockface of Windgate Crag —the sheer narrow pass between two bluffs that had been worn by the hot south wind Dehevol for a thousand years, no doubt by a now-dried branch of the Xanthus for a hundred thousand years before that. All this geology was no accident, or so patriotic Alanyans claimed. For a thousand centuries had gone into making the spot from which had risen the mountainous beauties of Hadrach.

"Beauties," however, would scarcely have been Brenn's word for them. Hadrach was a vertical city, ramshackled and tiered, smelling of incense and wine, of peppers and cinnamon and cumin. In all, the air was so spiced and smokey that the unexpecting traveler was likely to sneeze for the first hour or so after he passed through the Windgate.

The "Hadrach Pinch," they called it, when it lasted longer. Sometimes the sneezing would not go away, and the sufferer sought cure from any of the hundred mountebanks and oil-peddlers whose shops were sprinkled through the perpetual riverside market of Xanthian Banks—the intricate and corrupt trade center of the most intricate and corrupt city on the subcontinent. Each of these so-called healers had a cure for the Pinch: some were simple herbal cures from slippery elm to eucalyptus, while others were more complex, involving incantation, song, and in one case the placing of the sufferer's head beneath a large silver bell, the ringing of which was said to "frighten away" the Pinch. If finally the medicines failed, and the oils and chants and bells, the poor souls would either leave the city or quite literally sneeze themselves to death, for continual sneezing makes sleep impossible and sometimes banishes even the thought of food.

Delia, as Brenn imagined, was quite prepared for the Hadrach Pinch. As they passed through the Windgate, she handed him a white mask. Dutifully, Brenn placed it across his nose and mouth.

"I feel like a road agent," he joked to Delia, and when he spoke, suddenly he smelled and tasted an odd sweet fragrance —something mintlike and strangely familiar.

"Serpentine root," Delia explained. "That, and a little camphor. 'Twas, after all, Jimsett's gift to you, and pinch-warding is only one of its virtues."

"But I was supposed to—"

"Take it to the Aralu. I know. Do not worry, Brenn. There is root aplenty left for whatever need you will have of it."

"I'm . . . I'm growing worried, Delia," Brenn confessed, as

the wagon took a sharp turn and followed an incline up to yet another tier of shops and buildings. "I am *one lad*, mind you, no match for armed men or wild dogs or cwalu or indeed for any of the things I've run up against since I signed on with Terrance up in Maraven. How can anyone expect me to hold my own against the likes of a dragon?"

"You're here, aren't you?" Delia asked briskly, reining the horses around yet another turn. A brass railing, green with verdigris and bent from numerous careenings of carts and coaches and wagons, bowed out over a sheer drop of two hundred feet or so into the Eastmark River. Brenn looked out over the bluff and was suddenly dizzy. He swallowed hard and looked back at Delia.

"Here?" he asked. "Why, *of course* I'm here. Why do you . . ."

"Then you're a match for all of them," Delia said confidently, her golden eyes on the narrow road ahead of them.

"I don't—"

"Of course you do," she interrupted again. "The simple fact that you are still here, Brenn, means that you've not only held your own, but that you have triumphed over all those adversaries you've named."

She slowed the wagon and turned toward him, regarding him with a gaze both serious and beautiful.

"What do you think their intentions were? These armed men and raposa and cwalu. What do you think Dame Sorrow had in mind for you?"

"Why, to kill me," Brenn replied, and Delia nodded.

"So I would say you have won on all accounts," she proclaimed. "Your mask has done its work. Take it off now; you look like a road agent."

Around them and above them, dark-eyed Alanyans stared out of windows at this odd arrival: a brown-haired Palernan boy arguing with a dark Ruthic girl, both seated in a mud-covered, weed-draped wagon drawn to a complete stop on the Street of the Innocents. Soon, though, the sight had lost its newness, and the dark eyes looked away—up to the higher tiers or down over the Xanthus onto the flat muddy plains of Palerna.

* * *

Many were the adventures that Brenn and Delia had on the streets of Hadrach in the two days they stayed there. Hadrach is like that: dirty in the lower tiers, shimmering and decadent at the top of the city; but wherever you go it is never eventless, it is never the same, nor is it ordinary.

First of all, the travelers learned that it was a month later than they had imagined. The sky, as always, told the truth: it was June now, when it should have been May, and Spring had passed into summer on the road from Corbinwood.

At first Brenn thought it was a joke—an Alanyan lie designed somehow to part him from his money, though he had no idea how such a plan might work. But from shop to shop, from low streets to the top of the city it was unanimously June, and Brenn decided he had lost a month as they passed through the Plains of Sh'Ryll.

It was an odd feeling, an odd loss, but Hadrach did its best to repay him. For an afternoon he and Delia took up with a caravan from Jaleel. The Master, a man built like his crystals, angular and compact, turned out to know Ricardo—indeed, turned out to be a friend he had made in his furthermost travel into the regions of ice. The caravan, with the Crystalmaster Ianafitch keeping its time and plotting its course through his lenses and minerals, had passed not half a mile from the Aralu. Ianafitch claimed that the woodlands around it had been leveled, so that from all sides a flat, desolate land encircled the dragon's thicket of thorn and briar.

"Naturally leveled?" Brenn asked, leaning over Ianafitch's mug of ale. The Alanyan covered the mouth of the glass with his hand and looked through his eyepiece scornfully at the young man who had introduced himself as Furis, an enchanter from Aquila.

If he is an enchanter, Ianafitch thought, *then I am the King of Palerna*.

"Naturally leveled," he replied, "only if you think a dragon's natural."

He smiled, his dark face curiously handsome in the tilted green light of the Alanyan pub.

"But why should dragons be of concern to one of your . . . profession, Furis?" he asked. "Far better that you meet Sycorax the Enchantress. Next tier up, if I have my bearings in this heap of a town."

"We plan to stay only for the night," Brenn explained, his thoughts racing toward excuses. "And besides, enchantresses are prominent folk where I come from. It might take days, even weeks for an audience."

Ianafitch regarded him suspiciously. Alertly, Delia pressed the man with questions.

"This Sycorax . . . is she the famous one?"

"Famous?" Brenn asked, and Ianafitch regarded him ironically through the eyepiece.

"Of course, laddie. Famous she is, though far past prime, and tumbling into her dotage. They say she's seen all of nine hundred years, a great and terrible ancience even for a witch, and that the very spectra of her power—the reflections and the imprints and the afterglows—have kept her alive two centuries past her time. But she is the one."

"From Argier?" Delia asked with a half-smile.

"So they still teach Felix the Coblyn in the Ruthic Islands?" Ianafitch responded with delight. "How did it go?

> *This damn'd witch Sycorax*
> *For mischiefs manifold, and sorceries terrible*
> *To enter human hearing . . .*

How did it go from there, girl?"

"*To enter human hearing,*" Delia began, her eyes closed. "It goes,

> *To enter human hearing, from Argier*
> *You know was banish'd; for one thing she did*
> *They would not take her life . . .*

If the same one she is indeed, then 'tis worth the wait for audience just to set eyes on a nine-hundred-year-old creature."

She turned to Brenn, her lovely golden eyes imploring.

"Then again," Ianafitch urged, "you might gain audience at once. Indeed, you might keep her awake. 'Twould win you the thanks of the folk along the Corridor of Limes, where the enchantress lives." He sighed, downed the last of his ale, and pushed away from the table. "But 'tis neither here nor there to me. I have a shipment of cinnamon and pepper to guide to Rabia early tomorrow, and no time to spend over ale with strangers, no matter how charming or interesting."

He smiled a long smile at Delia, stood, and walked to the door of the pub.

"This begins to interest me," Delia whispered to Brenn when the door closed behind the crystalmaster. "All this talk about 'keeping her awake'."

"Words of caution . . . *alchemist*," Brenn declared, folding his hands gracefully on the table. "In case you have forgotten, Alanyans, and the people who deal with Alanyans, do not let information drop casually. There are strands untied in this story, and Ianafitch, for one, *wants* them untied."

Delia nodded. "I see. So the prospects are dangerous. We've enemies abroad, and of this Sycorax we do not know enough. And since we plan to be here only one night . . ."

She stared at Brenn. Slowly both of them began to smile.

"Why not spend that night," Brenn whispered, "tying the strands of the story?"

"My thoughts exactly, Your Highness," Delia replied eagerly.

It was then, as though it had appeared only when they had agreed to the undertaking, that they both saw the small oval mirror the crystalmaster had left leaning against his vacated chair.

Brenn picked up the looking glass and slipped it into the backpack he had purchased on the first tier so that he could climb with less encumbrance. It reflected the green pub light against the door, and for a moment the lad thought of will-o'-the-wisp, of the false fire on the Sea of Shadows.

"Lapis may want this glass on my return," he said lightly to Delia.

But he was not sure he would carry it all that far.

* * *

Ianafitch paused a tier below the pub. The moonlight spread across the rockface, and the moon herself lay refracted in the dark waters of the Random Shallows.

The father's eyes. Furis or Comus, Archimago or Merlin himself—whatever name the lad had chosen, he had his father's eyes.

And the sword on the hand. The lenses of his eyepiece had shown that.

Though he could not undo the harm he had done to the lad's father, the crystalmaster felt a very old burden lift somewhat that warm Alanyan night. He leaned against the brass rail, and drawing forth the spyglass at his belt, looked north over the bay to the edge of sight, where Random glimmered faintly on the water.

At least and at last, had come the chance to help the son.

He dusted his hands and moved quickly toward an alley that ended in a stairwell down to the next tier. Best to make himself scarce, he thought, before they tried to do something honorable and foolish like return the thing.

For now it was on to Rabia with the shipments. But before he descended the stairwell, Ianafitch turned, obscure in the shadows of the alley, and looked back at the pub. It would have taken a powerful, no doubt a magical lens, to guide the eye through the darkness and let an onlooker know that the man was smiling.

For the first time in a long time, the crystalmaster had done a very unbusinesslike thing.

>>> XXIII <<<

It was not difficult to gain audience.

The witch's guards led them through the narrow gate into the Corridor of Limes. Lumbering ahead of them in outrageous green armor and beaked helmets that made them look like parrots gone tragically awry, the soldiers lit torches at the door of the house and, carrying the brands into the front room, beckoned Brenn and Delia through the oily smoke, up two narrow flights of stairs to the quarters of the witch.

They found her sprawled across three mattresses, too large to leave her room by its narrow doorway.

Brenn had never seen so much woman assembled in one place. Sycorax weighed at least five hundred pounds, and seem to gain a dozen more as he stood in the entrance and watched as she adjusted herself into a posture both regal and grotesque.

This was a legend in the flesh, large of body and of consequence. For Ianafitch had been right: people along the Corridor of Limes had groaned when the name of Sycorax was spoken, had spat and made the warding gestures when they spoke of her in return.

For three of her nine centuries, the enormous woman had not left the dimly lit room in which she now granted Brenn and Delia audience. By candlelight, on a curious lap desk she lost weekly in the folds of her body, the old witch had written decrees by which she had once ruled all of Hadrach. Lately—or in the two centuries that stood for "lately" in the slow reckonings of the Alanyan culture—the decrees had become more and more bizarre, but less and less powerful.

The upper tiers ignored the commands at first, fully aware that Sycorax was isolated by her own largeness and unable to see what went on above her out the single oval window in her room. So when she banished from the city all girls of twenty who were more beautiful than she, the wealthy Hadrachans shrugged and told their daughters to avoid walking on the Corridor of Limes, and when the witch ordered that the hooves of the horses and the wheels of the carts must be covered in velvet so that passing vehicles might not disturb her sleep, the route from the twelfth to the fourteenth tier simply shifted down to Seven Stars Alley on the eastern side of the town.

Other decrees had followed: that only she could wear purple, that summer was outlawed because it made her perspire excessively, that all mirrors should be turned toward her face alone. Meanwhile, her power dwindled from precinct to tier to street . . .

. . . until Sycorax had begun to dream.

In those dreams the vestiges of her magic took on power and life. Dissatisfied each morning with her view of the Corridor outside the window, Sycorax would dream it otherwise on the next night—hung with gardens, perhaps, or with its streets curved into the letters of her name or with the Shallows much closer, covering the buildings at the far end of her sight.

And in the morning when she awoke, the dreams had come true.

Quickly the people along the Corridor of Limes had begun to pack and leave. Some left the tier. Some even left Hadrach entirely, possessed of the fear that the witch was regaining her powers. When Sycorax saw the migration, she had dreamt walls around the area. It did not work: soon the Corridor was a desolate, haunted place, where those who remained were afraid to leave because they might walk over a bluff that had not been there the night before, or they might not leave at all, taking a promising side street only to have it empty at the very place from which they had embarked.

All that were left were the very poor, the very ill, and the very old, but each of them told the same story. Meanwhile, the keeping of her street demanded all her attentions, all her energies, and Sycorax grew tired, and slept more, and consequently dreamed more, and awoke to find the corridor even more changed and even more difficult to manage and control, for each change demanded another change.

So the blue circles under her eyes and the linen pale of her face were not powder or kohl or any other cosmetic from her beautiful youth, but the blue of fatigue and the white of exhaustion. When Brenn saw her from the doorway she was as grotesque as her dreams.

"The wizard Furis?" she asked, her voice thick and garbled, as though it came to him through water. "And the alchemist. It is a pleasure to meet with those whose callings are . . . metaphysical."

Brenn looked about the room. The furniture—chests, desks, and chairs—lay capsized or broken, and the walls were dark and dreary, hung with moldy tapestries that represented the witch in various triumphant postures and mystical landscapes.

In all of them she was lithe and beautiful.

Finding no place to sit, Brenn remained standing in the doorway. Sycorax beckoned to him with a pale hand marbled pink and white.

"What may I do for you, laddie? What do you beg of the Witch of Hadrach?"

Brenn had prepared his story well. With a proper bow he began what promised to be a long and glamorous account of far-flung adventures it would take even a witch months to prove or deny. By the second sentence he had stopped.

Sycorax was not interested.

Listlessly, she swirled burgundy in a glass goblet, staring abstractly into its bowl.

"I did not grant you audience to hear of your exploits, enchanter. The Four Winds know that I have enough of them to tell, myself."

As if in emphasis, she raised her hand and displayed it, palm up, to her visitors.

Brenn gaped, for at the tip of each finger some long-dead tattooist had marked the sign of one of the winds. Sycorax smiled, bent her ring finger, and a hot wind coursed through the room as though the brick of the southern wall were but an illusion.

"You are here not to entertain, but to bring me sleep," the witch explained soothingly.

"Sleep?" Brenn asked. "When your dreams bring forth all your desires, what need have you of further sleep? Why not dream yourself asleep? You will have your wish then. You will have anything you want."

"Spoken like a mountebank rather than an enchanter," Sycorax said lazily, her eye on the oval window. Brenn followed her gaze and noted the teasingly familiar shape of the window, but from where he stood he could see nothing but sky and a solitary black bird.

"Do you not think I have thought of that before?" she asked. "Of all the tricks of dreaming, all the terrible circles and tiers of thought? I have tried all potions and salves, I have practiced the spiritual exercises of the Philokalians and Umbrian massage.

I have even tried mathematics, for there is a formula the Arabs know that brings you forgetful sleep after long contemplation. I had thought that an enchanter might know something . . . different. Something that the outside world conceals from my window and my eyes.''

Dramatically, she pointed toward the window. The curtains rustled as the winds of her fingers passed over them.

The shape . . . the size . . . Brenn thought. ''Have you tried lethe?'' he suggested.

''Seventy years ago,'' Sycorax replied laconically. ''Made things even worse. I would wake and find part of the Corridor gone entire, and I had changed it so many times that constructing it from memory was well-nigh impossible. It set me back years.''

''I beg your pardon?'' Delia asked.

The blue-rimmed eyes turned suddenly, brilliantly, toward the young alchemist.

If she is old and scattered, Brenn thought, *I shudder to think what she was in her prime.*

''Set me back years, my dear.''

''From what?'' Delia asked. ''Years from what?''

The reptile eyes of the witch clouded and strayed.

''Why . . . from gathering it all together. It changes too much beyond my eyes.''

Brenn shifted the pack on his back, felt Ianafitch's abandoned mirror jostle against his shoulder blade. Unthinkingly, he drew out the glass and turned around, intending to set the piece by the door until he and Delia left. Something about the mirror haunted and teased him. He looked at it closely, and saw the reflection of Sycorax over his shoulder.

She looked forlorn, lonely and lost within that mountainous body. It reminded him of the Goniph—of a strange empty sadness he recalled beneath all that weight and decadence and bluster—and he felt a sudden sharp pain. For a moment, dimly, Brenn thought he saw what Sycorax must have looked like eight centuries ago.

He thought she must have been beautiful.

''Is that a mirror?'' the witch asked, her interest suddenly fresh and her eyes focused.

''Indeed it is,'' Brenn replied, turning to face her. He wondered how he could have imagined beauty in the morass of flesh and corruption that lay before him.

"You know the law in Hadrach," the witch said coldly.

Brenn and Delia confessed that they did not.

So Sycorax instructed them how all mirrors must be turned to catch the reflection of the Witch of Hadrach. When her visitors complied, they were astounded to see the likeness of a beautiful woman in the glass.

"It is stunning!" Delia exclaimed. "Like one of your tapestries, m'lady!"

"Oh, that?" Sycorax asked noncommittally. " 'Tis but a painter's trick . . . the landscape behind me."

Astonished, the two looked at the witch, who continued to admire herself in the mirror. Slowly, the landscape behind her beautiful reflected image resolved itself into a garden, complete with topiary, fountains, and gaudy, mildly obscene and energetic Parthian statuary.

Delia chuckled softly.

"Stasis . . ." Sycorax murmured. "By the west wind Gorlewin, who brings autumn and rest, it is stasis behind me. See? Even the water in the fountains is still. I have done this for a hundred years, wrought portraits of my moving face in a still landscape, wrought—"

"But never like this, m'lady!" Brenn interrupted. Alarmed, Delia stared into his eyes and nodded almost indetectably toward the door. Brenn ignored her, set upon a dangerous venture. For melancholy thoughts of the Goniph had led to the core of the old thief's wisdom—a phrase rehearsed and repeated through Brenn's youthful apprenticeship in the gutters of Wall Town.

People, the Goniph used to say, *see exactly what they want to see*. It was the swindler's prayer, the cozener's article of faith, and Brenn breathed it quietly to himself as he set about to hoodwink a nine-hundred-year-old witch.

"For you see, this mirror is Gorlewin's own. From the ice regions of the Polis Glacialis, this is, where the Lapps reflect their homeland onto its surface and carry the image with them as a map of their return."

Panic-stricken, Delia nodded toward the door, this time more urgently. But Brenn continued.

"That is, at least, the common wisdom that surrounds this speculum, m'lady. But there are other, darker rumors . . ."

He leaned forward theatrically and whispered.

"Some say that there is a chant, said over the glass, that renders it *extrusive*, if you will, rather than *intrusive*."

Sycorax frowned. Delia's eyes gestured wildly at the door.

"By that, m'lady, I mean that I have heard the Lapp hunters would freeze their home, as it were. That the chant would hold both original and reflection in perpetual . . . what is the word?"

"Stasis," Sycorax replied. "Perpetual stasis."

Delia dropped her gaze and leaned against the wall. The lad's song and dance had found audience.

"Stasis, it is, m'lady," Brenn agreed, taking a deep breath and holding up the mirror. "And for a simple fee, I should be willing to tell you that chant."

"And that price?" Sycorax asked, narrowing her eyes.

"Tell me what you know of Amalek," Brenn stated boldly.

"The dragon? Why?"

"We have business and trade," answered Brenn.

"Trade with Amalek? You'll trade your life for a handful of thorns! D'you fancy yourself a wyrmslayer, wizard? D'you know how many of your kind have gone to the Aralu and never returned?"

"My fate in the face of the dragon is my own concern," Brenn replied bravely, though the words of the witch stirred his dark imaginings. "Teach me what you know."

"First the chant," Sycorax urged.

Brenn crouched by the monstrous woman. Slowly he toyed with the mirror he carried, looking once, twice, into his own face. It was a good likeness. The mirror was smooth, flawless —certainly no uneven Umbrian glass where the image enlarged the nose or receded the chin of the viewer.

And yet she had looked into it, and seen an altogether different reflection. He steeled himself, recalled the Goniph's words, then plumbed his memory through the hundreds of lines of poetry learned and recited in Terrance's toplesss tower.

It had better work, he thought, *or this time I'm a squinch fly for sure*. And he recited the first of the verses in which a mirror figured.

Leave lady in your glasse of christall clene,
Your goodly selfe for evermore to vew:
And in my selfe, my inward selfe I meane,
Most lively like, behold your semblant trew.
Within my hart, though hardly it can shew
Things so divine to vew of earthly eye:
The fayre Idea of your celestiall hew,
And every part remaines immortally.

"Lovely!" Sycorax twittered, her slablike hands folding daintily under her chin in a grotesque parody of prayer. "I love especially the words pertaining to my *celestiall hew*. Go away now, and leave the mirror."

The mirror. Suddenly it dawned on Brenn—the strange, teasing images which had plagued him in the witch's chamber. The size and shape of the mirror . . .

His thoughts hurtled from strategy to strategy.

"There is more," he stated quietly. " 'Tis a potion of which the user drinks. Without which, of course, the chant is only so much poetry."

"Where is it?" Sycorax demanded. "Give it to me."

Her hand rose and a scorching wind blew past them, charring Brenn and singeing Delia's bare arms.

"About Amalek," Brenn prompted, coughing. "The verse, of course, was a show of good faith on my part."

Ceasing the infernal blow, and sighing a huge billowing sigh that filled the room, Sycorax conceded that indeed he *had* shown faith, that indeed he was *owed* what little knowledge of dragonry her nine hundred years had brought her, but she would be more rich and searching of memory were he to produce the potion, let her see it, let her hold the vial in her delicate hand.

Brenn smiled. It was like the markets of Gaunt, the council of wizardry. Slowly, as if it were the hardest thing in the world he had to do, as if it brought him great sadness to deny such a magnificent and substantial lady, he informed Sycorax that the potion had yet to be mixed.

He nodded knowingly at Delia, who was already ahead of his gesture and had reached into her pouch and brought forth fragrant rosemary, juniper, and lavender.

Brenn knew them all by smell. Knew also that the mixture would have no more virtue or properties than a strong herbal tea. Finally, though, with a strange half-smile, the girl reached into her pouch for the last ingredient. At once Brenn recognized the egg-shaped leaves with the blunt notches, the small white flowers and the green berries just now turning to black.

Dwale. Delia had enough of it in her hand to stupefy a team of horses.

"He has been here as long as I have," Sycorax said, squinted at the flashing hands of the Ruthic girl, who prepared the potion with misdirecting rapid gestures and a flurry of fingers, "an old and dangerous presence ten miles to the east of here, in the midst of that thornbrake they call the Aralu. Taken with himself, he is, as are most dragons, but this one is fond of his wits rather than his beauty or strength—fond of his insight and talents. That last ingredient, m'dear . . . I don't believe I recognized those black berries . . ."

"The fruit of Memphis," Delia said tersely, her eyes on the bowl of the mortar. "A type of dried morel which gives the potion its particular flavor. A capital astringent, as I'm sure you know."

"Certainly," Sycorax replied, though her face showed she was none too certain. "Fond of his insights and his talents, I was saying. As a consequence, subject to flattery, I hear, and that may be his only weakness, except whatever else it is that arises from that fondness—I know not. The potion?"

Delia nodded and handed the black, sweet-smelling liquor to Brenn. He passed the mortar under his nose, nodded approvingly, and reaching for the bevelled glass goblet that contained the dregs of Sycorax's wine, mixed the whole thing together in the enormous jewelled bowl of the vessel.

When the witch awakened, her visitors were long gone. She tried to locate them out the window of her chamber, but all she saw was the Corridor of Limes, shadowed in the half-dark of the gloaming . . .

. . . and still. Still as marble sculpture, or as the landscape in the background of an enormous, well-crafted tapestry.

It was what she had wanted to see all along, this stillness in the city. Sycorax lay back on her mattresses and poured herself yet another glass of wine. Her sluggishness had not altogether left her, but surely that was a side effect from a potion that had worked remarkably and completely. Lulled by the drink and by the words of the chant she repeated and would repeat regularly, incessantly, she did not notice that the mirror Brenn had carefully lodged in her window reflected the candlelit landscape woven into the tapestry behind her.

Had her laziness permitted her to move to another spot in the room, perhaps the illusion would have been destroyed. Then again, the curtains were deathly still, unmoved by the breezes from the outside, and her wishes kept her from noticing. For what she had was what she had always wanted—surroundings she thought were forever past change. She had already forgotten the wizard Furis and the Ruthic alchemist.

Forever would she rule, the bride of quietness, the queen of silence and slow time.

Deep amid walls of black, glittering rock, below a thicket of thorns, Amalek raised his enormous head. For a moment the scales parted over one great eye, and with the dragonsight he saw all the way to the walls of Hadrach, though it was night and the city was ten miles away.

He rumbled in the belly of the dead volcano. Something had stirred him from his slumber.

Again it was the Great Witch of Maraven, summoning him with candle and spell.

The green scales covered his eye again. Under the lids her image fluttered, wavered in a distant candlelight. The pale face framed in blue-black hair, the fathomless eyes the color of which he could never quite determine—she was there again and summoning him, her voice riding the distant murmuring and drone of innumerable bees.

Again? he asked. *Th'art insistent on this lad, Ravenna.*

Insistent, because my birds tell me he approaches you within the day, she whispered, her eyes flashing gray and black and gray.

The dragon stirred, irritated at this awakening. But his curiosity had been roused as well, as it was when anyone ventured to his lair.

What does that mean to you? he asked curtly. His wings twitched as the huge muscles lengthened and stretched.

Wiser still to ask what it means to you, Lord Amalek. He comes for the Bag of Ladra.

Why bother thyself with this, Ravenna? he asked, probing for her intentions. *What if I should search my hoard and destroy the thing?*

The image of the Great Witch wavered.

This discomfits thee, Amalek said, puffing. The ravens in the thorn bushes about him arose with a flurry of boding and black feathers, startled by the onrush of dragonscent.

Not at all. But it might be less inspired than other choices, Amalek. The bag might be useful to you.

Or perhaps to thee? the dragon drawled. *What care I of Forest Lords or curses, Ravenna?*

Yet another pause. This time longer.

Destroy the lad, Amalek. Not the bag. He thinks he's a king, as you surely know.

And what are kings to me, Ravenna? What care I who rules the petty kingdoms of men? Kill him thyself.

The dragon smiled cunningly, and stirred back onto his side. He made his breathing leisurely and slow, thought of thermals and the wide expanses of the air.

Indeed, Ravenna thought he was passing back into sleep.

What I need, Lord Amalek, is to break his will. An inward destruction. And I shall see to that. Only let him have the bag, Amalek. It will draw Galliard and his family from Corbinwood.

How devious of you, Amalek teased menacingly. *Since you have been so . . . unsporting in your game with Terrance, I shall unravel the bag and dangle the string at your nose for my own amusement.*

No! Ravenna commanded. The candlelight flickered and wavered, as though a wind had passed through her faraway chambers. *I mean . . . dear Lord Amalek,* the witch coaxed. *Most insightful and ancient and all-powerful of living things . . .*

The dragon purred, savoring her transparent flattery.

Let this Pretender escape with the bag.

He listened deeply to the sound of her thoughts. She was dizzied by her own machinery and plotting.

Calmly Amalek thought of the peace of the mountains, the convenience of high winds.

He could not resist one last question of the Great Witch.

What says thy king of these matters?

The dragon felt a new coldness in the air. The corners of his mouth curled slightly. Clearly, even from a great distance, he smelled the fear.

The fear, and another smell. He knew it at once.

I speak for the King, Amalek, came the answer at last.

The dragon laughed softly, and a warm fetid wind filtered through Hadrach, the smell of ash and carrion disturbing the cinnamon and incense in the air, so that many in the town dreamt uncomfortably of death and tombs that night.

Oh, I am sure thou speakest for the King, Ravenna. It has come to a pass where someone else must.

The image of the Great Witch boiled angrily in his eyes, then faded in a flash of uncontrolled fear.

The dragon chuckled and stirred, this time toward a genuine sleep.

I am weary, Witch of Maraven. I trust thou art weary, too. Let me lullay thy weariness toward restful sleep, for I know all the songs in the world, and there is one I remember especial.

Had Brenn already started toward the Aralu that night—had he not remained in Hadrach in order to see Delia off toward home on the morrow—he might have heard the dragon singing softly over the plains.

Ianafitch did, on the Rabia route. He would tell his grandchildren how that song insinuated into the night and the wind on the grasslands, and how, though the June weather was temperate, when the song was finished the ground over which the caravan moved glittered with a harsh and forbidding frost.

The crystalmaster remembered none of the melody, and little of the words, but there was one refrain he would mouth to the grandchildren, to thrill them with a distant, ancient terror:

> *Is that the wind dying? O no;*
> *It's only two devils, that blow*

Through a murderer's bones, to and fro
In the ghost's moonshine.

>>> XXIV <<<

Galliard and Ricardo had regarded one another distantly to begin
with, and for good reason. Though the fight with the wyvern
had revealed to each of them that the other was a valiant, daring,
even formidable fighter, the caution remained, deep and unspoken. They mistrusted each other by instinct.

One look at the big Alanyan, decked out in green and orange
and four shades of gold, his long black hair twined in a single
scandalous braid, had made Galliard decide all that dazzle must
hide a great wound, a great weakness. He joked with Ricardo, and
passed time in amiable storytelling, but he was convinced
that the man was a fraud.

And one look at the young fellow who jested with him skeptically in the midst of the clearing, tall and thin and all too young
in his forest browns and greens, raised even greater doubts in
Ricardo. Surely the lad was brave: he had shown that, after all,
in the fight with the wyvern. But beyond physical courage, there
were deeper regions in the Forest Lord that seemed green and
untested. His forestry was good, as far as the Alanyan could
tell, and his battle tactics of skirmish and ambush suitable for
obscure terrain.

But if the curse is lifted, it is open ground for him and his
followers, Ricardo thought. *And against Helmar and Dragmond,*
I'd fancy a more weathered commander.

So they sized one another doubtfully, until Ricardo returned
from the Plains of Sh'Ryll with visions of Aquila and the sword.

Ricardo rode into Corbinwood from the west, crossing the Boniluce just downstream of Keedwater. Over the grassy Zephyrian
plains he rode, stopping twice to rest and feed his tired black

stallion, and one occasion eluding completely a squadron of the vaunted Zephyrian cavalry.

He concerned himself little with what was a remarkable feat of bravery and horsemanship, his thoughts dwelling instead on the sword Libra.

He broached the matter of the sword to Thomas first, for it was the bard who met him where the Boniluce emerged from Corbinwood, a good three miles from the clearing. Galliard had known he was coming, evidently, and had sent Thomas to guide him into the forest stronghold.

It was a fortunate choice of escort. The bard seemed closer to Ricardo's own temperament, closer to lore, and the most likely to listen to another's vision. Thomas nodded as Ramiro spoke, then crouched over the Boniluce, dipped his hands into the river, and holding a handful of water up to the moonlight, pored over its reflection as he would a book or an omen.

The sword's name was Libra, Thomas told the Alanyan. Its business was Galliard's alone.

Then with some reluctance, though he had figured it would come to this pass, Ricardo took his vision to the Forest Lord. Galliard regarded him skeptically at first, suspecting that the Alanyan might well have followed his vision because it seemed less perilous than accompanying Brenn into the Aralu. Nevertheless, the sword was Libra: there was no question about that. And something in the sword had joined his fate with the shifty, gaudy man who had seen it in the distant crystals.

Libra, Galliard explained, was an Aquilan heirloom. Its presence was wrapped up somehow with the duchy itself, with the promise that the sword should *single out the crown of the line*. He did not know, however, what the promise meant. Indeed, he had almost forgotten the weapon, supposing that its magic had run dry at the death of Mardonius and the end of the line of Danton—that the "crown of the line" had meant simply the end of a dynasty.

"The last I heard," the Forest Lord said, "the sword was Dragmond's. It hangs ceremoniously in the throne room of Kestrel Tower—regal in appearance, but useless. As so many things in that throne room are."

Ricardo smiled at the jest. "But unlike those other Maravenian ornaments, the sword Libra has appeared in my vision. So I propose . . . its retrieval.''

A hush spread over the clearing. The cousins looked at one another apprehensively.

The reciting owl at the Alanyan's shoulder stirred and trilled.

"Its retrieval?" Sendow asked, brushing pine needles from his hair.

Ricardo smiled mischievously, his eyes dancing from cousin to cousin.

"What would you have from us?" Ponder asked, moving to stand by Galliard.

"Your . . . support," Ricardo replied.

"You have that," Sendow insisted. "As friend of Brennart and of Terrance, you have our great good will. Would that some of us could go with you. But perhaps you were hasty in returning: Brennart might have used your help where the thorns twine in the Aralu."

Ricardo ignored the accusation. He looked at Galliard calmly.

"The curse will lift or the curse will not," he said. "And its outcome lies with Brennart in Alanya. Terrance told me long ago that the final steps of that journey would be Brenn's alone. What falls to us is not the waiting only, but the manner of the wait. What if the great events take place in a far-off country? What if others are the heroes? We need not be idle."

"We shall do our part, Alanyan," Sendow answered a little angrily. "But perhaps you have forgotten that the curse confines us to this forest."

"Is it the curse?" Ricardo asked. "Or scruples?"

It was not a popular question. Sendow stepped forward, his hand on the hilt of his sword. The owl squawked, and sprang from Ricardo's shoulder into the branches of the cedar.

Ponder hastened to step between the two men, for that space was charged and volatile.

It was then that Galliard laughed suddenly. The cousins turned to their leader in astonishment.

"Imagine," the Forest Lord said, "being schooled in ethics by the likes of you, Ricardo."

"As odd, sir," Ricardo said angrily, "as my accepting—"

"Come with me," Galliard interrupted, pleasantly but quickly. "And reveal to me alone what it is that you would have us do."

So it came to pass that the two of them rode north out of Corbinwood onto the Gray Strand. Galliard sat lightly in the saddle behind Ricardo, hooded and masked against the summer night. Again, ghostly and swift in the saddle, they eluded the Watch, and soon found themselves on black sand, racing up the Palernan coast.

"It is like my vision," Ricardo said loudly so that his companion could hear above the wind and the hoofbeats of the great black stallion. "This sand and the Gray Sea and the rocky coast of Aquila."

"Has Maraven changed that much in my absence?" Galliard asked.

"In ten years? Why, the whole *nature* of a city can change in the course of a year, sir. There is fire and flood and terrible neglect within the walls of the best of places. And these are Dragmond's years: the years of the Great Witch, of the Watch and the Death."

"You shall see to it, as you promised, that my hands stay in my pockets," Galliard urged. "That the good folk of Maraven will have nothing to fear from my lifting."

"I shall, indeed," Ricardo replied. "Which is why in the part of Maraven to which I intend to take you, good folk will be difficult to find."

They rode through the evening together, and the moon floated distant and low in the eastern sky above the Sea of Shadows. Two groups of horsemen passed them as they rode—one north and east of them, hurtling toward Maraven, and the other gray and moonlit and helmeted, moving more slowly south and west toward Corbinwood.

Galliard wondered again if he was doing the right thing. He had last seen the world outside the forest when he was still a child, when it seemed to promise all things glorious and adventuresome—the marbled streets of Constantinople, the great palaces of Roma and Londinium, the wine-dark seas where the gray leviathans danced in the spray. Now it was daunting—too large, too dangerous, and bordered on all sides by witches and dragons, kings and chaos.

Caution does nought against the likes of these, he told himself. Ricardo's long braid, lifted by the wind, brushed against his shoulder.

And yet witch and king will remain, regardless of whether the curse is lifted. Then, when I am most needed, I shall be no more prepared to treat with them than I am now, a hooded monk in a green glade.

He smiled and breathed deeply the rich and fragrant salty air. There was something sane in the seaside, whole and direct and completed.

Now, he told himself, *while the eyes of Witch and King are turned to the east, let someone strike from the west and south. For the real curse is fear and caution and waiting.*

From his sleeve he drew the engraved bowl and magnetized needle of the compass. Though he could not recall taking it with him, he was glad he had brought it: this open country was frightening, the landmarks so distant that he wondered how Ricardo was able to reckon their whereabouts.

Then he noticed that the names of each direction were written in Alanyan on the compass bowl.

Sheepishly, he slipped the device into a pouch at Ricardo's belt.

The Alanyan smiled, and spurred his stallion to a gallop.

They came to the ferry just after midnight, when the only lights apparent in the deep mist along the shoreline were the lights on the Western Gate and those high in the tower across the Causeway.

Bundled in gray blankets against the settling mist, Ricardo and Galliard managed to rouse a stubborn old Aquilan ferryman from a sleep well-oiled with Zephyrian gin. Once out of bed and fully awake, the man became even more stubborn, unmoved by persuasion or pleas or bribery. Barco, for so they called him, placed his pewter flask in his hip pocket and shook his head vehemently and finally. He claimed that the Gray Sea was haunted, that passage after sundown was foolish if not impossible. If that were not enough, the King forbade nightly crossing to all but members of the court, and if the King forbade it, they were all fools even to consider it.

Ricardo had endured enough. The man was impassable, he decided, as reluctantly he reached beneath his cloak for the dagger that would assure their crossing.

It was then that Galliard pushed back his hood and stood bareheaded before the man. The old Aquilan squinted, gaped, then bowed reverently, if awkwardly.

"Forgive me, sir," he whispered hoarsely, "for your eyes and your countenance mark ye for who ye are. Ye're Edmund's lad as sure as I'm alive and at the edge o' th' water!"

The Forest Lord closed his eyes, silently thanking the Four Winds that either recklessness or trust, or perhaps even both, would carry him across the water.

For after Galliard's unveiling, Barco needed little coaxing to ferry the men across to the Aquilan coast. Briskly he rousted his two strong sons, and the three of them donned gloves, passed the pewter flask among them once more, then pushed the craft into the Gray Sea, where, with Barco as steersman and the stout lads as rowers, the boat coasted swiftly through the choppy waters.

Galliard glanced back only once. The stallion looked forlorn on the Palernan coast, tethered beside the ferryman's shanty. It occurred to the Forest Lord that he had made no plans as to how they would return from Kestrel Tower once they had recovered the sword.

He hoped that Ricardo had more foresight.

"Look to the port side, Duke Galliard!" the old man called out much too loudly. Then, his voice muted by a warning look from Ricardo, he continued, his words scarcely audible above the regular splash of the oars.

"Up there in the Bay of Ashes, where the old ones lay to rest their fathers. That's where the haunting begun. 'Twas the Witch what done the most of it, coming out here with chants and incants and thoughts of raisin' the dead."

Galliard and Ricardo exchanged an uncertain glance and looked toward the bay. There in the far water, where the moonlight played over the spindrift, the sea would swell and buckle and break as though something unspeakable floated just beneath its surface.

"What's more, everbody knows she done it," Barco continued serenely. "I don't know where they get the idea that we *don't* know."

"They say that crowned heads are more visible than they could imagine, Barco," Galliard replied, his uneasy gaze still on the northern waters.

"Well, then they say right, Your Grace," the old man concluded. "Which is not to say that we know what you do down in Corbinwood among them cousins," he added hastily.

Galliard smiled. For the first time since they had left the woods, he relaxed a little, leaning against the side of the boat.

"If you knew, Barco, you would be disappointed," he maintained. " 'Tis forestry and boredom, and the wait for momentous things."

"Aye, sir," the old ferryman agreed drolly. "Compared to the princely style in which I am accustomed to conductin' myself, I expect it is poor fare indeed."

They came aground not a hundred yards from Kestrel Tower. Barco's sons helped their passengers onto the sand, and Ricardo and Galliard scaled the black rocks of the Aquilan beach, climbing steadily and nimbly toward Dragmond's stronghold.

"May the winds be behind ye, sirs!" Barco called out softly. Galliard turned and waved, then gestured Ricardo to a level spot in the rocks, where they sat and watched the ferry dwindle into the dark night and the darker seacoast.

" 'Tis surprising cold for a summer night," Ricardo muttered. "I could do with some of the gin you're hiding, Master Galliard."

Sheepishly, his eyes still following the ferry until, at last, he could see it no more, Galliard handed the pewter flask to his companion.

" 'Twould have been the death of old Barco, soon or late," he said with a crooked grin. "And besides, I left him its weight in gold for the trouble."

Scaling the tower walls with a makeshift grappling hook and twenty feet of rope that the Forest Lord had produced from nowhere, the two adventurers found themselves in Dragmond's throne room within an hour. The sword was where they expected it to be, hung valiantly high on the north wall of the chamber, crossed with another blade above a shield bearing the ancient arms of Aquila.

Clambering onto the mantle and from there onto a tapestry portraying one of Helmar's early victories, in which a cunning artisan had replaced the face of the general with that of King Dragmond, Ricardo scrambled along the weave like a spider until, reaching out over a giddy thirty-foot drop onto the stone floor of the chamber, he clutched the sword and held it aloft in triumph.

And then, the story goes, five Watchmen stumbled into the throne room. They did not think to look above them, where they would have seen the second trespasser dangling from the arras; instead, they must have thought they had burst in upon a solitary burglar—a young man, slight of build and armed with a rather tame-looking short sword. Confidently they moved forward, until the young fellow crouched in an Aquilan fencing stance—sword low in the left hand and hooked dagger held high in the right.

The burglar, it seemed, was schooled in the art of swordsmanship. That he was schooled well became apparent when a deft move of his sword hand disarmed one of the Watchmen, and then the dagger slipped quickly in until it rested with its point tickling the unbroken skin of his neck.

"Go back to sleep," Galliard ordered calmly, pushing the terrified man away. "This does not concern you." He backed toward the window and the rope, his eyes fixed on the Watchmen in front of him. The soldiers looked at one another in apprehension, then no doubt thinking of the punishment that awaited them if they let the trespasser escape, they pursued him, crouching and ducking and capsizing chair and table as they approached him across the ornate, candlelit room.

Finally, his back to the window, Galliard could retreat no farther. Silently, as lethally as a diving hawk, he sprang toward the nearest Watchman. Vaulting onto a table and somersaulting over a whirling sword, he landed squarely on his feet behind the baffled soldier. Before the man could raise his sword, the Forest

Lord caught him in the side with the edge of the blade. The Watchman toppled over with a groan, and Galliard turned to face the rest of his assailants.

It was then that Ricardo came hurtling down from the rafters onto the back of the Watch lieutenant, leaving torn tapestry and a fluttering owl in his wake. The dive itself was attack enough: the impact snapped the soldier's back, and he fell face forward onto the throne. Libra flashing above his head, the Alanyan felled another Watchman before the last two, quite overwhelmed by the skills of their enemy, spun and raced out the door through which they had entered.

The reciting owl perched on the back of the throne and sang merrily,

> *They dyd them to the tresoure-hows,*
> *As fast as they myght gone;*
> *The lokkes, that were of full gode stele,*
> *They brake them everichone.*
>
> *They toke away the silver vessell,*
> *And all that thei migt get,*
> *Pecis, masars, ne sponis,*
> *Wolde thei not forget.*

"We have no time for that!" Ricardo snapped at the bird, and gestured toward the window. Quickly Galliard grabbed onto the rope and lowered himself. The Alanyan stood at the window, watching the doors of the chamber until Galliard was safely on the ground below. Then he climbed over and followed out the window into the deep Maravenian night.

Safely on the ground, the Alanyan looked around him. Galliard was nowhere to be seen. For a moment Ricardo pushed down a rising panic, imagining all sorts of dire things that might have happened to the Forest Lord here in the enemy's stronghold. But soon, indeed before any of those nightmares could take root and flourish, the young man stepped from behind a dry brown cedar, a crestfallen look on his face.

"Just imagine, Ricardo!" Galliard exclaimed. "To neglect a grove of this wonder, these . . . *prospects*! All kinds of trees are planted here, and 'tis summertime, when they should flourish like Corbinwood!''

"Seaside soil is poor," Ricardo snapped. "Let us leave this place, sire!''

"Cedar, cypress, acacia, myrtle! By the Winds, 'tis a grove! 'Tis a forest, given a woodsman and a touch of care!''

"You'll find neither here, Galliard," Ricardo replied. "Make haste! the Watch is combing the grounds.''

Still the Forest Lord tarried. He crouched in the dark, at a business that both mystified and irritated Ricardo. Ricardo peered over Galliard's shoulder, but the deed was still obscure, the movements hidden.

"Just keep watch a moment, friend," Galliard urged, his smile mischievous in the moonlight. Exasperated, the Alanyan leaned against a ragged pine, looking up through its spare branches to the candle-reddened windows of the Tower. The owl settled on a low branch beside him, swiveling its head to regard him with wide, quizzical eyes.

It was then that Ricardo saw the King.

Dragmond stood on a balcony, framed in moonlight, his unkempt robe brushed idly by the night wind. He seemed distracted, bleary, as though aroused from deep sleep. There was something in his stillness that made Ricardo marvel.

Ricardo himself froze behind the trunk of the tree, but soon it was clear that the King's gaze was vacant and seaward.

"*He takis the campion in the stour,*" the owl muttered,

> *the capitane closit in the tour,*
> *the lady in bour full of bewte:*
> Timor mortis conturbat me . . .

"Hist!" Ricardo whispered, brushing away the bird and his incomprehensible song.

As quickly as that, the King vanished. But the sight of him stayed with the Alanyan for days, and troubled the sleep from his nights.

In the tower before sunrise, the commotion began, and with it the rumors that an armed force had seized the throne room, that

Zephyr had invaded, that the dead had returned to avenge themselves on the Witch. The Watch, an assemblage of wealthy and unblooded recruits, was understandably scattered and confused.

However, one veteran lieutenant—a man named Florian— soon discovered that the invasion was not as momentous as everyone had imagined. There were two trespassers, at most three or four. And with the Watch's numbers against them, they would be looking to escape.

Acting quickly, Florian combed through the barracks for the guards most nearly armed and assembled. Urgently and brilliantly, he sharked up a squadron of twenty or so, and at the head of this patchwork platoon stormed over the Causeway in pursuit of the trespassers, fully convinced that, the defenses of the Tower in Captain Lightborn's charge, over the Causeway and into the city was the only reasonable escape route.

Lieutenant Florian had done everything right. Too well, if it be known, for he had mustered his men too quickly. He had them through the tower gates and fifty yards up the Causeway when the last of his troops caught up with him—two volunteers, cloaked and hooded, who blended among the others unnoticeably, since haste had taken precedence over regulation, and nobody was quite in uniform.

Nonetheless, one of the men was helmeted, and from a distance that seemed good enough to Florian, as he turned and paced south along the Causeway, followed by a wave of men. Had he known, of course, that the helmet concealed Ricardo's long black braid of an Alanyan impostor, his search would have been over.

Nor did he count his men at departure or upon return, so when the squadron came back from Ships with two men less than when it left the Tower, he was no wiser for the change.

And from Ships it is a short way to the West Gate and the Gray Strand beyond. There the stallion waited, and Barco with another pewter flask, this one filled for the road with a hot herb tea. Galliard and Ricardo were exultant, triumphant, and though they really should have been more cautious, given the siege and the cavalry patrols, they were singing aloud over the Gray Strand as Corbinwood loomed into sight, the owl at Ricardo's shoulder the only creature among them in tune,

Ha ha! Ha ha! This world doth pass
  Most merrily I'll be sworn,
For many an honest Indian ass
  Goes for a unicorn.

          Fara diddle dyno,
          This is idle fyno.

Tie hie! tie hie! O sweet delight!
  He tickles this age that can
Call Tullia's ape a marmasyte
  And Leda's goose a swan.

          Fara diddle dyno,
          This is idle fyno.

In Kestrel Tower, the Great Witch paced the throne room in puzzlement. It was not Terrance, she told her companion. It was certainly not the boy.

"And perhaps I should rest easy, knowing that," she murmured, her eyes on the open window, on the rope still dangling from its sill. "Perhaps that should be enough. But 'tis not. By the winds and the darkness beneath them, 'tis far from enough!"

Ravenna turned and stalked from the room. Lightborn remained behind. Alone, he looked about him and walked slowly to the throne, resting his hand lightly on its arm. Then he sat, and with a long, insolent gaze surveyed the room. From door to window he looked, from floor to ceiling, his eyes finally resting in alarm on the shield adorned with the ancient arms of Aquila, on the single sword hung above it, and on the vacant, clean outline of the Sword of Libra.

>>> XXV <<<

The plains surrounding the Aralu were harsh, bare and desolate, as though drought had ravaged them, or the countryside was still trying to recover from an ancient fire.

Brenn stopped his horse at the edge of the cracked, dry plain. It was dawn, the sun just clearing the edge of the horizon, and before him, about half a mile away, the tangle of thorns and brambles shimmered in the heat already rising from the parched ground. Above that grim, writhing array of branch and briar rose the dark cinder cone of the dead volcano.

Brenn breathed deeply and looked in his knapsack at the strange array of belongings he had carried from Corbinwood. There were two small limbs from a rune tree, their markings already fading into the grain of the wood as the severed branches dried with time and the journey. There was a handful of serpentine roots, a silk map, a bow, and a dozen arrows.

Those things, the perfume bottle from Lapis, and the song in his memory were his earthly belongings, and if he could believe Terrance and Delia, they were enough even to overthrow old Amalek, the Great Wyrm of the Aralu, the Scourge of Alanya.

He leaned forward, the reins slack in his hands. It did not seem likely, such power from such odd and discarded things. He did not like puzzles, and the prospect of fitting these items together in a dragon-slaying plan seemed futile to him, almost silly.

Yet he remembered Delia's parting words as she stood on the deck of the boat to Random in the darkest part of the night. She kissed him lightly on the forehead, as though she bestowed a blessing. As the barge moved away into the Shallows on the only fair tide of the day, she waved to him and shouted over the calls of the bargemen and the racket of the never-sleeping harbor.

"*You lack for nothing!* Remember that! You have everything you need, and it only awaits your imagining!"

There was something else she said, something about caution, but Brenn lost it in the mist as the barge vanished around a squat peninsula, and reappeared as a bobbing lantern in open water, far from his hearing.

"Good luck, Delia," Brenn had murmured as slowly, a bit clumsily, he guided his horse through the narrow streets of seaside Hadrach, up and down the spiraling inland roads and out through the eastern gates. From there, guided by the skeptical directions of a green-clad Alanyan guard and then by his daylight memories of the silk map, he crossed the miles alone, steering the uneasy horse toward a hovering gray smoke on the eastern horizon, over which indignant black birds wheeled, crying like lost souls.

Brenn smiled grimly now as the horse began to pick his way more carefully over the hard borderlands toward the Aralu. It seemed as though his friends had a talent for leaving him, from the Goniph and Faye to Terrance and Ricardo, and finally Delia, sailing off placidly into the darkened Sea of Shadows.

Becoming a king was a lonely trade.

"I guess that's why there's so few of them," Brenn said through clenched teeth, and shifted in the saddle as the horse lurched and recovered.

Deep in the vent of the dead volcano, the dragon felt him approaching.

The green scales parted from his piercing eyes, and Amalek saw the lad on his horse, clutching the reins, headed east, more or less. Steering by old lights, the boy was, into a mystery he could not fathom, against an intelligence he could not hope to master.

Amalek growled lazily, his tail thrashing in the rubble, in the dry brambles.

He had waited for months.

Early, when Ravenna had first come to him in fear and uncertainty when the lad had slipped from her grasp, the dragon had listened quietly. Then, as the witch turned her sights frantically from Partha to Jaleel, he had closed his eyes amid the thorn and bramble of the Aralu, and he had called up the dragonsight and found the boy within hours.

Of course, he had not told her; he had let the witch come to that knowledge herself. By the time she knew that Brenn was in Corbinwood and had sent Amalek to look for him, the dragon knew more about the lad than she did—than perhaps anyone, except Terrance.

As the years shifted dreamlike in a soft light before him, the dragon saw the great events of the boy's life, paraded before his eyes in a series of scattered scenes: his father, his mother, the first time he picked a lock in a Grospoint millinery. He saw Brenn stumble into Terrance's tower, saw his first meeting with Faye and Ricardo, watched as he conjured elves and climbed an incandescent stairway on a timeless, sunlit adventure. He saw him stutter awkwardly before Faye, saw him trapped in the cellar of the Poisoners' Hall and wandering the honeycombed tunnels of the Guild beneath Maraven. Finally, he saw the lad fitful and fevered in the back of the wagon, bound for the forest fastness.

It was enough, Amalek decided. He knew all the events, and of course that was all he needed to know. Especially when he watched the events that brought the boy here—how his friends shed from him like skins from a snake, leaving the lad alone, a feeble opponent, but one of great importance in the eyes of the Witch and the Faerie Queen.

The dragon's wings stirred, and the settled birds rose in a new flurry.

Important to the Witch and to the Faerie Queen. It was enough for him. He was suddenly very hungry.

First the boy.

When he was scarcely a hundred yards from the thorns, Brenn saw the dragon rise.

Amalek burst from the volcano mouth with a crash, as the canopy of dry branches above him shattered against his powerful neck and wings. Birds scattered before him in alarm as he surged into the skies, and his shadow obscured the rising sun for a moment.

Brenn gasped and reined in the horse, fumbling for the bow.

Then the dragonscent reached him from across the barren plain, hot and fetid and overwhelming. The birds racing ahead of the monster lost all bearings, colliding with each other, crashing into the ground, broken. Brenn's arms fell to his side, the bow useless in his hand, and his thoughts tumbled past words into panic.

With an ungainly lurch, Amalek alighted. He folded his leathery wings and lumbered toward Brenn, the air shimmering around him. Iridescent red and violet, Amalek hoisted himself onto his hind legs and loomed over Brenn like a tower.

The horse threw Brenn and galloped wide-eyed toward distant Hadrach. The ground afforded a hard landing and, fumbling in the pouch at his belt, trying to cling to his swiftly unraveling senses, Brenn drew forth the perfume bottle. An absurd thought had struck him, and swiftly he brought the glass to his nose and breathed deeply.

Somewhere beneath the scalding, fear-inspiring dragonscent arose the faint odor of honeysuckle. Brenn savored it, turned it over in his mind, and slowly the dragonscent abated, and with it his bewildering terror.

Still, the creature loomed in front of him, fifty feet at least from tail to tooth, the wings fanning ominously. Though he had faced the gibbering, irrational fear and set it aside, Brenn had no intention of facing down the monster itself.

Leaping toward him in short, powerful bounds, the dragon bared its three rows of teeth, its hinged jaw opening, opening, until . . . it stopped, agape, sniffing the air.

Suddenly Amalek's rage seemed to subside. Hungrily, the monster lowered its snout and sniffed again. Rapidly recovering his faculties, Brenn reached behind him for a weapon, grabbed instead the serpentine root, and held it aloft.

How darest thou? something rumbled in his ear, so subtle, so insinuating, that for a moment he thought it was his own pulse. *How darest thou trespass in my country?*

The dragonscent arose once more, this time even stronger. Brenn brought Lapis's bottle to his nose again, searching for the smell to undermine the hot, dreadful stink around him. As he did so, he looked by chance through the red glass of the perfume bottle into the face of the dragon. The face was brilliant, menacing, unmoving, as the voice arose again in his ears.

*That root thou brandisheth is a soothing thing, but do not
pride thyself too famously. I am still here before thee, neither
tamed nor inclined to mercy. Tell me a reason why I should not
scatter thy members over the plains from here to Jaleel and
Rabia . . .*

Three dark spirals swirled and pulsed on the dragon's chest.
When Brenn lowered the glass bottle and looked at the beast
with naked eye, he could not see them: they were lost in the red
and violet iridescence. Curiously, almost idly, Brenn raised the
glass again.

I am waiting, boy, the dragon urged, the voice still calm, but
louder.

"W-what?" Brenn asked, lowering the glass. "Oh. I . . .
suppose I have something that . . . if you kill me, you can't
have."

Brenn's thoughts foraged wildly for what that thing might be.

In that packet of thine? The voice made Brenn giddy, nau-
seated. *Why, I shall take it myself. After I have disposed of thee.*

"But you can't. I mean, if you *dispose of me,* as you say,
you . . . you . . ."

The song.

"You won't be able to hear it!" Brenn announced triumphantly. " 'Tis a song. An ancient song yet unheard, because
for generations words and melody have been kept apart."

The dragon leaned forward onto all fours, then as gracefully
and effortlessly as a drowsy cat curls up on a rug, it settled itself
on the parched ground in front of Brenn, its long tail looping
behind the lad to cut off his escape.

A song. How . . . intriguing. But I know all songs already.

Brenn teetered, his ears ringing.

"But you can't have heard this one, sir," he replied gamely.
"It's the one about . . . well about the nature of things."

The nature of things, indeed! the voice exclaimed cynically.
*I know all the songs about the nature of things. Hast thou any-
thing to offer me?*

"Indeed, I do not, if you choose to kill me and scatter me,"
Brenn agreed. "But could it not be possible that this song of
the nature of things is, of the hundreds written and sung, the
only one you do not know?

What . . . dost thou seek in return? the voice asked, shrewdly and quietly.

Brenn paused. The creature before him was intricate in its evil, or so he had heard. If he disclosed that he was after the Bag of Ladra, for the life of him he could not figure whether it would help or hinder him.

Come, come, the deep voice coaxed with a cruel confidence as if it had reached inside him and held his thoughts to the light. *When wilt thou ask for the bag?*

The great iridescent tail thrashed the ground behind the wagon, and Brenn started at the thunderous sound.

"Well . . . I expect you know of it, then," Brenn confessed sheepishly, giving the dragon's tail a sidelong glance. All the items were still at hand—the map, the roots, the branches, the bow—but none of them offered themselves as an answer. Delia's words came back to him mockingly.

He had everything he needed, and it only awaited his imagining. But his thoughts were groping, his fancy strained.

And the dragon stood like a thousand deaths before him.

These cousins of thine, it said, its red scales mottling to a deep purple, then to a shallow black. *Why have they sent thee to lift their curses?*

"They didn't send me!" Brenn protested. "I took it on myself!"

Then it dawned on him that the dragon knew of the curses, too.

Is lifting the curse not a dangerous undertaking? Amalek asked. *Did Galliard try to dissuade thee? Did he offer to go instead of thee, since after all, the curse had marked him most painfully of all?*

"Galliard! How did you know about . . ." Brenn began. And then the drift of Amalek's questions struck him with all their dark logic. Ambushed by the sinister thoughts, the lad scarcely noticed the itching in the palm of his left hand.

"But he couldn't!" Brenn argued. "Galliard's lifting sickness! Were he to stray from Corbinwood, the property of even the most innocent folk would not be safe! He would not have that, and so . . ."

Where was he last night? the dragon asked, softly and coldly deep in Brenn's mind, where the sound of the question intertwined with his thoughts. *Does the sickness that keeps him from the plains of Palerna not keep him out of Maraven? Do you know what brought him to Kestrel Tower, where the Great Witch looked for him?*

And what business has that fast-talking Alanyan friend of thine with Galliard, or with Ravenna, for . . .

"Ricardo!" Brenn exclaimed. The voice was silent. "I don't believe you!"

Wilt thou spread thy silken map between us, lad? If I show them in the city itself, in the chambers of Kestrel Tower, wilt thou believe me then?

Cautiously, Brenn moved Ponder's map between them. Closer to the dragon, he could see how the scales along its back and flanks overlapped like shingles. The armor was seamless, thick and glittering.

At a nod from Amalek, Brenn cast the silk over the ground. The scene was mockingly cozy, as though he were spreading a cloth for a picnic. The map slipped from Brenn's left hand, which was throbbing now, and the fabric fluttered briefly above the dry ground. Then the dragon fanned his enormous wings slowly, and a green light rose from the midst of the silk, shimmering and wavering and resolving itself into shapes.

Two figures formed out of the light. Galliard and Ricardo, standing in the midst of a vaulted room. Galliard was cloaked and hooded, and Ricardo . . .

Ricardo was wearing a helmet of the Watch.

"But what . . . why . . ."

Is that not the great throne room of Kestrel Tower, the voice insinuated, *where the shields of five provinces hang? Art thy friends under restraint? Or do they stand there like welcome guests, admiring the tapestries, the beautiful work of the ornamental weapons?*

"Like guests . . ." Brenn admitted, his face cross and bewildered. Then, "No!" he exclaimed. "I see what you're trying to . . ." He paused, at a loss for words. The image of Galliard and Ricardo standing in the center of the throne room played dreamily through his imaginings in a strange green light.

A green light that seemed to be rising from the palm of his hand. Brenn shook his head, dismissed the image, and the questions of the dragon slowly insinuated their way back into his heart.

But then, thou hast known neither of them well or long, hast thou? Amalek asked, and stirred the surface of the map with his hot, fetid breath.

"Well, no . . ." Brenn replied uncertainly, again lifting the bottle to his nose. Through the glass he saw the scales of the dragon ripple and pulse—the perfect, invulnerable armor of the beast.

"Where are those dark swirls?" he asked himself silently. Then he recalled that he had seen them only on the breast of the monster. Quietly Brenn took it into account, and a strategy, though faint and ill-defined, began to form in his thoughts.

Are there others in thy company who have known thee longer and better? the voice asked, and at its return all schemes and tactics scattered before Brenn could master them. He startled and looked away guiltily, fearful that Amalek had entered his thoughts, had found out his scheming. But the dragon did not move, its eyes fixed on the silk map between them.

Is there a wizard in this story?

"There is indeed," Brenn replied. "Terrance of Maraven."

Ah. Lived in the court of Aurum, if I recall correctly. How long hast thou known him? Is he indeed as powerful as the legends say he once was?

"He is so, indeed," Brenn agreed, uncertain where the conversation was heading.

How dost thou think this Terrance would have availed against the likes of me? Amalek asked, and Brenn looked into his eyes, bewildered.

"He had reasons not to come with me," Brenn replied. "He . . . he had fallen unto dark acquaintance."

Oh, had he? the dragon asked, and a bleak, frantic dizziness passed over Brenn. *Dost you not think that visits to me bring dark acquaintance to many a man? Might prospect of that visit have done the same?*

The question hung unanswerable in the hot Alanyan air.

"But it wasn't like that!" Brenn protested. "There were plenty of reasons, short of cowardice, that Terrance could not come with me!"

Canst thou think of three? Two? Even one?

But he could think of no other version of things than the one the dragon's voice suggested. The words settled into his thoughts, and the silk before him shone with yet another scene, another green and luminous life.

On a southern road, Terrance handed a writ of apprenticeship to Dirk.

"He's . . . he's starting over again!" Brenn exclaimed. In anger he reached toward the map, seeking to pull it away, to shatter the image in front of him.

Hold! warned Amalek, and Brenn stopped, poised above the silk. *'Tis only eidolons thou seest . . . images past, though recent. Thy hand can neither change nor harm them.*

And after all, the dragon added soothingly, *are there not many reasons that a man doth what he doth? Even a wizard?*

Brenn scowled. He could think of none of them. "Replaced by my oldest friend," he muttered.

Your oldest? the dragon asked. *But is there not one soul thou hast known even longer?*

Again the lines on the silk map twisted and glowed. Brenn watched, dumbstruck, as the image of Faye appeared in the heart of the map—Faye, seated on a bed in a cozy, well-lit chamber, comfortably reading a book.

What is the nature of her work in Kestrel Tower? the dragon asked. *Why doth she answer only to the Great Witch of Maraven?*

And why would the Witch keep a young girl in the midst of a barracks of soldiers?

Could this Faye have forgotten thee? Could it be that she cannot even recall thy name?

"That . . . that is a lie," Brenn objected, though his voice was weak.

Have I lied to thee, like the others? asked the dragon.

Deep inside, Brenn knew the monster spoke truth.

Wilt thou sing to me of the nature of things?

In despair Brenn looked down, staring at his hands. On the

left palm glowed the long blue birthmark—the hereditary, sword-shaped scar that pointed toward his wrist, his arm, his heart.

No longer did it seem that important, this business of kings and lineage. Brenn closed his eyes. The plains seem to whirl, to rock in a harsh, uncomfortable light. He wanted to give up. He wanted to set it all aside.

He understood now why the dragon had saved the image of Faye for last. She was the first in his heart and the last to leave, but all the time his ambitions had set her aside, unnoticed and almost forgotten in the city he had left behind.

"I am sorry, Faye," he whispered hoarsely, opening his eyes. "Very well. Very well, Dragon. I cannot reason with the things you have shown me. The song, my belongings, myself—we all are yours to dispose of as you will. What difference does it make? I am king of nothing much."

The dragon purred and narrowed his eyes and began a slow, sinuous movement toward the lad.

What ground is it, when you have fallen into the great and abiding depths of yourself, buoys you and says to you *fall no farther?*

Where is it in the midst of the falling that the mind recovers, where the heart reckons and says, *This is all. By the winds and by the light there is something here to stand upon and for?*

It is the place where kings are born.

As the dragon moved toward him, Brenn retraced the betrayals in his memory . . .

He stood up. He decided they did not matter.

What if Ricardo and Galliard have gone to the side of Dragmond? And what of Terrance's cowardice, or Faye's more private betrayals?

Something in Brenn found his ground and turned. He looked at the scar on his hand as if for the first time. Blue and faintly glimmering, it was the sign of a heritage, of something given him, if obscurely and only by accident. And even if the others had betrayed him, there was yet a task set before him, a deed in which his ventures and striving and suffering were given direction and purpose.

"I may not be king of much," the young man muttered. "But

by the gods, I am king of something!'' Triumphantly, with a confidence he could scarcely imagine and could only in part believe, he set about to do the next thing.

First he stared fearlessly into the dragon's eyes.

"Amalek," he announced. "I have for you the song for which you hunger and wheedle and scratch . . ."

The dragon growled and purpled.

"But first . . .," Brenn continued, "you must put it together."

Put it together?

The creature grew deadly still. For it was knowledge that Amalek prized above all. It was number and deed and event that he hoarded, and his days were a continual asking, a ravenous hunger for fact.

The putting together was something new. Suspiciously, the beast arched his great scaled head and stared down upon the man in the wagon before him. Brenn neither flinched nor cowered, but looked straight at the monster with a calm, defiant gaze.

He also marked the dark swirls on the breast of the dragon.

Put it . . . together? the dragon asked again, and it occurred to Brenn that the balance had turned.

"Why, certainly," he said. "I shall sing you the melody. Then *you* must read the runes for yourself."

The invention was a gamble. And in the strictest of senses, one could not say that Brenn had lied. Nonetheless, the dragon listened alertly as Brenn piped out the melody, a beautiful, mournful song in a minor key, so lovely and fetching in its harmonies that the parched ground about him seemed to darken and bristle with new life.

In astonishment, the dragon watched the grass shoot up under Brenn's feet. A fanciful blue-green, burgeoning and flourishing, the grass lifted the silk map from the bare ground as it grew.

This is . . . promising, is it not? Amalek asked in excitement, as Brenn stepped aside and, drawing forth one of the rune-tree branches, tossed it toward the impatient monster. Secretly, he kept another in the knapsack, carefully concealed from the dragon.

Turning the limb in his talons, Amalek began to translate, to recite, to finally sing the words to the melody he remembered flawlessly.

I know you know I know you know,
And knowing descends to grief,
In the time when we know for knowing's sake
And knowing outknows belief.
There is no known catholicon,
No antidote nor cure
For needing to know what must be known
In order to know for sure.
And when the known is all revealed,
Forever the song will go:
We cannot rest in knowing, 'til
I know you know I know.

Unlike the voice that had brooded in Brenn's thoughts, the voice of the dragon aloud was thin, almost reedy. Amalek paused, and looked at Brenn in puzzlement. He had come to the end of the words, and yet the melody continued, having at least a measure or two to go before it was over.

"I know . . . you know . . ." the creature continued, and his singing launched him right back into the verse once more.

Again and again Amalek sang the silly song, each time with more urgency, as he sought the end of it, a harmonious final chord, a return to the dominant, a sense of resolution. But the song seemed to continue, the melody always a bar behind the last words until the dragon erupted in a shrieking chorus of *I knows.*

He has no invention, Brenn thought. *He lacks the imagining to finish the song he has begun.*

But Amalek did not lack for other powers. Suddenly, with a formidable swipe of his tail, the monster lashed at the new grass and sent it flying in bits. In the green rain, Brenn tumbled away as the dragon brought his tail down again, smashing and scattering fragments of rock and brambles.

Instantly, Brenn gathered his belongings, scrambled away from the site, and scampered into the Aralu, the dragon twisting and shrieking and stumbling in the music and rubble behind him.

Clambering through the harsh and clinging branches toward the volcano's mouth, Brenn heard Amalek singing, loud and shrill and jangling. It would not last forever: soon the dragon would disentangle himself from the makeshift song and come after him, his anger doubled at the treachery and wit of his quarry.

"But there is some time remaining me," Brenn muttered. "And I shall use it well."

So he ran, breaking through underbrush, hurdling branch and bole, the silk map billowing at his belt, until the ground sloped sharply upward before him, and he climbed over thorn and obsidian.

He had not thought what he would do when the Bag of Ladra lay in his hands. The decision would come at the moment and no sooner.

Behind the climbing lad, Amalek continued to sing, though the melody was lost entirely in the grating, hoarse, hysteria of the monster's voice. Skittering on gravel and dried wood he lurched after Brenn, now stumbling and recovering, now falling with a crash and a rumble as the song and the singing robbed him of balance and sense.

Nonetheless, he pursued relentlessly. Somewhere back in his unravelling mind, the dragon knew that the lad was cornered. Brenn had nowhere to go but down the vent of the volcano, into the heart of the Aralu.

Why, the fall alone would kill the sniveling brat.

Brenn skidded to a halt at the lip of the volcano. Shadows swallowed the ground beneath him—it was a good forty feet to the lair below, easily traversed by dragon wing, but perilous to the human trespasser.

Brenn huddled behind the fractured branches of a bare thorn tree, longing for flight, for the wings of eagles he had once worn in plague-instructed sleep . . .

. . . for the wings of that eagle there.

The bird perched above him, regarding him brightly, alertly. Something about it was familiar, though Brenn hadn't the time to ponder his memories. Instead, he spun about and nocked an arrow to Galliard's black bow.

For the dragon approached. Crashing through branches, dragging himself insanely over the slick obsidian, Amalek scaled the side of the volcano, sometimes crawling, sometimes borne on a hysterical lurch of his wings.

Brenn released the first shot. Rocketing through the air, it struck Amalek in the neck and bounced harmlessly away.

Brenn cried out in dismay and drew forth another arrow. Producing Lapis's bottle, he stared through it long and hard at the approaching monster. Then, as the dragon crept wickedly toward him, Brenn aimed again . . .

. . . this time where the bottommost dark spiral had appeared in the tinted light on the dragon's breast . . .

. . . and whooped in surprise and delight as the arrow flashed into the dark folds between the creature's scales.

Amalek roared and leapt backward, clawing a great, bloody swath across his breast in his agony. He stood on his haunches and beat his wings in the hot air, vainly nuzzling the wound, digging for the arrow with his rows of sharp teeth.

While the dragon thrashed and rooted at his chest, Brenn was not idle. Quickly he fixed another arrow in the bow and aimed again.

Then, for a moment, he paused, struck by the grandeur of the thing beneath him.

Evil though he might be, avaricious and vain and murderous and despairing, Amalek bristled with enormity and life, glittering green and red and purple below him as the colors changed and swirled on his smooth metallic scales . . .

. . . as they swirled darker still in the circles on his chest.

Resolutely, breathing apology to the winds and the gods and his own softer spirit, Brenn unleashed the arrow.

Amalek shrieked and tumbled to his side as the shaft buried itself in a second fold of his armor. His eyes glazed suddenly, and green scales formed on them like ice on a freezing pond.

"Now for the Bag," Brenn said, and started the descent. The eagle fluttered to an outcropping of rock and stared at the lad brilliantly as he took one downward step, then another . . .

. . . then paused.

But what if he follows? Brenn asked himself. *Not likely—he's badly wounded. What if he tells Ravenna my whereabouts? Worse yet . . . what if he destroys the lair just to keep me from taking the Bag?*

Curiously, the eagle leapt to his shoulder. Brenn startled, grasped for the rock, took one giddy look into the yawning crater behind him . . .

. . . and recovered his balance.

He clung to the dark obsidian, praying. The alarmed eagle hovered above him, its wings flapping.

"I wish I could understand you," Brenn murmured. "Whatever it is you're doing is confusing me to . . ."

A slow smile spread across his face.

"Confusion," he whispered. "Deception. The king becomes a thief again."

The eagle whistled and settled on a rock above him, its golden eyes bright and obedient and attentive.

So it was that Amalek, two of his three great hearts punctured and broken, looked up the steep Aralu and saw his enemy standing at the edge of the volcano.

The monster tried the dragonsight, but it told him nothing—a long, unlinked chain of events from a murky birth in the slums of Maraven to this crazed dance in the heart of Alanya.

None of it made sense. Amalek writhed on the black incline, pulling himself painfully higher and higher until the slight, shadowy form above him shifted and stood still . . .

. . . and a searing pain lanced through his third heart.

Then, his eyesight growing dimmer and dimmer, the dragon watched in helpless rage as the young man covered himself with a white sail of silk and seemed to step back . . . over the abyss . . .

. . . and he vanished entirely, white silk and all . . .

. . . and out of the abyss surged a sea eagle, his wings on fire with the sunlight. Wheeling over the head of the dragon, something clutched in his talons . . .

. . . *The Bag*, Amalek breathed bitterly . . .

. . . The bird flashed west over Hadrach toward the Xanthus, bound for Palerna and home.

An eagle, Amalek thought, abstractly, almost idly. *The king is an eagle.*

He turned once more, saw the black of obsidian, saw a deeper more desolate black that rose from his heart to swallow him.

* * *

In the reservoir of the dead volcano, forty feet below the surface of the Aralu, Brenn combed through the treasure of the dragon's hoard. He marveled at the chalices, the thousand rings, at a diamond the size of his fist, but he set them all aside, smiling in memory of the Goniph, impelled by a search more urgent.

No, the king was not an eagle. Yet for the moment, he was more magician than Terrance had ever fancied he would be.

For the only magic for which Brenn had a talent was simple Wall Town sleight of hand. It had been a tricky business, releasing the bird, knapsack in its clutches, as he dropped down the vent of the volcano, the silk map billowing above him like the wing skin of a flying squirrel, cushioning his fall. But there had been trickier feats when you climbed over rooftops in midnight Maraven, and long ago he had learned the thief's *esquilo*—the floating drop from a high place, buoyed by the fabric above him.

Brenn's mind was on the Bag of Ladra as he rummaged through the scattered coin and gems. He had a thief's sense of rifling a room; it was not long before the leather bag was in his hands.

He knew it was the Bag of Ladra, because there was no other reason that the dragon would keep such a plain and humble item. Made of simple dyed leathers, stitched together amateurishly and tied by a frayed rawhide string, it was the least likely thing of value in the whole horde. And yet it swallowed each of the cousins's stolen gifts—the branch from Sendow, the root from Jimsett, Lapis's red bottle. Brenn whistled Thomas's song into the open mouth of the bag, and he felt the wind being drawn from him subtly, as though the melody had caught some mysterious undertow of magic and wind, riding it deep into nothingness.

"Well, that is that," Brenn exclaimed, casting a glance toward a side vent in the volcano—a narrow, short tunnel that led out into sunlight and the other side of the Aralu. "All except the bow."

Reluctantly, he dropped the weapon into the bag.

Then for a moment he stood there in speculation, ankle deep

in unimaginable treasure. It had all seemed too easy, as though he had wandered a great distance to face a formidable enemy, bearing with him the prayers and dreams of innumerable others.

It did not seem that it should be over so quickly.

Brenn sat down and took inventory, retracing his steps over the last few miles of the journey. He closed his eyes and sighed.

Nothing was wrong. He had left nothing out, had forgotten nothing. Again, a trace of a smile passed over his face.

"Thank you, Delia," he whispered. "And Ricardo and Glory, and *you*, strange brother eagle, for being where you were. And above all, thank you Terrance, for your wisdom and your teaching and for the knowledge that you wrestled from the Great Witch and brought back to me out of that country of dreams and death."

At rest for the first time since he left the forest, Brenn tied the bag to his belt and climbed up to the side vent, and through the slim passage into the bare countryside east of the Aralu.

➤➤➤ **Epilogue** ⤙⤙⤙

Galliard was the last of the cousins to feel the curse lift.

Standing on the porch of his cabin, addressing his followers with an array of orders and mischief, suddenly he noticed Sendow shake his head distractedly, as though a mosquito whined in his ear. Jimsett did the same, and after him Thomas and Ponder. Lapis was last, as the company of woodsmen surrounding the cousins backed away from them, convinced that something unusual was coming to pass.

It was then that Galliard felt the change himself. A peculiar peace washed over him, a heaviness and drowsiness such as he had never felt, but that he later likened to the feeding of a great hunger. The Forest Lord sat upon his doorstep, birds and squirrels weaving excited paths through the windows of the cabin, and fell asleep sitting up.

It was a sleep that threatened never to end. Ricardo tried to prod him awake, then jostle him, but the Forest Lord slept on blissfully, his eyes tightly closed and a rapt smile on his face. Finally the Alanyan dragged him into the cabin and draped him over a cot, where he snored and murmured and laughed into the night.

Ricardo and the woodsmen feared for Galliard's health, and for the health of the others, for the cousins slept, too, and all the next day, the clearing resounded with their snoring and murmuring and laughing. A crowd of woodsmen gathered below Galliard's cabin, and a vigil began that lasted most of the afternoon. As the shadows lengthened near the end of the second day, a sea eagle roosted on the eaves of the cabin, staring through the window at the serenely sleeping duke until the next morning.

The herb woman reappeared soon after sunrise, quietly emerging into the clearing, a strange and vibrant glow on her face and in her hair the smell of sunlight and eastern perfumes. She climbed the rope ladder as nimbly as a twelve-year-old thief, and seated herself quietly by the duke's bedside, joining Ricardo.

"If I didn't know better," the Alanyan confided later to a group of the woodsmen, "I would have sworn she'd been journeying somewhere." But his companions swore in turn that Glory had not left the woods in his absence, and each man and woman claimed to have seen her deep in the forest's fastness, about some murky and no doubt herbal business.

Glory told them not to worry, that the sleep of Galliard and the others was no ensorcellment, but instead a long and much-needed rest after years of enchantment. She let the cousins sleep through the afternoon, then touched each brow with a sprig of rosemary, the herb of wakefulness and remembrance.

Galliard was the last to awaken. He laughed aloud at the cousins perched above his bed like a college of surgeons, then scrambled briskly to his feet, refusing Ricardo's aid. Taking Glory's hand, he walked to the entrance of the cabin. The eagle flew to his shoulder, and Galliard whispered to it. He removed his glove and offered it to the waiting bird.

Clutching the glove in its hooked beak, the bird took flight. Streaking from the clearing like a bolt, it vanished into a dappled sea of leaves. Galliard smiled, nodded, and turned to the expectant company of woodsmen assembled below him.

"Prepare yourselves to leave our accustomed home, lads and lasses," he began quietly, almost tentatively. "The time is coming when our welcome wears thin . . ."

He winked knowingly at Glory, who laughed with delight.

"I knew all along," Galliard whispered. "I have seen those lights for years."

"Not true on either count, you scoundrel," she whispered merrily. "But your return will always be welcome. Did you think your cabin belonged to any but you? We built it two centuries ago, so that the cedar would have time to grow around it. We prepared for you then, and we will prepare for you once more."

Galliard smiled skeptically. Faeries were known for their flatteries. He turned, cleared his throat, and resumed his speech, his voice raised with more confidence, more resolve.

"Tomorrow at dawn, Master Ricardo and I will ride west out of the woods onto the plains of Zephyr. Namid, the Count of West Aldor, is encamped not ten leagues hence with a company of Zephyrian cavalry. He has a score to settle with Dragmond, as do we. Perhaps we can settle them together."

The rough foresters and farmers and peasants assembled in the clearing murmured excitedly to one another. It was clear, even to the youngest and most naive of them, that Duke Galliard was talking war.

Among the ranks of woodsmen, there were few who would shy from a good fight. Many of them had served in the legions of Palerna or the cavalry of Zephyr, under Dragmond or Aurum or the fierce Zephyrian Counts Namid and Macaire. Some of the oldest men had fought under Albright, or against him. Most had been blooded in the brief, incessant wars that seemed to recur in Maraven, in Palerna, to all poor families who have the misfortune to live in the reigns of belligerent kings.

But somehow this seemed different. For the woodsmen had lived alongside the king they would serve. They had seen him sleep and eat, they had drunk from the same wineskin and gourd, and there were six of them who had seen him stumble and fall into the river in pursuit of the faeries they thought he imagined. Yet instead of diminishing their trust, that closeness had strengthened it.

King Brennart, they had decided early on, was one of them—Aurum's son or not.

"Prepare yourselves, my friends and captains," the Forest Lord concluded, wrapping one arm around the shoulder of the

Alanyan, the other about the waist of the herb woman. "Prepare, you who have stood and waited, for the end of your exile approaches. Your fields are tilled, and the new life blossoms in a dry place, watered with the blood of our enemies."

The oldest men murmured excitedly. This was general's talk, all bloody and visionary.

"Within the fortnight," Galliard shouted, "we march north from here, over the Boniluce and into Palerna. Whether the Zephyrians stand with us or not, whether Dragmond stand against us or not. King Brennart will ride at the front of our armies, and our eyes, our hearts, our resolve and our sacred honors we shall deliver into his hands, as he marches into walled and promised Maraven!"

A cheer rose from the tattered company in the clearing. Old hats were tossed into the air, catching on overhanging branches, and all Corbinwood west of the Boniluce shook with the sound of sword beaten against shield, quarterstaff against quarterstaff. Deep in the shroud of trees by the river, hundreds of dim lights fluttered and winked, their morning's sleep disturbed again by human commotion.

Ravenna stood in the throne room, oblivious to the scalding as the hot wax of the divining candle dripped over her hand.

Lightborn steadied the dead king on the throne, then turned to observe the auguring witch, in silent admiration and growing alarm.

She is single in thought and resolve, he mused. *Her passions will be difficult to bend.*

"An eagle," she murmured, cupping the flame behind her pale hand. Her gray eyes tumbled into bottomless black, and unnerved, Lightborn turned away.

His eyes rested on the window. Galliard's rope still hung there. But now, on the other end of the rope, dangled the two guards who had run from the room on the night the sword was stolen. They turned over the tower gardens, swaying wickedly in the first hot *alienado* wind of July.

Let the garrison take note.

"Eagle?" he asked idly. "What eagle, m'lady?"

"Amalek," she replied, striding toward the center of the room past Dragmond, whose red eyes followed her dully. "His thoughts were of eagles—of an eagle on the wing, carrying something away from the Aralu. The wizard's brat is a transmogrifier!" Ravenna spat, a rising hysteria in her voice.

"Absurd," Lightborn said flatly, walking to the window. He looked below, past the drying, swaying corpses into the garden, where, unexplainably, violets and primroses, sweetpeas and cowslips had sprouted miraculously and blossomed, surrounding the dead trees with new and variegated life.

"Absurd," he repeated, then turned to face the room. "Where is the boy, Ravenna?"

"In Palerna," the Great Witch muttered, "South of the Plains of Sh'Ryll, headed westward." She leaned against the throne, resting her hand absently on Dragmond's shoulder for a moment and then, suddenly aware of the cold body, removed it in disgust, as though she were touching ordure or fire.

"In Palerna!" Lightborn exclaimed, then quickly composed himself. Ignoring the cwalu seated on the throne, he paced to the center of the room. "I see. Well . . . if the power of magic cannot stop him, perhaps . . . the power of armies can."

He looked at Ravenna. Their eyes met.

"You will need a voice in the field," he observed. "Helmar will not take orders from you, and the king . . . well . . ."

With a crooked smile, he nodded at Dragmond.

"Thank you, Lightborn," Ravenna whispered huskily, extinguishing the flame of the candle.

He thinks I am helpless, she thought. *That I am daunted past all reason and sense. That I do not see him scrambling to the head of the armies.*

Smoothly, lightly, still holding the candle, Ravenna glided to him across the stone floor of the chamber. Her black-nailed finger touched lightly against his jaw as she passed, and at the doorway, she looked back over her shoulder.

"You, of course, will be that voice in the field, Captain Lightborn."

The Pale Man bowed dutifully, hiding a smile as the witch stepped from sight into the corridor. Hidden from the view of all but the ravens perched at the corridor windows, the Great Witch leaned against the wall beneath a torch, her pale hands shaking uncontrollably. Whirling through her head were a thousand schemes, each unravelling at the prospect of Dragmond dead and this upstart boy gaining power day by day.

Quickly, she relit the candle, held it before her, and drained the green vial of acumen. She thought of the lad, of the dragon, of the Aralu, focusing all her energy, passion, and intent on the center of the flickering candle. Clouds obscured the light in all the corridor windows, and the birds rustled nervously. Suddenly, with a vividness born of the drug and her familiarity with the dark, volcanic wastelands where Amalek dwelt, the flame of the candle turned black, obsidian black, and in its heart she saw the heart of the dragon's lair.

"Why?" she asked, dizzy from the drug and the vision. She squinted and looked closer. "Why this? Why not the boy? the dragon?" Weakened by the conjury, she slumped down in the corridor, and the torch above her gutted and went out.

"The Bag of Ladra," she whispered finally, her terrible smile framed in faint candlelight. "It is missing! The bag has been taken!"

She laughed, softly at first, and then more loudly. Lightborn heard her from his place by the throneroom window. He turned uneasily toward the door.

The ravens boded in the windows, and together the outcry of witch and birds cascaded to the ground floor of the tower, where Faye, poised above a mop in the kitchen, paused and shook her head, as though at that moment she remembered a dream.

"Brenn!" she whispered. "His name is Brenn!"

But they called him King Brenn on the plains of Palerna.

Brenn had emerged on the far side of the rocky Aralu, squinting at the sunlight, struggling for bearings. Climbing down out of the brambles, he had seen three horsemen below in the green of the Hadrach militia. They were armed, and they led a fourth horse with them.

At first the thief in him balked. He looked around him for cover, considered a quick retreat up the side vent. But then a calm settled over him. He thought of the last few days, of the struggle just completed on the other side of the mountain.

"After plagues and witches and dragons," he said aloud, "what danger is there in cavalry?"

He walked down to meet them. As he suspected, the fourth horse was for him. It was, however, a pleasant surprise to find that the animal was a gift from the residents of the Corridor of Limes, and the militia had volunteered to see him safely home. The four of them—Brenn and his three escorts—were joined by yet another ten riders—some militia, some civilian— and for the first time at the head of a column of cavalry, the young king rode westward toward the Xanthus, toward Palerna and Corbinwood and the friends he hoped would be there to greet him.

Two hundred peasants met them at the river. Twenty or so were on the Alanyan banks, and they crossed with Brenn and the riders to the Palernan shore, where fourscore others, armed with club, staff, and pitchfork, raised a cheer for the returning king and fell into line behind him.

Across the Palerna they gathered force—three hundred, four hundred, five hundred. From ruined farms they came, from desolate villages and hungry forests.

A hermit came north out of the Notches, impelled by a month-old vision that a king would pass this way and that times for contemplation had ended.

Two young women, their armor a patchwork of Palernan issue and ancient Umbrian bronze, joined with the company, setting their swords before the new king and offering their service. An Alanyan cavalry officer laughed and made a vulgar joke, but Brenn corrected him sternly, remembering the hardiness of Delia, the resourcefulness of Faye. Beaming, armed with a newborn purpose, the women joined the swelling ranks, and the column moved westward.

Past Tallow Tree they marched, through Ransom and Murrey and finally to Keedwater, where they passed the stone chapel, the smithy, and the Man of Law's house where the statue still stood inverted on the front lawn. Brenn took it all in; it was as though *he* remembered the places, they were that vivid. And each town emptied in support of the king: peasants picked up clubs, tanners polished well-hidden swords or spears, and the town militia to a man removed the red armor of Dragmond's

Watch and settled for old curie armor, for hides and skins, for simple padded cloth tunics.

At the head of a thousand armed and ready, Brenn rode, his thoughts on the woods and the days to come. Behind him, the clear tenor voice of a lad—a chandler from Murrey, as Brenn remembered, but a bowman now, and a commander of a handful of Palernan archers—sang out the new rallying song of the rebel army:

> The forward Youth that would appear
> Must now forsake his Muses dear,
>   Nor in the Shadows sing
>   His Numbers languishing.
> 'Tis time to leave the Books in dust,
> And oyl th' unused Armours rust:
>   Removing from the Wall
>   The Corselet of the Hall . . .

And on and on it went, in an elaborate chorus taken up by another and yet another, by those who did not know the words and those who knew the words but not their meaning . . .

. . . by the Man of Law who at last had found a way out of Keedwater, and by a brewer from Ransom who had distributed her wares among the infantry until some of them became lost on the plains . . .

. . . by an Alanyan gambler who had thrown away three decks of marked playing cards, vowing to lead the upright life of a rebel officer, and by the devout Brother Richard, a young priest of the Four Winds from the Braden Gorge in the eastern Notches, who had set aside his studies of Umbrian and Etruscan letters in outrage at the "moral misconduct" in Kestrel Tower.

North from Keedwater they went, then on to the west, until the gray-green borders of Corbinwood rose on the horizon. At the head of his growing army, Brenn stood in the saddle, shielding his eyes against the bright July midday. He squinted beyond the red lines of the Watch, who were already scattering in the face of superior forces, and into the vast, entangling sanctuary of the forest, where his cousins waited, no doubt. Perhaps Ricardo would be there, and Bertilak, and maybe even Terrance, though Brenn doubted that he would see the wizard again.

And though they were much too far away to see, Brenn could imagine the lands to the north, the black beaches and gray walls of the city he had left but never forgotten. Somewhere to the north of him Maraven waited. The streets of Wall Town and Grospoint waited, as did the black tower in which his enemies lay. And Faye . . . whatever Faye was turning out to be, she waited for him there, in the uncertain country toward which they all were headed.